Praise for the

M000188823

From the Ashes

I have been looking forward to reading *From the Ashes* by Stacy Lynn Miller since I read her first Manhattan Sloane novel back in April. I fell in love with Sloane, Finn, and all the other characters in this story while reading the first book, and I wanted more, especially since the story didn't completely end with the first novel. I'm happy to say I loved this book as much as the first one.

In this second tale, we find Sloane still struggling with her grief over her wife's death as she also deals with her growing love for Finn. Nothing is ever easy for Sloane and Finn, since the head of the drug cartel they battled in the first book is now looking for revenge, and he's quite willing to target Sloane and Finn's loved ones.

This is an action-packed story with a complex plot. Most of the characters in this book were introduced in the first one, so they are already well developed and we learn more about the different members of the drug cartel and their motivations. This is definitely a character-driven tale, and Ms. Miller has done an excellent job of creating realistic characters, both good and bad.

I enjoyed seeing the romance grow between Sloane and Finn, even with all the obstacles that could come between them. The author did a wonderful job weaving this romance into all the action and suspense in the overall story.

As I mentioned above, this book is the second in the Manhattan Sloane series and takes up where the first novel, *Out of the Flames*, ended. These books really need to be read together and in order to get the most enjoyment out of the story. I highly recommend both novels, though, so get them both. You won't be disappointed.

-Becky H., *NetGalley*

This was the sequel to this author's very good debut book, *Out of the Flames*.

I enjoyed how the author developed this sequel with realistic problems the characters faced after the loss of loved ones. The author also provided more answers to the car accident that killed Sloane's parents. This was a very emotional moment for those involved. The way it was described, I couldn't help but feel for those characters.

Similar to the previous book, there was a lot of drama when the characters dealt with the cartels. These scenes quickened the pace of the story and allowed for more anxious moments. The secondary characters, both good and bad, increased this story's emotional depth.

Since this was a sequel, I recommend reading the first book to get an overall understanding of the characters and their backgrounds. The author did allow some past events to resurface, but the emotional scenes from the first book were too good not to read and experience.

This book was very engaging with tense moments, emotional breakdowns and recovery, and most of all, tender loving scenes.

-R. Swier, *NetGalley*

From the Ashes is the sequel to *Out of the Flames* with SFPD Detective Manhattan Sloane and DEA Finn Harper. They're chasing after a Mexican drug cartel that is ultimately responsible for killing Sloane's wife. Sloane and Harper had a connection in high school but they were torn apart after Sloane's parents were killed in a car accident. Then they were thrown together on this case as the drug cartel seek revenge for the death of one of their own. Miller is a wonderful storyteller and this story had me sitting on the edge of my seat from start to finish. The first book in the series, *Out of the Flames*, was a 5-star read and *From the Ashes* is the same as it ducks and weaves and thrills and spills all the way to the end. The chemistry between Sloane and Harper is palpable…Miller certainly knows how to write angst into her characters. This book is a thrill a minute and I can't wait for the next one.

-Lissa G., *NetGalley*

I read Stacy Lynn Miller's debut novel *Out of the Flames* back in May, and couldn't wait to read the sequel to learn what happens to San Francisco police detective Manhattan Sloane and DEA Agent Finn Harper's relationship as well as the drug cartel they were chasing. *From the Ashes* resumes from the point that *Out of the Flames* ended.

The book was fast-paced with quite a few anxious and emotional moments. I don't think that you have to read the first book to enjoy this one, but I recommend it since it is a good story and it will introduce the background and characters in a more complete manner. I'd definitely recommend both books to other readers.

-Michele R., *NetGalley*

Firstly, if you've not read Stacy Lynn Miller's debut novel and first in the series of 'A Manhattan Sloane Thriller'... give it a read. It's called *Out of the Flames* and I can guarantee you will not regret it and be hooked like many of us who are now following her work.

From the Ashes follows on from the first book, you don't really need to read the first BUT PLEASE DO! Its fast-paced action keeps you on your toes and includes romance! What's not to love?

-Emma S., *NetGalley*

This is one amazing follow up to book one. The characters grow very well together, even though there are still mafia issues going on around them. I felt that the plot to resolve all issues was nicely provided. The finish was wonderful, and I feel like there will be a new set of stories (or so I hope) for the main characters who decide on their new adventure.

-Kat W., *NetGalley*

One of the things that Stacy Lynn Miller is skilled at is breathing life into her characters. Even important secondary characters. They all stand up as themselves, and there's never any difficulty remembering who is who. This is as true for Miller's previous book as this one. In fact, when I read the final passage, my first thought was for the future of a secondary character! Who worries what kind of future the daughter of a criminal will have? Me, apparently.

There is danger here, passion, secrets...all of the things that keep me reading long into the night. But this book wormed its way into me and wouldn't let up. I was quite literally unable to sleep because I was worried about one of the secondary characters—an autistic young man. I had to pick the book back up and finish it just so I knew what happened to him.

Miller wrapped up questions left dangling in the first book that I didn't know I had. There was a satisfying sense of completion and closure, and yet...there is still room for more stories to come from this fictional world. I do hope the author is interested in bringing us more from this made-up world of hers because I'll be among the first in line with my money out.

-Carolyn M., *NetGalley*

Out of the Flames

This is the debut novel of Stacy Lynn Miller and it's very, very good. The book is a roller coaster of emotion as you ride the highs and lows with Sloane as she navigates her way through her life which is riddled with guilt, self blame, and eventually love. It's easy to connect with all the main characters and sub-characters, most of them are all successful strong women so what's not to love? The story line is really solid.

-Lissa G., *NetGalley*

If you are looking for a book that is emotional, exciting, hopeful, and entertaining, you came to the right place. There are characters you will love, and characters you will love to hate. And the important thing is that Miller makes you care about them so, yes, you might need the tissues just like I did. I see a lot of potential in Miller and I can't wait to read book two.

-Lex Kent's 2020 Favorites List.
Lex Kent's Reviews, *goodreads*

If you are looking for an adventure novel with mystery, intrigue, romance, and a lot of angst, then look no further. ...I'm really impressed with how well this tale is written. The story itself is excellent, and the characters are well-developed and easy to connect with.

-Betty H., *NetGalley*

BEYOND THE
SMOKE

About the Author

A late bloomer, Stacy Lynn Miller took up writing after retiring from the Air Force. Her twenty years of toting a gun and police badge, tinkering with computers, and sleuthing for clues as an investigator form the foundation of her Manhattan Sloane romantic thriller series. Visually impaired, she is a proud stroke survivor, mother of two, tech nerd, chocolate lover, and terrible golfer with a hole-in-one. When you can't find her writing, she'll be golfing or drinking wine (sometimes both) with friends and family in Northern California.

You can connect with Stacy on Instagram @stacylynnmiller, Twitter @stacylynnmiller, or Facebook @stacylynnmillerauthor. You can also visit her website at stacylynnmiller.com.

BEYOND THE
SMOKE

STACY LYNN MILLER

BELLA
BOOKS
2021

Bella Books, Inc.
P.O. Box 10543
Tallahassee, FL 32302

Printed in the United States of America on acid-free paper.

First Bella Books Edition 2021

Editor: Medora MacDougall
Cover Designer: Judith Fellows

ISBN: 978-1-64247-237-0

Acknowledgments

A special shout-out goes to Barbara Gould, whose weird kernel popped into this beautiful story.

Thank you, Louise, Kristianne, Diane, Sue, and Sabrin, for giving me your two cents worth and then some. Every "wtf" and smiley emoji made the story sing.

Thank you, Linda and Jessica Hill, for believing in my work and holding a seat for me at the Bella Books table.

Thank you, Medora MacDougall, for throwing my words into your brilliant mixing bowl and shaking well. You made this story shine.

Finally, to my family. Thank you for braving COVID-19, wearing a mask, and for keeping me plied with ice tea and mama cakes.

Dedication

To Chris Waren.
My brother and partner in crime while growing up.
He taught me how to not get caught, but most of all, the
beauty of sacrifice.

PROLOGUE

San Francisco, California, twenty-two years ago

Nothing could have prepared thirteen-year-old Manhattan Sloane for the horror she witnessed weeks earlier on a twisty, foggy road. Her parents had died in a terrible, fiery crash, and the only life she knew burned up with them. In the aftermath, she'd been forced to live twenty miles away on the other side of the Bay Bridge with a grandmother she'd visited only once a year, but that wasn't where she wanted to be. She wanted to be home.

Her new home, Nana's suffocating, narrow, and cluttered townhouse, resembled nothing like the warm suburban ranch-style house she'd lived in since infancy. Without a yard to play in, Sloane spent her first afternoon in the only outdoor space available. The back deck wasn't much, but its hypnotic view of the bay and the life she left behind on the other side of it provided several minutes of comfort when she needed something to latch onto.

As much as her grandmother tried to make her feel welcomed, Sloane couldn't call her new surroundings home.

She lived off the items she'd stuffed into the two suitcases Child Protective Services had allowed her to take the morning following the accident. For weeks, the plain soap and shampoo her grandmother had loaned her were poor substitutes. Even her bed was an afterthought. She slept on the living room couch for ten nights until movers brought her bed and other things from her family home. Having the easy chair her father had sat in to read the evening newspaper and the dresser where her mother had stacked freshly washed clothes failed to dull the sharp sting of losing her parents.

Her only comfort came from her seventh-grade yearbook from Juan Crespi Junior High. Sloane looked at the picture of Finn Harper, her only friend, every morning when she woke and every night before going to sleep. She longed to see the one girl who made her palms sweaty by merely walking into her orbit. The question became how to make it happen. Without a phone number or address to go on, she'd have to become a detective in order to inhale Finn's sweet citrus scent again. Even if she tracked Finn down, she had another problem. Her grandmother didn't have a car and took the bus everywhere. What if buses or the train couldn't get her to Finn's? Sloane was stuck in a place with no future and no way of reaching out to her past.

In two days, Monday, she would mark her first day at a new school several miles away from her new home, the same place where her grandmother worked as an administrator. Like the townhouse, the school was nothing that Sloane was used to. The buildings were two stories tall and squeezed together like sardines, unlike the spread-out ones at the school she'd attended with Finn. The campus here had asphalt for physical education class, which meant the softball mitt her father helped her break in one weekend would now collect dust.

"What does it matter?" Sloane shoved the mitt underneath her bed, burying along with it the memory of the one fun thing she ever did with her dad. "It's not like I'd make any friends if they even had a team."

A knock on the door meant her grandmother wanted to tell her something. The only thing Sloane wanted to hear was that she'd been in a bad dream and all she had to do was wake up to have her old life back. When the door creaked opened after another knock and her grandmother poked her head inside, Sloane stabbed a brush through her long, thick brown hair to sweep away her ever-increasing frustration.

"Honey?" Her grandmother's voice was barely audible, frustrating Sloane even more.

"What?" Sloane barked without looking.

"You have a visitor."

Sloane froze. Who would visit her? No one knew she lived there. Her mind raced, picking at the possibilities. Could it be? Did that one special girl find her? "Is it Finn?"

Waiting for a response would've taken two or three precious seconds, time better spent running to greet her only friend in the world. She darted past her nana, feet pounding the stairs two at a time until she reached the top. "Finn?"

Bright afternoon sunlight silhouetted a figure standing near the sliding glass door leading to the deck. Every muscle tingled. It had to be Finn. The person stepped forward out of the blinding light. Her heart sank. The visitor was too tall and box-shaped to be Finn. Another step and a man came into focus. He wasn't in the uniform he wore when Sloane first had met him two weeks ago, but she recognized his kind face. His jeans and olive-green twill jacket worked well with his chiseled, light-skinned jaw and trimmed auburn hair. "Bernie?"

"It's good to see you again, Sloane."

"What are you doing here?"

"I told you I'd check on you, and I keep my promises." He closed within a step and placed both hands on her shoulders.

The night of the accident she wasn't sure how long she'd lingered roadside before Bernie scooped her into his arms and placed her in the backseat of his patrol cruiser. Numbed by watching the wreckage of her family car burn with her parents' bodies still inside, she'd welcomed his comforting arm while the fire trucks drenched the flames. As paramedics tended to the cuts on her hands she'd sustained when she failed to pry her mother loose from the devastation, he gave her a reassuring nod. When she refused to ride in the CPS woman's car, he drove her to the emergency foster care home. And before he left, he'd kneeled in front of her and promised to check on her when he could.

Today he did. Sloane's father had made one promise after another to spend time with her but rarely followed through. Bernie kept his promise, however, making her feel less sad for the first time since the accident.

"I didn't think you'd come." Sloane wanted to grin, but she couldn't. She wanted Finn.

Bernie's face softened with a sympathetic smile. "Why would you think that? How have you been doing?" When she lowered her head and shrugged, Bernie bent at the knees to look her in the eyes. "How about lunch, young lady?"

"I'd like that." When her eyes met his, she got a wild idea. He was a police officer. Maybe he could find Finn. But before she could ask, her nana's voice wheezed from the top of the stairs.

"You're a hard one to keep up with."

Bernie dashed over to offer his arm. "Loraine, would you like to join us for lunch?"

"That's sweet of you, but those stairs tuckered me out. Why don't you two go for a bite at The Tap? It's right down the street."

Phew! The last thing she wanted was an annoying grandmother around when she talked to Bernie. Maybe he'd agree to help her find Finn. Maybe Finn's parents would take pity on her and let her live with them. Any house in El Sobrante had to be better than this jail cell.

Following a short walk, Sloane and Bernie found a prime seat at the neighborhood pub and grill. Minutes later, the owner, who also doubled as bartender and server during peak hours, delivered their meals. The smell of freshly grilled burgers masked the stale scent of fryer grease wafting in from the kitchen.

"Extra pickles. Just the way you like it." Dylan placed Sloane's dish on the table in front of her.

Rubbing her hands together, she inspected her burger and fries and then Dylan's hippie-style ponytail and three-day stubble. He was the one bright spot of her otherwise dismal new life. "Thanks, D."

Dylan paused, cocked his head a few times as if shaking his memory loose before laying the other plate down. "And extra fries for Officer Bernie."

"Excellent memory. This looks great." Bernie accepted the ketchup bottle from Sloane and squirted a small red blob on the edge of his plate. "Thanks, Dylan."

"I'm pulling double duty today, so if you need anything else, wave me down." Dylan wiped his hands on his lightly stained white apron and gave Sloane a playful wink before sliding behind the bar.

She ate in silence and let the rock music Dylan had playing in the background fill the awkward void. While savoring the complementary flavors of pickles, raw white onions, and cheddar cheese mixed with a tangy sauce, she sized up Bernie. Did he visit all the kids he saved? Or did he consider her special? Either way, he made her feel that way.

Bernie soon swallowed the last bite of his burger, wiped his mouth with a paper napkin, and tossed it in the center of his plate. "I hear you start school on Monday, where your grandmother works. I think that's great. You already have someone there that you know."

She shrugged again, unsure how to respond without sounding like an uncaring brat. Other than Nana having a long-term feud with her father, she knew nothing about her grandmother. "Yeah, I guess."

"When I started with the police department a few years ago, we had to move. My daughter was about your age. It took her a few weeks, but she eventually made more friends than she had in the old place." Finally, something to give Sloane a little hope. "She told me the best thing about the move was that her new algebra class was weeks behind her old school, and the teacher thought she was a genius."

"Maybe, but I only had one friend." Sloane lowered her eyes, wondering where Finn was and if this was a good time to ask Bernie for his help.

"A pretty girl like you? You must be shy."

Shy wasn't it. She wasn't like the other girls. They only talked about makeup and clothes or how cute the boys were. Like Finn, she was interested in sports and singing. Should she ask? She opened her mouth to do so but stopped.

"You know, you can ask me anything."

"Can…" Her voice wavered, but she dug deep for an extra ounce of courage. "Can you help me find my friend at my old school?"

"Sure, Sloane. What's her name?"

Sloane's breath caught in hope. If he could find Finn, she was sure everything would be all right. "It's Finn Harper, but I don't know where she lives."

"That's okay. You went to Juan Crespi, right?" Sloane nodded hard enough to give herself a headache. He added, "I can get her address and home number through the school. I'll pass them along to your grandmother."

Sloane averted her eyes.

"Is that not okay?"

"Nana doesn't have a car."

"Maybe Finn can visit you."

Her stomach knotted on the thousand reasons Finn couldn't, or worse, wouldn't visit. Nothing was going right, and she thought nothing would ever again.

"Or, if your grandmother says it's okay, how about I take you on my next visit?"

"Really?" For the first time since the accident, Sloane's lips turned up in a genuine smile. Despite the horrible events that brought her to him, this kind man made her believe that everything would be all right.

"It would be my pleasure."

* * *

That hour at The Tap, combined with Bernie's weekly phone calls since, had taught Sloane one thing: fathers can keep promises. While homework over those three weeks kept her mind off the unbearable wait to visit Finn, school hadn't. Not one girl had made an overture to becoming friends. One blonde, though, with thick wisps trimmed around the ears like Finn had caught her eye in English class. But when Sloane worked up the courage to say hello, she discovered the girl wasn't worth her interest. Not one bit. She didn't have Finn's kind disposition and ability to put her at ease. Nor did she have a smile that made her feel like it was meant only for her. In fact, the girl was downright mean. That was it. Making friends wasn't in the cards.

This Saturday was *the* day, and the anticipation of finally seeing Finn had her springing from bed the instant sunbeams warmed her face—a first without an annoying alarm. She selected the perfect shirt and jeans and added the new denim jacket her grandmother had bought at a store near her school. Once dressed, she bolted up to the top stair where an alluring whiff of bacon drew her into the kitchen. "That smells great, Nana. Do you want me to get the plates out?"

"That would be great, honey." Nana paused from whisking the egg mixture. A slow-forming grin meant one thing: Sloane's first offer to lend a hand made her happy.

As if she'd been doing it for years, Sloane opened the cabinet neighboring the stove, retrieved the plates, and set the table. "Would you like orange juice, Nana?"

"That would be nice, Sloane." One of Nana's eyebrows rose to an exaggerated arch, putting a smile on Sloane's face.

At the small, rickety dining table, Sloane ate quicker than her grandmother. She chatted about Officer Bernie and her upcoming visit with Finn. He'd left a brief message on the answering machine earlier in the week, saying he'd pick her up first thing, ending it with, *"Let's surprise Finn this Saturday."* Sloane sat sentinel on the top stair leading down to the entry landing after clearing the table, bouncing a leg up and down like a piston.

After five agonizing minutes, her grandmother joined Sloane, standing near the step. "Why don't you wait for Bernie on the driveway? Just let me know when you two are about to take off."

"Thank you, Nana." Sloane gave her a quick peck on the cheek—another first. Before lunging toward the front door, she didn't take the time to consider the show of affection, other than it felt like she'd turned a corner.

An hour had gone by and then another while Sloane sat on the curb. Her excitement waned in the first hour, and disappointment formed in the second. The one thing that kept her interest was a smoke plume billowing over the rooftops and a cacophony of sirens blasting several blocks away. *Likely a house fire*, she thought. She didn't turn angry until her grandmother came out and sat next to her on the sidewalk.

"He lied."

Nana placed a hand on Sloane's back. Intended to comfort, it had the opposite effect. Sloane balled her fists and pressed them against her chin.

"Honey, why don't you come inside? I'm sure he got tied up at work and will call soon."

"He's not coming." Sloane stomped all the way to her room and fell on her bed facedown, screaming curse words into her pillow. "He lied," repeated in her head. She wouldn't see Finn today, nor any other day.

The next morning, a knock on her bedroom door woke her. "Go away!" she yelled before stuffing a pillow over her head. Talking was the last thing she wanted. Bernie had never showed, and she'd been holed up in her room ever since, refusing to come up for dinner.

The door slid open. Nana walked in, her face pale and eyes puffy red. A tear streaked her cheek and dripped to the half-folded newspaper she held in her hand. "Honey, I have terrible news." She moved to the bed and sat next to Sloane.

Sloane's empty stomach growled, making her queasier than she was yesterday when Bernie had disappointed her.

Her grandmother unfolded the newspaper to reveal the front page. A picture of Bernie in his uniform with the American flag behind his right shoulder, capturing his gentle smile, was emblazoned across the top. Above the photo in large black print read the headline: Off-Duty Officer Killed. She scanned a few words that hailed him as a hero who'd died trying to save a woman trapped in a burning Hunter's Point home before fire trucks arrived.

"Nooooo!" It had happened again. Sloane's body choked at the realization everyone around her was dying in a fire. She couldn't shake the feeling she'd become a death magnet.

Her grandmother wrapped an arm around her shoulders and pulled her tight against her bosom. Nana's soft voice spoke reassuring words but did little to soothe the sense of doom bubbling in her gut. She shook her head, hoping to cast off the plague of death besieging her, but nothing worked. She pushed Nana away and hurried across the room.

"No! I'm cursed." Sloane pulled at her hair. Her mind focused on death and flames and nothing else. "Everyone around me dies." Nana walked toward her, but Sloane called out, "No! Stay away."

Her grandmother didn't listen. She rubbed Sloane's arms. "Honey, what happened to your parents was horrible, but they didn't die because you're cursed. It was an accident. And Bernie died trying to save someone."

"No, I tell you." Sloane shook her head with the force of a tornado. "I was the reason he was in that neighborhood. Bernie was coming to see me. If I hadn't wanted to see my friend, he'd be alive. I can't do this to you. Or to Finn."

"Listen to me." Her grandmother's voice grew stern as she tightened her grip on Sloane's arms. "Your father punished me by keeping you away from me as much as possible. I'm not going to let anything separate us again."

Sloane's head stilled. She stared at her grandmother, having never understood the feud between mother and son. "Why would he want to punish you?"

"Because I sent his father away when he was young. He grew up, thinking I hated his father."

"Why would you send him away?"

"Because he beat me." Nana loosened her grip but kept her hands on Sloane's arms. "I took it twice, but not a third time."

"Is he alive?"

"No, child." Her grandmother shook her head slowly. "He drank himself to death years ago."

Why didn't anyone tell Sloane her dad grew up without a father? How ironic. He resented his mother for having no father, yet he worked so much Sloane didn't have one either.

"Listen to me, young lady. You are not cursed. I am not afraid to have you close. I've wanted to be a part of your life since the day you were born. We're all we have left." Nana pulled her into an embrace. "I love you, Manhattan Sloane."

Sloane pressed her head against her grandmother's frail shoulder and whimpered, "Thank you, Nana." She was a long way off from saying, "*I love you*," but for the first time, it felt possible. Tears dampened both their eyes. Sloane considered this the moment they became a family.

After dinner, while walking back from The Tap, Nana asked, "Would you like me to find your friend?"

Even if her grandmother was right, that she wasn't cursed, Sloane couldn't take a chance with Finn. Premonitions of doom haunted Sloane every step home, convincing her she couldn't risk the flames taking the one good thing left from her life before the accident. It was settled. Those hazel eyes would remain in the past.

"No, Nana. It's not important anymore."

CHAPTER ONE

San Francisco, California, present day

Stiff wind bit at Manhattan Sloane's cheeks and whipped long brown strands of hair from her ponytail. She drew in damp, briny air while taking in the white-capped waves beating the rocky shoreline of Lands End. Spectacular views of the bay like this one had comforted her the first summer following her parents' deaths. It was home. The word echoed in her head—home. Over the years, she never had thought she could feel more connected to anything, but the last five months, when she and Finn had become lovers following the kidnapping and rescue of their family members, had proved her wrong. San Francisco was home, but Finn Harper was her heart.

The thick picnic blanket Finn had thrown down near the edge of the cliffs softened the ground enough that Sloane barely felt the small pebbles through the thinning fabric of her favorite, well-worn blue jeans. She zipped her denim jacket further up to block the wind's chill before folding her knees close to her chest and wrapping her arms around them. A glance confirmed that Finn, sitting a foot away, was staring at the same remarkable scene and seemingly in the same trance Sloane had been in for the last few minutes. Even from that distance, Sloane felt her pull.

Sloane didn't have to wonder what her life would be like if her path and Finn's hadn't crossed again. She knew the answer. The fear of death would be gripping her. She'd be fearing everyone close to her would die in flames, like her parents and Bernie and her dear sweet wife, Avery. She'd be worrying the same fate would take her teenage stepdaughter, Reagan. That she'd either hold her at arm's length or ship her off to her grandparents— to the Tenneys, not the homophobic Santoses. *Assholes*, she thought. Luiz and Maria still had her panties twisted following their bitter custody and adoption battles.

Her rock now, Finn kept her anchored to the shoreline. Sloane didn't expect that leaving the San Francisco Police Department and navigating a new career would have so many twists and turns. But amid the uncertainty of getting their private investigation firm off the ground, Finn, with her experience as an executive in the Drug Enforcement Agency, kept them moving forward.

Sloane turned toward her new source of calm to focus on Finn's profile. An involuntary deep intake of salty air filled her chest with the same sense of peace she'd felt every morning for the last three months since Finn moved in. From Reagan to her career to her home, every thread of her new life had Finn's fingerprints on it. But if she had to pick the best part of her day, waking up next to this beautiful creature had become it. A late sleeper, Finn never woke before her, which, like now, provided several blissful minutes of taking in the soft curves of her face.

"I love family Sundays with you."

"I do too." The corners of Finn's lips stretched wide, forcing her nose to scrunch like it used to do in junior high. In an instant, Sloane knew that smile was meant for her. "You've been quiet since I told you Kadin wants to buy my condo. Are you concerned?"

"About you? No. Realistic about Kadin? Yes. She wants you back."

"Wanting and having are two distinct things." Finn leaned in. "You had me the day you walked back into my life."

Sloane's upper lip tingled at the thought of stealing another kiss like she did this morning before Finn opened her eyes in bed. She tilted her head forward to do just that, but Reagan's voice came up behind her, forcing that kiss to wait. "I'm starved. Anyone else ready to eat?"

"About a hundred stairs ago." Chandler Harper rubbed the sixty-year-old muscles of his right leg to ease what must have been a monstrous cramp. While running on his treadmill kept Finn's father in decent shape, it didn't prepare him well to hike the steep trails of Lands End.

Damn it. "You owe me a kiss." Sloane pulled back, wishing Reagan and Chandler had taken the long trail on their hike down the cliffside instead of the shorter one.

"Deal." Finn rose to her knees, retrieved the backpack behind her, and laid out the food containers.

"I guess those two-mile jogs haven't paid off, Gramps." Reagan smirked before she picked at the food.

"You'll never stop calling me that, won't you?" Chandler shook his head in a lighthearted retort.

"Nope." Reagan added a mischievous wink.

Since they had been kidnapped by the cartel, the playfulness between Reagan and Chandler had grown into a thing. Within hours of their terrifying rescue, they had begun needling each other and they had kept it up since. Sloane suspected they fell into it as a coping mechanism after their ordeal. Whatever the reason, it had helped Reagan work through the trauma, and she seemed no worse for the wear. For that, Chandler had her gratitude.

"You two will drive each other nuts by the end of summer." Sloane dove into the grapes and cheese they'd packed for their family day hike. She weighed the possibility that Reagan's summer internship at Chandler's law firm might be a well-intended mistake.

"A challenge I look forward to beginning tomorrow." Chandler raised an eyebrow at Reagan, throwing down the gauntlet.

"You're on, Gramps." Reagan joined Chandler in a high-five. *Definitely a bad idea.* Before Reagan started tomorrow, Sloane would have to talk to her about professionalism inside the office versus the familiarity of family outside.

While they ate, Chandler and Reagan continued their spirited banter, and Sloane soaked in the majestic power of the ocean beat. The rhythm of the waves came and went in a soothing pattern. Sloane soon closed her eyes and reached for Finn's hand. Together, their pulses matched the slow beating of the whitecaps. Home and heart were one.

Moments later, a vibration in Sloane's coat pocket, accompanied by a muffled musical chime, alerted her to an incoming phone call. Back to reality. She and Finn had only a handful of clients with their new investigation firm, and each expected the Sloane-Harper Group to answer their call, even on Sunday. Though, the six-month-long contract they won last week thankfully meant taking on no more clients until it expired. In another week or two, they'd be down to a single client—the City of San Francisco.

Casting her gaze toward the water again, Sloane let out a breathy sigh before fishing out her phone. "This is Sloane."

"Hi, Sloane. It's Morgan West."

"Morgan? This is a pleasant surprise." The personal call from her old boss picked up Sloane's mood.

"Do you have time to talk?"

"I'd love to, but we're on a family outing."

"This is important. It's about your city contract." Morgan's voice contained the same level of concern she had for Sloane following Avery's death. Sloane's antenna went up.

After giving Finn's hand a firm squeeze, Sloane snapped her stare toward her. "What about our contract?" Finn's eyes widened.

"I think you should know what's in store for you. Can we meet somewhere today?"

"Finn and I are at Lands End."

"I'm not that far from there. Can we meet you, say in thirty minutes?"

"Thirty minutes." Sloane gave Finn a questioning look. "We can meet you at the top. There's a café." Sloane muffled the phone into her chest and asked Finn, "What's the name of that place?"

"I think it's The Lookout."

Sloane nodded her concurrence and lifted the phone again. "It's called The Lookout Café. We'll start hiking up now."

After Morgan disconnected, Sloane filled in the others, and Chandler agreed to take Reagan on the last segment of the hike while she and Finn took their meeting. Sloane helped Finn pack away the picnic, recalling Morgan had said, "we." Who were we? Now her interest was really piqued.

Finn took the lead, following a gravel trail, most times wide enough for two people, other times only wide enough to walk single file. The mile trek brought them through areas of thick brush and others with weeds trimmed back. In between, several sets of steep wooden stairs dug into the hillside tested Sloane's ankle. Though healed from the nasty break in the explosion that killed her wife, it still stiffened with overuse. Trailing behind, Sloane struggled to keep up. "I think our next hike should be on flatter ground."

Finn glanced over her shoulder and stopped to let Sloane catch up. "Are you okay, babe?"

"A little sore." When Sloane reached the same step as Finn, she checked the pathway to make sure no one was approaching from either direction. She shifted the backpack containing the picnic food on her shoulder and snaked an arm around Finn's waist, pulling her in close. "I'll take that kiss now."

Finn's answer was in the form of another nose-scrunching smile.

Two inches taller than Finn in flat sneakers, Sloane placed a hand under Finn's chin and pulled her face closer. Her heart, still beating fast from the climb, fluttered when their lips touched. Finn's were cold from damp air, but they quickly warmed when Sloane pressed harder and wrapped her arm tighter. The orange scent of Finn's shampoo from earlier this morning had faded, replaced by salty sweat. It still sparked a desire to prolong the kiss. She parted her lips, inviting Finn to do the same, and then sent her tongue searching for its mate. The moment they touched, a twinge rippled her abdomen.

Breaking the kiss was the last thing Sloane wanted. She wanted much more. She wanted Finn's body to warm the rest of her and feel her skin to skin, but more would have to wait until later. Much later. After a reluctant sigh, Sloane pulled back.

"Wow." Finn's eyes stayed closed, but her mouth remained parted.

"We'll continue this later."

At the top of the hillside, the narrow gravel trail widened into pavement and the foot-traffic thickened, both signs the parking lot and café were nearby. Then Sloane recognized Morgan's cream-colored Camry, parked close to the building.

"She's here." Following a quick scan of the empty car, Sloane added, "She must be inside."

Sloane and Finn entered the café. Given that it had no tables or chairs, the owners should have labeled their establishment a food stand. The only place for patrons to rest their drinks and sandwiches was a series of counters not designed to accommodate a full meal that lined a thirty-foot-long wall of windows. Still, the space offered a beautiful view of the ocean.

At the far end, Sloane spotted Morgan's shoulder-length graying blond hair. Despite their three-year acquaintance, this marked the first time she'd seen Morgan in jeans and a dark peacoat. Casual clothes suited her well.

As she drew closer, Sloane recognized the bobbed black hair on the woman standing next to Morgan. Assistant District Attorney Kyler Harris looked as good in jeans and a casual coat. So, they *were* a thing. They made a handsome couple.

Sloane jabbed Finn in the ribs with an elbow. "Kyler's here, too."

"You were right. Good for them."

When Kyler ran a hand down Morgan's arm, the tender touch all but confirmed Sloane's suspicion. Morgan turned around. "Sloane. Finn. Thanks for coming." Following a round of hugs, Morgan offered Sloane and Finn each a paper cup with a plastic lid. "Hope you like latté."

"This is great, thank you." Sloane sipped, wrapping her hands around the cup to draw warmth into her chilled fingertips. Finn did the same. "You said this was about our contract."

"I think you should know what you've gotten yourself into." Morgan's narrowed brow suggested more than a passing concern, which simultaneously troubled and elated Sloane. The prospect of being in some sort of tight spot for her and Finn's first big contract was worrisome. Morgan, however, was bothering to warn her, which spoke to an affinity beyond their previous working relationship. They weren't merely former colleagues. They were becoming friends.

"We know looking into the department's cold cases will ruffle a few feathers." Sloane's concern drifted to Morgan. Was this where she was going? Was she concerned her and Finn's work would make her look bad?

"The new mayor wants to use your contract to do a lot more than ruffle feathers. She wants to clean house."

"She *did* run on a platform to hold the police more accountable for the use of force." Finn's reply knocked a memory loose in Sloane about Nicci Cole's mayoral campaign. Finn had followed the special election a lot closer than Sloane, who avoided politics as if it would give her herpes.

"She has a lot more planned." Morgan's pursed lips didn't bode well. "My contacts tell me she wants to dismantle department management and promote those who support her agenda."

"Which is?" Sloane's spidey senses were up. The vibe she got of Mayor Cole in her campaign ads was not one friendly to police.

"Only enforce victim crimes." Kyler's reddened face hinted at agitation, a reaction Sloane had observed on a rare occasion when the stakes were high, like when Reagan's and Chandler's lives hung in the balance. "She did the same thing when she was the District Attorney. If she had her way, vice, narcotics, and the gang task force would be history."

"That's insane. All those things lead to more crimes and more victims." Sloane's neck tingled as a disquieting hidden agenda took form. She and Finn were being set up.

"But we've been hired to review cold cases with victims. How does our work tie into the mayor's agenda?" Finn's stare bounced between Morgan and Kyler, but Sloane already knew the answer. She'd seen local politics at work in the previous administration—smear and blame everyone and everything for a long-standing mess.

"Incompetence is my guess." Morgan's face turned expressionless as if politics had drained all the joy she had for the job. "The SFPD has the highest cold case rate in the state. If you two solve even a fraction of the open cases, that's all the excuse the mayor will need to justify a complete overhaul of the department."

"So, if we do our job, half the investigations division will be out of theirs." Sloane ticked off in her head the names of detectives who didn't have a safety net. She counted at least two dozen in vice and narcotics alone. None of this was what she had in mind for the Sloane-Harper Group's first big government contract. If they defaulted on the project to protect her former colleagues, the city would simply rebid the contract. There had to be a way to neutralize the mayor while getting the job done, but she had no idea where to start.

"But if we don't do our job, our firm likely won't survive the hit." Sloane stared out the window to glimpse at the ocean water to calm her bubbling ire. She and Finn were pawns in a high-stakes political game, and she didn't like it. Not one bit.

"I hate this as much as you do, Sloane." Morgan briefly placed a comforting hand on her arm. "Expect resistance. Captain Nash has his eye on a deputy chief position, and he can get nasty when he feels threatened. And you and Finn threaten him."

"How about you? You could lose your job." The coffee in Sloane's stomach soured at her dilemma.

"I'm retirement eligible and never had aspirations of making captain or higher, so this only speeds up my plans. I'm worried, though, about the detectives who don't have their twenty in yet, like Eric Decker. If he's laid off instead of forced into early medical retirement, he'll lose his health insurance when he needs it the most."

A swell of sadness settled in Sloane's throat at her old partner's name. She hadn't seen him since the day she adopted Reagan and he dropped off a life-shifting gift. From reading the scrapbook he gave her, she learned that he'd kept an eye on her most of her life after her parents' accident. But that devotion didn't make up for him having played a part in their deaths. Tentatively, Sloane asked, "Have you partnered Eric up yet?"

Morgan furrowed her brow. "I'm surprised you don't know. He returns to modified duty tomorrow."

"Well, that's to be expected." Her old partner never liked being a straphanger. He preferred being the first one through the door. Sitting behind a desk, analyzing reports, crossing T's and dotting I's and doing the computer legwork for other detectives would drive him bat shit crazy. "Just don't stick him with Wilson when he's cleared. He's slower than molasses."

"You really don't know." Morgan frowned. "That round he took in the chest at Three Owls Vineyard did permanent damage to his left arm. He'll never work the field again and will ride a desk until he qualifies for medical retirement. Unless the mayor gets her way."

The news sucker-punched Sloane in the gut. She might no longer trust Eric after learning he kept the truth from her about her parents' accident, but she still cared about him. She never wanted him to be permanently disabled, and she sure as hell didn't want him to lose his health insurance because of her.

"Thanks for the heads-up, Morgan." Sloane swallowed the dry lump in her throat. She reminded herself that broken trust tore her and Eric apart. He was the reason she was an orphan and hid that fact for years. That meant he was no longer her problem.

"Watch your back, Sloane." Morgan's expression hinted that she suspected trouble wasn't just something to be expected, but inevitable.

CHAPTER TWO

Finn cringed when Sloane pressed a button on the driver's door armrest, retracting the side mirrors into the window frames. That meant a dance was coming after Sloane inched her gray metallic midsized SUV forward into the garage of their Hunters Point townhouse. The space was ample enough for two vehicles, but the stacks of Finn's things from her home office lining one side of the garage left little room for error. Sloane put the shifter in park, leaving an inch to spare for Finn to slip out, making sure not to scratch the midnight blue paint of her Audi sedan.

Other than the storage and parking situation, the townhouse was perfect for their small family—something to think about changing if she and Sloane stayed there for the long term. Inside, while Sloane added the picnic blanket to a pile and started their load of laundry, Finn and Reagan unloaded the food containers from their family hike.

"Are you set for your first day at the firm tomorrow?" Finn asked.

"I think so." Reagan's hesitant response made Finn think otherwise.

"You don't sound confident. Anything I can help with?"

"Maybe." Reagan peeked around the corner of the kitchen and then looked at Finn again. "Mom's great at giving advice with most things, but..." her voice trailed off.

"But?"

"She dresses cool."

"But she dresses soft butch, right?"

"You're more feminine like me." Reagan bobbed her head in agreement. "What do you think I should wear tomorrow?"

While Finn and Reagan had settled into a friendly relationship at home, this marked the first time Reagan had come to her for advice. They'd apparently turned a corner, making Finn optimistic that Reagan had accepted her as Sloane's partner. It felt good.

She fought back a grin before she spoke. "Daddy made sure everyone knows you're a high school student, so no one will expect you to wear a business suit, but you'll still have to look professional."

"That's the problem. Other than the dress I wore for Mom's funeral, I'm not sure anything I own is professional enough."

"You can pair those black twill slacks of yours with anything. And don't you have a black skirt that hits at the knee?"

"Yeah."

"That'll work too. We're about the same size. How about I loan you a few blouses? You can top it off with my plain black sweater."

"That would be great." Reagan's shoulders relaxed as if Finn had lifted a massive weight from them.

"Come on, you. Let's pick out a wardrobe."

Finn led Reagan into the master bedroom. She bypassed the stacks of moving boxes along one wall, some still unopened from the move before this one. At the closet, she sifted through her work blouses, the screech of metal hangers scraping along the rod sounding every few seconds.

"This one would look great on you." Finn pulled out a pale green silk button-down. "It'll bring out the green in your eyes."

"Just like yours."

"Yes, just like mine." Finn stopped her searching and turned her gaze to Reagan. Sloane had told Finn months ago she'd been looking for her in every woman she made love to and that it was no coincidence Avery closely resembled her. Now, Finn realized even with Reagan's darker skin, passersby could easily mistake her for Reagan's biological mother. Strangely, that made her more confident she and Sloane were meant for one another.

Before the tightness in Finn's throat turned into watery eyes, she cleared her throat and scanned the closet from left to right. "Now, where's that sweater?"

"Which sweater is that?" Sloane asked from the doorway.

Finn turned her head toward Sloane's voice. Sloane had let a bright smile stretch across her face as she propped a shoulder against the frame of the bedroom door. Finn matched her smile. "My black knitted cardigan."

Sloane pushed herself off the doorframe and walked inside the room. "I don't think you've unpacked it yet."

Finn snapped her fingers. "You're right."

"That's okay, Finn." Reagan gathered the blouses Finn had picked out for her. "I don't need a sweater."

"Oh, yes, you do." Finn arched her eyebrows. She couldn't have Reagan on display her first day there. "The firm is mostly men in suits, so that place is colder than an icebox. Unless you wear a padded bra, they'll be staring at your chest all day."

"You're wearing a sweater, young lady. That's final." In an instant, Sloane unstacked the top rows of boxes, looking for it. She muttered under her breath, "Where is that damn thing?"

Finn and Reagan laughed before rummaging through an open box. After one unsuccessful hunt, Finn paused to recall where she last wore the sweater—at her old office. "Babe, is there a box marked 'work'?"

Sloane scanned the remaining four boxes and then rolled her eyes. "On the bottom."

"Never fails," Finn said. Moments later, she had the box open and located the black cardigan.

Reagan kissed Finn on the cheek and whispered into her ear, "Thank you. You're a lifesaver."

"You're welcome." Finn gave her a wink. Who would've thought a sweater would bring them closer?

Before Reagan could leave, Sloane placed a hand on her arm. "You got a second, honey?"

"Sure. What's up?"

"I love the way you and Chandler needle each other on family day, but—"

"I know, Mom. Finn already gave me the scoop. It's Gramps at home, but Mr. Harper at the office."

Sloane kissed Reagan on the forehead. "I should've known better. You'll do fine tomorrow."

"Thanks, Mom." Reagan returned to her room to test out various combinations of the clothes Finn had loaned her.

Finn continued to sift through the box marked "work" and found items she hadn't seen in months. She pulled out the autographed photo of her shaking hands with the president, recalling how crazy that time was for her.

Sloane wrapped her arms around Finn's waist from behind and rested her chin on a shoulder. "I remember you telling me about that photo. You were in Yuma, right?"

"It was hot and miserable, but my hard work paid off and put me on the fast-track, eventually landing me in San Francisco and in your arms." Finn melted into Sloane's embrace. How could they make love this morning and that still not be enough to get her through the day?

"Do you miss it?" Sloane squeezed a little tighter.

"I don't miss the politics, which made the decision to resign an easy one. Though, after what Morgan said, it appears politics has followed us."

"I have a bad feeling about this project. The mayor is using us as pawns." Sloane kissed her on the cheek and released her hold, Finn instantly missing the touch.

"What do you want to do about it?" Placing the framed photo on her dresser, Finn continued to sift through the box while Sloane restacked the others.

"I'm not sure yet, but we need to keep our meeting with the mayor's chief of staff tomorrow. If we get a bad vibe, we should talk then."

"Agreed." Finn came across two unloaded spare ammunition magazines she'd kept in her office desk at DEA headquarters. She decided to store them in the gun safe as a reminder to clean them the next time she cleaned her personal firearm.

Finn unlocked her gun safe, which was mounted on the top closet shelf next to Sloane's. When she slid the ammunition magazines inside, her hand grazed a second gun next to her personal Glock. Finn had almost forgotten about the other weapon, but not how she had gotten it. Time and time again, she considered telling Sloane about it but discarded the idea as quickly as it popped into her head. Doing so would mean dredging up painful memories of the daring hostage exchange at Three Owls Vineyard, a topic Sloane had avoided discussing. Even now, as she considered returning the gun to its owner, she couldn't bring herself to tell Sloane.

Finn glanced at the alarm clock. It wasn't too late for a Sunday evening, and if she hurried, she could return the gun tonight. She just needed a believable excuse to leave the house without raising suspicion. Grabbing the second gun and locking the safe, she stuffed it into her jacket pocket before turning toward Sloane. "Hey, babe. We're low on eggs. I'm gonna run to the store so we can send Reagan off with breakfast tomorrow. Do we need anything else?"

"Why don't I come with you?"

Think fast. Finn stroked Sloane's arm as she walked past, making sure not to rub the hard, metal bulge in her pocket against her. "Rest that ankle of yours. I won't be long." Before Sloane could object, Finn had collected her purse and keys from the hallway table and was out the door.

A decade as a DEA agent had trained Finn to lie with ease and finesse. She didn't think twice about bending the truth on the job, but lying to Sloane was a different matter. While nothing she had said was an overt lie, omitting the whole truth felt like one. She told herself it was for the greater good. That alone should've sent up glowing red neon flags and told her this might come back to bite her. If she had to justify something to herself, it had to be wrong. Nevertheless, she had to complete what she started five months ago.

Twenty minutes later, following a quick text to Sloane that read, *Visiting with an old friend. Be back soon,* Finn knocked on the apartment door. She was doing nothing wrong, she reminded herself, but she couldn't shake the feeling of betrayal.

The door opened.

"Finn? What brings you here?" Eric's flat response contained neither joy nor annoyance over the unexpected visit. The apathy that had plagued him during her last few visits hadn't improved, neither had his pale complexion. Both suggested he hadn't climbed out of his funk after being shot in the chest at Three Owls and less than stellar recovery. The only positive sign was that muscle tone in his legs and right arm had returned. His left arm, where a Los Dorados bullet had ripped the tendons and muscles to shreds, was a different story.

"You're looking good, Eric. Can I come in for a few?"

"Sure." When he opened the door wider to let her pass, he still favored his left arm, holding it close to his side. Morgan was right. He'd probably never have full use of it.

Finn took a seat on his well-worn, beige cloth couch. A bachelor, Eric didn't put much stock into decorating. His furnishings—a sofa, worn recliner, cheap drapes, and a few tables, all in the same color palette—were intended for function, not appearance. He poured all his money into the toys: a sixty-inch ultra-high-definition television and high-end sound system that overpowered the room. The only personal touch was a handmade wall clock his father had created out of spent bullets and brass during his time on the police force.

"Can I get you something to drink?" The strides Eric took toward the couch seemed strong. At least that had come back to him.

"No, I'm fine. Morgan said you're returning to duty tomorrow."

"Modified." Eric rolled his stiff left shoulder before sitting in the nearby recliner positioned at a ninety-degree angle from the couch.

Finn pulled from her coat pocket his black .40 caliber Beretta automatic pistol. She pushed it across the wood coffee table, the muzzle ending up at a safe angle away from them both. "I thought you might have changed your mind about wanting this back."

Eric leaned back in his chair and rubbed his right hand across his stubbled chin. The lengthy pause hinted at an internal battle over the gun that saved all of their lives. "That was the second-worst day of my life."

"I guess the worst was the day Sloane's parents were killed." Finn felt the pain in his slow, silent nod. "She's still struggling, but I sense her anger subsiding a little every day."

"Sloane made her choice." Gritted teeth punctuated his reply. "I need to move on."

"Is that what you really want?" she asked.

"Do I have a choice?"

"Just give her more time."

"Sloane spent two decades thinking she alone was to blame for her parents' death, but I'm the reason they crashed." Eric's breathy exhale spoke to the regret behind his words. "That's not something you ever get over."

Finn had no comeback for the dilemma that had divided her loyalties. Eric had become a friend, and she hated seeing him pay a steep price for something he unintentionally did as a kid. But her first concern was for Sloane and getting her through her pain. Even if Sloane couldn't, Finn could see a time when she could get over what Eric did.

"I don't know what to say, Eric."

"You don't have to say anything. Like I said, I need to move on."

Finn leaned forward, placing her elbows on both knees to stress her next point. "I should warn you. Sloane and I won a contract with the city to work SFPD cold cases. Our paths might cross."

"Thanks for the heads-up." His ho-hum response made Finn think he held no hope that things would change between him and Sloane and that she'd worn out her welcome.

Finn had done what she'd come to do, so she stood. Eric had his backup weapon back but didn't seem to care about it other than it brought up lousy memories. Finn pointed at the gun. "No one knows I had this, not even Sloane. Unless Quintrell talks, no one will ever know what happened."

"Thanks. I hope that doesn't come back to bite you in the ass. You know how Sloane reacts when she finds out she's been lied to." Eric walked her to the door, the awkward silence speaking volumes.

Finn lowered her gaze. Inspecting the tops of her sneakers seemed like a better option than seeing the pain in his eyes again. "I hate this." When the door closed, a chill went down Finn's spine, telling her something had to give.

* * *

Evil, pure evil. Whoever invented the metal tape measure had a sadistic streak. Measuring anything longer than Sloane's arms' width with any accuracy proved impossible without a second pair of hands. All she needed to know were the dimensions of the unfinished storage area in the townhouse basement, but every time she let out more tape, the end moved from her starting point and snagged on boxes of holiday decorations. Compounding her problem, the only light came from the hallway through the opened storage area door, making it impossible to read the numbers without a flashlight.

"Why didn't I think of doing this half an hour ago before Reagan went to The Tap?" Sloane muttered to herself as if her complaining would move things along faster. A thumping on the stairs signaled someone was in the house. She heard her name. "Down here!"

"Babe?" Finn called out again at the foot of the stairs.

"In the storage area."

Finn shined her cell phone's flashlight onto Sloane, who was hunched over, fishing a long stretch of metal tape across the uneven concrete floor. Following a stream of curse words, Sloane looked up to see Finn sucking in her lower lip, failing to stifle a laugh.

"Can I help?"

After straightening her posture in the dark storage area, Sloane balled both hands and propped them against her hips. Pouting lips and all, she was as disappointed as the year her Nana gave her underwear for Christmas. "I wanted to do this before you came back."

A raised eyebrow marked Finn's curiosity. "What are you up to, Manhattan Sloane?"

"You'd never complain, but I know you miss your old home office. If we finish off this area and install some overhead storage in the garage, we could solve all of your problems. You'll have room to get out of both cars without doing the Shimmy, and, best of all," Sloane spread her arms wide as if surveying her kingdom, "this would make a great office."

Finn carefully stepped over the uneven threshold. She stopped inches from Sloane, breath tickling her cheeks. In a low, husky tone, she whispered, "Have I told you today how much I love you?"

"Just this morning."

Was it in bed or during breakfast when Finn whispered, "I love you" into her ear? Both. It was definitely both, and Sloane whispered the same words back. She kept the promise she'd made to herself when Reagan was missing. Sloane was now telling the people she loved how she felt every day—a dramatic departure from how she lived for her first thirty-five years. Thanks to Avery, Finn, Reagan, Chandler, and Reagan's grandparents, Janet and Caleb Tenney, she now embraced love, refusing to run from it.

Finn threw her arms around Sloane's neck. "After all this, it deserves repeating. I love you."

"I love you, too, and you deserve much more than words." She tossed the tape measure on a box before wrapping her arms around Finn's waist and pulling until their thighs, abdomens, and breasts converged. Finn's body had become her kryptonite. Every time she touched it, she grew weak and could think of nothing else. Why would she want to? It sparked and fed her every sexual desire.

The hallway light bounced through the open door and cast faint shadows on the side of Finn's face, setting the tone Sloane felt every time they were alone—everything she would ever need was right in front of her. She inhaled. Despite the room's musty dust scent and the smell of outdoors and a day's sweat, Finn still made her body tingle with anticipation.

The moment she pressed their lips together, she wanted to feel more. She slid her hands beneath the trailing edge of Finn's leather jacket and top until they found the soft skin of her back. A shudder of taut muscles where she'd grazed urged her to touch more. Tracing her hands around Finn's waist to her belly, she pushed them upward beneath more fabric until her palms covered both breasts. Finn's breathy release meant she wanted more as well.

Finn broke the kiss. "Upstairs."

The bedroom was way too far for Sloane's liking so she gave each breast an extra squeeze. If her internal clock was working, they had two hours until Reagan came home from her date. "Why wait?"

"Where's Reagan?" Finn threw her head to one side, giving Sloane more access to the spot behind her ear that drove her crazy.

"Tap 'til ten." Sloane clamped her mouth around the flesh of Finn's neck while she slid her hands to the jacket zipper. The basement wasn't sexy and didn't include soft sheets, but those things weren't on the menu. As much as Sloane enjoyed making slow, tender love to Finn, at this moment, she wanted sweaty, on-the-verge-of-getting-caught sex.

Unzipping and sliding Finn's jacket off her shoulders, she moved her lips down to the crook of her neck, alternating between kisses and licks. Finn's throaty moan was a clear indication she'd stoked her fire. In short order, shirts and bras flew in various directions to the cement floor. Breasts pressed together, each plunged a hand into one another's unzipped jeans. The stiff, unforgiving fabric required far too much concentration, and Sloane had none to spare. She muttered something incoherent in a futile attempt to not climax too soon, but her knees buckled to wave after wave of spasms.

Once Sloane's head stopped spinning long enough for her to regain her footing, frustration crept in. *Damn it! I never outlast her.* She quickly refocused on Finn's needs until she couldn't stand.

A thumping on the stairs. "Mom!"

Sloane's breath snagged in her chest as both their heads snapped wide-eyed toward the open door. A simultaneous, "Shit."

Heart pounding harder and no time for bras, Sloane reached for the first garment she found and slipped it over her head. Finn did the same, breasts flopping with their freedom. If not for the immediate danger of being caught in the act, Sloane would've relished the spectacle.

"In here." Sloane spun around to the sound of zippers.

"Why are you guys in the dark?" Thankfully, Reagan's silhouette in the doorway blocked most of the light from the hallway.

"Taking measurements. I'm planning to turn this space into a home office." A version of the truth worked best in embarrassing moments like this. Just in case, Sloane stuffed her hand in a pants pocket to hide the evidence. "Hey, I thought you were having a late dinner with Emeryn?"

"He was an idiot, so I left." Reagan squinted at her mom in the dim light. "Isn't that Finn's shirt?"

Sloane darted her eyes, searching for a plausible explanation. Not even drunk would she pick out a U-neck with ruffles. "Uh, yeah. Finn has me trying out new things."

Reagan wrinkled her nose and shook her head from side to side. "Definitely not you."

When Finn moved closer to the light, Sloane playfully slapped her on the arm. "See? Not me."

"I'm going to bed. Gotta be at the law firm at nine," Reagan said before turning on her heels toward her bedroom.

"Good night, honey." Sloane craned her neck out the door. After Reagan disappeared inside her room, she turned toward Finn, grinning like a teenager who got away with it. "That was close."

Upstairs, naked and sated, heart still pounding, Sloane lay in the center of the bed with Finn in her arms. Finn's head rested atop a breast, rising and falling to Sloane's rapid breaths, which were struggling to return to a regular cadence. Sloane walked her fingertips from Finn's bottom and up her spine in a straight line, the skin warm and damp from rounds two and three.

After spending nearly six months as lovers, feeling their bodies together, skin to skin, had become her addiction, requiring a daily fix. Though lust was a big part of it, her need went beyond desire. Finn's touch was the air she breathed, the water she drank, and the food she ate to sustain her every need.

"Do you think we made the right choice by taking the city contract?"

Finn's question brought Sloane out of her lazy trance. She stopped her trail at the midpoint between Finn's shoulder blades and focused on the ceiling. Dim illumination from the nearby streetlights seeped through the drawn faux-wood blinds, providing enough light for Sloane to make out the fan rotating at a slow pace above them.

"If we don't take it, someone else will. But I'm not sure if I want my fingerprints on it at all." Morgan's warning this afternoon had Sloane doubting the wisdom of being the new mayor's patsy. She told herself Eric had nothing to do with this. Still, the possibility of him losing his pension and health insurance gnawed at her like a dog working on a soup bone.

Finn poked her head up to look Sloane in the eyes. "What are you afraid of?"

Sloane shook off her doubts. She reminded herself that her priority was her family, not the man who took her first family from her all those years ago. "Nothing. I'm overreacting."

"Let's take the meeting tomorrow. If you still feel the same way, we can default."

"I can't let us do that. We'll never get a government contract again." Sloane rolled over to her side and coaxed Finn over to spoon her. "But I love you for the offer."

CHAPTER THREE

A high school field trip marked the last time Sloane stepped foot inside San Francisco's City Hall. Taking in its grandeur wasn't on the top of her list then, and despite Finn's probing, she couldn't recall much of its beauty. She liked the thought that Finn, an East and South Bay native, hadn't visited until today, so both could take in the architecture as if it were both their first times. They stepped through the building's east entrance and gasped at the interior, which stretched for almost a city block. At its center was a majestic rotunda.

"My goodness. This is so much bigger than I remember." Sloane's mouth gaped while her head pivoted in circles, taking in the ornate markings carved on the granite walls and four-story-tall ceiling. Some of the historical trivia she had learned on that field trip somehow worked itself to the surface. "Did you know that the top of this dome is higher than the US Capitol?"

"I can believe it." Finn bounced her head around at every angle while her heels clicked across the beige-toned marble floor and then up several steps of the grand staircase. "Damn.

We could park both our cars here, and I'd still have elbow space to get out."

Sloane took Finn's hand and gave it an extra squeeze. "We'll fix that. I promise."

"I'm not worried about it." Finn's closed-lip smile confirmed their parking arrangement wasn't on her list of concerns.

Sloane stopped their ascent two-thirds from the bottom, center from the sides. "But I am. It's your home too, and I want you to be comfortable in it." After angling Finn's chin upward by a hand, Sloane gently pressed their lips together. As warmth spread through her chest, she considered pulling away quickly when two businessmen descended, passing behind her. But, if any space made Sloane comfortable enough to kiss her partner in public, the home of the LGBTQ movement was it. She let the kiss linger in the perfect moment. *If I ever remarry, I'd like it to be right here.*

By the time she broke the kiss, several more people had passed them on the stairs. Their mouths inches apart, she whispered. "I love you."

"I love you too," Finn whispered back, her lips plump from the kiss.

"Let's go earn some money." Sloane cast her chin toward the second-floor mayor's suite and the adjoining chief of staff's office.

Following a quick greeting, Chief of Staff Mark Gandy led them to their meeting with the mayor. His tightly cut black hair with a hint of gray along the ears set off his equally tight maroon three-piece suit. Along the way, Sloane recalled how her sophomore civics teacher had pointed out the history as well as the intricate architecture. He'd marveled at eight-foot-tall dark cherrywood panels adorning the narrow hallway leading to the mayor's office and the framed images of every San Francisco mayor and Spanish alcalde since the city's inception. It took two decades, but today Sloane finally appreciated how those accents combined with the plush, red-patterned carpet to create a stately quality and sense of history.

"The mayor doesn't have much time today." Gandy slowed the stride of his short, skinny legs, his curt voice telling of an impatience for dawdling. "Keep the pleasantries to a minimum. Now, your job is to erase the city's reputation of having the highest cold case rate in the state. You are to review the evidence in cases involving homicide, arson, robbery, burglary, and rape and identify any that might now be solvable given technology changes. Highlight high-profile cases and prepare each case for state investigators to take the lead. Any questions?"

"None for you." Sloane remained skeptical. If the new mayor was anything like her no-nonsense public persona, Sloane would have to employ a straightforward approach to sniff out a broader agenda.

When the hallway gave way to a dimly lit private executive reception area, Gandy bypassed the two leather guest armchairs. He marched toward the perfectly coiffed and styled secretary seated behind an L-shaped oak desk. A light cream-colored sweater slung over her shoulders accented a double strand of bold Akoya white sea pearls. With a flawless posture and a stony expression, she projected the image of gatekeeper and protector no one dared sidestep.

"Is she ready, Doris?" Gandy softened his ego-inflated tone to a weak whimper.

Doris lifted her gaze from the glowing desk monitor before casting an affirmative nod punctuated by a daggered stare. "Tight schedule today. Don't go over this time."

"I'll herd everyone along." He smoothed his dotted Olympic blue silk tie atop a crisp white shirt. His nervous twitch confirmed Sloane's suspicion: Doris was the real muscle around here.

Doris eyed Sloane and Finn as if sizing them up for a casket in the event they went over their allotted time. She settled on a single arched eyebrow, telegraphing her warning. "Herding cats is not your strong suit." She paused at Sloane's smug smile and gave her a blank, unamused stare. "You may go in."

Gandy twisted the polished brass handle and pushed on one of the two eight-foot-tall wood-milled arched doors. This is where her taxes went, Sloane thought. He revealed an august office, walls adorned with the same dark, rich wood from floor to ceiling, with one broken up by two tall ornately draped windows, through which diffused sunlight was pouring. Between those windows sat the historic oak desk used by every San Francisco mayor since 1915. The one item in the room that didn't cost taxpayers a bundle.

The new mayor glanced up, discarding her pen and eyeglasses on a pile of paperwork. Dressed in black yoga pants, a white U-neck T-shirt, and a sweaty towel draped around her neck, Mayor Cole didn't resemble the polished politician she projected during the campaign. That woman never had a strand of her long brown hair out of place and always wore single-colored signature skirted suits in a rainbow variety of colors. She stood, extending a hand to shake Sloane's.

"I'm Nicci Cole. Pleased to meet you."

"Likewise, Mayor Cole. I'm Manhattan Sloane," Sloane said before Finn also introduced herself.

"I know Mark filled you in." Mayor Cole gestured for Sloane and Finn to take one of the three leather guest chairs in front of her desk. "I ran on a platform of holding our police department accountable to our citizens. Your job is to help me do that. Do you have questions before you clean up one of the biggest stains on our police department?"

Settling her elbows over the hand-milled armchair, Sloane steepled her fingers together. "Why us? Our company is new. We have no track record."

A slow grin formed on Mayor Cole's lips. "I like people who cut to the chase." She removed the towel from her neck and tossed it atop her desk before leaning into her high-back leather chair. "You're a bit of a San Francisco celebrity after taking down El Padrino and Los Dorados. Who better to help me clean h— clean up our department?"

Sloane shifted in her chair, recrossing her legs at the knee, sensing the mayor was less than forthcoming. "Define clean up."

"You are shrewd, Ms. Sloane. There's a reason our city has the highest cold case rate in the state. I intend to root it out and make changes."

"What kind of changes?"

"That depends on what you find. Your job is to identify those cases where victims in our city have needlessly waited too long for justice. Is this going to be a problem?"

Sloane opened her mouth, but Finn gently placed a hand on her forearm before she could get out her next shrewd question. "Of course not. We're happy to be part of this worthy pursuit."

What was Finn up to? Whatever it was, it meant leaving the mayor thinking they were on the same team. Finn stood after giving Sloane a light foot to the shin—time to go according to Finn's clock.

"It's been a pleasure, Mayor Cole. We'll have an initial report to Mr. Gandy soon." Sloane extended a hand, more skeptical than when she entered the room.

"I look forward to your findings." When the mayor shook her hand, Sloane sensed an underlying agenda, one that she had feared going into this meeting and one she wanted no part of.

On their way out with Mark Gandy in the lead, Doris harrumphed without breaking her stare from the computer glow. "Miracles do happen."

Down the grand staircase, past the rotunda, Sloane and Finn walked in silence. Crossing the Civic Center Plaza between Polk and Larkin streets, Sloane couldn't shake the uneasiness that followed her like a bad penny. "I got a bad vibe about this."

"I did too." Finn slowed her stride, pulling Sloane to a stop with her. "Morgan is right. There's more to this contract than just clearing cold cases. The mayor wasn't talking about cleaning up. She was talking about cleaning house."

"I caught that too."

"Then better we control the outcome than someone else." Finn's confident look meant there would be no going back. They were about to enter a quagmire.

Unable to envision a scenario where this ended well, Sloane fought against the foreboding shiver flowing down her spine. "This will get tricky and likely messy."

"Let it." Finn gave her a confident wink. "We'll land on our feet."

"This is why I love you." Sloane angled Finn's chin up an inch with a hand. She couldn't imagine taking this leap of a new career without her. "This wasn't how I pictured our first day on the contract, but you always manage to center me."

A smile crept up on Finn. "Speaking of first days, I wonder how Reagan's first day at the firm is going."

Sloane sighed. Reagan had experienced more trauma than a soon-to-be seventeen-year-old should and had decidedly matured. Still, Sloane feared working in Chandler's prestigious law firm might test that theory. "I shudder to think."

* * *

Nothing about Chandler's office matched Reagan's impression of him. Since the day El Padrino's thugs threw them into the back of that stuffy van and held them at knifepoint, she saw him as Gramps. He was the grandfather figure who preferred sneakers and sweaters and dripped mustard on his shirt during picnics. She never expected this.

"This is amazing." Her mouth fell open, her gaze soaking in the panoramic view of the Berkeley hills from across the bay. She lowered her eyes to the bustling Embarcadero landscape eighteen floors below his luxury high-rise office.

"Sometimes I forget how beautiful it is." Chandler's voice surprisingly contained a hint of amazement. The wonder, Reagan thought, should've worn off years ago.

She turned toward him. From behind his well-appointed cherrywood desk, he stared out the window Reagan was standing near. He appeared so professional. She'd never seen him in one of his thousand-dollar lawyer suits, perfectly shined leather shoes, and the ends of a gold pin popping off each side of a silk necktie. He then fiddled with the computer mouse and stared into the sleek flat-screen monitor nestled on the corner of his desk. She never considered him the techie type, but he seemed right at home with technology.

"Do you have questions before I send you into the trenches?" He gave her a wink, one that told her she had nothing to worry about.

"I wouldn't know what to ask." His laugh made her think otherwise—maybe she *was* in over her head. "Thanks a lot, Gramps. I mean, Mr. Harper." She rolled her eyes.

He scrunched his nose. *Kinda cute like Finn*, she thought. "That's a little too formal for us. How about Chandler in the office?"

"I can work with that."

"We'll make a fine lawyer out of you yet."

Becoming a lawyer was a suitable compromise. She'd be involved with the law like her moms but wouldn't be in any danger. While this internship would test her theory, she regretted saying yes to it so quickly. Despite its luxurious trappings, as she was discovering, being stuck inside an office wasn't how she wanted to spend her summer break. She'd rather be with her friends who were day-tripping to some cousin's backyard pool in the East Bay. Her choice now seemed like a poor tradeoff for experience and spending cash.

Now ensconced in the trenches, Reagan was on the verge of sleep, reading the voluminous electronic documents on office procedures and the filing system the office manager had assigned her to memorize an hour earlier. It was worse than Algebra II. Who the hell cared about file codes? The most exciting thing she learned today was everyone's coffee preference. Starting tomorrow, she was HMR's newest coffee gopher.

Her cubicle wasn't as bad as she envisioned. Relegated to the middle of a room not much smaller than her townhouse, she had a sliver of a view through a window that overlooked the neighboring skyscraper. She quickly learned that window spaces were earned and used as a visible sign of the pecking order. The smaller the window, the lower you were. She instantly knew her place. If not for the copy machine debacle, double-siding thirty copies along the long side and not the top, she would have called the morning a success.

A stomach growl told Reagan her usual lunch hour had come and gone. She grabbed her container of taco-mash leftovers in the office break room refrigerator. *Better than nothing*, she thought. Luck was with her. The microwave was a cinch to use, unlike the single-serve coffee machine the office manager trained her on this morning.

"Is that what they feed interns around here?"

The repeating beep signaled her food had stopped spinning inside, but Reagan turned toward the door, recognizing the smoky voice that had advocated for Sloane during the custody hearings that had pitted her mother's parents against her. Tall like Sloane with carbon copy wavy, dark brown hair, Kadin Hall, HMR's newest junior partner, had rested a hip against the doorframe. Her tailored dark gray pencil skirt and blazer highlighted an athletic body close to Sloane's slenderness.

"Hey, Kadin. Finn suggested I pack a lunch until I figured out the routine." Reagan retrieved the steaming container, gingerly lifting the sides to not burn her fingers.

"Of course she did." The blush of an unmistakable smile filled Kadin's cheeks as she pushed herself from the doorframe. She gave Reagan's food a quick sniff, her expression souring. "Leftovers, huh? I ordered way too much from The Pink Jade. How about you help me devour it?"

"Sure. Why not?" Other than Chandler, Kadin was the one familiar face in the place. Not that Reagan needed one. She got the impression that the staff had gone out of their way to be friendly to the young lady Chandler Harper considered his granddaughter. Nonetheless, she welcomed Kadin's gesture.

Unlike those of the other junior partners, Kadin's office had one hell of a city view, along with several extra square feet of space. Reagan surveyed the matching rich red cherrywood desk, credenza, bookshelves, and guest chairs. *Definitely high on the pecking order.*

"Wow!" Reagan punctuated her amazement with a whistle. "Max and Sabrin's offices aren't this nice."

"Perks of being the girlfriend of the founder's daughter when I was made a partner." Kadin doled out even portions of food onto two china plates she'd retrieved from a cabinet behind her desk.

"You and Finn used to date?"

"For a few years, but we drifted apart." Legs crossed at the knee, Kadin rested back in her chair and nodded with a faraway look of reminiscence. "How about you? Still dating that young man I met after the adoption?"

"Emeryn? Yeah, but he's going to New Zealand to visit family after my birthday tomorrow."

"Well, happy birthday. Special plans?"

"Dinner at The Tap with family and friends." Reagan dabbed each corner of her mouth with a thick paper napkin, not the cheap kind found in fast-food restaurants. Kadin had shown her great kindness this past year while her grandparents battled Sloane for custody, and it was about time she showed her appreciation. "You should come tomorrow night. Chandler and Finn will be there, too."

"I wouldn't want to intrude on a family event."

"Really, come. You played a big part in Sloane and I becoming a family. Please say yes."

Kadin tossed her napkin in the center of her empty plate, a grin stretching to her eyes. "I'd be happy to come."

* * *

Months had passed since Sloane was last at 850 Bryant—her stomping grounds for two-and-a-half years. As she stepped up to police headquarters, a growing sense of nostalgia of working and falling in love with Avery here surprisingly didn't have a sting to it. Perhaps the buzzing noise of power tools assembling scaffolding along the east exterior wall and the dozens of sweaty contractors in hard hats carrying supplies inside overshadowed her memories. This place was changing as much as she was.

Inside the public entrance, the urine and sewer scent invaded her sinuses and brought it all back. The inescapable smell was as strong as it had ever been. "Same shithole only with a coat of lipstick," Sloane said to Finn without prying her gaze from the building's interior. It was a far cry from the well-kept City Hall they had visited yesterday.

Sloane had read in the *Chronicle* that despite the new mayor's objection, the City Council had approved renovations for all police facilities. Why couldn't all of this have happened when she worked there? She was convinced, though, there wasn't enough drywall and paint in the city that could transform it into anything worth inhabiting. On the positive side, there were competing forces at play in the city—something she could use to her advantage if this contract went sideways.

Even with the habitual stench and a handful of familiar faces, walking inside seemed foreign. Today Sloane was a visitor, and she felt like one. She no longer had a badge and credentials to breeze through the security doors and restricted areas like she owned the place. Her squad room chair wasn't waiting for her to throw a jean jacket over, nor was her desk ready to bear the overpriced cup of coffee she was holding. This would take some getting used to.

Tossing the cup in the trash can, she queued in the nearby line to be screened through the metal detector. When it was her turn, she placed her satchel on the conveyor belt and cell phone and keys in a plastic tray. Over the years, she'd escorted in a handful of visitors who had to go through the screening process. Going through it now beat into her the fact that she was, indeed, a visitor.

Once she and Finn were through and lined up to check in with the desk sergeant, Finn whispered in her ear, "This certainly is different."

"Very." Sloane was the outsider now. Before they reached the front of the line, a voice called out her name from several yards away. She turned, recognizing the face. "Hey, Jim."

He waved her and Finn over the few feet toward him, but Sloane hesitated, hoping not to lose her place in line. He waved again. "I'm your escort today."

Sloane nudged Finn toward him. After approaching, she shook Jim Shaw's hand. "Great seeing you."

"I see civilian life is treating you well." Shaw hadn't changed. He had on the same department store midnight blue suit trousers, loose dark tie, and white sleeves rolled up an inch past the elbow. He was still fit for being in his mid-forties. His buzz cut and even tan hinted he'd recently returned from the beach vacation he took each year with his family. After signing a log and retrieving visitor passes, he extended his arm toward a door marked "Restricted Area." "Let's get you two inside."

At the elevators, he pressed the call button, prompting the door to swoosh open. "Scuttlebutt has it you and Harper landed the cold case contract. Gonna show us all up."

"With you still on board, that wouldn't be hard to do." Sloane stepped in, offered a snort, and patted Jim on the shoulder.

He lowered his chin and shook his head. "Same old Sloane."

Finn arched an eyebrow, riding out the rest of their verbal jousting to the fifth floor as a spectator until they reached the bureau captain's office. Jim knocked on the frosted glass door and waited for a muffled voice from inside. He peeled the door open and peeked his head around the metal frame. "Hey, Captain, the contractors are here."

"Let them in," a deep male voice sounded.

Jim let Sloane and Finn pass. "When you're done here, come get me in the squad room. I'll show you the space they've set aside for you."

"Thanks, Jim." Sloane gave him a pat on the arm, anticipating the welcome waiting for them wouldn't be as warm as his had been.

Inside, Captain Carter Nash didn't bother getting up from the high-back faux leather chair behind his oversized oak desk. Wood furniture meant he was brass. The twenty-plus framed awards, photographs of him with politicians, and news articles highlighting his stint in SWAT said he wanted visitors to know it, too. Not a quality Sloane admired. One picture caught her attention. The matching cardigan sweaters, youthful faces, and the same Greek symbols etched in their silver rings meant one thing—frat boys. Another reason he grated on her patience.

"Morning, Captain."

He barely raised his head from the papers strewn about the desk and motioned with his hand for Sloane and Finn to come closer. When he pushed his chair back, straining the hinges, his red suspenders bowed against the baby blue shirt covering his pronounced fast-food belly. He snatched his reading glasses from the bridge of his nose and met Sloane's eyes with a flinty stare. "I think this contract is unnecessary and a huge overreach. The money would be better spent by authorizing us overtime to attack the backlog."

Before Sloane could open her mouth, Finn did. "We know how overworked your detectives are and understand your position, Captain."

"I don't think you do." The rolls of skin above his collar reddened to a rosy shade. "The city understaffs us, refuses to approve overtime, and expects us to clear out cases decades old. We're barely holding our heads above water as is."

"I remember those days. Too many missed family meals." Sloane released a breathy exhale. "Look, Captain. We're here to do a job. We'll keep our footprint small."

"You do that, Sloane." He pushed forward in his chair, leaning his elbows atop the desk, a sign he was about to get more serious than he already was. "Let's set some ground rules. No evidence is to leave this building. If you need access to anything, including contacting any of my detectives, you do nothing until I've approved it. Got it?"

"Understood." Sloane straightened her back. *So, this is the way it's going to be—still with his panties in a wad.*

"Send your requests through Jim Shaw. He'll be your point of contact for the duration."

"Got it." Sloane kept one eye on the door to prevent the veins in her neck from popping. "Anything else?"

"You no longer wear a badge, Sloane. Remember that."

Asshole. Sloane motioned for Finn to move toward the door. "I think we're done here."

Once in the hallway, Sloane fast-marched out. Finn grabbed her by an elbow before she reached the elevator. "Sloane, slow down." They came to an abrupt stop. "What the hell was that all about?"

"Some of it had to do with the contract, but most of it was about me."

"What's his grudge?"

"Ever since the ass-chewing he gave me for leaving the scene after Padrino's men ambushed me, he's been icy. I'm sure pinning a medal on me after Padrino was killed frosted his ass. That was him putting me in my place."

Finn softened her expression. "You left that ambush scene because of me."

Sloane gripped her hands along Finn's hips an inch below the waistband of her dress slacks and pulled their bodies together. "And I'd do it again." Motion out of the corner of Sloane's eye caught her attention. "I want to kiss you, but I don't want to give Nash more reason to be pissed at us."

"Raincheck?" Finn winked her subtle message.

"Count on it."

Stepping into the sixth-floor squad room was like stepping into the past. Years of memories rolled like a movie on fast-forward: Eric greeting her the first day she pinned on her seven-point gold shield. Avery asking her out for their first date. Finn magically appearing in Morgan's office. Her colleagues welcoming her back after Avery's death. Finn embracing her at the news of Reagan and Chandler's kidnapping. The back of her throat thickened. Besides coming into her own as a detective, this was the place of countless emotional highs and lows, and she missed it.

"Look what the cat dragged in."

Sloane turned toward the gravelly voice, drawing a smile. Three of the old-timers, loose ties and sleeves rolled to their elbows, raised their coffee mugs in a warm welcome.

"Just couldn't stay away," another said.

The last time she made her way through this gauntlet, she was saying goodbye on her final day wearing the badge. That was a bittersweet day. Today, she weaved her way through the clusters of desks, shaking hands and patting the shoulders of each detective along the way. At the lieutenant's open door, she knocked on the frame and stuck her head in.

"Morgan?"

At her desk, Lieutenant Morgan West poked her head up from her computer monitor and leaned back in her chair, a grin matching Sloane's. "Thought I heard your name bantered about out there."

"Got a minute?"

"For you? Always." After closing the door and settling in the chairs around her conference table, Morgan pointed at the badge dangling from a chain around Sloane's neck. "Visitor badges look different on you two."

Sloane flipped the badge up, inspecting its meaning and how it marked her new role. "Can't go back now."

"I'd take you back in a heartbeat."

"Not gonna happen." Sloane glanced at Finn, who gave her a concurring wink. "Besides, you were right about the mayor. We got the feeling she plans on using us to justify sweeping changes in the department. Ones I don't think we'll like."

Morgan rubbed a hand across her chin. "I was afraid of that."

"Unfortunately, we're not sure if there's anything we can do to mitigate the mayor's agenda." Finn's pinched face confirmed she was just as worried about Morgan's future as Sloane was.

"I wouldn't ask you to." Morgan shook her head. Her deep sigh signaled she understood something inevitable was coming.

"But—" Sloane said.

"No buts." Morgan pointed at Sloane's badge. "Remember, you're a visitor now. This is our problem. You two just concentrate on your job."

Finn patted Morgan's hand. "Enough about this. I'm more interested in hearing about you and Kyler. When did you two become a couple?"

"Were we that obvious at The Lookout?"

"To us." Finn's broad smile gave Sloane the impression that she was equally vested in a blossoming friendship with Morgan. "Sloane suspected something was going on between you two before she quit."

Morgan shifted her stare toward Sloane and softened her voice to a curious tone. "And you said nothing?"

Sloane slumped her shoulders when she averted her eyes. "How could I? After Avery died, you went out of your way to reach out to me, but I pushed you away. I had no business asking about your personal affairs."

"Let's get something straight." Morgan extended her smile. "You were grieving and coped the best way you could. Since I'm no longer your boss, I'd like to think we're friends now. So feel free to ask about personal things."

Relief warmed Sloane like a tender embrace. She met Morgan's gaze and extended her hand. "Thank you. Friends."

"Friends." Morgan grasped her hand before eyeing Finn. "Kyler and I have been seeing each other for about six months."

"You two make a handsome couple," Finn said when Sloane gave Morgan's hand an extra squeeze before letting go.

"Thank you, Finn." Morgan's cheeks turned a shade rosier. "Our bosses know, and though our relationship isn't against department policy, we're not going public to avoid the appearance of a conflict of interest."

"We're a private investigation firm now. Discretion is our middle name." Sloane had never seen Morgan this relaxed or happy. Morgan's relationship with Kyler must be more serious than she'd let on. "We'd like to have you and Kyler over for dinner one night soon, though."

"Yes, please. We'd love to have you over." Finn's face lit up when she glanced at Sloane. "This woman is a brilliant cook."

"I'll pass it by Kyler, but I'm sure we'd love to come." Morgan had added an extra pep to her tone.

"I hate to cut this short," Sloane stood, wishing they had more time to catch up, "but we gotta meet with Jim. He's supposed to show us our temporary office."

Morgan placed a hand over her mouth, failing to stifle a laugh. "Good luck with that."

Sloane cocked one eyebrow high. "Why? Where are they sticking us?"

"I'll let you discover that for yourselves," Morgan laughed.

Sloane reached the threshold of the office door. When she stepped out, she T-boned someone crossing her path. "Sorry."

"Sorry."

Sloane recognized the voice that had been a constant in her life for years. It had been the voice of calm, comfort, and strength. Her heart sank when he turned around. "Eric."

"Sloane?" His voice was as hollow as his eyes. The sparkle behind them was gone, replaced by deep creases of sadness. His once muscular frame had all but disappeared, and if she had to guess, she'd estimate he'd lost twenty pounds. Remembering the adrenaline rush he used to get from lifting weights, she noted his chest had shrunk at least four inches and guessed he missed it as much as she missed this place. "Jim said you'd be around starting today."

She swallowed the emotion building in her throat. At least Eric had his color back, and the black circles around his eyes had vanished. So much needed to be said, but the one word that flowed from her mouth was "Contract."

"Yeah, well, I'll get out of your hair." He retreated to his desk, next to her old one where they spent two-and-a-half years together. He held his left arm close to his body, shoulders slightly hunched, a sign of his limitations. Morgan was right. With the strict department standards, he'd never work the field again. Because of Sloane.

* * *

"Fucking great. The Pit." Sloane had heard about the basement offices of 850 Bryant, but until now, she'd never walked into one. Whether deserved or not, they had the reputation of serving as the building's bottomless pit—once thrown in, you never got out.

"Sorry, Sloane. Captain's orders." Jim shrugged. "I bribed the facility manager with a fifth of scotch to make sure he didn't stick you under the men's room."

"This will do fine." Finn tested the wheels of a desk chair. They worked fine, but an arm was bent a good thirty degrees outward. Sloane could live with that, but the seat fabric had been sliced in two, revealing a section of missing cushion the shape of a watermelon wedge. They'd have to scrounge up a replacement.

The rank air wasn't the worst Sloane had experienced in the building but it came in a close second. The flickering fluorescent overheads, however, would either drive her nuts or give her a seizure within a week. She ran a hand across the clunky computer tower shoved against a front leg of her dented, rust-stained metal desk. "I think this is the same model I had when I first started here. Why isn't this thing in the junk heap?"

"We'll make do." Finn nestled the chair back under the desk before rubbing Sloane's arm. She whispered so Jim couldn't hear. "I know seeing Eric rattled you. Remember, none of this was Jim's doing."

"You're right."

"I'm always right." A sly grin built on Finn's lips.

"Yes, you are." Sloane cleared her throat and focused her attention on Jim. "Be sure to tell Captain Nash thank you for us."

"Sure thing, Sloane." Jim laughed, switching the lights off on his way out and returning the musty, windowless pit to its darkness. "Let's get you two contractor badges so you'll have full run of the joint."

"Oh, come on." Sloane scrutinized the photo on her shiny, new official building pass. Hands down, worst picture ever. A muffled chuckle from the seasoned uniformed desk sergeant pissed her off even more. She snatched Finn's ID badge from the four-foot-high countertop and flashed it in his face. "Hers is beautiful. Mine is ridiculous."

"Thank you." Finn shifted her gaze to Sloane's picture. She studied it, tilting her head to one side. "Yours isn't so bad."

"I look hungover." This was worse than the high school freshman photo that earned her the nickname "Headlights"— something she still refused to talk about to this day. Sloane imagined the six-month-long torture of having to show the picture from hell anytime she was asked for her credentials. She doubted she'd have the restraint to not coldcock the unlucky guy who embarrassed her one time too many.

"Sorry, Sloane." The sergeant pressed his lips together in a failed attempt to hide a laugh. "Unless you lose or damage it, I can't make you another one."

"I'll have to introduce this damn thing to my garbage disposal."

"Let's go, Sloane." Finn snickered, pulling her out the door.

CHAPTER FOUR

Even with enough dinner crowd noise in The Tap to drown out a Sherman tank gunning its engine, Finn melted at Sloane's shenanigans. Over the last half hour, Sloane had griped to everyone who would listen about her official picture that looked more like a booking photo than a security pass. She now had her next victim in her crosshairs.

Sloane had waved Dylan over after he delivered the neighboring table's orders. Dylan politely nodded his head up and down, wiping his hands on his freshly washed cook's apron. Sloane then slapped the badge on the table, flapped her arms in the air, and ended by burying her face in her hands when Dylan's pooch of a belly jiggled to a loud guffaw. So freaking cute. Both of them.

From the other end of the table, Finn's father made her laugh—something he'd done all her life. Challenged to a high-stakes game of checkers, he refused to let the birthday girl clean his clock for the third time in a row. Around here, a dollar a game was big money.

Chandler hovered his hand over one of the black pieces, rubbing his chin as if the wrong move would set off a nuclear bomb. When he reached for another round disk, Reagan shook her head. "Uh-uh. I don't think you want to do that, Gramps."

Chandler scanned the board again, pursing his lips. "Well, poop."

Everything was perfect for Finn. For two decades, she'd chased the echo of Sloane, and now somehow she'd stumbled into a life where her teenage crush was at the heart of it. They'd blended their families and their home, and now the one thing missing was a ring that signified the commitment they'd already made to one another. Was it too soon? Was marriage even something Sloane would consider again? Whatever the case, Sloane would have to do the asking.

Her stare darted between Sloane and Chandler. They were so much alike. Both had lost a wife who left a daughter as a living reminder. If anyone could advise her, her father could—sooner than later.

"Sorry I'm late." The voice behind Finn was unmistakable. That sexy timbre had woken her for two years, but it had lost the effect it once had on her.

As Kadin slipped past, Sloane whispered into Finn's ear. "I didn't know she was coming. Did you invite her?"

Finn shifted into Sloane's lean. "Not me. Must have been Daddy or Reagan."

Sloane harrumphed. The last time she narrowed her eyes like that was after Chandler ate the last of her Oreo cookie ice cream. She was grouchy for days until he replenished her supply.

When Kadin continued down the table, Reagan popped from her chair. "You made it."

After a warm hug, Kadin handed her a small gift bag. "Happy birthday."

"You didn't have to bring me anything."

Kadin waved her off and watched Reagan pull out a matching gray wool scarf and beanie set. "I saw these in a shop today and thought they would look perfect on you."

"You shouldn't have, but thank you. They're beautiful."

After Kadin settled into a chair next to Reagan, Finn nudged Sloane on the shoulder. "That was sweet of Kadin to bring her a gift."

"Yes, sweet." Sloane's sharp tone and refusal to break her stare at Kadin broadcasted in big flashing lights that she wasn't impressed.

Finn pulled Sloane's chin around until Sloane was forced to focus her gaze on her. "You're jealous."

"What if I am?"

"I think it's hot."

"You do, huh?"

Finn pulled Sloane's face closer until their mouths were a whisper apart. "Absolutely." She hovered, inviting Sloane to kiss her.

"Then I think I'll do a little territory marking." In one slow, sweeping motion, Sloane pressed their lips together in an unhurried, tender kiss. Finn thought it would last only two seconds, but it lingered for five. Then ten. Sloane's fingers grazed her cheek, starting from below an eye, ending at the base of her neck. Every one of Finn's lovers had quickly discovered touching certain spots on her neck drove her crazy. Sloane was no exception. Now she inched her fingers back until they sparked the first pangs of desire. This had to stop, or Finn would insist on going home early to fan the embers Sloane had stoked. Well, maybe a few seconds longer.

At the first pulsating twinge, reluctant and ever so aroused, Finn pulled back. "Another raincheck?"

A naughty grin formed on Sloane's face. "I know where Dylan hides the key to his office. Just sayin'." She finished with a slow, suggestive wink.

As tempting as it was to say yes, if she agreed to a sweaty office romp, Finn could never walk into The Tap again without a guilty conscience. She pushed Sloane back with a fingertip to the breastbone. "You're bad."

Sloane's adorable pouty lips almost made her miss Kadin as she sped past. Was she upset? Kadin was a master at hiding her emotion in the courtroom and in public but not to Finn. She recognized the pained look, straining to hold back an avalanche.

She rested a hand on Sloane's forearm before she let Kadin get too far out of sight. "I'll be right back."

She'd forgotten how fast Kadin was in heels and a pencil skirt, a skill born out of necessity while working her way up the pecking order at Chandler's law firm. Finn lost her in the crowd toward the back of The Tap. The kitchen was unlikely her destination, so Finn continued deeper down the dimly lit wood-paneled corridor, the walls littered with mirrored beer signs.

Pushing the ladies' room door open, Kadin came into view, perfect posture, dabbing her mascara with a paper towel. Under the poor bathroom lighting, her reflection in the mirror revealed red-rimmed eyes. Less than a minute later, the one other woman in the restroom finished at the neighboring sink and left. Finn edged up to the counter, resting a hip against it to face Kadin.

"Are you all right?"

"Allergies."

Finn tilted her head to one side. "That line may work with most people, but you're not fooling me, Kadin Hall."

After trimming the smudged black lines from below her eyes, Kadin wadded the paper towel and tossed it in the trash bin beneath the counter. "It's nothing."

"I've never seen you shed a tear over nothing." Finn took a step forward and rubbed Kadin's arm. "Is it your girlfriend?"

"You're one behind. It's boyfriend now."

"Really?" Finn shifted until her bottom leaned against the Formica counter. "Do I know him?"

"Four B."

"Not the stud with the beagle? I thought you said he was too vain with his weekly manicures."

"I changed my mind." Kadin's halfhearted shrug led Finn to think there was something more behind Four B.

"Did you two have a fight? Is that why you didn't bring him?" Kadin lowered her head but failed to hide her quivering chin. Finn pushed herself from the counter and bent at the knees to get a better view of Kadin's face. She softened her words. "What is it then?"

Finn straightened, and Kadin raised her head to lock gazes. "It's you. It's hard seeing you with someone else."

"It's been almost a year." Sloane was right. Kadin wanted her back. But as she told Sloane at Lands End, wanting and having were two different things.

"I know." Kadin's long, breathy sigh forecasted deep-rooted regret, a tricky emotion that worried Finn. "I thought I'd moved on. Then when Chandler was kidnapped, you held me like this."

Without warning, Kadin swept her into her arms, pulling their bodies together. Kadin's chest heaved up and down at a sprinter's pace. Before Finn could pull back, Kadin tightened her grip and maneuvered her lips over an ear, her moist breath tingling the surrounding skin. "I never stopped loving you." Kadin's tone was absent her usual husky foreplay. Instead, her words, like her breathing, contained a sense of pained desperation.

Finn's hands hovered inches above Kadin's shoulders. Unsure what to do or say, she feared anything would conjure up reciprocation in Kadin's mind. Finally, she placed the pads of her palms on the front of Kadin's shoulders and whispered her name, but even that encouraged a tighter squeeze.

"I've missed you." Kadin slid her mouth around until her lips covered Finn's. They were hungry as if she hadn't eaten in a year.

For a moment—a fraction of a second—Finn hesitated. Those lips were as familiar as her favorite pair of old jeans. Both were smooth and made her feel ever so sexy whenever she tried them on. Then, in a flash, she told herself to push back. She did, but Kadin refused to relent. Finn strained against Kadin's determination to not let go. *You were so right, Sloane. I should've seen this coming.*

"How could you? Both of you?" The voice was enough to knock Kadin out of whatever trance she was in and loosen her grip. Both their heads turned toward it.

"Reagan." Finn's stomach knotted when Reagan jerked her head back, throwing a hand over her mouth. "It's not what—"

Before Finn could finish her sentence, Reagan rushed out the door, potentially taking Finn's perfect life with her.

She imagined everything she'd built with Sloane falling apart because of something she should have had her eyes wide open to days ago. Finn snapped her head toward Kadin. She tried taking in a cleansing breath to quiet the seething anger, but her words came out like razors. "Fucking great, Kadin."

"I'm so sorry, Finn." Kadin's chest caved in like Finn's world. "I'll tell Reagan and Sloane this was all me."

"You've done enough for one night." Finn wrenched the restroom door open, slamming it against the wall. She made a mental note to arrange for repairs of whatever damages she just caused.

Blurred by a mixture of bubbling anger and gloom, Finn marched down the hallway. She was pissed for letting herself get into the situation and dreaded the virgin territory she and Sloane were about to tread. Sloane's hypersensitivity about Kadin would likely make this worse. Right now, Finn's chief worry was Reagan.

In the main dining room, she weaved through the sea of tables, her heart beating so hard it drowned out the noise of the wall-to-wall patrons and background rock music. She was too late. Sloane appeared confused and concerned at what Reagan was telling her. Sloane had wrapped her hands around Reagan's upper arms, and her body language signaled Reagan was getting her message across.

"Fuck." The closer Finn approached, the tighter her stomach twisted. Was she too late? Had Sloane jumped to the conclusion any sane person would believe? Finn hoped for the best but prepared for the worst. Then, from a yard away, Sloane locked eyes with her, the pain of betrayal popped in them. "We need to talk."

"How could you?" Reagan snapped her head around, her stare hot enough to boil the paint off the walls.

"Let's talk about this at home." Finn scanned the room. Other customers had begun to stare at the spectacle, just the thing she didn't need. "It's not what you think."

"What I think is that I caught you making out with your ex," Reagan ended on a loud note, drawing Chandler's attention.

"All right, Reagan. Let's not do this here." Sloane's face turned pale as if her knees had been cut out from under her.

Kadin appeared through the crowd. All the color had drained from her contrite face. Every gaze at their table and some from a few of the neighboring ones followed her, still perfectly postured, as she retrieved her large leather purse. Before stepping past Sloane, she paused. "It was all me. She did nothing wrong."

Sloane's body and mind numbed more with each step of the quarter mile home. She silently reminded herself about the panic she flew into on the eve of her wedding when Avery saw Michelle throwing herself at her. *Don't jump to conclusions*, she told herself. *Don't assume the worst.* At the townhouse door with only the porch light for illumination, she fumbled with her key, missing the lock twice.

"Let me, babe." Finn cupped Sloane's hand before taking the key and opening the door. When she handed it back, Finn locked gazes with Sloane. "Do you trust me?"

Every synapse screamed that she should, but any answer she gave would alienate either Finn or Reagan, so she said nothing. The defeated look on Finn's face said that wasn't the response she needed.

Sloane wanted to believe that what Reagan saw was another Michelle debacle. That Finn was an unwilling victim and gave Kadin a what for in the ladies' room. Everything she and Finn had been through told her to trust her completely. She glanced over her shoulder at Reagan, whose raised chin, tapping foot, and crossed arms in front of her chest signaled that trust was the last thing Finn deserved. Her passive-aggressive reaction was louder and more lethal than an atomic blast.

Inside, Reagan stomped toward the head of the stairs, presumably to sulk in her room. Finn yelled, "Wait," but Reagan continued her march down the stairs.

Sloane dropped her chin close to her chest and sighed at the war of wills that had begun. "Reagan, wait. We need to talk this out as a family."

The clomping stopped. "Family?"

"Yes, family. So, please, come back up."

After several tense, silent moments, Reagan reappeared, her stare lasering a hole right through Finn's skull. She plopped down on one end of the couch, Finn on the other, both refusing to break their angry death stare at one another. That meant Finn had reached the end of her patience.

Instead of the injured party, Sloane felt like a referee when she positioned herself between the combatants. She focused on a spot on the coffee table a few feet away, so she didn't have to look either of them in the eye. "Reagan told me she saw you and Kadin kissing in the restroom. Tell me what happened."

"You were right. Kadin wants me back. I'm sorry I didn't listen to you." Finn's voice started off shaky but ended confident. When she placed a hand on Sloane's arm, she offered the same strong yet comforting touch she did at the vineyard when they escaped sure death twice and when she faced her painful past at her parent's accident site. At that moment, Sloane knew she was telling the truth.

Finn continued, "I excused myself because she looked upset. I followed her into the restroom to make sure she was all right. Then she pulled me into an embrace, and before I knew it, she kissed me. That's when Reagan walked in."

"Oh, sure." Reagan leaned back on the cushion and crossed her arms in blood-boiling, dagger-throwing defiance.

Sloane shifted and crumpled her nose when she locked gazes with Finn. "I believe you. Something similar happened to me the night before my wedding. Avery believed and forgave me."

"Just like that, you believe her?" Reagan's eyes rounded in clear-cut bewilderment.

"Yes, honey. That's what love is. Unconditional."

Finn clutched Sloane's hand. "I love you. Only you."

"I love and trust you." Sloane squeezed it tight. "You've never lied to me." The sudden arch of Finn's brow made Sloane pause. She'd conducted enough interrogations to recognize a tell, and that was Finn's. She believed her about Kadin and would stand by her word, but Sloane's gut told her Finn was holding back something else. *What aren't you telling me, Finn?*

Later, in the dark, lying in their bed with scant illumination from the night sky and nearby streetlights, Sloane held Finn in her arms. Inching the soft covers down, she nuzzled Finn's neck from behind and inhaled her potent citrus scent. "You smell good."

"I should after the shower you insisted on."

Sloane shifted closer. "I didn't want to get Kadin on me."

Finn squirmed and twisted until she faced Sloane and entwined their bodies. "Kiss me."

"Did you gargle like I asked?"

"Twice."

"Hmmm. You better make it three times."

Finn rolled on top of Sloane, pinning her arms to the mattress. "I can think of better ways to spend my time." The weight of Finn's body atop hers sparked the first twinges of passion. Sloane knew where this was going—their first hot make-up sex. And she wasn't disappointed.

Finn was soon in her arms again, only this time, her gentle now-and-again snoring broke the peaceful silence. She loved Finn. Of that, she was sure; she couldn't imagine a life without her. But her instinct told her this wasn't the last time she'd have to deal with Kadin Hall.

CHAPTER FIVE

The furthest out aisle of the visitor's section of Bryant's underground garage with its narrow parking spaces was virgin territory to Sloane. It was day one, and already she didn't like it. Weighed down by laptop satchels and a shopping bag with an impressive collection of office supplies, she mumbled her frustration under her breath every step toward the basement entrance.

Finn, on the other hand, appeared content with their new lot in life, carrying a box with personal items and the ever-important coffeemaker.

"Are you actually humming?" Sloane asked.

"Yes, it's a beautiful day."

"We're about to begin our sentence in The Pit. I wouldn't exactly call it beautiful."

"I would. Today I get to embark on a new job with the woman I love. Definitely beautiful."

"If you put it that way," after pushing the access door open with her bottom, Sloane adjusted her load to grab the god-awful security pass dangling around her neck. "I'd have to agree."

She swiped the backside of her badge over the card reader, earning her a buzzing noise. A promising sign—something actually worked in this building. The security door unlocked. Sloane butted it open, and Finn led the way down the narrow, musty hallway. With only half of the overhead lights working, willowy shadows on the linoleum floor followed them to their destination.

Finn pushed the second to the last door open, the one leading to their dungeon for the next six months, and flipped on the wall switch. The lights flashed on. One continued to flicker while the other came to life with a continuous low whirr.

"Great, more humming."

"First things first." Finn laid her load atop the single desk in the center of the twelve-by ten-foot room. "Coffee. You're cranky."

After putting her things down, Sloane kissed Finn. A quick peck on the cheek would have signaled that Finn was right and that Sloane was ready to move on. But this kiss was on the lips. Intended to last two seconds, the kiss turned into five, and then ten just like the one Sloane had initiated at The Tap last night. This time, instead of marking her territory, she was marking her apology for misbehaving on their first day. "I'm sorry."

Eyes still closed, Finn purred, "You should be cranky more often."

"Be careful what you ask for." Sloane pecked her on the lips.

Over the next hour, they organized the new workspace, adding a feminine touch to their bleak surroundings. Sloane's scavenger hunt in the Pit's underbelly scrounged up another chair and a small table that doubled as their coffee bar and second desk.

"Knock, knock." A voice came from the direction of the open door.

"Morning, Jim. Spying on us already?" Sloane welcomed the visit. Besides Morgan, he was their primary ally in the building. She threw a soiled cleaning rag into a packing box to properly greet him. "I'd ask you to sit, but as you can see, we have few accommodations for guests."

"Still complaining, I see." He snickered. "I'm here to give you these." He handed Finn a cardboard carrier containing two large coffee house lattés.

"You shouldn't have, but thank you," Finn said.

"I didn't. I'm just the delivery man." Jim rubbed the back of his neck—his tell that he was nervous about something.

"Spill it, Jim." Sloane clipped her words, topping them off with a smile and wink. He was always the peacemaker in the squad room, mending fences whenever the opportunity presented itself.

"They're from Decker. He wanted to walk them down himself, but he wasn't sure how you'd react."

Sloane swallowed past a growing lump in her throat at Eric's peace offering. *Of course, he'd reach out first.* "Thanks, Jim." Eric was trying. Despite her reluctance to do the same, she still hoped doing her job wouldn't cost him his, which made her a walking contradiction.

After retrieving login credentials to the SFPD data system, hours later, Sloane and Finn made lunch their next stop. Sloane had snagged a decent parking spot four blocks from their destination. Along their walk, three of the city's homeless had set up sleeping accommodations with blankets and stacked tattered backpacks along the sidewalk where it buttressed the building facade. Sloane squeezed Finn's hand when they sidestepped them.

"It's a shame we can't do more for them." Finn glanced back at makeshift beds when they stepped up to the threshold of Sally's Café.

"I used to see it every day when I wore the badge, but I was always too busy working to really notice." Sloane spied an open table near the back and away from the clatter of the wall-mounted oscillating fans. She steered Finn toward it. "I guess I had become immune to it."

"Most people ignore it as a survival mechanism." Finn frowned before walking inside. "If they don't see the mentally ill, then they don't exist."

At this time of day, Sally's was winding down from the usual lunch crowd. Along the wall opposite the service counter, where the grease-tinged air was more breathable, most of the rickety Formica tables for two were empty. Sloane picked out one along a wall, making sure it wasn't a table she and Eric had sat at during one of their many visits. She didn't need another reminder of him.

"It's time to introduce you to the best pie in the city." Sloane picked up a menu and eyed Sally's collection of tempting desserts first.

Halfway through their meals, Sally dropped off a large slice of lemon meringue with two spoons. In between bites of chicken salad, the plate of sugary goodness taunted Sloane. She swiped an index finger across the whipped topping and popped it in her mouth.

"You're like a little kid." Finn laughed.

"It's so good. Here, try some." Sloane stole another finger-full of topping, this time offering it to Finn.

"Mmm. You're right. It's delicious." Finn licked the last of the cream from her lips.

"Hi, Sloane."

A tightness built in her chest before she turned toward the familiar voice. "Eric."

"Still a sucker for Sally's pie, I see." His tone contained a sense of hope that talking about pie might serve as the perfect icebreaker, but he was wrong. Even the best pie in the world couldn't repair the rift between them.

Finn rose from her chair and gave Eric a warm, welcoming hug. "It's good to see you."

"Thanks, Finn. How's the new job? I hear you two are in The Pit."

"It's great. Why don't you join us?" Finn extended an arm toward an empty chair at their table. Sloane drilled her with her eyes. She wasn't ready to talk to him, let alone share a meal.

Eric locked stares with Sloane for several beats. His chest rose and fell to a longing set deep in his eyes. The lines between his brows had become more pronounced since the last time she studied his face, and if she had to guess, he was an emotional mess.

Eric slowly returned his gaze to Finn. "I don't think Sloane is ready for that yet, but thanks anyway."

"By the way, thanks for the coffee this morning." Finn added a pleasing lilt that made Sloane uneasy. Cordial was as far as she was willing to go. "It was very considerate."

"We're all office rats on the same ship and are bound to run into each other a lot. I didn't want it to be awkward."

"We appreciate the gesture." Finn reached out to rub Eric's forearm a few inches above the wrist.

"I should go." He straightened his posture, looking a little stronger than he did yesterday, and returned his gaze to Sloane. "See you around, Sloane."

When he turned and took several steps toward the door, so many questions about her parents' accident came to mind, but only one needed an answer. "Why didn't you stop?"

Eric paused. His shoulders slumped when his head dipped forward. He didn't turn and kept his back to her. A heavy sigh preceded three words before he walked away. "I didn't know."

Sloane's chin quivered at the empty spot he left behind. When Finn made a path on the table by shoving several plates to the side, she reached a hand across. Sloane grabbed it. Strong, warm fingers wrapped around hers, sending comfort. She and Eric had exchanged only seven words, but the unearthed pain ran deep. Whether or not he was aware of the accident at the time, he had made her an orphan. That fact would never change. His answer, though, at the very least, told Sloane he wasn't a coward.

* * *

For the first time in Finn's adult life, her father's text read more like a summons than an invitation. *Dinner 7pm at Shay's.* Though, following last night's commotion at The Tap, she deserved it.

After pulling her SUV to the drop-off curb, Sloane slid the shifter into park. "Want me to come in with you? I can valet the car."

"As much as I would like the reinforcements, this is a conversation I need to have with Daddy alone." Finn leaned in, ready for a kiss. "But I appreciate your offer."

Sloane leaned in the rest of the way, and in that brief second when their lips pressed, Finn felt so damn lucky. Not every woman would've taken her version of last night's story at face value, but Sloane did. "Call me if you need the calvary."

With its precious woods and fabrics, Shay's hostess station presented an elegant atmosphere, the type Finn was comfortable in but never sought out for herself. She craned her neck past the shorter of the two tuxedo-clad hosts. "I don't see my party."

"You must be Ms. Harper." The taller one snapped to attention as if royalty had arrived or a hefty tip was in his future.

"Yes, I am."

"Your father insisted on a private table." He extended an arm to his right. "Please follow me, miss."

Oh boy. Daddy expects fireworks. Finn felt like she did as an unruly third-grader when her teacher led her to the principal's office for pulling Toni Jensen's hair in class. Her anxiety over the expected grilling peaked when she rounded the double-sided stone fireplace, dividing the main dining room into the private area.

"Miss." The host gestured toward her father's table before making a speedy retreat.

At the table for four, covered with fine white linen and adorned with two place settings, a single lit glass lantern in the center cast a warm glow on her father, who had leaned forward in his chair. Reading glasses low on the bridge of his nose and an expensive fountain pen in his right hand, he was focused on the papers laying to the side of his plated filet. The creases on his face hinted whatever he was reviewing troubled him.

"Daddy."

He glanced over the rim of his glasses. "Pumpkin, have a seat. I ordered the chicken piccata for you." The nickname and her favorite dish were a good sign. "I'm almost done."

Minutes later, after giving the papers several more swipes of the pen, he stacked and returned them to a satchel that had been hiding in the neighboring chair. The waiter delivered Finn's chicken piccata, placing it next to her glass of Bordeaux. She gave him a smile and a nod when he glided away.

After her father finished putting away his things, Finn sipped on her wine. "Your text made it sound like I didn't have a choice about coming tonight. That's unlike you."

The kidnapping and rescue, during which they thought they might lose one another, marked a sea change in their relationship. Since that day, Finn and her father hadn't let three days pass without being in each other's company. Now, without the disagreement of her dangerous career choice with the DEA between them, they'd become closer than they had been after her mother died.

"I'm sorry, but last night was upsetting." Chandler pursed his lips, a quirk he'd reserved for her on rare occasions. The last time was when she'd backed her car into a light pole during college, a careless act that disappointed herself more than him. She loved that little hand-me-down Infiniti G20. It was old, but thanks to her father's midlife crisis years earlier, it had all the bells and whistles.

"So you summon me?"

"I wanted you to know I've scheduled a meeting of the partners. I'm calling a vote on Kadin's partnership."

Finn drew her head back, a disquieting feeling settling inside her. "Please don't, Daddy. That would devastate her."

"I knew she was still in love with you, but last night she crossed a line." He flared his nostrils as he tossed his napkin on the plate of his half-eaten dinner.

"I think you're overreacting." Finn used a calm voice to defuse the tension. "Sloane and I are fine, and Kadin knows to never try something like that again."

He shook his head hard. He was a riled-up papa bear. "Why are you defending her? Kadin's conduct was unprofessional. She's burned a bridge with me."

"Daddy." She caressed his hand. "I don't want to see her hurt."

He fixed his stare on her. His silent examination felt like an interrogation had begun—something he had never done with her. It was an uneasy feeling. "Are you still in love with her too?"

Finn recoiled, not because it was true but because she didn't dislike the kiss for a brief second last night. "Of course not."

"Then I need to protect you." He had perfected the "papa bear protecting his young" persona, something she'd never seen in her father before. She appreciated how deep their bond had become, but this was too much.

"I can protect myself. Don't do this."

"She knew you were off-limits. Sloane and Reagan are family now, and I won't stand for her threatening that."

"Daddy, please."

"I love you, pumpkin, but I have to do this for the firm's welfare as well."

"Don't write this off as a stain on the firm. You're overreacting because it's personal."

"Of course, it's personal, but I can't have the partners thinking they can defy my explicit instructions, and she did."

Minutes later, walking down the Embarcadero, Finn pulled her cell phone from her jacket pocket and dialed. On the third ring, the call connected. "We need to talk."

* * *

The cornerstone of the LGBTQ community, Red's seemed like a safe, neutral place for a delicate conversation. It was public and only a few blocks away from her earlier grilling. As an added benefit, Kadin couldn't mistake this no-frills bar with its bare walls and thirty-year-old seating as romantic.

The last time Finn was here, she'd given Sloane information to track down the makers of the drug Kiss. It was a regretful act that led to the death of Sloane's wife Avery, but one that ultimately led her into Sloane's arms. That marked the single worst and best thing she ever did. She grabbed the same table where she and Sloane sat that night. Within minutes, Finn skimmed a hand across the length of it, wondering whether, if she hadn't broken the rules and Sloane hadn't lost Avery, she would have stuck it out with Kadin.

Soon Kadin walked through the door. She didn't look like herself, not at all. Sweats, a wrinkled T-shirt under a light warmup jacket, flip-flops, and tousled hair were entirely out of character. When she approached, her pale, unmade-up face appeared sullen.

"Are you all right, Kadin?"

"That same question last night put me in this state."

"Kadin." Finn's soft tone served as her white flag. "Please sit."

Once in a chair, Kadin averted her eyes. "I'm so sorry about last night. I don't know what came over me."

"Are you sure about that?" Finn angled her head to better see her. "Look at me, Kadin." Their eyes met. "I know you. You do nothing without carefully thinking it through."

"If that were true, and I'm not saying it is in this case, I obviously didn't do enough thinking."

Finn smiled. That was as much of an admission she'd likely get out of her. "Why now, Kadin? What brought on last night?"

"The way you looked at Sloane. You used to look at me that way. Make me feel sexy, wanted, and loved in a single glance."

"Then why did you break up with me? When I moved out, I told you all I needed was space."

"A mix of stupidity, impatience, and short-sightedness. If I were as smart as all my degrees suggest, I should've never let you go."

"I'm with Sloane now."

After a lengthy pause, Kadin locked gazes with Finn, searching for something. "That final night, when you came to our apartment, and I let you go, you told me you still loved me." The pain in Kadin's eyes deepened. "Do you? Still love me?"

"I love Sloane."

"You didn't answer the question."

Any answer Finn gave would either break her heart or encourage her, but she needed to put a stop to this. "You know the answer, but it doesn't change the reason we fell apart."

"Don't you see? All of that has changed." Kadin reached for Finn's hand across the table, but Finn retreated. "You're no longer in a dangerous job. I wouldn't have to worry about you every time you walked out the door."

"My problem with you wasn't about my job." Dare Finn say the rest of what was on her mind? She'd regretted how they left things. So much was left unsaid.

"Then what was it?"

"A part of me will always love you. We were perfect for each other. I even considered proposing, but it came down to one thing."

"I have to know. What did I do to drive you away?"

"You never accepted my choices. Always tried to change me. Sloane has never done that."

A tear rolled down each of Kadin's cheeks. Finn hoped the brutal truth had hit her in the gut because there would be no going back to the way things were. Kadin carefully wiped each streak. "Then it's time to move on. Maybe I should consider starting over in a new city."

"You may have to."

Kadin furrowed her brow. "What do you mean?"

"I had dinner with Daddy tonight. I've never seen him that angry."

"He was as cold as the North Pole at the office today." Kadin shook her head in clear disappointment. "I'll try to smooth things over tomorrow."

"I'm afraid you're too late. Daddy scheduled a meeting with the partners. He's calling a vote on your partnership."

"Damn." Kadin slumped back in her chair. "I really fucked things up."

"You can fight this."

One corner of Kadin's mouth tilted upward. "You do love me."

"Of course, I do." Loving her and being in love with her were two distinct notions. A fact, Finn hoped, Kadin had understood and accepted for both their sakes.

CHAPTER SIX

One word came to Kadin's mind—pissed. Pissed at herself for hurting the woman she still loved. And pissed that she'd put her livelihood in jeopardy. She'd done some stupid things in her thirty-eight years, including that near-miss in Santa Cruz during law school that could've landed her a marijuana charge. But going after Finn the other night topped the list. The word "sorry" had twice crossed her lips, but she wasn't, not really. She'd never regret telling Finn she still loved her, but she sure as hell regretted the consequences now hitting her like a nuke.

Kadin had started building her bomb shelter the minute she got home last night, and it all started with a list. Lists always provided structure to her day in both her personal and professional lives. She never shopped without one and never worked an issue for a client without her trusty catalog of to-do items. She hoped the list she'd made last night would protect her from the hell storm Chandler and the other partners would rain on her later today. When the morning fog thinned, she took a deep, hopeful breath, optimistic this wouldn't be the last day she'd gaze at the best damn view of the bay she'd probably ever have in her career.

"Thank goodness athletes start their day early," Kadin mumbled over the droning telephone dial tone as she cradled the handset between a shoulder and an ear.

She studied the first name on the list—an up-and-coming assistant professional basketball coach for whom she was resolving a contentious contract dispute with the team owners. If anyone would follow her to another firm, Bill Jeffers would. She hated doing this to Chandler. He'd shown her nothing but faith and kindness for seven years, but self-preservation had kicked in stronger than her loyalty.

The call connected after several rings. "This is Jeffers."

"Bill, this is Kadin Hall from HMR and Associates."

"Kadin? Don't tell me the team's front office is still whining over my contract."

She laughed. "No, Bill. They're still licking their wounds, and I expect that three-year extension, plus bonuses. I'm calling for personal reasons."

"Well, this just got interesting. Does this mean you've changed your mind?"

Bill was a gentleman through and through, and Kadin counted on that trait continuing. She put on her "game face," hoping her words would come out as confident. "I'm afraid not. Mixing business and pleasure is never wise."

"I've never been known to do the prudent thing, which is why I often require your services. I'm holding out hope you'll take me up on that drink one day."

"Maybe—"

"Before you finish that sentence, I'll take that as a good sign. Now, what has you calling me at eight thirty in the morning?"

"I hate making this call, but I find it necessary. You're my first call. For personal reasons, I might leave HMR."

"Holy hell, Kadin. No one knows my contract inside out and can handle the team owners as you do." The panic in his voice was the response she wanted.

"That's why I'm calling. If I leave, do you have a preference for my replacement?"

"I don't trust anyone but you. You picked the worst time to chase a bigger paycheck."

"I'm not chasing more money, Bill. All I can say is that I'm not in control of all the circumstances."

"Are you saying HMR is letting you go?"

"I'm not at liberty to discuss the specifics."

"This is a fucking mess, Kadin. I know at least a dozen other coaches and athletes in the same boat. They'll hit the roof when they hear you're leaving."

"I'm so sorry about the timing of things, but your other option would be to change representation and follow me to my next firm."

"Then that's what I'll do. There's no time to get someone else up to speed."

Bingo! That was precisely what she needed to hear. If Bill followed, she hoped the rest of her clients would too. HMR couldn't afford that big of a hit all at once. Over the next three hours, she worked her way through her list of clients, finishing with a sore ear and hoarse voice.

A knock on the door drew Kadin out of her self-preservation focus. "Come in."

Reagan entered, carrying her third load of client folders of the day. The long brooding face announced she still wasn't over the events at The Tap. And on her birthday of all days. Kadin had pulled a classic asshole move, and she couldn't blame Reagan for the Cold War reception. No sense in apologizing. Reagan likely wouldn't believe her. Hell, Kadin barely bought her own apology when she bared her soul to Finn last night.

"You asked for these." Reagan's eyes narrowed, forming a now-familiar death stare. She dropped the files on the corner of her desk, resulting in a swoosh of air gusting several loose papers toward Kadin.

When Reagan turned on her heel, Kadin had had enough. "Stop." She waited for Reagan to turn around. The same stone-pelting glare remained. "You don't have to like me, but I'm a partner here, and you will respect that."

Reagan opened her mouth to fire back, but before the first word tumbled past her lips, Kadin raised an index finger in indignation. "Chandler may have hired you, but any partner may fire you. Remember that."

When the door closed behind Reagan, Kadin slumped forward, thumping her forehead atop her dark wood desk and likely leaving a mark. "Damn it." She'd torched every bridge around here and wondered if her circling the wagons today was worth it.

The chime from her phone reminded her she was to face the executioners in five minutes. No time to change course now. She'd wallowed enough. She needed this job and the money that came with it. The title company's email this morning read, *"Congratulations! Escrow on the Market Street condo is scheduled to close in two weeks."* She wasn't about to go back on her word with Finn about buying her place. Not about anything. Not now. Not ever.

After swiping her phone quiet and rising from her chair, Kadin placed the final client folders in a file box. She squared her shoulders and puffed out her chest. A quick tug on her dark gray designer suit jacket, and she was ready for battle. She picked up the overstuffed box and strode through her office door with a purpose, leaving her doubts behind.

At the double oak doors leading to the conference room, she paused and put on her game face again. It was time to go toe to toe with the big boys. With a single hip thrust, she pushed through. Seven other suits and sets of eyes evenly spaced in a U-shape around the oblong conference table instantly focused on her. Under any other circumstance, she expected the one other skirt in the room to back her up, but not today. This was personal to Chandler, and everyone would have his back. He was that kind of leader. That meant the tack she'd chosen was her best option.

She plopped the box on the table opposite Chandler, who was positioned fifteen feet away at its head—the seat of power. Taking a seat herself seemed pointless. She didn't intend to remain on the chopping block long enough for him to sharpen his blade.

"I suppose this meeting is about me." A scan of the other partners confirmed it. They refused eye contact, all except Chandler.

"Your conduct was unprofessional and cast this firm in a bad light." Chandler's fighting mad, unblinking response sent a chill through Kadin.

"I disagree and think you're overreacting, but considering the other person involved, I know nothing I say will change your mind."

"Then the only thing left to say is that I'm calling a vote on your partnership." Chandler broke his stare and glanced down both sides of the table at the other partners. "Shall we vote?"

"Before you do that, I think you should see something first." She retrieved the first client folder from the box and laid it on the table. "Bob Jeffers. Thirty thousand dollars."

In succession, she laid out each client's folder and recited their names and the fees they paid the firm the first half of this year. Over two million dollars in total. She pointed to the neatly stacked files. "Each client has pledged to follow me if I'm forced out. If you think HMR can take a potential four-million-dollar hit this year, by all means, call a vote on my partnership. I'll be happy to throw up a shingle of my own."

An indistinct murmur simmered in the room as each row of partners darted their heads back and forth, consulting one another. She hated doing this. Every word that spewed from her mouth flew in the face of everything her own father taught her. That trust and loyalty, above everything else, formed the foundation of every business arrangement. She'd burned Chandler's trust the moment she kissed his daughter in that bathroom, and now she threatened to blow up the one thing she had left to offer—her loyalty.

"I don't like where this is going." Chandler spun and then tapped his fountain pen. The fact it was a gift from his daughter didn't escape Kadin.

"I don't either." Kadin's rough Richmond roots had prepared her for this moment. Game face, she reminded herself. Don't show one ounce of weakness. The hum of whispering grew again because the battle of wills had taken a turn. Kadin had stood her ground. Fervently. Resolutely. She refused to break her stare with Chandler.

Several tense, silent moments passed while Chandler spun his daughter's gift numerous times. "It appears you have us over a barrel."

Their history tugged at her, but she kept her walls up and showed no emotion. "You took a chance on this girl from the wrong side of the tracks who took twice as long to work her way through law school. I want to repay your loyalty in kind by remaining with HMR, but if you force me out, I'll do what I must to survive."

The other partners shook their heads in apparent disagreement with Chandler's proposed vote.

"You've won this one, but I caution you, Ms. Hall." Chandler stood, buttoning his suit coat over his crisp white dress shirt. His expression stern. "Bottom line or not. Don't press my patience a second time."

"All right then, I'll get back to work."

Moments later, Kadin slid inside her office, closing the door with a kick of her heel and then slumping against the smooth, cold wood. She'd outflanked Chandler, but she wouldn't catch him off guard a second time. Even if she toed the line, she got the impression he would still gun for her and would work at stripping away those pledges she'd racked up today.

She feared all she accomplished was to buy herself time. It was time to organize her finances and time to set up her own practice. She had one person to thank for that—Finn.

After placing the box on her desk, she leaned her bottom against it and whipped out her cell phone. Her fingers quickly tapped the keyboard. She pressed send and returned the phone to her jacket pocket, feeling a smile slowly emerging. The text message read, *Thanks for heads-up. Dodged a bullet today because of you.*

Seconds later, Finn replied, *I'm sure Daddy isn't happy, but I am.*

"So am I, Finn. So am I."

* * *

Sloane swiped her access badge over the card reader to her and Finn's office in The Pit and listened for the unmistakable unlocking click. As she pushed the door open, she hoped enough time had passed over the weekend. She inhaled deep and wasn't disappointed. "Ah, linen." The multiple air fresheners they'd installed on Friday had done their job. The musty smell had disappeared.

"See, I told you it would work." Finn lowered her laptop satchel from her shoulder and placed it on their worktable.

Sloane slid up behind Finn and wrapped her arms around her torso, nuzzling her chin atop a shoulder. "I should've never doubted you." *About the air fresheners nor about Kadin*, she thought.

Finn squeezed Sloane's arms with her own. "Remember that when we start analyzing the next set of case files."

After preparing the requisite pot of coffee, she and Finn dove into the day's work. Today's focus—cataloging and collecting metadata on unsolved homicide cases of the last twenty-five years, including dates, locations, type of victims, type of suspects, cause of death, and investigating officers. Hours later, Sloane popped up from her workstation, rubbing the kinks from her stiff neck. "I'm getting more coffee. Want some?"

"Absolutely." Finn also rubbed her neck. "This cataloging sure has been revealing."

"You're telling me." After stirring in two sugars, Sloane handed Finn a full cup. "With the nature of the crimes, I expected to see high unsolved rates for robbery and burglary, but the trends we unearthed last week surprised me."

"How's that?" Finn asked.

"The same few detectives kept popping up. It's a wonder Ferrara and McNichol are still collecting paychecks." Sloane curled her lips at the sad fact that some cops never seem to carry their weight. "I long suspected those two were slugs, but this data proves it."

"At least they collected DNA from the crime scenes that might make their cases solvable now."

"That was all Avery. From her first day as a CSI tech, she insisted on collecting it at every scene despite budget constraints. Most of the time, we didn't have the money to test the sample, but she ensured we'd have something to go on if we ever got the funding."

"That's an amazing legacy. Avery's forward-thinking will help solve crimes for years."

Sloane's throat thickened at the word legacy. A reminder Avery was gone. A reminder Avery would never see Reagan as the beautiful woman she had evolved into. Sloane was proud as hell of that amazing wife and mother and the legacy she'd left behind. She cleared her throat, but her voice still croaked when she said, "Yeah, it will."

After grabbing Sloane's mug from her hand, Finn placed both their cups on the table. Her eyes softened as she caressed Sloane's arms. "It's okay to miss her."

Sloane's lower lip quivered when she nodded. "I know. It's awkward with you. I don't want to make you feel that I loved her more, because—"

Finn placed an index finger over Sloane's lips. "You don't have to say it. You make me feel loved every day. I never doubt that."

Sloane pulled Finn into her arms. "I've always loved you."

Where their bodies touched, every nerve ending tingled. That sensation had become a drug, one Sloane craved more and more every day. Of all the women she'd made love to, Avery was the first to leave her wanting more. But with Finn, that want turned into a need. The powerful connection took two decades to complete, and it seemed to grow stronger with each passing day.

Sloane squeezed until a knock on the door forced her to let go and return to business. She grabbed her coffee mug, its contents still warm. "Come in."

Jim Shaw pushed the door open. "Afternoon, ladies."

Afternoon? Sloane glanced at her watch. She'd lost track of time. "Hey, Jim. What brings you to The Pit?"

"I was typing up an email to send, but then I missed yelling across the squad room at you, so I did the next best thing." He extended his arms wide, presenting himself as if he were a shiny present wrapped in a bow. "Here I am."

"I miss it too, but family comes first."

"Yeah, I get it."

Did he? True, Sloane had left the department for her family but she couldn't say what she really missed. She missed walking into that squad room every day, knowing she and Eric would hit the streets together to do their part in the never-ending drug war. But if she had to boil it down to one thing, she missed her best friend.

"I wanted to let you know it's the first tomorrow, so I put you two on Captain Nash's calendar for ten. He's expecting your first status report." Jim arched an eyebrow. "Please tell me you have something to report."

Sloane raised her coffee mug and took a leisurely sip. "Report? I thought we were here to drink coffee all day like the rest of you."

Off to her left, Finn chuckled when Jim's eyes rolled. "Yes, Jim." Finn grinned when his cheeks puffed. "We'll have a robust update for the captain."

"See?" He gestured toward Finn while staring at Sloane. "That's how you give a direct answer."

After Jim left, Finn retrieved the food and bottles of water she'd packed for her and Sloane and laid it out on one workstation. "After lunch, we better work through the rest of these homicides and arson cases before we leave tonight."

"Can't disappoint the all-powerful Carter Nash." In Sloane's experience, the captain would jump on any little thing to make their job impossible to perform. And poor performance meant an unhappy Mark Gandy. And an unhappy Gandy suggested no future city contracts for the Sloane-Harper Group.

Hours of shifting from one computer screen to another had muscles in Sloane's neck screaming for a break. One more reason she hated deadlines. Whatever happened to investigations where cases were solved on their own timeline, not some bureaucrat's? God, she missed those days.

She took another sip of bottled water, rubbed the back of her neck, and entered the next case number into the SFPD system. When the details populated the screen, she mechanically focused on specific data fields, copying the relevant information. Then a name caught her eye. Bernie. She looked closely. Bernie Sellers. It *was* him.

She couldn't remember the last time that name had crossed her mind. Maybe it was when she was explaining to Finn why she became a cop. No, that wasn't when. It was six months ago. She'd just adopted Reagan, and Finn was by her side when she had gone through Eric's scrapbook memorializing her life after her parents' accident—the one he caused. That was the moment Sloane had gained a new perspective about that horrible day. Anger had replaced guilt. Nevertheless, six months was too long to go without thinking about the man who rescued her.

Her hand shook against her lips as she read the scant summary. *Arson-Murder. Home known hangout for drug users. Suspected arson. Three deceased: unidentified WFA, unidentified MA, Bernie SELLERS, off-duty San Pablo police officer. Cause of death: Smoke inhalation SELLERS and WFA. Gunshot MA, burned beyond recognition.*

She gasped. "Oh, my God."

"What is it, babe?" The wheels on Finn's chair scraped along the linoleum floor as she moved closer to Sloane.

"It's Bernie."

"Not your Bernie?"

"Yeah." That one word stuck in Sloane's throat. With considerable effort, she cleared it. "His death is unsolved. I assumed it was accidental, trying to save that woman from the fire."

Finn stood and cozied up behind Sloane, resting her forearms atop her shoulders, peering at the computer screen along with her. "Why was he at a house fire in the city?"

"Because of me." Twenty-two years had yet to erase the sting of his death. He'd left behind a daughter that she knew of and likely a wife. She grabbed one of Finn's hands and squeezed. "He was picking me up to make a surprise visit." Sloane spun around on her wobbly office chair and hugged Finn, pressing her head against her chest. "He died because I wanted to see you."

Finn cradled Sloane's head. "He died because he was a hero."

"My nana said the same thing." Sloane tilted her head up and locked eyes with Finn. "I want to find out who set that fire."

"We'll make sure this one gets to the state investigators."

"No." Sloane shook her head with a purpose that was twenty-two years in the making. "I never thought to look up his case, so I want to investigate this myself. I owe him that."

Finn lifted Sloane's chin with two fingers. "How about we do it together?"

"Another reason I love you." Sloane checked her watch. "It's almost seven. We can finish our findings in the morning. I don't want to miss dinner with Reagan."

"You *have* changed." The sparkle in Finn's hazel eyes reassured Sloane her transformation was for the better. Family always came first.

"I figure we'll have plenty of days ahead of us when we won't control our hours. Until then, I'm not missing any family dinners. Especially not for Nash."

* * *

Dinner wasn't what Finn had hoped for, but it was what she expected—a cold war with no end in sight. Reagan had refused to make eye contact since the moment she and Sloane walked through the townhouse door and had kept it up all the way through dinner. If anything, the young woman was persistent.

Seated next to Reagan, Finn had glanced at her several times since they filled their plates. Over the stubborn silence, Reagan remained fixated on the chicken and carrots, shifting them around her plate in no discernible pattern. *She's still pissed*, Finn thought.

The pit in Finn's stomach made her less interested in eating, and like Reagan, more interested in forming chicken and green bean geometric patterns on her plate. She couldn't blame Reagan for her frosty reception. They had yet to develop the deep trust Reagan shared with Sloane, and what little they had, the incident with Kadin blew up. The problem—Finn had no idea how to fix it.

Finn felt pressure on her fork-laden hand. From the head of the table, Sloane had wrapped a hand around hers. Sloane spoke in a muted tone. "I think your food has had enough playtime. How about taking a few bites?"

"I'm sorry, babe. I'm a little distracted."

"I bet you are," Reagan mumbled.

It took every ounce of restraint to not offer a sharp retort. Finn dug deep and asked in the most pleasant voice she could muster, "Could you pass the salad, Reagan?"

After an obligatory five-count, followed by another five, Finn reached for the salad bowl herself. Sloane placed a hand on her arm. "Don't." Sloane narrowed her eyes toward Reagan. "I've been overly patient with you. Finn did nothing wrong. I can't force you to like her, but you will be civil. We're a family, and families treat one another with respect."

Reagan's eyes welled up. Then her lower lip quivered. "I'm sorry. May I be excused?"

"Yes, you may." Sloane's expression softened.

After Reagan hurried downstairs, followed by the slam of her bedroom door, Finn asked, "What was that all about?"

"After our wedding, Avery gave Reagan the same speech when she gave me the cold shoulder."

"Thank you." Finn stole a brief yet passionate kiss. "I'd like to think we are a family."

"We are. Give Reagan time. She'll get past this."

After Sloane and Finn did the dishes and after ice cream on the couch, all the problems of the day melted away. Sloane held Finn in her arms beneath the covers in the darkness and in the silence of their bedroom. Where their bodies touched skin to skin, the warmth eased Finn into a twilight moments before sleep. As her mind began to fade, she whispered. "Do you think Nash will give us access to what we'll need to look into Bernie's case?"

"Hmmm," Sloane's voice was soft on the edge of slumber. "Probably not, but I have a plan."

CHAPTER SEVEN

Striding down Bryant's fifth-floor corridor, Sloane realized she'd have to get used to talking to the brass, which, in her experience, meant unpleasant things—reprimands and politics. As a contractor answering to the mayor, she didn't fear Captain Nash's admonitions. She did, however, cringe at his political ambition, which meant not revealing anything that would put a stain on his leadership.

"Babe?" Finn gripped Sloane's forearm in mid-stride, bringing them both to a halt.

"Huh?" Finn's hazel eyes were enough to bring Sloane out of her thoughts.

"Where were you just now?"

If Sloane had her way, she'd be back in bed, nuzzled next to Finn's warm body. She'd rather do anything than stand in front of a man who'd only looked down on her. "You know Nash will block us at every corner."

"Which means what?"

"We don't tip our hand. We need to go around him to the mayor." Sloane would rather deal with the snake paying them than the one fighting them.

"I don't trust Nicci Cole."

"I don't either, but we need to forget politics, and use our cover story to get access to work Bernie's case."

Sloane waited for Finn to nod before tapping her knuckles against the frosted glass door. A deep male voice ordered them inside. As expected, Nash ignored her and Finn, not glancing past the papers on his desk. This time, though, Sloane played his game of manipulation and remained silent. When Finn gestured toward Nash as if to speak, Sloane shook her head, signaling the game wasn't over.

Sloane's wait reminded her of the standoff she and Finn had at Red's the night Finn handed her Diego Rojas on a platter. Both Sloane and Finn had tested each other's patience like she was doing with Nash. She expected to win this battle as well.

After ten, twenty, and finally thirty seconds of awkward silence, Nash looked up from over his metal-framed glasses and squared his chair with the desk. "I'll expect updates on your progress the first of every month until the work is complete."

"We report to the mayor." Sloane's brusqueness earned a brush on her thigh from Finn's hand.

"You also need access to SFPD systems." Nash leaned back in his chair as if he had the upper hand. "This is the price of admission."

And there it was—the opening salvo. Sloane and Finn were sandwiched between Captain Nash and Mayor Cole in a power struggle. She was never one for politics and wanted to turn back the clock. Given the opportunity again, she'd never sign this contract with the city.

Tension built in her neck over the thought of having to claw and scratch for every inch of ground. Finn must have sensed it, because before Sloane could utter her next quip, Finn brushed a hand against hers and inched forward.

"We understand, Captain." Finn's reply was better-mannered than what Sloane had in mind. It was also a gentle reminder of what Eric had taught her early in her career as a detective—give the impression of cooperation even if it's the furthest thing from her mind. She silently snorted. People from outside agencies were rarely helpful and primarily out for their own best interests. Captain Nash was the poster child for it.

"We've spent the last two weeks getting the lay of the land." Sloane bit back her distaste for the man and continued in a businesslike fashion. "We cataloged all the unsolved cases where the statute of limitations was still in effect and about three-quarters of those in the last twenty-five years without the limitations."

"The list we provided wasn't enough?" Nash lowered his brow, just the response Sloane didn't want.

"It was a good start," Finn said, "but we needed to collect additional metadata to identify trends and rank each case's potential solvability."

"And what have you found so far?"

"We're still in the early stages," Finn added, "but have found several opportunities where available technology might solve more cases."

"Anything else?"

"Yes." Sloane gave Finn a faint nod. Time to test the waters. "We need unrestricted access to NCIC."

"Why?"

"Limiting our access to the unsolved cases hampers our abilities. To complete our mandate, we need to analyze how other cases were solved while similar ones were not." Once the words tumbled out of Sloane's mouth, she realized their cover story had merit and should be part of the contract.

"We've provided you everything your contract stipulates. If you need something more, then I suggest you work it through the mayor's office."

Of course, this wouldn't be easy. Nash only responded to force, and Sloane expected his patented resistance. She stiffened her spine and resolve. "Then that's what we'll do."

* * *

Sloane closed the door to their small office in The Pit after she and Finn entered. The linen aroma of the plug-ins was losing the war against the closed-in stale air. Instead of reclaiming a chair like Finn, Sloane leaned her back and bottom against the smooth cream-colored surface of the beat-up pressed-wood door. Options rolled in and out of her head. How much should she and Finn let on during their next phone call? Should she come right out and tell Gandy they unearthed a disturbing trend among the unsolved homicide cases? Tipping her hand would lead to questions she wasn't ready to answer.

She let out a heavy sigh. "We need to stick to our cover story with the mayor's office. If they get wind that we're investigating a case ourselves, we could lose the contract."

"Then who knows who the mayor will hire and use to clean house." Finn sifted through her purse and pulled out a business card. Minutes later, she disconnected her call with Chief of Staff Mark Gandy. "He didn't suspect a thing. Gandy says he'll push our request through and that we should have access to everything we want in the morning."

"I don't like this, Finn." Sloane pushed herself off the door and joined Finn at the desk. "Both Captain Nash and Mayor Cole have competing interests, and we're stuck right in the middle. If we're not careful, we'll be locked out of future contracts or several good cops will lose their job. Maybe both."

"We'll figure it out, babe." Finn rubbed Sloane's arm, but the gesture did little to shake the disturbing feeling this job wouldn't end well.

* * *

The following morning, when the red and white mechanical arm guarding the underground parking area at 850 Bryant rose, Sloane stretched her mouth into a full, throaty yawn. Sleep had fought her most of the night, her mind bouncing between the job and the growing rift between Reagan and Finn. At the bottom of the ramp, she turned left.

"Where are you going?" Finn asked from the passenger seat. Her voice ended on an uptick.

Sloane checked her surroundings and stomped on the brakes. Two-and-a-half years of driving into this parking garage had her on autopilot, and she'd turned toward the police-only area, not the visitor section. Her face grew long. "Shit. Force of habit." She backed up and weaved her way to a set of spaces in the visitor section's last row. She'd discovered that two slots were six inches wider than the rest in that section, though, they were still narrower than the official PD spaces she'd grown accustomed to. And since her SUV still had that new car smell, the thought of catching a door ding gave her the shivers.

Once parked and walking toward the underground entrance, Finn pulled on Sloane's arm, bringing her to a stop. "You miss it, don't you?"

"Being a cop?" Before Sloane turned, she carefully thought out her words so Finn wouldn't mistake her feelings. "Sometimes I miss the job, but you and Reagan are my priority now. I was fine when we had private clients. But working here, it's hard seeing the same people I worked with for years. I'm worried about what might happen to them when we finish our contract."

"I am too. If we only had some leverage over the mayor."

Sloane's mind churned at the possibility of turning the political tables. She inched closer to Finn and then scanned the surrounding area, making sure no one else could hear. "Nicci Cole is a former district attorney. Since we'll have access to the full SFPD database, why don't we poke around her old cases? See if we can come up with anything."

"You want to dig up dirt on the mayor?" Finn curled her lip. "I hate politics."

"I do too, but if you can think of another way, I'm all ears."

Finn tapped her lips with an index finger as if summoning the brainpower to solve the riddle of the Sphinx. "She must have prosecuted hundreds of cases. Where would we start?"

"I bet Kyler Harris could point us in the right direction."

One corner of Finn's mouth inched upward. "You're a genius."

Sloane resurveyed the parking garage. They were still alone. She pulled their bodies together until their thighs and hips touched, and the warmth of Finn's breath tickled her lips. "Say that again."

"You're impossible, but you're also a genius."

Sloane's surroundings faded into a blur. She and Finn had been a couple for six months, a blink of an eye to most, but in reality, their connection spanned decades. This, she was sure, would last a lifetime. A wedding on the grand steps of City Hall seemed more than a possibility. "I love you, Finn Harper."

"I love you, Manhattan Sloane."

When Sloane leaned in for a kiss, movement in her peripheral vision caught her attention. She pulled back and focused on it. The way he held his left arm close to his body as he walked was unmistakable. She swallowed to a hard lump.

"Good morning, Sloane."

"Good morning, Eric." His eyes lit up at her greeting, a sparkle she hadn't seen in them since before he was shot.

A memory took over, one Sloane would rather forget. The last time she and Eric met in this parking garage, she had protected him. Their off-book investigation into Avery's killer put their jobs at risk, so she'd decided to cut him out. Back then, Sloane would do anything for him, and he would do the same. She inhaled at the mutual trust she missed so much.

"It's nice seeing you two so happy." A sense of regret in his voice almost broke her resolve. He stared at her as if hoping for something more, but she offered the same indifference she'd shown him for months. As much as she missed what they had as partners, she wasn't ready to forgive him.

"We are."

"I'm glad." Eric's chest heaved before he walked off toward the entrance.

When he disappeared behind the door, Sloane's breaths turned rapid and shallow. She placed both hands on her hips and leaned forward at the waist to steady herself. "Damn it, Eric. Why did you have to tell me?"

Finn's hand fell to the small of her back and gently rubbed away her pain. "It'll get easier. I promise."

"I hope so."

* * *

Sloane had scrounged up worthy opponents against The Pit's stale air and blinking fluorescents on Finn's suggestion. The addition of an oscillating fan kept the air moving, and strategically placed table and desk lamps provided a softer, unblinking light that made it easier to work. Without those annoying morning distractions, Sloane brought the computer workstation to life. The hard drive spun and creaked, adding to her suspicion that this heap was on its last leg—another thing Sloane would have to address sooner rather than later. She impatiently tapped her fingertips against the blue ceramic coffee mug she was holding.

"This thing is ancient."

"I fully expect us to need a replacement before this contract is over." Finn took the neighboring seat and fired up the company laptop, booting it in fifteen seconds.

"Finally." Sloane could've baked a cake in the time it took the damn login screen to appear. She positioned her mug beside the keyboard, and several clicks and keystrokes later she was in the SFPD data systems. She rubbed her hands together with the eagerness of a child on Christmas morning. "Let's see if Gandy pulled those strings."

She tested the security controls by entering the number assigned to her last case—El Padrino. The dreaded "Access Denied" message popped up. "I guess Gandy doesn't have as much juice as he'd like us to think."

"I'll text him." Finn tapped on her cell phone.

"Wait. You have Tight Pants's personal number?"

"Uh-huh. When we talked yesterday, he said our contract is the mayor's number one priority and that I should contact him if there's any problem." Before Finn returned the phone to her suit coat pocket, it dinged. "It's Gandy. He said he'd light a fire."

Two hours later, a light rap on the door broke Sloane's focus from cataloging the remaining unsolved cases with Finn. "Come in," she yelled.

Jim Shaw emerged when the door pushed open. His expression telegraphed this wasn't a simple social visit. "I don't know what you two did, but Nash is on the warpath."

Sloane glanced at Finn, earning her a satisfied grin. "Tight Pants came through."

Jim laughed. "I'm not sure what that means, but it seems you have some pull. Next time you log in to our systems, you'll have full access, even to compartmentalized cases." He fished two security access badges from his front pants pocket and handed them to Sloane and Finn. "You'll like this. Here are your new building passes. Access to everything. Nash drew the line at an official PD parking pass."

"Damn it, Jim. You should've given me a heads-up." Sloane flashed her pass to Finn. "They used the same hangover picture."

After Jim left, Sloane put aside the awful picture of the century, reclaimed her chair, logged into the law enforcement system, and reentered her last case. In an instant, data populated the screen. She smiled so broadly that it hurt. "We're in."

Within seconds, she focused on the case summary, which detailed Padrino's cartel affiliation, the kidnapping of Reagan and Chandler, the shootout at Three Owls Vineyard, and Eric's injuries. Her back stiffened, reliving the events of the day Padrino was killed, the day that changed everything. She'd told Finn she loved her, almost lost Reagan to a ruthless drug lord, and ended up losing her best friend, not to a bullet, but to a twenty-two-year-old truth.

Her eyes scanned the photograph displayed in the upper right-hand corner—a color still from Valley Hospital's security footage. Even then, Padrino had an evil look about him. The camera had picked up his cold, steely stare, the same one Sloane had faced down the night the hostage exchange went awry at Three Owls Vineyard. The same night she almost lost Reagan and Finn. She glanced at Finn, confident with her choices. No matter how much she missed the badge, she'd never put those two at risk again.

She redirected her attention to the screen and focused on a data field labeled *Related Cases* that she hadn't noticed populated before she left the force. The plus sign beside it meant someone had linked another case to Reagan and Chandler's kidnapping. She clicked on it, and a new window opened. Three cases were listed in chronological order from newest to oldest. Sloane recognized the first two case numbers, Avery and Shellie Rodriguez's deaths. The third, with its 1998 identifier, seemed oddly familiar. She opened the link to a second pop-up window.

"What the hell?"

"What now? Did Captain Nash revoke our hall pass?" Finn asked.

"Bernie's case is linked to Padrino's."

Finn closed the lid on her laptop and walked the few steps until she peered over Sloane's shoulder. "How can that be?"

Sloane drilled down and read. Her breath caught on the words, forcing her to clear her throat. "The bullets removed from Padrino and one of his bodyguards match the one removed from the unidentified adult male vic in Bernie's case."

Finn's silence prompted Sloane to glance at her. Her face had turned blank and pale. Sloane recognized that look—something had troubled her. "Are you all right? Is something wrong?"

"That can't be right." Finn's eyes darted back and forth, and she swallowed—hard.

"Avery trained her team well. They wouldn't get something like this wrong. I bet Quintrell picked up one of the guns Padrino's goons dropped in the brush before everything went haywire. Bernie's case could be a cartel hit. Did Los Dorados have a presence here back then?"

"I don't know. Prichard might know."

Sloane rolled her eyes. "Not Prickhead."

Finn swiped her cell phone screen. "Shoot. I forgot I promised to have a late lunch with Daddy today."

"Should I come with you?"

"I think he wanted to talk about something personal." She slung her purse over her shoulder. "I'm not sure how long I'll be, so I'll Uber over." She kissed Sloane on the lips. "See you at home tonight."

Before Sloane could get in a word, Finn hurried out, slamming the door behind her. "Strange. Very strange." She suspected something was amiss but couldn't pin it down. "What aren't you telling me, Finn?"

Sloane returned her attention to the computer screen and the mystery begging to be solved. She'd lost count of how many cases she'd worked on as a detective, but the ones that stuck with her, besides Los Dorados and El Padrino, were the few she couldn't close. This one was personal, and she wanted to solve it. The only other case she'd taken personally had led to a dogged pursuit that cost her Avery. She couldn't bear losing Finn and silently vowed to be careful and recognize when it was time to call it quits.

CHAPTER EIGHT

A pang of guilt worked its way through Finn, faster than she cared for. She couldn't remember the last time she was in this elevator but recalled it was when she was still raw from breaking up with Kadin, which was a year ago. She should've known better than to visit her father at his office back then because passing Kadin in the hallway had surfaced a grab bag of hurt emotions. After that, she'd stopped coming. Today's urgent need for her father's advice, though, forced her to put all of that aside.

The reception area of the sprawling office suite hadn't changed. The furniture and flooring of varying shades of dark woods juxtaposed against crisp white accents and fabrics imparted a luxurious atmosphere. They were an interior designer's selections, definitely not her father's. If Chandler had his way, the office would be a mix of dark leather, oak, and golf memorabilia.

Finn strolled up to the receptionist, a man in his mid-twenties, dressed in a navy and white windowpane-patterned blazer tailored tightly over a white button-up shirt patterned with small navy butterflies. The white pocket square of the same shirt material completed the young gay professional male look.

"Afternoon, Brian. Is Sharon out today?"

"Lunch." His gaze fell to his computer screen. "I don't have you down. Was Mr. Harper expecting you?"

"No, but I was hoping he wasn't with a client or in a meeting."

"Neither, but I should announce you." He reached for the phone receiver perched on the corner of his sleek glass-top desk.

Finn raised a hand in a subtle stopping motion and continued past his desk before he could object. "I'd like to surprise him if you don't mind."

"Ms. Harper," he called out.

She waved a hand over her head, Brian still calling out her name. After she turned the corner, the entrance to her father's private office came into view. She'd used this door dozens of times, taking advantage of her father's open invitation. He'd said that if he wasn't with a client, she was welcomed any day and never needed an escort to see him. Today was one of those days.

She tapped her knuckles on the door and waited. No answer meant her father had stepped out or was on the phone. Either way, she decided to tiptoe in. After twisting the knob, she slid the door open, revealing the window side of his office where his desk sat empty. *Maybe he went to the bathroom*, she thought.

Pushing the door open further, she stepped in. Motion to her left caught her attention. She turned. Jacketless, her father pushed himself up from the leather couch he was stretched across, one leg flat, and the other bent, reaching the floor.

Three feet away, Sharon was standing at the side of the couch, straightening her white slip-on silk blouse and yellow pencil skirt with her palms. Her usually perfectly styled wavy, shoulder-length black hair was mussed.

"What the—" Finn had yet to process the scene in front of her.

"Pumpkin." He bounced from the couch. "I can explain."

A compulsion to flee set in when two and two finally added up. Her father was having an office romp. At first, she squirmed at the thought of him having clichéd hot office sex with his secretary. She turned to retrace her steps. "I'll come back later."

"Pumpkin, wait." He edged around the low coffee table parallel to the couch. "It's about time we told you."

About time? That meant whatever this was, it had been going on for a while. Why didn't she have a clue her father was seeing someone? Then again, maybe they weren't dating, and this was about sex. Finn froze, her body quivering at the disturbing images flying through her head. They were thoughts no daughter should ever have of her father, under any circumstance.

"I'll let you two talk." Sharon gracefully exited through the main door, leaving an awkward silence in her wake.

He tightened his low-hanging tie and rolled down the shirtsleeves that had been resting halfway up his forearms. "I've meant to talk to you about Sharon, but we were waiting until we knew this was going somewhere."

"Your love life is none of my business, Daddy." Finn remained statue-like, still unable to close the door nor make her feet move.

"It is when we're thinking about moving in together."

"Moving in? How long have you two been a thing?"

"Ever since the kidnapping." After he sat again, he extended his arm, offering her a seat on the couch.

"Uh-uh." She shook her head with the energy of a racehorse. The thought of what Sharon and her father may have done on that couch minutes earlier made her queasy. "I'll stand, thank you very much."

"It's safe, I promise." He laughed while patting the cushion next to him. "Sit."

A shiver shot through when she sunk into the leather. She tried to shake it off, thinking this was something she'd have to get accustomed to. "Six months, huh?"

"It came as a surprise, but the kidnapping had a dramatic effect on me. I realized I no longer wanted to go through life alone. You had Sloane, and I wanted that same love in my life again."

"Does she make you happy?" Finn had guessed her father was five or ten years older than Sharon. Still, she never considered the possibility of those two as a couple.

"Very." The twinkle in his eyes confirmed the answer. "I never thought this old man's heart could race again at the thought of a woman, but she—"

"I don't need any details." Finn briefly put up her hand in a stopping motion. "I'm glad you've found someone. You should bring her on our next family day."

"She would love to see the Giants game with us." He shifted on the cushion and slung an arm over the back of the couch. "Now, what brings you over? You haven't visited here in ages."

Finn blew out a long, lip-sputtering breath. "I've gotten myself into the middle of something, and I need your advice."

"If your expression is an indicator, I'd say this something is quite troubling."

"It is, Daddy." When his hand fell upon hers, Finn was sure he'd guide her through this, as he'd done when she didn't know how to help Sloane through her grief. "Sloane and I have been cataloging all the unsolved SFPD cases as part of our contract. We stumbled upon a case that's linked to Sloane's past."

"How's that?"

She pursed her lips. "The police officer who rescued her after her parents' accident died while saving a woman from a burning building. Another man was found dead at the scene, but he had been shot in the head. But that's not the most important part. The bullet from that case matches the bullet taken out of Padrino's chest."

"That's an interesting twist. Do you think the old case was some kind of cartel assassination?"

"Sloane made the same assumption, but—"

"But you know something that you're not telling her."

"Am I that obvious?"

"To someone who knows you."

Shit. Did Sloane suspect she lied earlier? The day she moved in, she promised Sloane to always be honest with her, but even then, Finn knew that was a promise she couldn't keep. She'd been lying to Sloane since the night Eric was shot.

"I never told Sloane how Quintrell got the gun he used to kill his father."

"It wasn't from one of Padrino's men?"

"No." She slowly shook her head, letting the reality of her predicament soak in. "Eric gave it to him in the car. It was his backup weapon."

Her father eased his arm from its perch and leaned back. "You're saying Eric's gun was used in an unsolved murder. When was that?"

"Twenty-two years ago."

"That makes little sense."

"You're telling me. I don't know what to do."

"Is there a chance Eric could've been involved?"

"He would've been a teenager back then, but yes. Sloane once told me he thought the law and justice were two separate things. I'm not sure what to think." She barely believed what she was about to say. "What if he did? What if he took justice into his own hands?"

"He never struck me as the type. I never spent much time with him, but the way he protected Sloane all those years to make up for what he did gives me the feeling he has a deep sense of right and wrong."

Finn's breathing deepened. Her father didn't know it, but Eric was capable of extreme violence when he thought a greater good was at stake. As they all did, Eric had believed that he was in the right to beat Agent Barnes into the jail infirmary in order to find out where Padrino had taken her father and Reagan. Violence may not have been his trademark, but it was in his wheelhouse.

"But when pushed to his limits, his tendency to blur that trait makes him a suspect. What do I tell Sloane? I've been hiding the truth about Eric's backup gun for six months."

"Why didn't you tell her?" he asked.

"At first, I didn't because Eric had been shot and Sloane was a mess when he confessed about causing her parents' accident. Later, I didn't tell her to protect him. If the PD found out he gave a weapon to a prisoner, it would cost him his job. How do I tell Sloane now?"

"This is a tough one, pumpkin, but she's your life partner and deserves your honesty."

"I know, Daddy, but we just went through the Kadin thing and a major trust issue. Telling her that I've been holding something this big back from her will make her doubt me again." Motion of someone either stepping away from or walking past the open private entrance caught Finn's attention. She couldn't be sure who it was and silently chided herself for leaving the door open.

Her father's soft expression turned stiff. He apparently shared her exasperation at having painted herself into a corner. "Then I suggest you stop giving her reasons to doubt you and take your medicine. You haven't broken her trust yet, but you soon will. Once you do, it'll be hard to get back."

* * *

Hours of walking the Embarcadero had cramped Finn's calves, but it also gave her time to figure out how to break the truth to Sloane. First family dinner, followed by dessert if everyone was in the mood, and then off to bed. She'd tell her when they were the closest in each other's arms. That way, Sloane wouldn't have a chance to pull away and could feel her regret.

The Uber driver had taken off, leaving Finn at the curb of her and Sloane's Hunters Point townhouse along with her worry over Eric's future, as well as her and Sloane's. She stepped up the driveway, her gaze falling to the left side where a large tarp covered the stacks of sheetrock and other supplies the contractor had delivered. If all went according to schedule, she and Sloane would have a basement office in two weeks. Finn imagined herself in that office, working side by side with Sloane, stealing glances and touches like they'd been doing in The Pit. Here, though, in the seclusion of their own home, they could take their desire to its natural conclusion. What a perfect life that would be.

After repocketing her keys and closing the front door behind her, Finn expected the sound of pop music Sloane liked to play when she cooked, but tonight, the townhouse was silent. *Maybe Sloane ordered takeout or delivery*, she thought. Light glowed at the top of the entry steps, suggesting the main level was occupied.

"Babe?" Finn called out as her foot landed on the final entry step.

When she turned the corner, Sloane and Reagan each shifted their stare toward her from their positions on the indigo blue couch along the living room wall. She predicted Reagan's narrow eyes, a remnant from the misunderstanding at The Tap. But Sloane's blank expression scared her. She'd seen that look before. Sloane carried that look for months after Eric's confession.

"Babe? Did something happen?"

"You happened." Reagan's words came out as sharp and as deadly as her glare.

Finn suspected something more than Kadin had Reagan riled. Her stomach muscles tightened when she focused on Sloane, whose expression remained unchanged. "What's going on?"

"You tell me." Sloane pushed herself from the couch. Instead of approaching Finn, she retreated, pacing the floor with both hands propped on the backs of her hips. Sloane stopped. "What secrets are you hiding?"

Finn slumped. Reagan must have been the person outside Chandler's office listening to their conversation. Everything was about to unravel, and it was her own damn fault. Sloane held trust and honesty in high regard, especially after Eric's betrayal. She needed to fix this before everything came undone.

"I can explain."

"You've been doing a lot of explaining these days." Reagan's crossed arms provided the final confirmation.

"Enough." Sloane snapped her head toward Reagan. "I need to talk to Finn alone. Can you go have dinner at The Tap? Tell Dylan to charge it to my card."

"But—"

"Please, Reagan. This is between Finn and me."

"Don't believe her." Reagan snarled at Finn when she stomped past.

When the door slammed shut, Finn's legs turned weak. She thought back to when she faced death during the raging wildfire and expected her father's death when Padrino kidnapped him. She was scared beyond belief then, and right now, she was just as petrified. She couldn't move. Several anxious moments passed, with Sloane's deep breathing breaking the silence.

Her back to Finn, head held low, Sloane finally said, "Tell me about Eric's gun."

Finn took a step toward Sloane. She resisted the urge to throw her arms around her and take away the hurt she'd created. She raised a hand a few inches, aching to touch her. "I'm sorry."

Sloane turned, raised a hand as if reaching out to her but lowered it a moment later. Her internal battle was evident. "Start from the beginning."

The pained tone in Sloane's voice tore Finn's heart in two. Since learning Eric's dark secret, Sloane viewed holding back the truth as being the same as lying. Finn couldn't fault her for that. Now, here she was, faced with having to explain a deep secret of her own. Good intentions or not, her having hidden the truth from Sloane spoke to a matter of trust between life partners, and Finn broke that trust. Now she'd have to earn it back.

"After you followed the paramedics with Eric on the stretcher at Three Owls, Quintrell pulled me aside and handed me the gun he used to shoot Padrino and one of his men. He told me Eric had given it to him in the car."

Sloane offered a slow, almost mechanical nod. "I assumed he used one of the guns we made Padrino's men drop."

"I originally did too. Quintrell said Eric thought Padrino would never suspect he'd be armed since he was a prisoner. Eric's hunch saved our lives. I didn't think of telling you that night because it seemed small in the scheme of things. We'd rescued our family that night, and Eric hung to life by a thread. The first time I visited him after he was released from the hospital,

I tried to return it, but he refused. He said he'd lost everything important to him that night."

Sloane glanced up. "So you still have it?"

"No. I gave it to him the night before he returned to duty."

Sloane's eyes darted back and forth as if searching for a memory. "So that was the old friend you visited after our trip to Lands End?"

"Yes." When Sloane pursed her lips, Finn had to summon the courage to tell her everything. "I didn't tell you because I'd have to explain why I was there."

"The lies keep mounting."

"I'm sorry, but Eric said he'd lose his job if word got out that he'd given a gun to a prisoner."

"He's right. He would."

"Now you know why I promised to not say anything. I needed to protect him."

Sloane stared at Finn, her upper lip twitching. "You thought you needed to protect Eric from me?"

"It wasn't like that. It wasn't my secret to tell."

"So you thought lying to me was the better option?" The hurt in Sloane's eyes was enough to confirm Finn's greatest fear—playing fast and loose with the truth could cost her the best thing that ever happened to her. The only thing left to her was the truth as she knew it.

"I never lied, but I never told you what was going on."

"You're my partner. Not telling me says something." When Sloane paused, her lower lip quivered. "I'm not sure which hurts more: the fact you didn't trust me or that I can't trust you."

As Finn feared, as her father had warned, everything had unraveled. She buried her face in her hands as her world crashed down around her. Keeping secrets used to be part of her job, but it had become a death knell as a life partner.

When she looked up, she saw that tears were swelling Sloane's eyes. She threw off her caution, closed the distance between them, and drew Sloane into her arms. The quaking from both their bodies rumbled to a crescendo. She wouldn't let this be the last time she'd feel the warm softness of Sloane's body. "I won't let this break us."

Sloane tightened her grip around Finn's back, clutching the fabric of her blazer. They had been on the precipice of saying goodbye, and that was the best signal Finn could've hoped for.

"I'm so tired of secrets." Sloane nuzzled her cheek into Finn's shoulder. "Avery kept secrets about her parents. I kept them about the accident. They got us nowhere. The secrets have to end."

"No more secrets." Finn pulled back enough to look at Sloane. "We tell each other everything important."

"No matter what." Sloane searched Finn's eyes, which must have told her she had more secrets to reveal. "What else haven't you told me?"

Finn averted her eyes and released a deep sigh to relieve the tightness in her shoulders. If she were to earn back Sloane's unconditional trust, the entire truth about Kadin needed to come out. "When Kadin kissed me, I didn't pull back right away. I could say she caught me off guard and leave it at that, but that wouldn't be the entire truth."

Sloane's arms dropped to her side. Her eyes closed. Finn instantly felt distance growing between them, and she needed to reverse its course. She braced herself to pull off the Band-Aid of secrets in one tug.

"The kiss was familiar, and for a second, it reminded me of the time we spent together. It also made me sad because I once loved Kadin enough to consider marriage, but we fell apart."

"Do you still love her?" Sloane's voice cracked, thick with emotion.

"Yes, but not romantically. I'll always care what happens to Kadin. That's why when Daddy told me last week that he was calling a vote on her partnership at the law firm because of that kiss, I asked him not to do it. I didn't want to see her hurt. He refused, so I met her at Reds later that night."

Sloane kept her eyes closed and clenched her fists.

"I told her what Daddy had planned. She thanked me, and then we talked about why we broke up. I had pulled away from her back then because she never accepted my choices and tried to change me. I told her you've never done that, which is why I love you so much."

The back of Finn's throat swelled, making it hard to swallow. "That's when she told me she still loved me. I told her the same, but only as a friend."

Sloane's chin slumped to her chest, and in a glum, breathy voice, she asked, "Is that it?"

"Yes."

Sloane's blank expression was impossible to read. Was she numb? Or had the lies drained the love she had for Finn. "I need to think about all of this."

Finn's hand shook when she raised Sloane's chin. "I've loved you since we were thirteen. You're the one I want to grow old with. Please tell me we'll be okay."

"Give me some time."

Finn had known grief, but tonight she finally understood what a broken heart sounded like. It didn't sing like it had in choir because Sloane had entered the room and glanced her way. It didn't swell because Sloane gave her a smile meant only for her. It didn't beat like a drum because a single caress had sparked a burning desire to touch and be touched. Her heart was silent, broken in two.

The rest of her shook when she lowered her hand. "I'll pack some things."

When Finn stepped toward the bedroom, Sloane wrapped a hand around her wrist, pulling her close. Her skin tingled where their bodies touched, reminding her how strong their pull was. She couldn't lose Sloane, not over this.

"Don't leave." Sloane's soft tone begged. Finn had the sense she felt the pull too. "This is your home. I'll sleep on the couch."

"If anyone is sleeping on the couch, it should be me."

"I did it for months. It'll give me time to think." Sloane's vigorous head shake told Finn not to argue.

An hour later, after Reagan had stormed downstairs without a word upon returning from The Tap and Sloane had crawled into a makeshift bed on the couch, Finn closed the bedroom door, separating them. They were thirty feet apart, but the distance felt like three thousand miles. Finn settled beneath the sheets and stared at the ceiling, ticking off the times she should've been open with Sloane. If given another chance, she wouldn't make the same mistake again. She'd lost count how many times she'd turned and fluffed the pillow. Her lies of omission had made the bed too empty, and guilt fought her for hours, making it impossible to surrender to sleep. Finn turned over, back to the door, unable to face the tight spot she'd put herself in.

Then the floor creaked, the stiff silence of the night magnifying a dull snap. Then another and another. Someone was up. Soon the covers lifted behind her, the night air cooling newly exposed patches of skin. Her breathing labored in relief when Sloane's warm body slid next to her. She got the sense all was not forgiven, but that the arm Sloane slung around her torso represented a temporary white flag.

The night silence remained, but this time, the gentle, rhythmic rise and fall of Sloane's chest pressing against her back assuaged some of the nagging guilt. Sleep quickly appeared on the horizon, along with the hope she hadn't shattered the love that had taken a lifetime to find.

CHAPTER NINE

A crisp light morning breeze and a mesmerizing stubborn pale fog from the tranquility of her back deck were just what Sloane needed, or so she thought. She'd had her elbows resting atop the wood railing long enough for the half-full coffee mug in her hands to go cold, but she still had much to unpack from Finn's revelation last night. Under any other circumstance, the break in trust would've stood out as the most compelling issue, but this thing about the gun had a double-edge. Was Eric somehow involved in Bernie's death? If not him, the gun was.

She did the math and asked herself a question: At sixteen, would he have been capable of shooting someone in the back of the head execution-style? Before she quit the police department, when she thought she knew him, the answer would've been a resounding "no." But discovering he could hide the truth for decades had taught her that he was excellent at deception.

"You know the difference between the law and justice and that the two don't always mean the same thing." He had said those exact words to her at their first crime scene as a detective, making it

clear there was a distinction between the two in his view and that going by the book didn't always yield the desired result.

What was she supposed to do with this information? Homicide Division had yet to pick up on it, which meant she had two options: ignore it or report it. Both had a bitter taste. If she did nothing, she'd never look at herself in the mirror and not think she'd possibly let a killer go loose. If she turned the information over to Captain Nash as her contract required, he'd suspend Eric in a heartbeat. No matter how that department investigation unfolded, Eric and his lousy publicity would end up on the mayor's chopping block.

Behind Sloane, the sliding glass door skidded open across its tracks. She glanced back at the wood decking level as the door slid closed and recognized Finn's ankle-length leggings and blue slip-on sneakers. If this were any other day, she'd expect Finn to come up behind her and snake her arms around her waist. But this morning was their first real test. Finn was walking on eggshells as she sidled up a foot to Sloane's right, leaving a polite buffer between them.

"Good morning." Finn's voice lacked the playfulness or flirtation Sloane had fed off every morning since she moved in. Sloane caught Finn's profile from the corner of her eye, enough to see she was staring at the now receding fog. She had leaned at the railing, mirroring Sloane, her elbows resting on the wood and her hand holding a coffee mug. Heavy creases outlined the side of her mouth, marking her worry.

"Good morning." Those were the first words they'd exchanged since Finn closed the bedroom door last night. Sloane's tiptoeing in the dark was about feeling, not forgiving. This morning, though, she was ready for both. She couldn't let the love of her life go without a fight.

She placed her cold mug atop the railing, took Finn's and did the same to it, and then swept her into her arms. Clutching the fabric of her sweater, Sloane pressed their bodies together, desperate to let her know the need for eggshell walking was over. The distrust hadn't disappeared, but resentment had given way to the fear of losing Finn. "I love you."

Finn collapsed into Sloane's embrace as if all the tension that had built up overnight had washed away with the fog. "I'm so sorry."

They remained in each other's arms until the sound of morning traffic and angry drivers broke the quiet. Sloane pulled back. "I don't trust Kadin."

"I get that. After escrow closes on the condo, I'll ask her to keep her distance."

Sloane nodded her agreement and dropped her arms to her sides. She'd dumped street snitches for less subterfuge and what Finn had done was testing her limits. This didn't come easy, but Finn deserved, if not her trust, her understanding.

"Thank you." Finn paused. "What do we do about Eric?"

"He's involved. We need to talk to Morgan."

"He was once your friend. Don't you think we should talk to him first?" Finn asked.

"And give a potential suspect a chance to dump a murder weapon? That breaks a cardinal rule. We talk to Morgan."

"But—"

"I'm not arguing about Eric." When Finn pinched her lips together as if deflecting a jab, Sloane realized her words had come out harsher than she intended. If there was one thing that could bring her and Finn closer together, it was doing what they did best. She rubbed Finn's arms and smiled. "But I would love to find out with you who killed Bernie."

"I'd love that too."

Inside at the dining table, Reagan had dressed for another workday at the law firm. She glared at Finn over her bowl of cereal.

"Before you start anything…" Sloane sat next to Reagan, squeezing Finn's hand atop the table as she did. She hoped the show of support would blunt her icy behavior. "Finn and I talked everything out, and we're both good."

"Unbelievable." Reagan dropped her spoon in the bowl, sloshing drops of milk over the rim. "So she gets away with it again?"

"Reagan—" Sloane said.

"No." Finn put up a hand, stopping Sloane in mid-sentence. "She deserves an explanation. What I told your mom about that kiss with Kadin was the truth. And about Eric, I never lied to Sloane, but I held back the truth to protect him because he asked me to."

Sloane locked eyes with Finn, giving her an affirmative nod. There was no need to explain further about Eric or the kiss.

"I think Eric needs protecting from you." Reagan folded her arms over her chest. Her posture turned even more defiant.

"Enough, young lady," Sloane raised her voice. "Let us worry about Eric. You need to work on respecting Finn."

"I wouldn't be surprised if Finn planted that gun. She twists the truth about everything. Even Eric said there's no way his gun would match that other case."

Sloane froze. What did she say? "Eric knows?"

"Yeah. I texted him last night." Reagan shrugged.

"Damn it, Reagan. He's involved in a murder." Sloane rubbed the muscle that had tensed in the back of her neck. Not only had Reagan tipped him off, but she'd also forced Sloane's hand.

"I'm sorry, Mom, but I thought he should know."

"You shouldn't have done that." Sloane turned toward Finn, a sinking feeling seeping into her pores. "We need to get ahead of this."

Finn pulled out her phone and dialed. "We need to talk," she said when the call was picked up.

* * *

Ever since Sloane chased after Los Dorados and her wife's killers, Sally's Café had become her favorite meeting spot for delicate discussions. Several miles separated it from the nearest police station, ruling it out as a cop hangout. As a bonus, it had sinfully delicious pie, pie that she was about to devour. The two slices of tangy key lime she ordered were worth the waitress's cocked eyebrow, not to mention the extra hour she would need at the gym.

"You're not going to eat both of those for breakfast, are you?" Finn asked.

"Yep." Sloane forked off an ample mouthful. "I don't get here enough."

"He's late." Finn checked her watch and then returned her gaze to the café entrance. "He said eight thirty."

"I know." Sloane glanced at a Coca-Cola wall clock behind the cash register—two minutes before nine. She savored another mouthful to take the bite off waiting and the reason she had to. Eric was never late. Never. She hated to think it, but she'd seen Eric go off when he suspected a perp had gotten away with something big. The last time it was DEA Agent Barnes, the man who planted the bomb that killed Avery. True, he'd put Barnes in the infirmary because Reagan's life hung in the balance, but that demonstrated the level of violence he was capable of. Did something like that happen when he was sixteen?

"He's here." Finn gestured toward the main entrance. Sloane refused to glance up at the door. While one fear was allayed, another ignited. Did Eric bring the gun? If not, why not?

"Good to see some things never change. Best pie in town." Eric took a seat directly across from Sloane and to Finn's left. He still favored his left arm, holding it close to his chest.

His playfulness didn't last long. The grin that formed when he first locked eyes with Sloane had disappeared, and those eyes narrowed to thin lines. He'd changed, and Sloane couldn't read him like she thought she could when they were partners. His warm center was hidden by an icy outer shell. What she couldn't figure out was if his change stemmed from their falling out or if it had been there all along, and he was merely good at hiding it.

"Now, what's this bullshit about my backup?" Eric leaned forward until his right elbow rested on the Formica tabletop. His gaze steadied on Finn.

"I had to tell her." Finn's shoulders dropped a few inches. "I didn't have a choice."

"Ah." His expression remained unchanged, still unreadable. "I'd do it again in a heartbeat."

"Would you like to order, sir?" The waitress's sweet voice matched her bubbly appearance. On the plump side, she'd wrapped her long ebony hair into a ponytail and tied it off with strands of shimmering silver stars.

"Just coffee, please."

After the waitress scurried off, Finn said, "Look, Eric, ballistics matched the bullets that killed Padrino and one of his men to one that killed a John Doe found in a burnt-out drug house in 1998."

His eyes widened, catching Sloane's attention. *So, the year means something.*

"So? Quintrell used one of the goon's guns instead of mine." Eric shrugged.

"No." Finn frowned as she briefly pressed her eyes shut, shaking her head. "Quintrell was clear when he gave me the gun. He said he shot his father with it."

"I don't trust a thing he says." Eric straightened—his tell that he was on the defensive. "And there was a time you wouldn't either."

"Do you still have the gun?" Finn asked.

"Whether I do or don't is none of your business."

"Damn it, Eric." Finn threw a wadded-up napkin on the table. "We're trying to help you."

"I believe *you* are." He cast his chin toward Sloane. "But I'm not sure about her."

"What the hell does that matter?" Sloane bit back the thing she wanted to ask: What else are you hiding? "Either you have the gun, or you don't."

Eric turned her gaze toward her. "She speaks." A bold cockiness had replaced the tentativeness he'd displayed since his confession.

"Eventually, we'll have to report our findings to Nash." Sloane took some of the edge off her tone because a nagging question haunted her: Did he give up on reconciling, or did he have something to hide? She didn't like either option. "When he starts asking the questions, you'll need better answers."

"But somehow, without knowing the answers, you consider me a suspect, don't you?"

"I follow the evidence." Sloane had no other choice because… "You taught me that."

"Eric." Finn touched his forearm, shifting his focus toward her. "I can't believe you're capable of murder. Do you have any explanation about the gun?"

"Would it matter?" He stared at Sloane.

Sloane never thought she'd consider her next question, but Eric had proved himself capable of not only deception but violence. "You taught me from day one that the law and justice aren't the same thing. Did you mean it?"

"Yes. And I thought you understood the difference too."

"It doesn't justify murder."

He sent Sloane a long, pained look. "Then I guess there's nothing else to say."

"We're briefing West at ten. She'll tell us what to do with the information." Sloane refused to break eye contact.

"Please be there to defend yourself. And if you have the gun, bring it." Finn's begging tone hinted that she doubted he'd show. Sloane held the same doubt.

Eric stood, eased the chair back to its original position, and threw a five-dollar bill on the table. After he left without another word, Sloane picked up her fork and stuffed another bite of key lime into her mouth to ease the strain in her jaw. Everything about that conversation bothered her, from Eric's caginess to Finn's unequivocal support. He was a master at deception. Why couldn't Finn see it?

"You couldn't put your anger aside for one damn minute, could you?" Finn's narrow eyes told Sloane she'd pay a price for the rest of the day for her coldness.

"You saw how evasive he was. He's hiding something."

"He was defensive. I would be too."

A sharp clank sounded when Sloane dropped the fork on her plate. Sally's pie or not, she'd lost her appetite. "Too defensive if you ask me." She wiped her mouth with a paper napkin. "Why are you defending him?"

Finn covered Sloane's hand with one of her own, their forearms resting on the tabletop. She softened her voice. "I don't want to fight with you."

"I don't either. Let's brief West and see what she has to say." Sloane shifted and clutched Finn's hand as a white flag, but Eric still bothered her. Deep down, she wanted to believe he wasn't involved. Six months ago, she would've rousted every junkie and snitch to prove it, but today her anger wouldn't let her lift a finger.

* * *

Eric had less than an hour to get some answers. Before the glass door at Sally's flapped closed, he whipped his cell phone from his suit pocket and swiped the phone app that had four numbers on speed dial—two of those had to do with work and one was for Sloane. The remaining one came with a price tag—guilt. He hadn't called this number since the week he returned from the hospital after he was shot.

He stretched his stride and turned the corner to get out of Sloane and Finn's view once the call connected. It did after four rings. "I need to ask you something."

"Don't I deserve a better greeting than that?"

"You're right. I'm sorry. Hi, Dad."

"Hello, son. It's great to hear from you. How's that arm of yours?"

"Still stiff. It's about as good as it's gonna get."

"Sorry to hear that, but I'm proud of you for taking a bullet to save your partner and those hostages. I'm not sure if I would've done the same thing when I was on the job."

"You were a great cop, Dad. Don't sell yourself short. I'm sure you would've done the same thing."

"About the only thing I'm willing to risk my life for these days is to get a decent tee time."

"Retired life getting you down?"

"Hell no. There are too many silver-haired ducks like me retreating to the sunshine state. I've had to learn how to game the system to get the best tee times."

"Sorry to cut this short, Dad, but I need to ask you a question."

"Shoot, son."

"That Beretta you gave me when I graduated from the academy, did you buy it used?"

"Are you thinking about getting a different backup? I thought you liked the model your old man used on the force."

"I do. Something's come up, and I need to know its history."

"I don't like how this sounds. What's going on?"

Eric exhaled, slow and deep. Of course, this wouldn't be easy. He got his suspicious nature from his dad and had learned at an early age that he could get nothing over him. "Just answer the damn question, Dad."

"Fine. I bought it new from a dealer when the department switched to them in the mid-nineties. Then I gave it to you. Now, are you going to tell me what's going on?"

"Ballistics show a bullet from it matches one found in a dead vic from an unsolved 1998 case."

"That can't be. I never shot it outside the department firing range. Something is screwy."

"Don't worry, Dad. I'll sort this out. I gotta go."

After retracing his steps, Eric rushed inside Sally's. At Sloane and Finn's table, the plump waitress was sliding a few dollar bills from the tabletop into her apron pocket and gathering the dirty dishes. Sloane and Finn were gone.

"Damn it." If he had any hope of stopping them, he had to hurry.

* * *

The drive from Sally's was chillier inside the car than out. *One step forward, one step back*, Sloane thought. This morning, she and Finn had come to a truce following their first real argument. Now, Eric was at the center of a second argument. Or was it a continuation from the first one? It didn't really matter because she and Finn weren't talking.

Everything about this morning stunk. Even the air fresheners in The Pit had lost their kick when Sloane stepped in. "Fucking great. I'm tired of this shithole."

Finn dropped her purse and jacket on a worktable. When Sloane jerked a chair out from beneath a desk, Finn spun her around by the shoulder. Before she could object, Finn grasped her cheeks with both hands and gave her a deep kiss.

The sharp irritation that had formed into a finely honed blade since the confrontation at Sally's now melted into a soft liquid. Finn's silky tongue drove its way past her lips and darted against Sloane's. One tense muscle after another relaxed with each long stroke until the need to touch overpowered her. She clawed Finn's cotton shirt until its flaps gave way to skin and lace. Every arm hair tingled when her fingertips slipped under both cups and squeezed. Even the walls she'd erected to protect herself from losing Eric crumbled.

Hands and tongue working in unison, she rushed Finn against a wall, resulting in a vibrating thud she was sure their office neighbor would be curious about. In a frenzy, she pushed fabric out of the way and latched her mouth to a breast. A guttural moan rattled in her throat, followed by one from Finn.

A knock on the door startled them apart.

"Damn it." She *had* thumped the wall too hard. She cocked her head and yelled. "Everything's okay. Go away."

Through the door, a muffled voice sounded. "Sloane. Finn. We need to talk."

"I think…it's Eric." Finn's chest heaved in between words.

"Go away!"

"Sloane, open the damn door." Eric's muffled voice was louder.

"Hold on, Eric!" Finn pushed Sloane back and straightened her clothes.

"You're criminal with that tongue of yours." Sloane kissed Finn on the lips. "We'll finish this later." Sloane leaned a hip against the desk and waited for Finn to respond.

"I guess I'm getting the door." Finn walked toward the door. Her hip sway was too enticing for Sloane not to tilt her head to one side and watch her each step of the way.

"How else can I enjoy the best view in the city?"

Finn opened the door. "Are you okay?" The glacial stare Eric had given Sloane at Sally's had been replaced by the long, pale look of fear.

"Can I come in?" He turned his head left when someone passed in the hallway and then Finn let him inside. She closed the door behind him. "Have you talked to the L-T yet?"

His darting eyes hinted at either desperation or a ploy. Sloane crossed her arms at her chest. "Why?"

"Never a straight answer with you." Eric shook his head. "I don't have time for your games."

"No, Eric." Finn shot Sloane a short but distinct glare. "We haven't seen Morgan yet."

"Good. Hear me out."

"You had your chance an hour ago." Sloane pushed herself from the desk. She wasn't sure where this was going, but she suspected he was trying to talk her out of going to Morgan. "Now, if you'll excuse us, we have a meeting."

Eric placed both hands on his hips with his right elbow akimbo. His left arm struggled to bow outward, and that gnawed at Sloane's conscience. He took that bullet helping her daughter, but somehow it came up short of making up for her parents.

"Damn it, Sloane. This isn't only about me. It's about my father."

In two-and-a-half years as his partner, Eric had mentioned his father only twice, and she had assumed they weren't that close. "At least you still have one."

"That's enough." Finn stepped beside Sloane. Her reproach felt like a swat on the bottom, so Sloane bit back her next words. "What about your father?" Finn asked.

"My dad bought the Beretta in the early nineties. He used it as a backup weapon until he gave it to me as a gift when I graduated from the academy about ten years later."

"Like father, like son, killing someone close to me." Sloane was too angry to hold back those words.

"Sloane." Finn's breathy response suggested disappointment in her comments. They were low even for her and disappointed her too.

Eric's blank stare meant he had ignored Sloane's jibe. "My dad is a retired cop. He spent twenty-five years on the job and never fired his service weapon or backup outside the firing range."

There was a time when Sloane would've believed Eric without question. Now, staring into his pained eyes, she recognized the look there of unwavering determination. She missed that grit he brought to each of their cases.

"Retired cop, huh?" Sloane softened her tone but still kept it distant. "What do you want from us?"

"Time. Time to sift through the reports and evidence and see if this is a mix-up or if the detectives missed something back then."

"How much time?" Finn asked.

"Two weeks." Eric rubbed the back of his neck, his tell that he was desperate.

Finn gave Sloane a questioning look. "Babe?"

"I'll give you three days." The glacier inside Sloane shifted enough to show some mercy. Three days weren't much but represented a good start. "After that, it's up to Morgan."

"Thank you."

After Eric left, Finn sagged her back against the door. "I believe him."

"I want to." Sloane's voice trailed off. Besides saying "I love you," first to Avery and then to Finn, those were the most authentic words she'd ever spoken.

* * *

"*Like father, like son, killing someone close to me,*" Sloane had said. Eric needed to find out what she meant. In less than five minutes at his desk, he navigated the SFPD data system, brought up the Padrino record, clicked on related cases, and had his answer. Sloane had said the name only a handful of times; nevertheless, Bernie's name had stuck with him. If not for what Eric had done, Sloane wouldn't have known Officer Bernie Sellers. This old case was personal to Sloane, something they had in common. They had competing motivations, but they were after the same thing—solving it.

He studied what little data was stored in the electronic file and quickly determined he needed information beyond a summary. That could only be found in the original case file and evidence. In the next five minutes, he hit his first two stumbling blocks. Everything he needed was in a twenty-two-year-old cold case file that was sitting in county storage with all the other old cases. A phone call to the warehouse clerk started with, "Unless it's a priority, we can't get to it until Tuesday." He ended the call with "asshole."

"Of course, this wouldn't be easy," he grumbled.

He was stymied. He couldn't make this investigation a priority without Lieutenant West's signature, and he couldn't do that without raising questions. The case summary wasn't much help either. Other than Bernie, the other two victims were unidentified. Until Tuesday, the only thing left to him was talking to the original investigating officers. Following a quick search of the data system and several phone calls later, he hit his third stumbling block, discovering that one detective was dead and the other was in a nursing home with dementia.

He was screwed. Tuesday wouldn't be soon enough, leaving him two options: wait for Sloane and Finn to tell all to Lieutenant West or tell West himself. At least he had a few days to mull it over.

CHAPTER TEN

Television never captured the alluring smells of ballpark food or the electrifying buzz of cheering fans. For Sloane, catching her first glimpse of the Giants' playing field each time she attended a game never got old. The ballpark was striking with its lush green grass, rising stadium rows of seats, larger-than-life scoreboard, and nostalgic brick and ironwork. She hoped the din of the Sunday afternoon crowd and festive atmosphere would rally her dull mood. The dilemma of dealing with Eric or reporting him to Morgan West had conflicted her more than she anticipated.

Chandler glowed with infectious amazement, transforming into an excited kid, a side of him that Sloane admired. He spent all day in thousand-dollar suits, staring down sports team owners, yet he was a sucker for garlic fries and the occasional foul ball heading his way. And to think Reagan considered him a grandfather made Sloane like him even more.

Legs churning up the steps, he reached the top first. "Best damn park in baseball," he bellowed, arms raised over his head.

"Is he always like this at games?" Sharon asked as she adjusted her purse strap over her replica white Giants home jersey. The shirt prominently displayed the number "35" and the name "Crawford" on the back—her favorite. As she had explained during the car ride over, "He looks so much like Uncle Jesse from *Full House*."

"Ever since I can remember." Finn leaned into Sharon's shoulder when their feet reached the top step. "He turns into a little boy at the ballpark."

Sloane was a pace behind. She tried to focus on family day, but she couldn't get out of her head the notion that Eric or his father might be a killer. Her thoughts kept wandering to her last meeting with him and the resolute look on his face.

"You okay, Mom?"

Reagan's voice pulled her back. "Yeah, honey. I have a lot on my mind."

"Eric or Kadin?"

Sloane halted her stride to a deep sigh. Both bothered her, one more than the other, but she couldn't let that spoil family day. "It's work." She draped an arm over Reagan's shoulder and guided her up the last step. "Let's enjoy the game."

By the sixth inning, the Giants were behind by two runs. But seeing them win wasn't the point of attending the game. Today was all about the experience. Snippets of deafening interlude music and pricy garlic fries distracted Sloane from all things Eric and Kadin and had her in a good mood.

The constant flow of seat vendors racing up and down the steps blended in with the crowd noise, but none had interested Sloane until now. The sight of white pressed clothes, a navy blue halter apron, and a pleated soda jerk paper hat had her bouncing in her hard metal seat. "Ice cream!" She motioned him over to their row of seats before leaning toward Reagan. "I've been waiting for this all day."

"Me too." Reagan rubbed her hands together in what Sloane would describe as sweet anticipation.

Sloane glanced down the row of seats toward Finn, Sharon, and Chandler. "Anyone else want a Ghirardelli Sundae? It's heaven in a cup."

Chandler and Sharon shook their heads no, but Finn answered, "Ooh, yes. I haven't had one in ages."

Sloane held up three fingers. Minutes later, she dipped her spoon inside the plastic cup, bringing up a sizeable glob of hot fudge and vanilla ice cream. "Reagan and I get one of these at every game."

"Finn Harper. I thought that was you." A short, curvy brunette dressed in ghastly L.A. Dodger garb above the waist and form-fitting jeans below ascended the aisle stairs closest to Sloane. She was an obvious SoCal transplant—because no self-respecting San Franciscan would wear that to a Giants game. An orange tutu maybe, but never Dodger white and blue.

"Liz." Finn stood long enough to reach across Sloane and shake the woman's hand. Her face lit up. "It's good to see you. Are you still at the Shipyards?"

"Still there, but all my friends are moving away." Liz extended her lower lip into a pout, an expression that looked cute on Finn, but one that appeared childish on any other grown woman, including this one. "First you, now Kadin. When she told me she was buying your condo, I thought that meant you two were getting back together. It's a shame that's not the case. You were the perfect power couple."

Sloane shifted in her seat, earning a reassuring thigh-to-thigh graze from Finn. "Liz, I'd like you to meet my partner, Manhattan Sloane."

"Ah." Liz extended her hand, which Sloane accepted. At a minimum, her smile seemed forced, as if she were greeting a teenage nemesis at her high school reunion. "I read about you in the papers, helping Finn take down that cartel drug lord."

"Yes, I'm quite the helper." Sloane wrenched her hand extra hard, sending a clear and concise message. *Leave.*

When Sloane loosened the vise, Liz flexed and wiggled each finger, proving the challenge came short of permanent damage. "Yes, well, I should be going. It was nice seeing you, Finn. We should get together for a drink soon."

"I'd love that. Give me a call next week." After Liz disappeared up the stadium stairs, Finn turned to Sloane. "I'm sorry about that, babe. Liz lived across the hall from Kadin and me when we lived in Oakland."

Sloane's back muscles spasmed at Kadin's name. "Can we not talk about her today?"

"I agree. She's caused enough trouble." Chandler stabbed a hand into his box of popcorn and stuffed some into his mouth.

"Daddy." Finn stabbed the spoon in her ice cream. "You're overreacting."

"No, he's not. I don't trust her." Reagan leaned forward, ensuring everyone understood that she and Chandler were on the same side.

Sloane had had enough of Kadin Hall and everyone picking sides. She needed something more potent than ice cream. Plopping her dessert into the seat cupholder, she maneuvered down the row, squeezing past two spectators. Once she was up the twenty steps and through the glass doors leading into the club level, Sloane queued in the three-person-deep bar line and stewed. She wanted nothing more than to put Kadin in the distant past, but Finn's unwavering defense had pushed every button in her. Some she didn't know existed.

When she reached the front of the line, she stepped up to the bartender. "Scotch, neat."

"Make it two." Finn tossed thirty dollars on the bar, grabbed the two tumblers, and walked toward a glass door leading to an outdoor patio overlooking King Street. She held the door open with her body and motioned with her head for Sloane to follow.

Sloane stepped away from the bar and dipped her chin. The good mood that had taken most of the game to build was ruined, and she wasn't up for more talking about Kadin. Retreat seemed like the logical approach. After walking up to Finn, she grabbed a tumbler from her hand, downed its contents in one swig, turned, and stepped in the opposite direction.

"You don't get to walk away." Finn's voice was firm.

"This isn't the time or place, Finn."

"There's never a good time for a difficult talk, but the place thing I can fix." Finn walked outside, the glass door wobbling shut behind her.

"Damn it, Finn," Sloane mumbled. She reminded herself of the lessons she learned after her and Finn's near brush with death during the wildfire. The most important was that love could get her through anything if she placed her trust in it. "You win."

A chilly bay breeze bit at her cheeks the moment she stepped through the glass door. Finn had taken a seat on the circular concrete bench surrounding a gas-fueled fire pit. Artificial logs glowed a deep orange on a bed of one-inch dark blue glass beads in the center.

They were alone, but the look on Finn's face made Sloane unsure if that was a good thing. She sat beside Finn and warmed her hands by the flickering flames. Finn's full glass suggested she hadn't reached her breaking point yet.

"I thought we were past this thing with Kadin." Finn's stiff posture meant she was as frustrated as Sloane, for which Sloane couldn't blame her. Losing trust in a relationship could send it into a death spiral.

"I thought so too."

"Then what is it?"

"I'd rather do this at home, Finn."

"We've been home for two days, and all you've done is mope."

"Obviously, we're doing this here." Sloane jutted her jaw out and slid it left and right, churning up the words that had needed saying for days. "You knew I stopped trusting Eric, yet you hid the truth about his backup from me for months. You told me you did it because you were backed into a corner. That I'd misjudged Eric. Have I misjudged you?"

Finn recoiled. "Where is this coming from?"

"Kadin. You defend her at every turn. Things aren't over for her. I wonder if they really are for you."

Finn's jaw quivered for a moment. The pained look on her face resembled Eric's when she first shunned him. "Either you trust me or you don't." She pushed herself off the bench and drank the scotch in one gulp. Sloane's words had just driven her over the edge. "I have the condo for one more night. I'll sleep there."

Finn disappeared inside. Sloane slumped forward, elbows to her knees. She couldn't figure out what had her more upset— the fact she couldn't trust Finn or that she couldn't trust her own judgment.

* * *

Finn thought moving out of her Market Street condo months ago meant she'd escaped the elevator torture. Another Barry Manilow earworm had wound its way into her head. One step out the elevator, she mumbled, "Sorry, Barry, but I haven't missed your mini-concerts."

Void of her personal things, the condo still had the sleek, modern bedroom and living room furniture that came with the original lease. The place looked dull and sterile, nothing like the night when she and Sloane made love for the first time. The bedding they'd laid waste to was in some box in their garage. That was if she still had a garage after tonight. The lamp Sloane had broken in her haste to undress had long ago been tossed in the trash heap, a fate Finn hoped their relationship wouldn't mirror.

Finn tossed the overnight bag she'd hastily packed onto the bare mattress. She'd put little thought into what to bring and stuffed triples of everything. This one-night cooling-off period, she worried, might stretch into more. Once she placed her toiletries in the bathroom and spread a throw quilt across the bed, she sifted through the kitchen junk drawer where she'd left menus from the neighborhood restaurants and delivery services. Starved but with no craving for anything specific, she picked one at random and dialed the number.

"I'd like to place an order for delivery."

"May I have your phone number, please?" Finn recognized the sweet, singsong voice on the other end. The woman repeated her number. "Miss Harper, it's been quite a while. We thought you moved away."

"I had, but I'm back at my old place for tonight."

"Welcome back. I hope you'll stay longer. Would you like to order your usual?"

"Please, and can you toss in paper plates, cups, and utensils? I packed up my kitchen months ago."

"Anything for you, Miss Harper. Give us thirty minutes."

Finn hung up. Staying here longer was the last thing she wanted. But for tonight, at least, she needed a brief break from Sloane's doubts and time to figure out how to repair this growing rift between them. To do that, she needed a shower to wash away the grimy feeling of the day.

She lost track of time as the pulsating streams of hot water needled the tense muscles along her back and shoulders. The events of the last few weeks played in her head, starting with the gun she'd secretly held for Eric and ending with today's latest defense of Kadin. Each misstep had bled into the next, compounding Sloane's distrust, a trend that needed reversing.

Without a hairdryer, one of the many niceties she forgot to pack, Finn towel-dried her shoulder-length hair and ran a brush through it, deeming it respectable for a quick phone call before the delivery service arrived. She hit the third saved number in her speed dial list.

"Kadin. I know we weren't supposed to meet for the condo walkthrough until after work tomorrow, but I need to do it first thing in the morning." She'd rushed her words without their usual friendliness, a level of politeness she wasn't in the mood for.

"Hello to you, too."

"I'm sorry, Kadin. Hello."

"Much better. Now, care to tell me what this is all about?"

"It's nothing. I have something important to do tomorrow."

"I'm buying your condo, but not your excuse, Finn. You sound upset."

There was a time when Finn welcomed Kadin's ability to read her every emotion, but that time had passed. Now it complicated what she had to do. She modulated her voice to remove all emotion. "Whether or not I'm upset is no longer your concern. Can you meet me in the morning?"

The moments of silence meant she'd made her stinging point. "I have to be in the office by nine." Experience told Finn that Kadin's flat tone said she'd given up on her effort to be cordial.

"How about eight? We can do the walkthrough, and I can give you the keys."

With that agreement, Finn ended the call, scrolled to her speed dial list, and deleted the third stored number. It was time to put Kadin in the past.

At the door, a fresh face she didn't recognize handed her a bag of aromatic delectables in exchange for a signature and a sizable tip. She closed the door and took two steps inside, but a knock forced her to turn around. She opened. "Did you forget—"

"I brought our favorite pick-me-up." Chandler held up a pink and white paper sack from Finn's go-to ice cream joint. Despite the unexpected but not unwelcome invasion, it was just the comfort food she needed.

"Daddy? How did you find me?"

"I peppered Sloane with questions until she spilled. Now, are you going to let in your old man?"

She stepped aside to let him pass and raised her own bag. "Have you eaten? I ordered Chinese."

"Haven't you learned by now I never turn down food? I'll stick these in the freezer."

After filling their plates with food and paper cups with water, Finn dragged two dining chairs in front of the picture window and the Bay Bridge's eye-catching nighttime orange glow. Sitting in one, she extended her legs and propped her feet on the other. "Join me, Daddy."

"Since when do you put your feet up on the good furniture?"

"Since Sloane. All furniture is meant to be lived in."

"I really like her." Chandler grinned and dragged two more chairs over, matching Finn's setup. He took several bites of the takeout she'd ordered. "This thing with Sloane must be serious if you're spending the night here. Do you want to talk about it?"

"It comes down to trust, Daddy."

"Secrets can test its limits. How do you plan to fix it?"

"Besides no more secrets?"

"An olive branch usually works when love is still there. Is it?"

"Yes. I can feel it when it's just us."

"Then that's where you start. Make sure Sloane knows it's just the two of you."

After orange chicken, fried rice, and vanilla ice cream with swirls—a combination she decided she'd rather not repeat anytime soon—they rearranged the furniture, replacing their chair setup with the sleek white couch. Leaning against her father's shoulder, gazing at the crawling lights of the cars zooming in and out of the city, Finn welcomed sleep, but it fought her. Chandler, though, didn't last twenty minutes.

She slid off the couch, draped the one throw quilt from her bedroom over him and tiptoed back to the bare mattress. She knew what she had to do tomorrow. Once she handed Kadin the keys to this place, she'd say goodbye and never look back.

Sleep had evaded Finn from the moment she fluffed her backpack into a makeshift pillow and lay down with a hoodie for a blanket. Without Sloane's arms and radiating warmth, she tossed until night turned into morning. Bright streaks of sunlight reminded her she had a mission today—cut Kadin out of her life and regain Sloane's trust.

She scooted her phone toward her on the mattress and thumbed it awake. No call or text alerts. Nothing from Sloane, saying she missed her and wanted her back in their bed. Finn couldn't blame her. She was the one who'd pushed Sloane to her limits, as her father had put it.

In a few hours, Finn could start Operation Olive Branch. After another shower, brushing her teeth, and fixing her hair, she entered the living room. The smell of fresh coffee perplexed her. Her machine was wedged deep in a box between packing paper and spatulas somewhere in Sloane's garage.

"Morning, pumpkin. Two sugars, one cream." Chandler offered her a tall paper cup, warm to the touch. "I picked up breakfast while you were in the shower. Hope you're in the mood for blueberry."

"Perfect, Daddy." She sipped and nibbled on a sliver of muffin. "You looked so peaceful last night. I didn't want to wake you."

"Other than a stiff back"—he placed a hand along his flank and stretched—"I'm glad I stayed."

"I am too. I didn't realize how much I needed my dad last night." She settled onto a stool at the breakfast counter that separated the kitchen from the dining room. "Do you need to get going? Or are khakis and a golf shirt the new lawyer's attire."

He checked his watch. "I'll shower and change into my emergency suit at the office, but I should be on my way."

After donning his Windbreaker, he kissed Finn on the forehead. "It'll take some work, but you two will be fine, pumpkin."

"I hope so, Daddy."

Once he left, Finn packed up her things, taking more care this time by folding each piece of clothing. After she put all the furniture back in place, tidied up the kitchen, and placed the trash in a single delivery bag, the doorbell rang. *Right on time*, she thought.

Finn slid the door open wide and let Kadin in. "Always punctual." She looked good in her tailored dark gray pencil skirt and blazer. Every brown hair was perfectly brushed in place, a sign she was over her funk.

"You used to like that about me."

"And I still do." Enough chitchat. Finn needed to put Kadin behind her. She walked further into the entry hall. "We should probably do a walkthrough. Make sure I didn't take or leave anything I wasn't supposed to?"

"Sure." In the living room, Kadin ran a hand across her new white couch. "I love the furniture that came with this place."

"I did too. Part of the reason I exercised the buy option last year."

Kadin approached the large window where Finn and Chandler ate next to last night and gazed toward the cityscape. "Not to mention this spectacular view."

Finn joined her. "Probably one of the best views in the city."

"I'm surprised you're giving it up. Why didn't you and Sloane move in here?"

"Her townhouse belonged to her grandmother. I couldn't ask her to sell it."

Following a quick check of the empty kitchen, guest room, and bath, they entered the master bedroom with its floor-to-ceiling window peering directly out to the bay.

"We had a few wonderful nights here." Kadin ran her fingers across the foot of the plush mattress.

"Please don't make this hard, Kadin."

They locked gazes. "I'm trying. Letting go usually isn't this difficult for me."

"Which is why, after today, I have to say goodbye for good."

Tears pooled along Kadin's lower eye rims and trickled down each cheek. "I know."

Comforting Kadin was out of the question, but their two years as a couple made seeing her this way tougher than Finn expected. Tears rolled down her cheeks as well.

"I'm sorry, Kadin, but I have to—" The doorbell rang. Finn wiped her face dry with the back of a hand. "Let me get the door. Then we can wrap this up." Finn walked past the living room, into the entry hall, and opened the door.

"Hi." Sloane's meek tone matched her crumpled posture. "I missed you last night."

Finn's overwhelming sense of relief manifested in a deep intake of air. She hated fighting with Sloane. She hated why it started, but she had only herself to blame. "I missed you, too."

"Can we talk?"

"Of course."

When Finn opened the door wider, Sloane took one step in but came to a sudden halt. Her face turned pale before they locked gazes.

"Babe?" Finn turned her head around, her breath catching in her throat.

"Finn, I need to get going." Kadin ambled down the entryway toward them, her head buried in her purse looking for something.

Finn whisked her head back around. "Sloane, it's not—"

"I wanted to trust you."

The pain in Sloane's eyes was eerily familiar. Finn had seen that look once before—at Avery's wake. Had Finn made Sloane feel like she'd lost her for good? That there was no coming back from what she'd thought she'd seen?

"Babe, listen to me."

Sloane whipped a hand up in a stopping motion, her eyes flinty. "Don't. I've seen everything I need to."

Sloane turned on her heel and stomped down the building hallway toward the elevator, sending a rush of panic through Finn. When she moved toward the door to chase after Sloane, a hand fell to her shoulder and stopped her.

"Let her go. She needs to cool off," Kadin said.

Kadin was right. How could she get Sloane to understand that nothing happened? Like she told her father last night, it came down to trust. Nothing Finn said at this point would make a difference.

Finn slammed the door shut. She gritted her teeth. "Kadin, if you did that on purpose…"

Kadin stiffened her spine and assumed her rare fighting posture. "I may regret letting you go, but you know I don't play petty games. I give you my word. I am not out to sabotage you and Sloane."

Sloane may have had trust issues, but Finn didn't. Kadin never gave her cause to doubt her, and she wouldn't let Sloane's mistrust spill over. "I believe you, but this is a mess."

"I'd offer to talk to her, but that would make things worse."

"Yes, it would." Finn rubbed the tension building in her neck. Despite her instinct to give Sloane time, she needed to do something. "I have to fix this."

Finn trotted toward her collection of things on the kitchen counter. She fished through her purse and retrieved the set of condo keys. "Here." She slung the leather bag and backpack over her shoulder and grabbed the quilt. "Can you take care of the trash?"

"Sure." Kadin accepted the keys with a confused expression.

"If there's anything wrong with the place, let me know. I'll take care of it. I gotta go."

Finn sprinted down the hall, but Sloane was gone. Gone was the hope of stopping this from spinning out of control. She thought of calling, but even if Sloane did the miraculous thing and picked up, a call wouldn't fix this. Finn needed to look Sloane in the eye and tell her that hers was the only touch she needed. Hers was the only kiss she craved. And that she'd spend a lifetime saying it until she believed her. But where would she go on a Monday morning? The Pit? That musty office wasn't the ideal place to work this out, but it was the best location to start looking.

Morning traffic didn't help Finn's agitated state. She inched forward on one side street after another, swerving to bypass several lumbering buses. Once she pulled into Bryant's visitor's parking garage, she crept around the aisles, craning her neck. She looked left and right, hoping to spot Sloane's SUV, but her hopes faded when she reached the last parking row.

Finn parked in the first available slot and dashed toward the building entrance. Inside, she swiped her access badge over the card reader. The door buzzed. She pushed it open. With each fast-paced stride, she conjured up words that might knock down the wall Sloane had likely built. Each version ended in "I love you," but considering her recent track record, she feared neither would get through to Sloane. The twisting sensation in her gut convinced her this was worse than their first argument about Kadin and that everything they'd built over the last six months was about to crumble.

Another swipe of her ID badge, and she opened the door to their office. Her hopes sank. It was empty. "Damn it, Sloane. Where are you?"

She could spend all day tracking Sloane down and still come up empty. At this point, a call would have to suffice. She dialed Sloane's number, but it went to voice mail. "Babe, I love you. You're the only one I want. If you stop and think, you'll know it's not what you assumed. I'll wait for you at home."

Finn slumped in a chair. Her life was unraveling, and she felt helpless to do much about it. She had sold her condo an hour earlier, and she'd likely not be welcomed in Sloane's townhouse after today. But having a place to live was the least of her problems. She was losing the love of her life. That was scarier than staring down El Padrino and outrunning a wildfire. She needed to do something, anything to make things right.

She dialed her only hope. After three rings, the call connected. "Daddy, it's all gone horribly wrong." Her voice cracked on every word.

"Pumpkin, tell me what happened." After Finn explained the events of this morning, her father asked, "Are you sure Kadin didn't intentionally torpedo things?"

"I know you don't like her, but I'm sure. She's not like that. And how could she have known Sloane would come by at that time? *I* didn't."

"Uh-huh." He didn't sound convinced.

"This isn't the time, Daddy. I need your help."

"How?"

"I've never asked you to get involved in my love life, but you know I didn't spend the night with Kadin. Sloane respects you. Can you talk to her?"

"I'd be happy to. Where is she?"

"I don't know, and she's not answering her phone."

"Don't worry, pumpkin. I'll find her."

"Thank you, Daddy. If I lose her, I don't know what I'll do." She hung up, hoping she'd never find out.

CHAPTER ELEVEN

Sloane wasn't ready to face Finn, who was likely waiting for her at the house. That meant she couldn't go to the one place she could count on to help her find answers—her townhouse's back deck. There was no other place she wanted to be, so she aimlessly drove San Francisco's bustling districts in a fruitless attempt to get her bearings. Despite feeling the breeze on her face and getting glimpses of the bay, she never achieved the solace she was seeking. Nothing felt like home because she had no idea what her home would look like after today. Her life was shattering, and she felt like that scared child who twenty-two years ago had lost everyone dear to her.

Sloane found herself drawn to the one other place that held meaning. The one location that got her through those childhood fears. Now well into the noon hour, she pushed open the heavy wood door with its streaked glass window and trudged through the threshold. The recognizable smell of grease filled her nose, welcoming her like an old friend.

It had been a while since she'd visited The Tap at this hour on a weekday. The last time, she realized, was when she was mourning Avery. The memory triggered a spreading numbness. She was just as lost now, mourning the loss of Finn.

Her gaze shifted to one particular table near the far wall. It felt strange to be intentionally seeking it out. She hadn't done that since before the wildfire, when she still felt connected to Avery. She didn't know why, but she needed that connection again today.

A regular patron occupied her target, but she didn't think he'd mind. Condiments and a soft drink cup populated the tabletop, but not food, so she tapped him on the shoulder. "Hey, Ray."

He craned his neck. "Oh. Hey, Sloane. What's cookin'?"

"I'm having one of those days. I was wondering if you could do me a favor."

"Sure, Sloane. What do you need?"

"This table has special meaning to me. I hate to ask, but could you move to another one?"

Maybe it was the weariness in her voice or the drained feeling that likely was manifested in her face, but he didn't question her. He picked up his drink, grabbed the jacket he'd slung over the back of his chair, and patted her on the shoulder.

"Hope your day gets better, Sloane."

"Thanks, Ray."

He took a table on the other side of the room, creating a significant buffer between Sloane and the next patron. She silently thanked him for his thoughtfulness before claiming his old chair. When she sat, she gripped the edges of the table, remembering the significance of this square of metal, pressed wood, and thirty-year-old Formica. It was where she and Avery shared their first kiss, where Sloane proposed to her, and where they dined after their wedding.

"I could always trust you, Avery," Sloane whispered, rubbing a hand across her forehead.

Surprisingly, she didn't feel angry, only stupid that she'd been agonizing over her behavior at the ballpark yesterday. Finn was right when she said, "either you trust me or you don't." Today, Finn had proved she wasn't worth Sloane's trust.

"What can I get you?"

Sloane looked up toward the familiar sultry voice. She tilted her head, expecting something different. "You've gotten blonder."

"I thought you stopped noticing." Michelle arched an eyebrow in a way that said Sloane's attention was welcomed and long overdue.

"Commenting, yes. Noticing, no."

A glimmer of hope appeared on Michelle's face. "So you like it?" She puffed the bottom row of locks with a hand.

Until now, Sloane hadn't thought twice about her old fuck buddy beyond ordering food and drinks, but with nothing left to lose, she inspected her from head to toe. Her trim, shapely body was as pleasing the last time she shared a bed with her three years ago. "Who wouldn't? But I'll take a scotch first. Make it a double."

"Coming right up, sexy." Michelle walked away with an extra sway in her hips, clearly intending to catch Sloane's attention. It did, which made Sloane feel empty.

In short order, Sloane took care of her double. Then another. Their dizzying effects soaked up her sorrows to the point she felt like her old self. Not the person she was before today, but who she was before Finn and Avery. The one where the walls she erected let no one close enough to hurt her as Finn had. The one where sex was a drug that satisfied a need and nothing more.

Half an hour later, she flushed the toilet and finished buttoning her jeans. The room spun a bit when she opened the stall door. *Only four drinks in*, Sloane thought. Life with Finn had made her a lightweight. She figured it would take a month to remedy that problem. She walked unsteadily to the sink and splashed a little water on her face.

As she reached for a paper towel from the dispenser, the restroom door opened and Michelle entered. Sloane watched in the mirror as she braced an arm on the metal stall frame and cocked a hip to one side and into a tempting stance.

"Ready for dessert?" Michelle had an extra button undone on the top of her blouse, exposing more than a hint of cleavage.

"I haven't even had lunch yet." The walls and floor oscillated in slow, intoxicated waves, taking Sloane's self-restraint out to sea. She turned around, allowing Michelle to lower her arms over her shoulders.

"This hot dish is ready to eat."

Sloane needed to forget why she'd come to this place. Why she'd downed four drinks in the middle of the day. She needed the one thing she could count on before she was stupid enough to let a woman rip her heart in two.

Sloane pulled their bodies close until they touched in several places, arousal coming to life. She slammed Michelle against the flimsy stall, the vibration echoing off decades-old subway tiles. After pinning Michelle's arms over her head against the smooth, painted metal, she pressed their hips together, the scent of stale cigarettes wafting upward. "What do you want, Michelle?"

"For you to fuck me." Michelle thrust their centers together, the friction from the thick denim seam of her jeans swelling Sloane's folds. She let Michelle kiss her neck, sucking her flesh with vigor, not with passion as Finn had done to her a hundred times. Michelle released long enough to force Sloane's hand to the fly of her jeans.

"I want your fingers inside, like before."

Before? Before her heart shattered when Avery was killed? Before Finn put it back together only to rip it in two today? Sloane sobered enough to ask, "You mean like last time?"

"No. I mean before those bitches got their claws into you."

Avery and Finn were anything but bitches. Besides Reagan, they were the best part of Sloane's life. Michelle wasn't what she needed to forget her pain. No matter how much Sloane was hurting, she needed Finn. She pushed herself back and forced Michelle's hands off her. "They are not bitches. They were and are ten times the woman you'll ever be."

"Then why are you with me and not bitch number two?"

Sloane thought the sight of Kadin in Finn's condo before nine o'clock in the morning was the answer to that question. But it wasn't. The explanation for why she was there was herself. Finn may have been why her heart was hurting, but Sloane's self-pity was the reason she was pawing her old fuck buddy.

"You know what, Michelle? This was a colossal mistake. Just bring me my fucking bill." She straightened her clothes and walked out, regretting the rancid smell of cigarettes on her and how it had gotten there.

Sobered enough by her own disappointment, Sloane navigated the hallway, her glance alternating between linoleum floor and neon beer signs. With each step, she grumbled, "What the fuck was I thinking?"

No matter what Finn may have done, allowing Michelle to dig her claws into her again was a major blunder. She needed to crawl into bed and sleep off the stink and sting of the last few hours. Instead of waiting for Michelle to slink over with the check, she cut out the middleman and bellied up to the bar. She waved Dylan over.

"Hey, D, close me out."

He acknowledged with a strong cast of his chin.

"I got this one, Dylan. Can you bring one coffee? Black."

Sloane turned toward the male voice behind her. Suddenly, her temples throbbed. "I'm not in the mood for this, Chandler."

Finn's father pointed to a hundred-dollar bill he laid on the bar, catching Dylan's gaze.

"I appreciate it, Chandler, but I prefer to pay my own bills."

"My guess is you racked up a hefty bar bill this early in the day because of my daughter. The least I can do is cover the expense." He waved two fingers, telegraphing he wouldn't need change nor any more of Dylan's services besides the coffee.

"Sure thing." Dylan scurried off and quickly returned with a steaming paper cup.

Chandler slid it in front of Sloane. "This is for you. You'll want to sober up when you hear what I have to say."

Sloane ignored the coffee. "She had the guts to tell you?"

"She told me you jumped to conclusions this morning, which makes for a damn good cop but for a piss poor life partner. You need to learn to stop and listen."

"I know what I saw, Chandler. I didn't want to stay for the morning afterglow." Sloane stared at her cup of joe and wished it had magically turned into scotch. If she had to dredge this up, she'd rather not be sober.

"Trust me. There was no glowing involved unless you think having coffee and blueberry muffins with her old man might have caused it."

"What are you talking about?" The remaining alcohol fog cleared in an instant. Had he thrown her the life preserver she so desperately needed?

"Look at me, Sloane." He waited until they locked gazes. "Have I ever lied to you?" She shook her head in the negative. "I'm no fan of Kadin these days, but she's innocent in this one. Finn didn't spend the night with Kadin. She spent it with me. After I left, Kadin came to pick up the keys to the condo. It closes escrow today."

A sinking feeling pulled Sloane's insides toward the bottom of the abyss she created today. On the basis of an assumption, she'd turned away the love of her life and fallen into the ash-smelling clutches of a well-worn standby. When reality fully settled, she rubbed her temples as flashes of her and Michelle in the restroom pelted her like a prizefighter. "What have I done?"

"Whatever you've done, there's time to fix it." He rested a palm on her shoulder. "I don't know what you said to her yesterday at the ballpark, but last night, I never saw her more torn up, not even when her mother died. That should tell you something. I know this Eric thing makes it difficult to trust her, but you can bet the farm she wants only you. With every fiber, she loves you, Sloane."

"Where is she?"

"She's waiting for you at home. I'll take Reagan out for the evening after work. That should give you two time to work things out."

"Thank you, Chandler." Sloane didn't need the coffee. The shame of her near-tryst and the uncertainty of how she would explain it to Finn were sobering enough.

* * *

After squeezing her car next to Finn's in their garage, Sloane placed a palm on the hood of the sedan. It was cool to the touch, which meant Finn had been home for a while, waiting and likely hoping Sloane would make her way back to her. But had Sloane pushed her too far? Despite Finn's pleas, she'd refused to listen, refused to trust. Now apprised of the truth, she felt ashamed. She'd acted the fool for days, letting hurt feelings dictate unthinking, unpleasant, and unfaithful responses.

Once up the stairs, she called out, "Finn?" No answer. Further in, she peeked out the deck's sliding glass door, but still no Finn. She tiptoed into the bedroom. There, on the bed, covered with a throw blanket, lay the woman she couldn't live without.

Sloane's breath hitched when she studied Finn's face. Though her eyes were shut, she could tell they were puffy. She'd caused that. Like her, Finn had spent hours thinking they were over. The one difference, Finn had cried herself to sleep while Sloane sought solace from a scotch glass and another woman's body.

She knelt beside the bed, soaking in Finn's features. So damn beautiful. She was so lucky to have found her after all these years. Now, they were on the precipice of shattering into pieces, something neither of them could repair. She didn't want this to be the last time she would feel Finn's breath on her face but feared it could be.

After Finn shifted and rolled to her other side, Sloane lifted the edge of the blanket. She slid onto the mattress, scooting across until her thighs and torso touched Finn's backside. That simple touch, even through layers of fabric, felt like perfection. This couldn't be the end.

When she draped an arm over her, Finn trembled. Soft whimpers broke the silence as she clutched Sloane's hand and pulled it to her lips.

"I love you," Sloane whispered into her ear. Finn wiggled to turn over, but Sloane squeezed her tighter. "Not yet. I don't want to see the disappointment in your eyes when I tell you what I did."

Finn froze. Though they were touching, a distance was growing between them. Even Finn's grip felt nonexistent.

"I won't try to excuse what I did but simply explain that I was hurt and lost. After I left your condo, I drove around for hours and ended up at The Tap. I drank...a lot. When I went to the bathroom, Michelle was there. She made it clear she wanted me. I pressed our bodies together and let her kiss my neck."

Sloane felt every muscle in Finn tense. Her legs straightened, and then her spine stiffened as if Finn were bracing herself for the worst. Sloane did too and cleared her throat.

"Even though I thought I'd already lost you, it didn't feel right. I stopped, and I swear that's as far as it went."

Sloane heard a long breath escape Finn's lungs and felt her rigid muscles slowly relax.

"Then your father found me and told me everything. I'm so sorry for not trusting you. I'm so sorry I walked away. I'm so sorry for doing the very thing I accused you of in my head. I have no right to ask for your forgiveness, but I am. Please forgive me."

After several silent beats, Finn lifted the blanket. Then Sloane's arm. She slid out and lumbered to the door as if weights were chained to her ankles. After Finn placed her hand on the knob, she craned her head over a shoulder and said in a sad, soft tone, "I love you." She walked out, taking Sloane's hopes with her.

Minutes passed. Soon an hour. An agonizing hour of pacing and cursing herself behind that closed door. An hour to imagine a life without Finn when the only thing she wanted was her. The garage door hadn't opened, which was a good sign, but the fact Finn was still sorting out things was not. She didn't have the right to press and resigned herself to patience. She'd wait and hope like Finn had earlier today.

The stink of the day weighed heavily on Sloane, as did the stale smell of The Tap's cooking grease, cigarettes, and Michelle's cheap perfume. Within minutes, steam had fogged the glass shower door, and the hammering spray of hot water had beat Sloane's shoulder muscles into submission. The day had taxed her strength, and she needed to brace both hands against the slick tiled-wall to help her stand.

She closed her eyes, thoughts of what she should've done differently flooding her head as the steam thickened. When she saw Kadin in the hallway, she should've stayed and asked questions. When Finn pleaded for her to stay, she should've relented. When Michelle threw herself at her, she should've run. Should've run back to Finn and told her she believed her and wanted only her.

A click sounded behind her, followed by a rush of chilly air. She didn't have to look, nor did Finn have to speak. She felt Finn's forgiveness the moment their bodies touched skin to skin. Finn pressed harder against Sloane's back and snaked her arms around Sloane's torso until each hand claimed a breast.

"I'm the only one who gets to touch these." Finn's voice was as possessive as her hands, which were squeezing with the pressure of a lion's jaw engulfing its prey.

Relief seeped from Sloane's pores as Finn reclaimed what was rightly hers. From the first time they made love, Sloane had reserved her body only for Finn. The thought she'd violated that trust even in the smallest of ways sickened her. She pitched her head back until she nuzzled Finn's cheek.

"Only you."

Finn released a hand and drifted it down Sloane's water-slicked torso. Her palm and fingers didn't softly glide as they'd done a hundred times across her skin. Not in her patented way that made Sloane feel loved with a single stroke. This touch had a domineering force behind its descent, compelling Sloane's flesh into obedience.

Finn's hand clutched her sex, sparking a pulsating rhythm within. "This is the body I want. This is the pussy I crave," Finn roared, warning off all other predators.

At that moment, Sloane turned from skin, bone, and blood into a pile of clay ready for Finn to mold into whatever form she wanted. Sloane flung an arm backward, hooking Finn's neck in a desperate need to be owned.

"It's yours." Sloane's gravelly words were the last things she controlled. Finn commanded every reflex, every intake of breath, and every heartbeat. She was entirely hers.

Finn spun her. As they stood breast to breast, core to core, water cascaded from one body to the other. Lips collided in a burning passion as arms and legs entwined, triggering a downward stream of arousal. Sloane pressed harder with every body part that moved, begging Finn to take her.

The clank of the faucet twisting shut forced the water to a trickle. Then it stopped. Finn dropped to her knees and inhaled Sloane's scent. She flipped one of Sloane's legs over her shoulder, giving her access to the prize Sloane wanted her to take.

"Mine," Finn growled before latching her lips onto what was hers.

"Yours. It's all yours." Slamming a hand against the shower wall, Sloane crested in shuddering waves.

Finn clamped her hands on Sloane's bottom, keeping her steady when her quaking legs threatened to stop holding her in place. After claiming every drop of arousal, Finn rose and captured Sloane's limp, panting body in her arms.

Sloane let Finn wrap her in her arms, and when her core and breathing settled, she whispered. "I love you. Only you."

Finn tightened her hold. "Never again, Sloane."

"Never."

Never again would Sloane doubt Finn's love. She melted into Finn's embrace and into her second chance.

CHAPTER TWELVE

As daybreak slipped over the eastern hills, Sloane gripped the steering wheel and kept her focus on the dark city street ahead, anxious about her plan. If not for her second chance with Finn, she wouldn't have considered going. She had hoped that Reagan would've done the same for Finn last night after her and Finn's show of a united front, but it never came. Perhaps she just needed a bit more time.

"You're right about this."

"You've held this pain for too long. It's time to let it go." From the passenger seat, Finn drifted a hand to Sloane's thigh, caressing it.

It was time, but was she ready? The hurt had cut deep, and for that very reason, she had avoided facing its roots for months. Sloane pulled Finn's hand up to her mouth and kissed the back of it. "You'll stay, won't you?"

"If that's what you want. Then, of course, I'll stay."

Sloane considered releasing Finn's hand, but she'd come so close to losing it she couldn't bear letting it go. She drew it to her chest and held it there until she pulled into the Daly City apartment complex.

Once parked, she unbuckled and tugged Finn's chin toward her with a hand before she could escape. "I always want you with me." She pressed their lips together in a brief, tender kiss. It wasn't nearly enough. She needed to say those words and kiss those lips a thousand times until the unpleasant parts of yesterday evaporated with the morning bay fog.

By any standard of decorum, it was too early for visiting someone, but she didn't have a choice. She'd set the artificial deadline of finding answers before she and Finn went to West, and now she had to head it off. Minutes later, at the apartment door, she waited for it to open. The sound of the deadbolt sent a sour taste bubbling up to the back of her throat. When the door was pulled ajar, silence settled in like the thick fog she'd woken up to this morning.

Hair mussed, dressed in long plaid pajama pants and a ratty white T-shirt, Eric took several deep breaths. "I know my time is up."

"May we come in?" Sloane's voice remained steady without emotion. He nodded.

Finn entered first, rubbing a hand along his bad arm as she passed. Sloane followed. She'd spent enough time with Eric to see that he was curious. She had some questions of her own and hoped they both would soon get the answers they needed.

Inside, she was ashamed to think this was the first time she'd ever set foot in his apartment. They had been partners for over two years, and not once had he extended an invitation nor had she asked for one. Now she understood his reluctance. The space was cramped and had the feel of a low-rent hotel. The one touch of personalization was the big-screen television and a small wall clock made of spent ammo mounted next to it.

Without many options, Sloane and Finn sat on the years-old couch, while Eric took a seat on the nearby recliner. His stare alternated between both women, eventually settling on Finn, historically his ally. Of course, he'd looked to her. Finn was there for him when he was at his worst when Sloane wasn't.

"Wanna tell me what's going on?" Eric asked.

"Sloane should answer that." Finn rubbed Sloane's thigh, giving her the last push she needed.

"All right." He shifted his gaze and waited.

How to start? Sloane had put no thought into it, having fixated only on the expected challenging parts. She said the first thing that came to mind. "I don't want to see you hurt, Eric."

"Thank you." Eric's eyes got glassy at the same time as his Adam's apple floated up and down, a sure sign he meant it.

"Before we talk about the cold case"—Sloane's voice started strong, then cracked—"I need to know what happened that night."

Eric's breathing turned ragged. "I've waited twenty-two years for this day."

Sloane reached for Finn's hand, gripping it for courage. For strength. For the love she needed to get through this.

Eric began. "I met my cousin at the gas station he was working at in Richmond. He bought me a case of beer for the weekend, so I went to pick it up."

Heat built inside Sloane, enough that her cheeks burned. As she trembled, the unforgivable went through her mind. She had to know. "You were drinking?"

He locked eyes with her. He didn't flinch. Didn't blink. "No, I wasn't. I didn't have a drink that night."

Her shaking dwindled. "Why were you on that road?"

"The accident on the freeway. I had to take the back way home."

Sloane nodded, shaking loose twenty-two-year-old memories. "I remember my dad saying something about an accident."

"I was changing the station on the radio when I came around a curve. All I saw were headlights. Then I realized we both had crossed the line—me more than the other guy. I swerved back into my lane, and the other car did too. I continued around the curve and drove home."

The image of those oncoming headlights made Sloane's breath hitch. Nothing Eric said entirely lifted the weight of blame from her shoulders. They both were at fault. Her singing was why her father took his eyes off the road, but Eric was the reason he overcorrected.

Tears trickled down Sloane's cheeks. She clutched Finn's hand tighter. "You didn't hear the crash?"

"God help me. I wish I had. I would've helped." Tears threatened to fall from his eyes. He formed a fist with his right hand and slammed it against his thigh. "The windows were up. I had the music blasting." He rocked back and forth before burying his face in his hands. "I didn't know, Sloane. I didn't know."

Processing the truth proved more difficult than Sloane expected. She wanted it all to be his fault. Maybe then she could absolve herself of the guilt she'd carried for decades. But there was no escaping the truth. They both were careless, and both carried guilt. The one thing that made it easier to swallow was that he did something about his guilt.

"We're both to blame."

His head rose, eyes reddened with emotion. "What do you mean?"

She understood the weight he'd carried all these years because she'd carried the same sadness and self-loathing. But life with Finn had opened her eyes, and she could now see a day when she could finally let it all go. But today's discussion was about him, not her.

"We can talk about that another day. Did this have anything to do with you becoming a cop?"

"Yes. Before that night, I wanted to be nothing like my old man. But once I learned what I'd done, the only way I could make up for it was to save lives. It made my dad proud, but not me. I knew why I put on the badge."

Sloane recalled all the times she shared a car with Eric behind the wheel. One question came to mind. "The accident? That's why you never play music in the car." He offered a slow, affirmative nod. "I believe you, Eric. I believe you spent all these years making up for your part."

He gave another slow nod.

"Now, it's my turn to do a good thing for you." His eyes met hers. "We both essentially want the same thing. You want to solve the case to prove your innocence and your father's. I want to prove who killed Bernie. If we alert Morgan and Nash, they'll have no choice but to take over the case, and we'll lose control of the outcome. I don't want this to sit unsolved for another twenty-two years."

"Me neither."

"Then I propose we work together, find out as much as we can until we have to turn it over to Nash, or Nash shuts us down." His eyes lit up. "But you have to do one thing first."

"What?"

"Give us the gun. We'll hold on to it for safekeeping."

Eric retreated to another room and returned minutes later. He handed Sloane the Beretta in its waist holster. They exchanged no more words. None needed to be said after the seed Sloane had planted. She left, holding Finn's hand along with the hope this marked the beginning of a new chapter.

Walking down The Pit's corridor of blinking overhead fluorescents with Finn this morning marked the first time 850 Bryant didn't haunt Sloane. She'd thought she simply missed the camaraderie and putting bad guys away, but in reality, she missed Eric. They weren't partners again, but focusing on the cold case with a vested and shared interest in its outcome almost felt like they were. She welcomed that feeling. It was, at the very least, a start.

Once inside their office, she and Finn fired up the coffeemaker and computers and settled into a comfortable rhythm of cataloging the remaining cold cases. Soon a knock on the door broke their concentration. Sloane checked her watch. Enough time had passed for Eric to retrieve the evidence box and records from county storage. She cautiously opened the door.

"Morgan?"

Damn. Sloane thought her earlier phone message was enough to reverse her knee-jerk idea to reveal this mess with Eric, Quintrell, the gun, and the cold case. Morgan West's wrinkled brow told her the attempt likely fell short, and this wasn't a social visit. *Get on your dance shoes*, Sloane told herself.

"You canceled our meeting at the last minute without much of an explanation," Morgan said. "I wanted to make sure everything was okay."

"Everything's fine. Like I said in my message, the problem solved itself." Sloane moved to one side and motioned with her arm. "Come in."

Morgan scanned the width of the room, her upturned nose telegraphing her impression. "Your accommodations certainly reflect how Captain Nash feels about your oversight."

"We're making the best of it." Finn pointed toward the air fresheners.

"A necessary but nice touch for The Pit." Sloane wrinkled her nose too. "You should've warned us."

"And take all the fun out of you discovering your dilemma?" Morgan waved her off, smiling.

"She was grouchy for days." Finn chuckled at Sloane's expense, but she was right. Sloane had been a grouch.

"I'm sure she was." Morgan cast her chin toward the glowing computer monitor. "How's the work coming along? Any hidden gems yet?"

"We're not ready to discuss specifics, but we can see the potential for new technology solving several cases." One was life-changing, but Sloane couldn't tell her yet. She regretted not being forthcoming, but too much was at stake. Sloane wanted answers, as did Eric. And if Morgan knew the truth and took no action, she'd likely lose her job too.

"That won't bode well for the department." Morgan exhaled a weighty sigh. "The mayor will dismantle investigations and management for sure."

"I hate being in the middle of power struggles." Sloane pursed her lips. "I'm afraid our work will cost you and a lot of other good detectives their jobs."

"You two are doing important work. Maybe the PD needs some shaking up." Morgan dipped her head, reality perhaps sinking in. "I should get back to the squad room."

When Sloane opened the door for Morgan to exit, she saw Eric in the hallway with one of the building janitors, who was pushing a handcart loaded with three boxes. She locked eyes with Eric and shook her head from side to side like a dog shaking off its bathwater. She stepped back inside the office and jerked the door closed.

Think, think, think. Sloane put her dancing shoes on. "Morgan, I meant to ask. Since you're not my boss anymore, it's time we get to know each other better. Would you and Kyler like to join Finn and me for dinner at The Tap?"

A glint appeared in Morgan's eyes, augmenting her dimpled grin. "I'd love to. We were doing takeout tonight, but I'm sure Kyler wouldn't mind the change of plans. How about seven?"

"It's a date." Sloane smiled at Morgan's infectious delight. "Kyler will love The Tap."

As Morgan stepped toward the door, Sloane peeked again into the hallway. Empty. Eric had thankfully caught on, so she slid the door open wide. "All right then. Send me a text to confirm."

After Morgan disappeared down the hallway and through the double doors, Sloane called out in the opposite direction, "Eric? The coast is clear." Seconds later, he appeared from around the corner, followed by the man with the hand truck.

"Nice save," Finn said from inside the office.

Eric drew even with her. "That was close."

"Too close." Sloane moved into the hallway, making a path for the janitor. "Anywhere will do," she told him.

After the janitor dropped off the boxes and turned to exit with the dolly, Eric handed him a folded twenty-dollar bill and shook his hand. "Thanks, Harry. I appreciate the help. I still owe you that bottle of scotch."

He's changed, Sloane thought. Before the shooting, he wouldn't have needed help to carry in three evidence boxes. With his superior strength, he likely would've carried them by hand, never resorting to a hand truck or another man's help.

She recalled Avery's wake when he had swooped her into his arms and carried her to her table at The Tap. She'd welcomed his sturdy arms around her, shielding her from the anguish swirling in that place. But all that strength was gone, taken by a bullet that could've killed her daughter.

She studied his face after he closed the door behind Harry. His resolute expression told Sloane he might have changed, but only physically. Underneath, he was the same determined man, ready to turn over every rock to help someone he loved.

"Where should we start?" he asked.

"Where you taught me. With the evidence." Sloane wasn't ready to show it, but it felt good working with him again. More of her glacier fell into the sea.

The first case she had drawn as a detective remained vivid in her mind. Besides allowing her to make a fool of herself in front of Avery Santos, the woman she'd later marry, Eric taught her to make up her own mind about the evidence. *"Don't listen to the first-on-scene patrol officer rant on about his or her opinions. They are often wrong,"* he had said. *"Instead, take what the CSI techs unearthed for what it was—a clue."* A clue that, when pieced together with all the others, painted a picture. In most cases, that picture would reveal the truth.

In this case, she hoped the original detectives had either missed something or couldn't decipher the picture. She hoped to do better. Instead of delving into the investigative report and let the original detectives' findings and conclusions taint their objectivity, she, Finn, and Eric would first dive into the evidence.

She and Finn unstacked the boxes, distributing them on a desk, worktable, and chair. Each person attacked a box, unveiling rows of file folders with reports and photographs and two collections of sealed clear plastic bags of various sizes.

Sloane emptied the contents of her box. Each evidence bag was well preserved, considering its long dormancy in a dank warehouse along with the other unsolved cases. She logged in details, noting who collected what item, when, and where.

Each time she picked up an item identified as coming from Bernie's body, she held it with reverence then placed it in its separate pile. A gold wristwatch. The remains of his shoes. Melted credit cards. His service weapon, a Colt .45. Finally, his badge. Parts of it were smudged by ash, but its shape and color were unmistakable—a seven-point gold badge, not unlike the one she used to wear. His was more ornate, imprinted on each point with olive branches and in its center with the City of San Pablo emblem.

Sloane cocked her head several times, absorbing the badge's surface details and drawing on her decades-old memory. Twenty-two years had passed, but the accident was crystal clear. She had first seen the now smudged badge when flames from the nearby burning wreckage had shimmered an orange reflection. That was the moment she knew she was alone in the world.

"Bernie had such a kind face. I wonder whatever happened to the daughter he left behind."

"When we figure this out, we'll track her down. Give her closure." Finn spoke as if it were a promise.

"I remember the day Bernie died. It was a Saturday, his day off." She locked her stare at Finn. "He promised to take me to see you. We were supposed to surprise you. I waited for hours on our driveway. I remember watching billowing smoke rise beyond the roofline of the houses across the street. The sirens sounded close, and I thought it must have been a house fire." Sloane contorted her face and averted her eyes to keep the regret she'd carried for years from overtaking her. "I was so mad at Bernie for not showing up. He broke his promise, and I called him every name in the book that night."

"You didn't know." Finn rubbed Sloane's arm, sending a warmth radiating up and through her chest. Her gentle touch had returned.

"I learned what happened the following morning. It was all over the news. Witnesses said he tried to save a woman from that burning house."

Sloane shook her head, remembering the newspaper headline hailing a fallen hero. Then it hit her. When she had focused on that newspaper photograph of Bernie in his uniform with the American flag behind his right shoulder, that was the moment she let go of Finn. *Never again*, she silently prayed. Never again did she want to feel that lonely.

"How is it we spent over two years as partners and you never mentioned this?" Eric asked in an uncertain tone.

Sloane turned her gaze to him. Not hard, but sad. The irony of his question made her realize she and Eric weren't that different. "For the same reason you never mentioned the accident. I felt responsible. He wouldn't have been in that house if I hadn't asked him to help me find Finn."

They continued to work and tape crime scene photographs on three walls, grouping them according to each room from the partially burned-out crack house. The exterior pictures had an exclusive location on the back of their office door. Next, Sloane and Finn grouped the evidence bags according to where they were found, placing them near the corresponding photographs. Collectively, the pieces already painted a rudimentary picture.

Eric's gaze fell to the photo of John Doe's burned corpse. Sloane's followed. Ends of finger and toe bones poked out of charred black covers that used to be skin. Blackened ribs outlined what used to be his torso, and holes in the charry skull were left where eyes once resided.

Below the picture lay two pieces of evidence. Eric lifted the first bag and inspected the bullet encased inside. "How did you get from my gun to inside someone's head?"

"That's the sixty-four-thousand-dollar question." Sloane picked up the other bag. "This gold-plated tooth could have some DNA in it."

"Wait. I remember seeing another evidence bag marked 'tooth.'" Finn sifted through the larger pile of evidence bags on the table situated below a picture of the partially burned bodies of Bernie and the unidentified woman. She pulled out one bag. "Here. This one was taken from the Jane Doe, which was great forward-thinking. DNA sampling was in its infancy back then. At least your CSI team knew enough to take samples even though they had nothing to compare against."

Sloane shifted her attention to the stack of evidence bags containing items from the woman Bernie tried to save. "Our first step is to figure out who Jane and John Doe were." She stabbed a finger on Jane's photo. "They are the key."

Following concurring nods, Sloane and Eric began organizing the various evidence bags. At the same time, Finn brought up a blank spreadsheet on her laptop. They worked like a well-oiled machine, rattling off descriptors of each piece of evidence and logging it into a file. When they were done, Eric leaned back in his chair, rubbing the back of his neck. "Nothing here screams identity. We need to dig deeper."

"Damn." Sloane earned a like-minded eyeroll from Eric. Digging deeper meant digging through a brick-sized case file and separating the wheat from the chaff of the original report.

"I'm the office rat now. I'll go." Eric grabbed the thick case file and left the office.

Finn knitted her brow at Sloane. A smile punctuated her amusement. "You two have a shorthand that's hard to keep up with."

"It kinda feels like old times." The last hour sifting through evidence made Sloane remember the unspoken cues she and Eric once shared. A simple nod or use of a name or code word was all it took for them to get through dicey situations. She missed it.

Finn stepped closer until the scent of her shampoo tickled Sloane's nose. Citrus, her drug of choice. "It's good seeing you two working together again."

"It's a start." Sloane inhaled Finn's fragrance for its medicinal properties, clearing a residual tightness in her lungs and lifting the underlying uneasiness of having almost lost her.

"A significant one." Finn drew Sloane's chin closer and gave her a gentle, lingering kiss, the type that made her know yesterday was forgiven.

Soon Eric returned with two thick case folders. Finn arched an eyebrow.

"We work better when we're looking at the same information at the same time." Eric handed one folder to Sloane.

"More shorthand." Finn grinned. "What do you want me to do?"

Sloane spun one of the office chairs around and patted its seat. "Take notes while we all spitball."

"Got it." Finn took her position and readied her fingertips at the keyboard.

For the next hour, Sloane and Eric peeled back every line in the original report. They discarded assumptions and focused on the evidence, looking to unearth anything the detectives may have missed. Sloane ignored the crick in her neck until they'd questioned each entry and posed one what-if after another to identify paths that could be rich with more clues.

When Sloane reached the last line of the last page, she pushed herself from her chair, rubbing the stiffness that had spread down her shoulders to her lower back. "Geeze."

"You're getting old, Sloane. Thirty-five is right around the corner." Eric's mischievous grin was like old times.

"Yeah, well, forty isn't that far off for you." She walked toward their makeshift coffee bar but kept her smile hidden. For the first time since she discovered the truth of her parents' accident, she could see a day when that wasn't her first thought when she saw Eric.

Sloane finished pouring three cups of coffee. She handed one to Eric on her way to Finn's workstation. He gave her a quick, but what sounded like a genuine, "Thanks." She waved the second cup in front of Finn's face.

"You read my mind." Finn took a long and apparently satisfying sip.

Sloane peeked over Finn's shoulder at her computer screen and studied the notes she'd taken during their spitballing session. She bent at the waist and inhaled another dose of Finn's remedy for all of her pain. Moments later, her stiffness disappeared.

"You had a great theory about the crime scene, Eric." Sloane turned to face him, as did Finn.

"A drug deal gone bad like the original detectives surmised didn't sit right. I buy their theory that whoever shot John Doe," Eric pointed to a picture of the charred body he'd tacked to a wall, "and set the fire didn't know the woman was there, but why didn't anyone hear a shot?"

"That didn't sit well with me either." Sloane reviewed one of her handwritten notes. "The detectives said they offered a get-out-of-jail-free card to anyone who heard or saw anything, yet they got nothing. Every junkie I know in the city would've jumped at the offer."

"Which is why I think there was no shot." Eric pulled the picture from the wall and studied it for several beats. "The body was dumped, and the fire was set to cover it up."

"Okay. So, we have a working theory." Sloane stared at the extensive collection of evidence bags. "But we're no closer to identifying our Jane and John Doe, are we?"

Sloane fixed Eric with a stare. They both said the same name at the same time, "Todd."

"Who's Todd?" Finn asked.

Sloane smiled. "Shorthand."

CHAPTER THIRTEEN

A good start—that was how Eric labeled the last four hours with Sloane. They had different motivations, but it didn't matter to him. What mattered was that she'd put aside her anger, at least for now, and worked with him. Last week, he thought that impossible. He'd violated every aspect of trust on which they'd based their partnership and friendship and deserved her resentment. Today was more than he could've hoped for.

"How's that ankle? You up for stairs?"

"Since when do you take the stairs?" Sloane asked, tucking two evidence bags under an arm, snug against her body.

"Since I got shot. Too many months in bed and on the couch. Stairs are great cardio."

"Stairs it is."

"Beauty before age." Eric waved his good arm, inviting her to lead the way up the stairs from the basement to the sixth floor.

Sloane didn't quite have the playful, teasing expression he'd seen over the years, but it was much better than the scowl she'd thrown his way the few times he'd seen her since taking that bullet.

He followed and, surprisingly, kept up step for step. The two months he spent in the gym on the leg press to get his strength back had paid off. But if he were honest, he took the stairs once a day out of guilt, forcing himself to not fall into an office rat rut. Today, he'd also suggested the stairs to prolong his alone time with Sloane. Because he'd likely not have another chance. This wasn't the fire department where the firefighters used the stairs religiously to keep up their climbing muscles. Hence, he counted on them being alone.

While ascending the first four flights, only one person passed them in the stairwell. When they reached the next landing, he gently grasped Sloane by the elbow. They both stopped. "Thank you for not up-channeling this case and that whole thing about Quintrell and the gun. It means a lot to me."

"You want to clear your father. I want to find justice for Bernie." She shrugged. "We can't do either if it becomes an active case again."

"You keep saying that, but I think there's more to it."

"Well, there's not." She turned and continued her ascent in silence.

When she reached the sixth floor, he called out, "Wait, let me see if the coast is clear. I called in sick today." He glanced at Sloane. "You better give me the evidence bags. Otherwise, it might look odd."

She silently chuckled. Eric scanned the hallway through the shatterproof glass window of the door before stepping into the hall. After a dozen quick strides, he and Sloane slipped inside the CSI lab.

Sloane froze, her stare arcing from one end of the lab to the other. "It looks so new."

"The funding Avery asked for when she first took over finally came through."

Old metal workbenches were gone, swapped out for state-of-the-art modular workstations. The archaic computers Avery had grumbled about had been replaced by flat-screen monitors attached to hinged retractable arms so they could be shared between multiple stations. Most of the equipment appeared to be new, and the room had a fresh coat of paint and brighter overhead lighting.

"I wish she could've seen this." Sloane's voice didn't contain the melancholy it had the last time Avery came up in conversation, but that was five months ago. Eric was happy to see how far she'd come.

"She would've loved it," Eric recalled when Sloane and Avery first crossed paths at a makeshift meth lab. Anyone could see Sloane was smitten, which had influenced him to stall at the crime scene to give those two extra time together—the single best thing he'd ever done for her.

Seconds later, he tapped his knuckles against the frame of the open office door. A voice called, "Come in."

He stepped inside with Sloane on his heels. "Hey, Todd."

Todd leaned his head around his glowing desktop computer screen, tipping his reading glasses lower on the bridge of his nose. A fresh haircut had tamed his unruly curly red locks. "Hey, Decker." A bright smile formed, and then he dashed from around his desk and gave Sloane a hug, crumpling his white lab coat. "So good to see you, Sloane. How's civilian life?"

"Hours are a lot better. Mind if we close the door?"

"Sure." After Eric closed the door, Todd asked, "What's up?"

Eric raised the evidence bags chest high. "I need DNA run on these."

"No problem." Todd accepted the bags. When he inspected the labels, his brow narrowed. "Nineteen ninety-eight?"

"It's from one of the cold cases Sloane's company has been contracted to look at."

Todd placed the bags on top of his desk before retaking his chair and swirling his computer mouse to bring his monitor back to life. "Let me look it up."

"Todd." Sloane had softened her voice. "We need you to run the DNA without raising red flags."

"Exactly what are you guys asking?" Todd's ear thumbing meant one thing: he was miles away from being convinced.

Eric straightened his posture, debating what and how much to tell him. They had a cordial working relationship that had taken a turn for the better following Avery's death, but a favor of this magnitude would test its limits. "It's like this—"

"Todd," Sloane interrupted. They couldn't very well tell Todd that Eric was implicated in a murder, so that left only the part personal to Sloane. It would be more convincing if she explained. "The case involves three unsolved homicides. One was a police officer who rescued me from the accident that killed my parents. He's the reason I became a cop. Our contract gives us the authority to look into all unsolved cases. If Homicide gets wind of what we're doing, though, they'll think I'm stepping on their toes and might take it over. I'd like to be the one to identify the killer and bring him or her to justice."

Todd looked at Eric. "And you're okay with this?"

"She has the clearance, and yes, I'm okay with it. Can you run the tests personally and associate them with one of my open cases?"

"I can definitely run the tests. Tinkering with the case number might not be possible, but I'll see what I can do."

* * *

The thick late-dinner crowd din at The Tap combined with the Eagles playing softly in the background to create a sense of privacy. Sloane couldn't make out conversations at the neighboring tables, which meant the nearby diners likely couldn't hear her either. After sipping her scotch, she didn't bother whispering in Finn's ear nor filtering her words according to social graces.

"I'm glad you suggested I wear my crew neck tonight."

Scooting her chair closer to Sloane at their rectangular table for four, Finn hooked the high-scooped front of Sloane's top with an index finger. She pulled it out a fraction of an inch, exposing a patch of her neck. Finn's gaze focused on the reason for Sloane's wardrobe choice. "I got a little carried away when I was marking my territory."

"In several places." Sloane's words spilled out between deeper breaths.

Last night in the shower had brought out a carnal side in Finn that Sloane never knew existed. It wasn't about love or lust, but dominance. The reason for it was painful, but the result was beyond erotic.

Finn released the fabric. "Are you complaining?"

"Absolutely not." Sloane's breathing picked up. "It was hot as fuck."

"If that bleached-blond slut so much as looks at your cleavage tonight, I won't be responsible for what follows."

"You're super sexy when you're jealous." A loud clearing of a throat prompted Sloane to look behind her.

"Did we arrive at a bad time?" Morgan's apologetic smile was cute by any measure.

"Not at all." Sloane rested an arm across the back of Finn's chair and gestured for Morgan and Kyler to sit. In her forties, Morgan was striking in her not-too-tight jeans, white crew neck silk top, and dark blue cardigan. Beside her, Kyler was just as fetching, dressed in similar jeans, a low-scooped T-shirt, and a black leather jacket. "I was telling this beautiful woman how incredible she is."

Kyler removed her jacket and draped it over the back of her chair before sitting. Her head turned slowly, taking in her surroundings. "I love places like this. Ones that only locals know about. They have the best food at great prices."

"Then The Tap is for you," Sloane said. "I've been coming here since I was thirteen."

"Thanks for inviting us." Morgan helped push Kyler's chair in and caressed her shoulder as she took her seat. "After we met that time at Lands End, I've been looking forward to doing it again under better circumstances."

"So have I." Sloane reached across the table and briefly squeezed Morgan's hand. "You were nothing but kind to me when I worked for you, but I wasn't ready for friendship. I am now, thanks to this wonderful woman." Sloane kissed Finn on the cheek.

Finn turned and greeted her with a smile. It only took a moment, but Sloane committed to memory every feature in her face. The wave in her dirty blond hair, the high angles of her cheeks, the smoothness of her porcelain white skin, the depth of her hazel-green eyes. She couldn't help but think of that face at thirteen with the roundness and innocence of youth. Sloane had dreamed about it during her adolescence and chased it throughout her adulthood. She fast-forwarded and imagined that face after decades of aging, and it made her want Finn even more. Sloane was sure. They were meant to grow old together.

"Enough of this mushy stuff." Morgan scanned a menu on the table. "What do you recommend?"

"You can't go wrong with anything, but we're both partial to Dylan's burgers." Sloane handed Kyler a menu Dylan had dropped off earlier.

After chatting about things unimportant and devouring most of their burgers, Morgan wiped her mouth with a napkin and fixed her stare on Sloane. "Care to tell me what Decker was doing in your office most of the day after calling in sick?"

Finn stopped in mid-chew, while Sloane didn't skip a beat. After taking one more bite, Sloane wiped her mouth with a napkin. "So you saw him?"

"I was flattered by your invitation this morning, but you rarely do anything out of the blue, Sloane. What gives?"

"Eric and I are addressing our differences." She shrugged. She'd hoped she wouldn't need her dance shoes again, but the truth, as partial as it was, served as a plausible cover.

Morgan's face grew long when she shook her head. "I never understood what happened between you two, but I'm glad you're working things through. You were my best team. The division took a big hit when you quit and I had to place him on desk duty."

"Maybe someday we'll tell you everything, but for now, it's too raw." Sloane nervously shook her thigh, but Finn slid a hand to calm her. Within seconds, it stopped.

"Still with your walls." Morgan gave her head a slight shake. Her kindness deserved a better answer, but that was the best Sloane could do for now.

"This is Eric's story to tell as much as mine. Give us time." Sloane turned to Finn and whispered into her ear. "Should we?" Finn nodded. "Morgan, we know you're concerned about the mayor dismantling the department. We think Kyler can help."

"Me?" Kyler pointed to herself.

"You used to work with Nicci Cole in the DA's office, right?" Finn asked, receiving an affirmative nod. "Mayor Cole is a savvy, cut-throat politician. Odds are she's had political aspirations for a while. We have the feeling she wasn't squeaky clean during her fifteen years in the DA's office."

"And you want me to help you find out if she was dirty." Kyler's tone sounded skeptical. The slow, hesitant rub to the back of her neck confirmed it.

"We're only asking you to gather information, which is what you do all day long." Finn gave Kyler a reassuring smile. "What harm could it do?"

"Where do you suggest I start?"

"District attorneys have the power to prosecute and the power not to." On more occasions than Sloane cared to remember, an ADA had refused to proceed on one of her arrests. Not based on lack of evidence, but a lack of spine. Most young prosecutors didn't understand that Sloane had already given the perp a second and third chance on the street. "I'm more interested in learning about the cases she declined."

"Those are a matter of record," Kyler said. "Anyone can request that list."

"Lists don't tell you why she declined to prosecute. That would take some digging." Sloane added a sly grin. "And that's where you come in."

"If she's as ambitious as we think she is," Finn leaned in, "she can't afford bad press."

Kyler looked at Morgan as if asking for permission and received a firm nod. "All right, ladies. If it means saving a lot of good cops their jobs, including this one right here," she kissed Morgan's hand, "I'll do some digging."

Sloane felt a hand rake across her shoulder, from one side to the other. Its direction meant it wasn't Finn's, yet it still had a feathery, flirtatious touch. She glanced toward it and recognized the strawberry blond hair.

"Anything else I can get you?" Michelle asked, her eyes suggesting she was tonight's special and all Sloane had to do was say the word.

"Just the check." Sloane slung her arm over Finn's chair to emphasize that yesterday's encounter had been a mistake, one she wasn't going to make again.

Michelle reached into the pocket of her black waist apron, sifted through several slips of papers, and pulled out one. She laid it on the table in front of Sloane and walked away, sliding her fingertips across her shoulder again.

Finn shifted in her seat and crossed her arms over her chest. Whether her audible sigh was from jealousy or frustration, Sloane had to quell it. She pulled Finn's chin toward her and kissed her lips, lingering without deepening until she sensed Finn's muscles relax. When Sloane pulled back, she lowered her voice into a seductive timbre. "Only you."

"But does she know that?"

"It doesn't matter, but I'll make sure she does." Sloane kissed her again, quick and light.

"Let us get the check." Morgan reached for the slip of paper.

Sloane thumped her hand on the bill. "We asked you out. How about you get the next one?"

"Deal," Morgan added a wink.

"I'll take care of it." Before Sloane could object, Finn picked it up and walked toward the bar.

Sloane settled into more chitchat with Morgan and Kyler, agreeing on a once-a-month double date while alternating who would choose the location. A commotion behind Sloane, involving the sound of breaking glass followed by laughter, compelled her to turn toward it. She arched her brow so hard that her eyes hurt.

"What the hell?"

Finn marched toward their table. Behind her stood Michelle, who had the look of a Midwestern farmer who had endured a direct tornado hit. Some unknown liquid dripped through soaked and twisted blond strands down to her shoes. Dylan was kneeling beside Michelle and collecting the broken glass, shaking his head and mumbling under his breath. His niece apparently had some explaining to do.

Finn approached the table. Her narrowed eyes and cocked-to-one-side grin telegraphed her roguish satisfaction. Half-shocked, half-amused, Sloane asked, "What did you do?"

"I paid the damn bill."

CHAPTER FOURTEEN

Sloane sat, arm bent at the elbow atop her desk in The Pit, head resting on her palm, staring at Finn and pondering the challenge that had been issued by the morning radio host. In light of Finn having marked her territory for the second night in a row, it deserved serious thought.

Finn ripped her gaze from the computer monitor long enough to ask, "Are you planning on working today?"

"I'm thinking." Sloane added a wistful tone to her voice.

"About what?"

"That radio DJ this morning. Describe your partner in six words or less."

"You've actually been thinking about that?"

"After the last two nights? You bet."

Finn rose from her chair to straddle Sloane in hers. Sloane gripped her by the waist while she draped her arms over Sloane's neck.

"How would you describe me?" Finn asked, her voice an octave lower than usual.

"I've put a lot of thought into this. You're my confident, smart, fiery, sexy, warrior princess."

"Warrior princess?"

"You have incredible fighting skills and are my sworn protector."

Finn's cheeks blushed to the tone of her rosy lipstick. "Michelle needed to learn boundaries."

"I think she knows not to trespass anymore." Through the fabric of Finn's top, Sloane kissed the top of a breast. "How would you describe me?"

Finn drew back and tapped a finger against her lips as if considering and throwing away several options. "I would've chosen Xena for you, but you already took that. Though you do have some Gabrielle qualities." She tapped her finger again. "I'd have to say you're my strong, courageous, passionate, irreplaceable, authentic soulmate."

"Soulmate, huh? Like Xena and Gabrielle?"

"Just like them."

Finn kissed her, slowly at first. When Sloane sent her hands searching beneath her top, up the toned muscles of her backside, Finn's fiery side ignited. That was the side Sloane wanted, the side that sparked her own passion. Tongue searching, she pressed a palm against the breast she kissed earlier. She'd promised herself not to take their touching too far in this smelly dungeon, but after their shower encounter, self-control was something she had little of.

Sloane raised her other hand to find the other breast, but one of their phones rang. She broke the kiss. "Damn it."

Finn reached for the buzzing phone on Sloane's desk. After Sloane thumbed it to accept the call, Finn held it near her mouth. "This is Sloane." She forced herself to concentrate on the other end of the call, not the sexy warrior princess on her lap.

"Sloane, this is Todd. I have your DNA results."

All sexual desire suddenly took a backseat. "Todd." Sloane motioned, prompting Finn to dismount. Sloane spun in her chair and faced her desk. "What did you find out?"

"We got nothing on our John Doe but got a lead on Jane Doe. She didn't match anyone in the system, but I got a familial match in CODIS, likely a brother."

"Do you have a name?"

"Bruce Thompson. I'll email you everything I have."

She jotted down the name. "You're the best, Todd. This is what we needed."

"Sloane, I have to warn you. When I ran the familial search, I had to give DOJ the real case number. The match should pop in the SFPD system by tomorrow or the next day at the latest. I'm sorry, Sloane, but I couldn't take a chance on this blowing back on the lab if it went to court."

"I understand, Todd. Avery taught you well." Surprisingly, the memory of Avery came sweetly, without a sense of sadness. Could it be that Sloane had finally let go?

"Yes, she did."

"You've given us another lead and at least another day to investigate. I owe you one."

After wrapping up her call with Todd, she dialed another number. "Eric, DNA is back."

"On my way."

By the time Eric arrived, Sloane had Bruce Thompson's address and phone number in Daly City. A search of the National Crime Information Center data system revealed Thompson had a single arrest for assault with the intent to commit robbery twelve years ago but wasn't convicted. She silently thanked the law that compelled DNA sampling during intakes for all felonies.

"The fact he's been clean since bodes well. He'll likely provide us the information we're looking for," Sloane told Eric. "But according to Todd, we have little time."

"Let's just call." Eric pulled out his cell phone and dialed. A few silent moments passed. "I'm looking for Bruce Thompson …I'm Sergeant Decker of the San Francisco Police Department. I need to ask you some questions."

Several minutes later, with his cell phone cradled between his cheek and shoulder, Eric jotted down some notes. "Thank you,

Mr. Thompson. We'll keep you apprised of our investigation."

He hung up and raised his notes for Sloane and Finn to read: Carli Thompson, junkie missing since 1998. "This is our Jane Doe."

"One down, one to go." Before Finn finished her sentence, Sloane had entered Carli's name and some additional details into NCIC. Seconds later, she had a match.

"Got her." Sloane's pulse buzzed with excitement. This part of police work, the hunt and the puzzle-solving, always energized her and kept her mind sharp, particularly through emotional lows. Every line of information she read on the screen got her one step closer to solving this mystery. "Arrested multiple times in Daly City and San Francisco for possession."

"Pull her arrest records." Eric leaned in, wide-eyed. "She may have been arrested with someone."

A quick glance from Sloane confirmed she and Eric were in sync and alive with anticipation, a feeling she missed. And, if she were honest with herself, one she wanted back. She manipulated the mouse and navigated deeper into her electronic file. "One name pops up: Julie Powers. She was arrested twice with Carli." Sloane clicked several more times and typed in Julie's name. "Got her. Nexis search shows she lives and works in Vacaville."

Sloane and Eric locked gazes with each other, and like old times, simultaneously said, "Road trip."

* * *

Sloane peered at Eric with his right hand on the wheel, concentrating on the road ahead, and then returned to reviewing notes and case documents from the passenger seat. Her silence stemmed from muscle memory, not bad blood. If not for the absence of her Sig Sauer and seven-point gold badge, she would've sworn the clock had turned back to a time before the shooting. To a time before Eric confessed his deep-seated guilt of being responsible for making her an orphan. Like old times, they were on their way to squeeze information out of a witness that could make their case. The familiar feeling made her believe forgiveness could be within reach. Almost, but not entirely.

He parked in the crowded shopping center lot, but not too close to the storefronts, pulling through to the adjoining slot. *Good to see he hasn't changed*, Sloane thought. When they were partners, every choice he made in the field was chosen to give him and Sloane some tactical advantage. *"You never know when you might need to make a quick getaway,"* he once taught her, *"so always park to leave yourself an easy egress."*

Walking through the credit union's front doors gave Sloane hope that Julie Powers's junkie days were a distant past. She glanced at Julie's DMV photo on her phone. The teller standing behind the plexiglass at the furthest end of the service counter dressed smartly in a crisp white blouse matched Julie's medium height, stocky build, and short brown hair. "Over there." Sloane cast her chin in that direction.

Eric acknowledged with a quick nod and lined up behind the last patron waiting for service, earning a raised curious brow from Sloane. "Honey and flies," he winked. Eric was right. The badge he carried could command cooperation in most cases, even with the unwilling, but a bit of politeness, he'd taught her, often went a lot further. A woman like Julie, making every attempt to put a sordid past behind her, deserved such courtesy.

When the line cleared and their target was available, Eric stepped up to the window with Sloane steps behind. He discreetly displayed his badge at the level of the counter. "San Francisco Police, Ms. Powers. We need to talk to you about Carli Thompson."

She froze but not before the blood rushed from her face, leaving her as pale as the white countertop separating her from the public. In that instant, Sloane was sure they were on the right track. The next moment, Julie's hands shook. Her world was crashing. Sloane leaned in and spoke softly, "We don't want to make trouble for you, but we need to ask you a few questions."

Julie cocked her head left and right as if looking for a predator onto her scent. "Not here. I'm due for a break. I'll meet you in the parking lot in ten minutes."

Two doors down, Eric had leaned against an overhang post near a storefront, one leg comfortably crossed in front of the other at the ankle. His relaxed posture meant he was as confident as Sloane was that they'd get what they came for. No words needed exchanging. They were on the verge of a change in their bitter estrangement. Maybe not now, but the possibility was there. For now, or for at least the next fifteen minutes, she would pretend that she was still a cop and that they were still partners.

The credit union glass door swung open, and Julie stepped out, clutching one straight arm with her other hand and holding it close to her body as if it would fall off if she let it go. She was holding on to whatever part of her life that she could. Locking eyes with Sloane, she approached, trembling and in desperate need of a cigarette if she were a smoker.

"Thanks for meeting with us, Ms. Powers." Eric's gentle voice set the tone that their ensuing conversation would be more cordial than confrontational.

"What is this about?"

The next five minutes revealed two things: the name of Julie and Carli's dealer from twenty-two years ago and a healthy dose of regret. The now mother of two had cleaned up her act after her high school best friend went missing. It was the wake-up call she needed. She regretted it didn't come sooner. If it had, Carli, and Bernie by extension, might still be alive.

Sloane took long strides back toward Eric's car, cell phone pressed against her ear. "Julie gave us a name, Finn. She confirmed she and Carli used to meet their dealer at that crack house for a fix. His street name was Hewey."

"That's not much to go on, but I'll run the name." Moments later, Finn said through the phone, "Nothing shows up for Hewey or Hugh during that time frame. Let me call in a favor with Nate Prichard. Maybe that street name will pop in some federal case file."

"Let us know what you find out."

"I should have an answer by the time you two come back."

Sloane ended the call and tapped her phone against the dash. The race against time was catching up to her. She doubted if she could dredge up enough twenty-two-year-old clues before the Homicide Division caught on. The DNA report that Todd ran and the bullet match would soon catch their attention.

"I'm guessing Finn didn't get a hit on the name." Eric's voice contained the same disappointment that was hitting Sloane.

She shook her head. "She's checking with the DEA."

With no other leads to go on, all they could do was return to Bryant and wait. They settled into a comfortable silence again in the thick Bay Area traffic. With no radio or conversation to steer Sloane's thoughts elsewhere, she focused on the awkward rift between them. She hated it, and the reason for it, and until now, had avoided even the thought of forgiving him. How could she when she hadn't forgiven herself?

When they neared the Dam Road exit, Eric flipped on the turn signal and took the off-ramp. He didn't say a word, nothing about a bathroom stop or a fast-food drive-thru. Soon they were on the last road she wanted to be.

"What are you up to, Eric?"

He ignored the question and drove. He crested the El Sobrante hills and began the gradual winding descent to the bottom. She knew what he was doing, but the direction of travel initially confused her. He hadn't taken the route her father did, but the one he must have been on that horrible night.

He rounded a curve. "I've taken this route at least a thousand times since the accident, going over everything I did wrong."

"You don't have to do this, Eric."

"Yes, I do." He didn't take his stare off the road. As the car slowed to about half the speed limit, he gripped the steering wheel until his knuckles turned pale. "Right about here, I took my eyes off the road for two seconds to change the radio station. I was about halfway over the line by the time I looked up and saw headlights."

He slowed the car even more. "If I'd waited another five seconds to fiddle with the radio, I would've been on a straightaway and wouldn't have crossed the line." He pulled the car off to the shoulder, out of the traffic lane. The muscles in his jaw rippled as he pounded the wheel with his right hand. "Five fucking seconds and they would've lived."

A sharp intake of breath steadied Sloane's shaking hands. "It wasn't all your fault."

"Yes, it was. I took my eyes off the road."

Images from that night flashed at blinding speed. Glaring headlights. Jerk of the wheel. Roll of the car. Floating shards of glass. Jolting stop. Bloody arms and faces. Fiery explosion.

Her voice thickened with emotion. "I never told you what happened in the car that night."

He turned his head to face her. His eyes begged for forgiveness.

"I knew my dad was in a foul mood, but I couldn't help myself. I told my mom about the song Finn and I had been practicing for a school concert and she wanted to sing it with me. Our singing must've made him mad because he looked back to yell at me, and that's when he crossed the line."

"That's what you meant the other day when you said we're both to blame? That we both did this." His eyes glistened with tears. "That day at the college career fair when you said your name, I was shaken to my core. Then you said you wanted to be a police officer. I knew right then we were connected for life."

"That's why you requested me as your partner."

His slow nod confirmed what Sloane already knew—Eric was a good man. "I couldn't bring your parents back, but as your partner, I could protect you. I know I created a debt I can never repay."

"But you have. You saved my life at the drug lab explosion, and Reagan's and Finn's at the vineyard."

Several silent moments passed. Eric raised his gaze. "You may not be my partner anymore, but I consider you family, Sloane. I'd like to work on being friends again."

She locked eyes with him. "I'd like that."

Self-blame, rank from two decades of rotting their cores, permeated the air in the car. It was time to start fresh. This was the moment to forgive him and to forgive herself. So she did. She let it all go.

She finally felt free of her past and the guilt that had weighed on her for too long. Though the guilt hadn't been wasted. While it made her hold people at arm's length, it had molded her into the woman she was today, someone who now loved profoundly and could forgive what she previously thought was unforgivable.

Sloane recognized the chime from Eric's phone. The unique tone meant it was an incoming call from Lieutenant West. "You better answer that. When we're in the field, the L-T only calls when it's important."

"We, huh?" Eric's shy grin meant he was hopeful. He swiped the screen of his phone. "Decker...What's this about?...About an hour." Eric slid his phone back into his pocket and let out a breathy sigh. "I have to report in ASAP."

"Did she say why?"

"No."

"Uh-oh." Sloane was sure that their run of remaining one step ahead of the homicide detectives had come to an end.

"Uh-oh is right."

* * *

Steps into the DEA command suite, Finn stopped when a twinge of regret tapped her on the shoulder. For months, she'd missed carrying her gold special agent badge. As a federal agent, her jurisdiction ended at the border, not the city limits like Sloane's. Nothing was beyond her reach, and that badge trumped any local, state, or other federal agency when drugs were involved. She didn't realize until now just how much of a rush that kind of power had on her. Maybe the last two nights with Sloane filled with surging carnal desire had something to do with that.

As she walked down the hallway toward Nate Prichard's outer office, she reminded herself why she gave it up—to protect her loved ones. She stopped at the desk of his secretary. From what she remembered, the clutter on it was very much out of character. Carol's appearance was more haggard than she remembered too. Her bobbed dark hair had more than a few strands out of place, and the deep creases between her brows hadn't been there the last time Finn had seen her.

"Hi, Carol. Is Agent Prichard in?"

Carol looked up from her glowing computer monitor and peered over the reading glasses that were propped low on her nose. "Ms. Harper. It's so good to see you." She stood and gave Finn a hug. "I was delighted when Agent Prichard told me to pencil you in."

"It's good seeing you too. And it's just Finn, please."

"We sure miss you around here, Finn." Carol returned to her seat and ran both hands through her hair. "Okay, I sure miss you."

"That bad?"

"You have no idea. Agent Shipley replaced you, but he's no Special Agent Harper. He writes reports his own way even though Agent Prichard wants them differently. I spend most of my day cleaning up after him. Frankly, he's worse than my kids."

"My father would have a simple solution, but you may not like it."

"I'm open to anything."

"Be passive-aggressive. Give him enough rope to hang himself. Give Shipley exactly what he asks for, nothing less, but more importantly, nothing more. If Shipley doesn't pick it up himself, eventually, Prichard will realize he made a terrible choice."

"You're a genius, Finn." Carol peeked over her shoulder into Prichard's office. "He's ready to see you."

"Thank you, Carol." Finn patted her on the shoulder as she passed.

"If you change your mind, I'll personally walk your reinstatement paperwork through," Carol said before Finn slipped through the doorway.

Her old boss had changed little since her farewell luncheon six months ago unless she considered the extra inch around his waist. He wore the same white business shirt with the sleeves rolled up to the elbows that he always did, topping it off with a black tie hung loosely around his neck. If she had to guess, his hairline had continued its slow retreat.

His office hadn't changed at all. Photos of his family adorned his dark wood desktop and credenza directly behind him. His walls proudly displayed his commendations, degrees, and newspaper clippings detailing his accomplishments. "I love me" walls never impressed Finn, but she had to admit Prichard's was tame compared to some she'd come across during her visits to the DC headquarters.

"Thanks for seeing me, Nate. Mind if I close the door?"

"Sure, Finn. Come in." He beamed as he gestured her over. "I was surprised when you called."

"I'm sorry I haven't called before now, but Sloane and I have been busy getting the firm off the ground."

"Well, you look great. We sure miss you around here."

"Carol said the same thing."

"Shipley hasn't picked things up like you did."

"He better figure it out soon. Carol seems rattled."

"That's just it. I'm not sure he ever will. What can I do to convince you to come back?"

"I don't think that's in the cards, Nate, but thanks for the compliment."

"Well, if you ever change your mind, the job is yours." He gestured toward his guest chair as he returned to his own and scooted his belly up to his desk. "You said it was important."

"It is. I normally wouldn't ask, but this is personal to Sloane." After Finn explained the details, she added, "We're looking for information on a San Francisco drug dealer from 1998 who went by the street name Hewey."

"Why does that name ring a bell? Let me run the alias." He turned in his chair, typed on his computer keyboard, and stared into the monitor. "Several Heweys, but only one in San Francisco in the nineties. Now I remember." He spun his computer flat-screen around so Finn could see. "Jesse Houston, a.k.a., Hewey. He was suspected of the unsolved murder of undercover FBI Agent Jared Walker. He was on the FBI Most Wanted List when I went through the academy at Quantico."

"Interesting. Can you email me everything on that case and Jesse Houston?" Finn asked.

"Happy to if it would help solve the murder of an agent."

First, John Doe, Officer Bernie Sellers, and Carli Thompson. Now, an FBI agent. The bodies were piling up. Finn had a sinking feeling this could get dangerous.

CHAPTER FIFTEEN

Peeling paint and scuff marks had plagued the door leading to the narcotics/vice division locker room since the first day Eric had walked through it seven years ago. Today, he stopped caring. He knew the drill when a cop was suspected of a serious crime, and as those went, murder topped the list. He'd likely not see that peeling paint again nor anything else in this shithole after today.

He retrieved one of the beat-up cardboard boxes from atop the wall of lockers with his right arm and placed it on the wood plank bench that ran parallel. His mind jumped between years of memories of his time as a detective, making it nearly impossible to dial the combination on his lock. It clicked on his fourth try. He pulled on it, and the rickety metal door rattled when he opened it. He visually inventoried the contents, his gaze settling on the bulletproof vest he gave to Quintrell the night of the hostage exchange. The heavy metal plate had been replaced, and the hole in the fabric cover had been sewn over. Placing it on the bench, he ran his left hand over the black cloth, thinking if he'd worn it that night, he'd be whole, Quintrell would be dead, and Finn wouldn't have linked him to the gun.

He shook off his melancholy, stuffed his belongings into a well-worn blue duffel bag, including the combo lock, and shoved the vest back in the locker. After slinging the bag over his right shoulder, he grabbed the box and trudged into the squad room. Surprisingly, his load didn't attract attention.

In the corner, near the seclusion of his desk, he stared out the window for what he assumed would be the last time. To think he opted for this spot because of its unique view of the city and suffered through years of leaks seeping from the toilets on the floor above with the regularity of Old Faithful. He harrumphed; the occasional stench had been worth it.

He shifted his gaze to the empty desk and chair next to his. Lieutenant West had used a budget constraint as her excuse for not filling Sloane's position, but he figured, like him, she was holding out hope Sloane would return. Ironically, even if Sloane did, it was likely now that he wouldn't be there.

He rifled through his drawers, pulling out anything that wasn't SFPD property and placing it into the box. He didn't realize how much crap he'd accumulated since becoming a detective. He swore to himself at his next job he'd become a minimalist.

"Eric."

He recognized Sloane's voice and was buoyed by its supportive tone. He turned toward her. "West didn't have a choice once Homicide Division got wind of the bullet match. She's suspended me."

"I know. I just saw Morgan and gave her your gun. She said the fact you turned it over right away is one thing in your favor. She couldn't say one way or the other, but I could tell she believes you."

"I'm still out of a job for now." He struggled to lift the box, heavier now with his personal things in it.

"Let me get that."

Sloane took the box from his hands, something he wouldn't have allowed without argument before being shot. The old Eric would've juggled that and held the door for Sloane on his way out. Instead, they split the tasks. She carried, and he got the doors. When the elevator door swooshed opened at the lower level, Sloane boosted the box with a knee and stepped toward The Pit.

"I'm not in the mood." Eric aimed himself toward the parking garage.

"Trust me." Sloane continued down the hallway, holding his box hostage. Moments later, she waited at the door to her and Finn's office, casting her chin toward it.

"Damn it, Sloane. I just want to go home." He twisted the knob and pushed the door open.

When she stepped inside, Finn bounced from her chair and cleared an area on a desk. "Did you tell him?"

"Tell me what?" Eric was confused and still unamused.

"She has a name." Sloane's smile said they had a hell of a lead. Hope sparked inside him because he'd be at least one or two steps ahead of Homicide Division.

"What did you find?" he asked Finn.

"Hewey was a drug dealer by the name of Jesse Houston. He was suspected of shooting an undercover FBI agent in 1998 and was on the FBI's Most Wanted List for a few years."

"Looks like he reaped what he sowed," Eric said.

"Two dead cops." Sloane pursed her lips. "Who was the agent?"

Finn checked the notes in her hand. "Jared Walker."

Eric jerked his head back. He'd heard that name a few times in confidence after one too many beers at Eddie's among the camaraderie of fellow cops. He thought he'd never hear it again after Sloane became his partner, but this couldn't be a coincidence.

"Does that name mean something?" Sloane asked him.

"It might be nothing, but my old partner mentioned that name a few times."

"You don't mean Peter Rook?" Sloane's expression soured.

"Afraid so."

"Is this more shorthand?" Finn asked.

"No. Rook is a chauvinistic pig." Sloane sucked in her upper lip.

"Peter was a good cop. He was just old school." Eric bit back the memory when they parted ways, which was less than amicable. First Peter, now Sloane. Maybe Eric wasn't as easy to get along with as he once thought.

"Don't excuse his boorish behavior, Eric," Sloane said.

"He joined the department when women wearing the badge was still an anomaly." Peter's jaded attitude toward women had worsened his last year on the job. It was a good thing he retired when he did. Eric had struggled to brush off Peter's antiquated way of thinking because the two of them had the highest case closure rate in the department. "Peter was pissed that physical standards were lowered so the department could meet the city quota."

"And he let every woman cop he came across know it." Sloane shook her head as if dispelling a bitter taste in her mouth. "He treated Avery like shit."

"I know he could be an ass."

"Could be?" Sloane's voice growled.

"Okay, he *was* an ass, but he was still a good cop."

Eric couldn't knock Sloane's hostile response. She knew the cynical Peter, the one who had spent too many years on the job. Eric knew the Peter that his dad raved about when they were partners and the fun guy who went to baseball games with him when he was a kid and an adult. Most of that bright-eyed exterior had left Peter by the time they partnered up. Eric had chalked it up to twenty-three years on the job. His gut hardened now as he realized that his last hope to clear him and his father lay with an old partner with whom he hadn't seen eye to eye on their last day together.

"Look, Sloane, this may be our one chance. You and I both know he doesn't like women cops. Let me talk to him."

Sloane agreed, following him to his car, loading the box into its trunk, and then retreating to The Pit. Eric remained parked for a while, twisting his fingers around the leather wrap on the steering wheel and recalling how cryptic Peter would get when he drank too much and retold the circumstances of Jared Walker's death. He never talked in detail about the scum who killed him, only about the fallen hero.

Questions swirling in his mind, Eric dialed his cell phone. After several rings, the call connected. "Peter, this is Eric. We need to talk about your brother."

Eric wasn't an outsider, yet he felt out of place sitting on a barstool at Eddie's among the sea of cops. Without a badge and service weapon, he was no longer one of them, and the beer he'd downed failed to soften the sting. Checking his watch, he estimated he'd have less than a half hour to wallow, so he wagged his right hand in the air to catch the bartender's attention.

"Second round?" The handsome, young butch came into view, dressed in Eddie's required all-black employee attire with sleeves rolled to the elbow. Eric was sure her athletic build and fashionable buzz cut made her excellent eye candy for the femmes. *Damn it, Sloane, get out of my head.*

He nodded. "Throw on a whiskey chaser."

Moments later, two glasses, one large, one small, teased him with promises of a temporary diversion. He gripped the shot glass and threw back its amber liquid, savoring the burn as it trailed his throat. He made short work of half the beer, anticipating relief would come soon if he kept up the pace.

"You better slow down, tiger," said a soft voice behind him. Eric turned.

"Kadin Hall." Fueled partly by alcohol, partly by attraction, he drew out her name. Her classy dark business suit and skirt, along with her Hollywood perfect curves, had caught his attention the first time they met. "Can I buy you a drink?" He gestured for another round.

"Why not?" She focused long and hard on the butch. "Sex on the beach."

After the bartender dashed off, Eric lowered and shook his head. "Knew it. Eye candy."

"She's cute." Kadin gave Eric a slow once-over, brushing back her long brown wavy hair as she did. "But I've switched teams until further notice."

"Good to know." Eric tipped his beer toward her, thinking, *possibly*. "What brings you to a cop bar?"

"I needed to corner one of my clients for a signature." In one alluring move, she mounted the neighboring barstool, crossing her legs at the knee. A very sexy knee at that. "He was having drinks with his brother."

"Which one?" She pointed toward a young uniformed officer and a tall, brawny man a few tables over. "Must be a rookie. Never seen him before."

"Tell me, Decker. Why are you drinking alone? Sorrows to drown?"

"Waiting for an old friend, but yes, plenty of sorrows to wash away."

"Don't tell me. These sorrows go by the name Manhattan Sloane."

"Not this time, but she hastened my misfortunes."

"She tends to be at the center or on the periphery of our respective troubles."

"I'm living proof." He raised his third round and tilted it toward Kadin's glass.

"This has the makings of a pathetic club." Kadin took a long sip of her drink. "We should hold weekly meetings after work."

A week ago, he would've been president of that club. But today he hoped to permanently terminate his membership. "That's if I still have a job." He opened his suit coat flap, displaying the vacant spot where he used to clip his badge. "I've been suspended."

"Sorry to hear that. My firm takes on labor disputes." She pulled a business card from the purse she'd rested atop the bar and scribbled something on the blank side. She traced a fingertip across the back of his hand when she handed it to him. "Call me if you need a lawyer or if it's time for another meeting."

A dark figure claimed the stool next to Kadin and leaned into the bar. "Shot and a beer," the raspy male voice ordered, catching Eric's attention.

"You have no idea how much I hate cutting this short, but my friend is here."

"Call me." She slung the purse over her shoulder, stood, and then twice tapped an index finger on the business card before grabbing her drink and walking away.

Eric gave his friend a death stare. "You have the worst timing, Peter."

"Who's the ten, Junior?" Peter Rook slid over one more stool next to Eric, repeatedly coughing into the back of his hand.

"Lawyer."

Peter leaned back and leered at Kadin's disappearing frame. "Nice rebuttal."

"Still as crude as ever."

The four years since their parting hadn't treated Peter well. The deep lines along his cheeks and brow made him appear much older than fifty-five. What little hair was left had turned gray, and the bloodshot eyes reflected a troubled life.

"I hear you're an investigator for the Medical Examiner."

Peter downed his shot of whiskey. "You didn't ask me here to shoot the breeze about my job working with stiffs."

"No, I didn't." That last day with Peter hadn't exactly been a warm send-off, but it was what Eric's old partner deserved. Apparently, he still held a grudge.

"Then why am I here?" Peter drank half of his beer.

"When we were partners—"

"Partners have each other's backs like your old man did." Peter's jaw tensed, signaling that his bitterness was as strong as ever. "We were never really partners."

"We were until you went too far."

"I was trying to save your ass." Peter coughed when his voice turned sharp.

"My ass didn't need saving. It was a good shoot. I wasn't about to plant evidence."

"I was trying to save you from the lengthy Internal Affairs investigation that could've gone either way because of that IA bitch."

As every vein in Eric's neck fired like pistons, the sour taste of their turbulent past bubbled up his throat. The last thing he wanted tonight was a rehashing of their falling out, especially when he was three rounds in. "Look, Peter, I need to talk to you about your half-brother."

"What about Jared?"

"You never talked about the guy who killed him."

"That's what's been bugging you? You force me to retire and wait four years to ask why I never dwelled on the ·dirtbag who put a slug into the back of my brother's skull?"

The muscles in Eric's jaw strained. The only reason he gave Peter the option of retiring instead of facing an Internal Affairs investigation of his own was because of his dead FBI brother. "I'm asking because the guy suspected of killing him is dead from a bullet to the back of the head that came from my backup gun."

Peter cocked his eyebrow before raising his second glass of smelly concoction. "Good. I appreciate the swift justice."

"Aren't you curious about how it happened?"

"He's dead. Why would I care?" Peter waved at the butch for another round—whiskey solo.

"Because I didn't put that bullet there, and neither did my dad. Whoever shot him did it in 1998."

Eric had all but forgotten the depth of Peter's indifference. The mark of a good detective was to remain detached, but Peter took it to an extreme. He never showed one ounce of regret over using high-handed tactics, nor any sympathy over a death. He almost seemed immune to it.

"Wasn't your backup a present from your old man? I guess I have him to thank."

"He had no reason to kill Hewey, but you did."

"What are you suggesting?" Aged and worn, Peter's face was unreadable. It was a handy trait when he had to bluff his way through an interrogation, but right now, it made it impossible to infer a damn thing. *What are you thinking, Peter?*

"I'm suggesting you know something."

"If I did, what would it matter? He deserved what he got. I'm glad he's dead."

Eric's patience gave in to his anger. He slammed his fist on the bar with a loud thud. "Damn it, Peter. My father is implicated in this. He was your partner for six years. Don't you care what happens to him?"

"He was a lot better partner than you ever were." Peter downed the whiskey and lazily wiped his mouth with a coat sleeve. "But what's done is done. You need to give this up."

Eric's stomach twisted, a knife of doubt slicing its way through layer after layer of flesh. *Dad swore he wasn't involved. Was he covering for Peter? For both of them?* "Even if I walk away from this, Sloane won't."

"What does the broad have to do with it? I thought I read she quit like all the cunt cops do."

"You need to stop while you're behind. If you weren't old—"

"You'd what?

Eric had enough. Nothing had changed, and he'd get nothing from him. He stood from his barstool and turned to walk away.

"You've been hanging around those cunts for too long. You've turned into a pussy."

That was it. Old or not, that was the last straw. Eric cocked back his right arm and let it rip toward his target. The cracking sound of bone on cartilage meant he landed a direct hit on the bridge of that asshole's nose.

Peter rocked backward and stumbled off his stool to the dirty, beer-stained wood-laminate floor. He groaned, blood trickling from his nostrils.

Eric towered over him, thinking he deserved a lot more than one good shot. Two cops at the neighboring stools jumped in and pulled him back by the arms. He grimaced when one tugged too hard on his waste of a limb.

"You're already suspended, Decker," one said. "Don't make it worse."

"I'm good, fellas. He's not worth it."

When two other nearby cops lifted Peter from the floor, he pressed a thumb and index finger against his bruised beak. "Sounds like your world is crashing down around you. Now you know what it feels like."

"You just can't let that go, can you?" Peter was pushing him to his limits. Eric clenched his fist, preparing to pelt him between the eyes again. "I did what I thought was right."

"I thought you knew the difference between law and justice, but I was wrong."

"I did and still do. I just never bought into your brand of it."

Eric almost laughed at himself. The quality he came to loathe in Peter Rook was the very quality he loved in Sloane. The difference between the two was that Sloane knew where to draw the line.

"My brand of justice is swift." Peter's eyes narrowed into a frosty stare, sending chills down Eric's spine.

* * *

Peter fumbled with his car keys as he shuffled down the sidewalk toward his beat-up, fifteen-year-old domestic sedan, parked several blocks from Eddie's. The bleeding from his nose had stopped, but it was throbbing from the thumping Eric gave him minutes ago. Hell, his entire face felt like a Mack truck hit him head on, backed up, and rolled over him for good measure.

Sliding into the front seat, he inspected Eric's handiwork in the rearview mirror. Red, swollen, and misshapen, his nose was definitely broken. He didn't need to touch it to know it hurt. "You always packed one hell of a punch, Junior. Too bad you were such a boy scout."

He pulled out a flip phone, grumbling about the past finally catching up with him. The full year hadn't passed since the last time he dialed this number, their agreed-upon check-in date. He thumbed to the contacts list and brought up the only number saved. It was marked "Insurance Policy." He pressed Send and let it ring three times before hanging up. Their signal that something was amiss.

He waited.

Within five minutes, his phone rang. He pressed the green button and pulled it up to his ear and mouth.

"Why are you calling? It isn't time." The male voice on the other end remained steady and didn't reflect the degree of concern he'd expected.

"We have a problem." For twenty-two years, they had been in a quagmire. Their once-a-year phone call on the anniversary of the day they crossed the forbidden line reminded one another they were in this together until one of them died. After Eric's prying questions, Peter knew deep down those check-in days were over.

"What kind of problem?" The voice slowed, apparently coming to the same conclusion.

"The kind that could get both of us a death sentence. I was questioned about my brother today."

"By whom?"

"Junior." Peter inspected his throbbing nose once more in the rearview mirror, regretting his choice of diversion to stop Eric's grilling.

"What does he know?"

"He knows where the bullet came from and that John Doe is Hewey. I thought you took care of that."

"I could only do so much." The voice remained strangely calm. "Did he say how he found out?"

"No." The silence on the other end was smothering. The name Hewey linked back to only Peter, and he figured he had a few days before the walls closed in on him. "Do I have to remind you about my insurance policy?" Peter asked.

"No, you don't. Nor should I have to remind you about mine." That bullet was Peter's ticket to the death chamber. "Junior came to you. You need to take care of it."

"What do you mean?"

"You've already killed once. You need to do it again unless you want to be strapped to a table and injected with a lethal dose."

Peter's stomach soured. Accidental or not, capping Hewey after what he did to his half-brother still felt right. Hewey was a dirtbag, and the world was better off without him. But killing Junior was a whole different kind of wrong. Killing a cop to save his own ass was a line he never fathomed facing. "I won't kill a cop."

"You already have."

"That part was all you. I had nothing to do with that."

"You know the law, Peter. It doesn't matter if you started that fire or not. It was a continuation of the original crime. All those bodies are on both of us."

Peter gritted his teeth so hard that Junior's handiwork bled down his lips. He'd had enough of this.

"You need to eliminate the threat, Peter. For both our sakes. If you don't, I will."

Fuck. Fuck. Fuck. Why did Junior have to dredge this up now? His only hope was to talk some sense into him. "I'll handle it."

* * *

Not since he had been shot had something like this crossed Eric's mind. The recovery, followed by the certainty of a lifelong handicap, had drained everything out of him. But tonight, his suspension and the dust-up with Peter had his dander up and, along with it, new vitality.

He considered calling but estimated a bottle of red would be more enticing. After knocking, he leaned against the doorframe, still feeling the effects of the whiskey shot he downed after Peter left.

This is nuts, he thought, and considered turning tail. When he pushed himself off the frame, the door cracked open. Thankfully, the situation didn't call for a smile. He couldn't manage one if it did. He was too busy admiring all the right curves in all the right places. "You said to call."

"And you thought what?" Kadin turned up the corners of her mouth as she rested an arm high on the doorframe, accentuating her trim, five-foot-eight body. "This would save some time?"

"I've never been one to waste time." He raised the wine bottle in his right hand.

"A 2015 Saint-Emilion. Interesting choice."

"How so?"

"Not your bottom-basement Bordeaux, but not the kind behind lock and key either." She gave him another glance from head to toe. "You figure it would be enough to impress, but not too expensive in case your boldness was for naught."

Her teasing was a good sign, so he raised the bottle higher. "Well?"

She pushed the door open wide. Eric walked through.

Half an hour later—the bottle three-quarters empty, two half-full glasses on the coffee table, and clothes forming a trail to the bedroom—he confirmed his choice of wine had sent the right message. With limited mobility in his left arm but the rest of him working as advertised, he hadn't quite thought through how to make this a mutually pleasurable experience. Kadin, luckily, had some ideas of her own. She soon lay skin to skin with him, an arm and leg draped over his prone body, both their chests still heaving for more air.

Between ragged breaths, she forced out, "How are you still on the market?"

"I always considered myself as the B&B type—overnighters and long weekends." He slung his right hand under his head, palm up and elbow bent.

She rolled on top, her hard nipples dragging against the fine hairs of his chest. "With amenities like yours, you should be booked up for years."

"Not anymore." The stiffness in his left shoulder reminded him he'd never be the lover nor the cop he once was. He twitched it to shake off its bite.

She kissed the dimpled quarter-size scar he despised. "Does it hurt much?" she asked.

"Some days." Actually, most days, but he'd never let on, especially not to the department doctor who had signed off on his return to desk duty. How ironic a hole so small could wreak so much damage. "But that's the least of my problems."

Kadin slid back to the mattress, this time flat with her left arm positioned similar to Eric's under her head. "What's going on? Why were you suspended?"

His eyes focused on the white ceiling with its mounted fan and lumbering blades pushing air down as he mulled over how to condense today. "Half of it, I can't figure out. The other half? I fucked up helping Sloane."

"Why is she always involved?"

Kadin pulled her legs up, knees bent with her feet flat on the bed. Her right leg lazily fell to Eric's midsection. Under any other circumstance, that would've posed an arousing tease, but the alcohol had finally taken its toll. A second round wasn't in the cards at the moment.

"She's the least of my problems."

"Sounds like you need a lawyer."

"Are you offering?"

She rotated to her right side and rested her head in her palm, arm bent at the elbow. "Yes."

He cocked his neck to meet her gaze. "If it comes down to it, you'll be the first one I call."

"Good."

She rolled to her other side. Eric scooted his body close, drawing the covers over them as he did. Tucking his useless left arm and hand around his belly, he draped his other arm over Kadin's waist and pulled her closer. Thoughts of Peter Rook made sleep elusive, but when he sensed Kadin's breathing soften and felt her limbs go limp, he let go of his anger, if only for tonight.

Sometime later, Eric's eyes fluttered open to the darkness, the image of Peter and his cold eyes still burning in his mind. Motion on the bed nudged him awake further. Then in an instant, a dull throb in his arm, the side he'd been sleeping on, forced him to shift and roll to his back. A pained groan escaped his lips.

"Hangover?" Kadin's groggy voice competed with the whoosh of ceiling fan blades.

"Shoulder."

She rolled to one side, facing him. "Can I get you anything for the pain?"

"I'll be fine." His vision adjusted, the swell of a breast coming into view. He ran a hand up the curve of a toned leg after Kadin slung it over his thigh.

Maybe it was his sigh or distant tone that prompted Kadin to ask, "This suspension really has you worried, doesn't it?"

"It does, but..." He trailed off.

"But what?"

"Something Peter said."

"Was Peter the friend you were meeting last night?"

"Yeah. He said something about what's done is done."

"What do you think he meant?"

"I'm not sure, but I'm going to find out."

CHAPTER SIXTEEN

If Eric had his way, he'd still be in bed with Kadin, enjoying her long, wavy brunette hair and even longer, angular legs, but she had to work. It was odd being kicked out of her bed when he had no schedule to keep and no workplace to hurry off to, but memories of the previous night soothed the mild hangover during his early morning drive of shame home.

He'd forgotten how much he missed skin-to-skin contact with a woman. Quick hookups had become his go-to for as far back as he cared to remember, but last night was different. It marked the first time he'd had sex since the shooting. His injury had wholly altered the experience, forcing him to focus on Kadin's needs, not only his.

How pathetic. It took being partially handicapped for me to become a more thoughtful lover.

Parking his car in the only available slot at his apartment complex, Eric dragged his exhausted body across the lot in the moist, chilly morning air. He grumbled at the weeds growing tall and wild, just like, well, weeds. The apartment manager was skilled at reminding him when he was a day late with the rent, but not so good at keeping the property presentable.

He cursed himself for taking care of Kadin's needs for a second and third time and not getting enough sleep. There was no way he could meet up with Sloane and Finn for breakfast and provide them an update on last night's meeting with Peter. He stopped in the parking lot long enough to text Sloane. *Late night. Won't make breakfast. Meet for a late lunch. You pick where.* He considered the early hour and didn't wait for a reply.

Ascending the exterior concrete steps to the second floor, he turned toward his apartment door but stopped after a single stride. A man in casual dress, not street garb, had taken a comfortable position leaning against his door and was inhaling long drags from a cigarette.

Peter.

Was he here to get in a good lick or to come clean about Hewey and the bullet? Eric wasn't in the mood for either but braced himself for both options. He resumed walking, balled his right hand into a fist, and prepared mentally to question everything Peter might say.

Peter dropped the cigarette to the ground, put it out with his shoe's sole, and pushed himself from the door. When Eric closed the distance, Peter coughed into a jittery hand. "We need to talk."

The morning light was soft but strong enough for Eric to see the results of last night's lucky punch. He snickered. Peter would have a shiner for a week or two. "You look like shit."

"You're not looking so rosy yourself."

"Yeah, well, life's a bitch." In the old days, Eric would've commented on his recent conquest over the "ten" as Peter had rated Kadin. Such crass talk would've earned him a slap on the back and a command that he was buying the next round. Times had changed, though, and so had Eric. Sloane saw to that, and he liked the man he'd become. There would be no more bragging about last night and this morning, only silent crowing with a satisfied grin.

Eric jabbed his key into the keyhole. "Come in, Peter. I'll make us a pot of coffee."

"Coffee sounds good." Another cough.

Steps inside, Eric tossed his keys on a pressed blond wood coffee table and made a straight line for the kitchen. He dumped the quarter pot of day-old coffee into the sink and gave the carafe a good rinse before filling it up with fresh water. Minutes later, he had two steaming cups of brown liquid that could pass for coffee.

"You'll have to settle for black. I'm out of everything."

"You *have* changed." Peter accepted a mug. "You always had your shit together."

"Like I said, life's a bitch." Ever since his injury, Eric had let many things drop by the wayside. House cleaning and stocking the fridge were the first to go.

After taking a seat on the couch, Peter cast his chin toward Eric's injured side. "What happened to the arm?"

"Took a bullet. Tore up the muscle and ligaments."

"During that hostage rescue that I read about?"

"Yeah." Eric sat in his recliner. He wanted to forget everything about that night, but the ache and limited mobility of his arm served as its constant reminder. "Why are you here, Peter?"

"We got off on the wrong foot last night. I know you're worried about your old man, and I made things worse."

"You were an ass, but what else is new?"

"I wasn't always an ass." Peter bowed his head in an unconvincing show of contrition. "I'd like to bury the hatchet."

Three years as Peter's partner made it easy for Eric to recognize his tells. Hand movement meant he was nervous, but his twitching right eye said much more. He was desperate, not sorry. Peter never wanted to bury the hatchet with anyone, even if he was clearly in the wrong like now.

"Look, Peter." Eric softened his expression to put his old partner at ease. "I never had it out for you. Planting drop guns on a perp may have worked in the old days, but—"

"It was good enough for your old man."

"Are you saying he was involved in a bad shoot?"

"I'm saying he knew when the law wasn't enough to get justice."

What the hell is Peter implying? Was Dad involved in the murder of a cop, or is Peter trying to make me think he was?

"Spit it out, Peter."

"Tell me this, Junior. Cops gossip. Word has it you're tight with Manhattan Sloane. I wouldn't be surprised if you're in love with her. How far did you go to protect her? Far enough to catch a bullet?"

Of course, he loved Sloane but not in the way Peter thought. Eric owed Sloane happiness in whatever shape she needed it. "What are you driving at?"

"I'm trying to make you understand that sometimes we go too far for the ones we love." Sweat beads had formed and were trickling down the sides of Peter's face. He was on the edge of confessing something and needed one last push.

"Is that what you did? Did you go too far?"

"We were supposed to beat Hewey to an inch of his life, but something in me snapped when he said my brother cried like a baby begging for his life. He executed my brother, so I executed him." The muscles in Peter's face turned taut. Experience told Eric his nervousness had turned into anger. "He killed a federal agent gangland-style for God's sake."

"Who's we? You said we."

"Does it matter? Hewey got justice."

"If it were only Hewey, I could turn the other way, but two others, including a good cop, died in a fire *you* set to cover up what *you* did." Peter's chest heaved into a roaring coughing spell, so hard Eric thought he was having some sort of attack when his face turned beet-red. "Are you okay?"

Peter sprang from the couch. His voice croaked, "Damn summer colds are the worst. Where's your bathroom?"

Eric pointed with his right arm toward the short, narrow hallway. "On the left."

Peter staggered down the hallway. The noose was closing around his neck; it was only a matter of time before it choked the life out of him. Shutting the bathroom door, he hobbled to the counter and fumbled with the faucet until water gushed out.

He couldn't splash his face fast enough to soothe the burn of what Eric had said.

He stared into the mirror, face dripping and shirt and jacket soaked along the front, cursing the haggard man he had become. Palms gripping the edges of the vanity, he held back the coffee that threatened to make a reappearance.

"You did this, Carter. It was only supposed to be Hewey."

He'd never wrapped his head around the consequences of a crime he committed. Sure, he cut corners and didn't give a rat's ass about perps, but a cop? The fact he was the reason a fellow police officer was dead had twisted his life into knots for decades. Every cop in the state would want his head on a pike. No wonder Eric and Sloane were acting like a bloodhound onto a scent.

"They'll never give this up."

Carter was right. He'd be labeled a cop killer. Peter had no proof he wasn't the one who set that fire, but that didn't matter. The coverup was a continuation of Hewey's murder. He was as guilty as Carter. How ironic. His dark past had caught up with him three weeks after the doctor said he had but six months to live. Fuck lung cancer. He wasn't about to spend what little time he had left in a ten-by-seven-foot cell. He needed to do what Carter had demanded—control the outcome by getting Eric on his side or wrapping up loose ends.

Peter reached into his damp coat pocket and pulled out a small unmarked, sealed evidence bag containing his insurance policy—the only thing that could prove he wasn't alone when he killed Hewey. It was no longer safe to keep it with him. He needed to stash it in the last place Carter would look.

He searched the bathroom for a not-so-obvious, yet not-hard-to-find hiding place. The toilet tank was out of the question. That's the first place detectives look, not to mention the risk it posed of water washing away the DNA evidence it contained. He hadn't held onto this damn thing for twenty-two years just to fuck it up now.

The tissue box atop the tank caught his eye. He pulled out several sheets, dropped the bag inside, and then returned the tissues, fluffing them to their original state. If anything happened to him, Eric would eventually find it and know what to do with it.

"You can do this." Peter gave himself a weak, if not essential, pep talk in the mirror. He squared his sagging shoulders, sucked in his middle-aged gut, and retraced his steps to the living room.

"Feeling better?" Eric asked.

Peter nodded. "Junior—"

"I hate it when you call me that. Call me Eric."

"I've been calling you Junior since you were eight." Peter retook his seat on the couch. "Hell, you look so much like your father when he was your age, I needed something to separate you two."

"Whatever."

"Look, Eric. I admit I killed Hewey because he deserved it. I need to know. How did you piece it together?"

"Like you taught me. Through good old-fashioned detective work. Sloane and I sifted through the evidence and figured out that new technology could help us find more leads. Modern DNA testing led us to the woman."

How ironic—teaching Junior everything he knew would be his downfall. "And from there you tracked down known associates and got another name. Does anyone else know?"

Eric shook his head side to side. "We've been working this off-book. Now, I need to know. How did you swap the bullets?"

"You know how your dad was at the firing range, always collecting his spent brass and bullets from the catch bin for his art projects."

"He's an artist." Eric cast his chin toward his big-screen TV and the one reminder that he had a life outside of the job and Sloane. "That wall clock is one of his. He's so proud that every piece is made from bullets he shot."

"That's how I knew where to get a bullet of the same caliber to substitute."

"So you tampered with the evidence."

"Not directly. My partner. After we disposed of the body, he said he could substitute the bullet and needed one of the same caliber that wouldn't point back to either of us." Peter sighed. Besides a dead cop, framing Eric Senior—a good man, just like his son—was his only other regret. "So I gave him one."

"You were my dad's partner for six years." Eric clenched his right fist but didn't make a move to throw it at him. This boy scout had twice the self-control Peter had ever dreamed of having. "How could you implicate him in a murder you committed?"

"I had two hours to make it happen, and your dad was convenient. I'm sorry about that."

"But not about the woman and cop who lost their lives."

"That wasn't me. I had nothing to do with that fire."

"Who then?"

Peter coughed hard enough that he thought he'd lose a lung. *Cancer is a bitch*, he thought. The look of concern on Eric's face might be the break he needed. It was time to put all his cards on the table. "Look, Eric. Doctors say I have a few months left. I won't spend the time I have left in a courtroom or jail cell. If I give you his name, I need you to back off until I kick the bucket to go after him."

"My dad always said you were his best partner. You always had his back and made sure he never had to use his gun in the line of duty. He told me I couldn't have drawn a better partner when the brass paired us." Peter sensed that Eric was caving. Despite the horrible thing he had done and the shell of a man he'd become, Eric still had a soft spot for him.

"Maybe killing Hewey changed you, but I never saw the man my father did." Eric's eyes softened, but when he shook his head, Peter's hope sank. "I can't do what you're asking."

"Same old boy scout." Peter lamented the corner he'd painted himself into and the fact that Carter was right. If he had any hope of avoiding a prison cell for what little time he had left, he had to clean up this mess. He stood, nudged his jacket upward on his right side, and pulled a Beretta from his hip holster—the same gun he used to kill Hewey. He'd thought about tossing it into the bay over the years, but it had become a symbol. It represented the best and worst things he'd ever done.

Now he'd stoop even lower. He pointed it at Eric. "You still packing cuffs?"

"What do you think you're doing, Peter?"

"What I have to." He waved the muzzle toward Eric.

"You're fucking crazy." Eric reached around to his back and pulled out a pair of chrome-plated Smith & Wesson handcuffs.

"Put them on." Peter brought both of his hands together on the grip of the Beretta.

"This will never work." Eric slapped one cuff over his left wrist and tightened it. Then maneuvered to do the same to his right.

"Unh unh. Hands behind your back."

Eric dangled his left arm behind his back as far as it would stretch. After considerable grimacing and body contortions, Peter heard the click of the second cuff.

"Show me." Eric twisted at the waist and displayed his perfectly cuffed hands. "We're going for a little ride." Peter snatched up Eric's car keys from the table and marched him out the door, one hand on the back of his jacket collar and his Beretta to a kidney with the other.

When they reached the exterior stairs, Peter shoved the muzzle hard against Eric's back. "You and I both know I have nothing to lose, so don't try anything." He coughed several times before Eric safely descended the concrete stairs.

He steered Eric toward the weed-laden parking lot at the rear of the building, shielded from the already busy street at the front. Peter pressed the lock button on Eric's key fob. At the far corner, parking lights flashed.

Navigating through the aisles of parked SUVs, sedans, and the occasional motorcycle, Peter popped the trunk. Besides an emergency kit, a roll of tape, jumper cables, and bottled water, it was relatively empty. "Get in."

"You've got to be kidding."

"Do I look like I am?" Peter patted Eric's jacket pockets and pulled out his cell phone. *This is gonna be easier than I thought.*

Eric muttered one foul word after another while he crammed himself inside, facing the opening.

Peter held out Eric's phone. "Unlock it."

Eric shifted his shoulder. "I can't, dumbass."

"Rollover."

"Damn it, Peter. I'm too big for this shit."

Peter pressed the tip of the gun against Eric's leg. "Perhaps I didn't make myself clear. Roll the fuck over."

After copious amounts of swearing, Eric rolled inches at a time. On his final shift, Peter maneuvered the phone until Eric's right thumb grazed the home button and unlocked the phone. "Thanks, Junior." Peter cocked his arm and whacked Eric on the skull. His body slumped and stopped moving. "Sorry, but I'm not taking any chances."

Surprisingly, Peter wasn't anxious. He'd gotten all of that out of the way in the bathroom. He wasn't looking forward to what he had to do next, but he was out of options.

After taping Eric's ankles together with duct tape, he slammed the trunk shut, slid into the driver's seat, and inspected the phone—not one application beyond the standard crap that came with it. "Glad to see I'm not the only one who hasn't fallen into the social media trap."

He opened the messaging app. As expected, the number of text strings didn't fill the page. Eric had always lived a solitary life, he thought. The top string was between him and Sloane with the last message reading: *If you change your mind, will be at Sally's with Finn.*

Peter threw the phone on the passenger seat. "Now, to take care of business."

CHAPTER SEVENTEEN

Sloane slowed her stride as she read Eric's text, shivering at the unexpected sense of disappointment she felt. Nearing the main entrance of Sally's, she repocketed her cell phone. She told herself it had nothing to do with him. That she was just eager to hear what connection Peter Rook had to the dead FBI agent. Deep down, though, she knew there was more to her melancholy. Working with Eric these last few days had made her nostalgic for the time before their rift.

She held the door open for Finn. "Eric's not coming. He'll meet us for lunch later."

"It's probably a good thing, since Morgan suspended him," Finn said.

"You're right. He took it hard."

They stepped inside. Morning at the popular café meant crowds. Crowds at the counter for the solos. Crowds along the walls for the couples. And crowds in the center of the restaurant for friends. Despite the early hours and the accompanying morning chill, wall-mounted fans churned at their full measure from all four corners. Their rattling, however, wasn't enough to overpower the crowd's din.

Familiar with Sally's layout, Sloane placed a hand on the small of Finn's back while she scanned the center of the room. She applied slight pressure when she spotted their party. "Right center, Finn."

Finn shifted her gaze. "Got 'em."

They waded through the rows of tables, squeezing past pushed-out chairs and bypassing servers and bussers as they zipped by.

"Morgan. Kyler. So glad you suggested breakfast today." Sloane pulled out Finn's chair, a habit she'd fallen into since they moved in together. The courtesy was never discussed, simply practiced and received with the care intended.

"We figured with our busy schedules that this would work better than lunch." Morgan closed the laminated menu and returned it to the table. "I know we said breakfast, but I think I'm going for coffee and a slice of pecan. Last time I was here, Nate Prichard devoured mine."

"He never passes up dessert." Finn smirked as she slung her purse over a chair. "I think I'll follow your lead, Morgan. Pie sounds perfect."

Kyler picked up Morgan's left hand and kissed it. "She has great ideas, which is why I asked her to marry me."

Finn's mouth fell open. "That's wonderful news."

"Yes, wonderful." Sloane glanced at Finn, recalling how hollow she'd felt when she thought she'd lost her to Kadin. Maybe Kyler had the right idea—put a ring on the woman she loved before she slipped away.

Rita, a full-bodied brunette, took their orders—four coffees and as many slices of pecan. "Whoever said you can't have pie for breakfast needs to be shot."

"I can help with that." Morgan pushed back the flap of her suit blazer, exposing her badge and the service weapon clipped to her belt. She ended her display with a playful wink. Morgan was polite and professional in the squad room, but Sloane was tickled to see this lighthearted side.

"Another lovely lady in blue." Rita glanced between Sloane and Morgan.

"I'm a civilian now, Rita." Sloane kissed the back of Finn's hand. "And enjoying every minute."

"After that ordeal several months ago, you've earned it, Sloane." Rita slipped her order pad inside her decorated, colorful apron. "Four slices of pecan coming up."

Once Rita sped off, Kyler released Morgan's hand and pulled several documents from a leather satchel she'd rested against her chair. She laid them on the table for Sloane and Finn to read. "You asked me to do a little digging, so I dug."

Kyler's confident expression boded well. Sloane scanned the computer printouts listing various criminal cases, numbering in the hundreds. "What are we looking at?"

"The first set is a list of prosecution declinations grouped by Assistant District Attorney for the last two years, including Nicci Cole's last year as an ADA."

The list was long, summarizing the crime, defendant's name, defense lawyer, and reason for declining. Most of the offenses involved drug possession, prostitution, possession of illegal firearms, and gambling—all considered victimless crimes. Nothing on the list stood out on the cursory scan; each ADA had racked up similar numbers of declinations.

Kyler pointed at the next set of documents. "The second set is a list of prosecution declinations grouped by crime during the same time frame."

A picture formed. Under each type of crime, each ADA declined approximately the same amount of crimes—except for two. Under gambling and sex trafficking, Nicci Cole lay claim to the lion's share.

"The third set is Nicci Cole's declinations, including those in which she overrode the ADA when she was the DA. I've marked what's key." Kyler had highlighted the defense lawyer for each gambling and sex trafficking declination, along with several of the drug and prostitution cases. There were a few names in common.

"What's the trend here?" Sloane asked.

"They are all from the same law firm, Colby and Jones." Kyler leaned back in her chair, folding her arms triumphantly across her chest.

"And the importance of that firm?" Sloane sensed bringing in Kyler was about to bear fruit.

Kyler's smile provided enough energy to power every oscillating fan in the joint. "Drum roll, please. That law firm was Nicci Cole's largest political donor for her mayoral campaign."

"You're thinking payoff," Finn said, voicing the conclusion any sane person would come to.

"Exactly." Kyler nodded toward the papers. "If you look at the fourth set, you'll see about ninety percent of the declinations represented by that law firm were from then-ADA and DA Cole."

"That's no coincidence." Sloane smelled a five-foot-three-inch rat by the name of Nicci Cole. How far back did this connection go? How much money had exchanged hands? More importantly, what did Colby and Jones now expect in return?

"That's what I thought." Morgan gave Kyler's hand a gentle squeeze and then released it. "She should've been an investigator."

"I'm just a paper detective. I'll leave the real sleuthing to the professionals." Kyler rubbed Morgan's arm, the kind of tender touch that spoke to genuine love.

"This may not be enough to convince the mayor to back off her plan to dismantle the PD, but it's a great start." Delighted with Morgan and Kyler's public affection, Sloane stretched her arm over the back of Finn's chair and whispered in her ear. "These two are so cute together."

Finn grinned and mouthed, "I know."

The smiles coming from Finn and the others swept Sloane up like a whirlwind. This female friendship thing had become more than a novelty. She'd assumed the energy between the four of them at The Tap the other night was an anomaly, but it was even more potent this morning. Sloane silently declared Eric's no-show a good thing. She wasn't ready to resume socializing with him, and the invasion of a male fifth-wheel would've tinkered with the group dynamics.

Sloane let a smile form when she focused on Morgan and Kyler's matching white gold engagement rings. They featured rainbow sapphires and gemstones on either side of a single diamond. Simple yet elegant, they simultaneously displayed their gay pride and love for one another. How different they were from the vintage engagement ring, a single diamond flanked by two white gold infinity symbols, she'd given Avery. She glanced at Finn. *What type of ring would you like? Silver, maybe. You love silver.*

After devouring Sally's best pie, Kyler dabbed her mouth on each side with a cheap paper napkin. "I hate to cut this short, ladies, but I still have to prep for court this afternoon."

Morgan eyed the check Rita had dropped off and threw enough cash on the table to cover it plus tip. "We got this one."

Everyone collected their things and pushed back their chairs to stand. Sloane slung her jacket over her shoulders and stabbed both arms into the sleeves. "We should make breakfast a regular thing."

"You mean on top of monthly dinners?" Finn asked as she hooked her purse over a shoulder. Sloane glimpsed Finn's bare ring finger and thought again that she'd have to remedy that sooner rather than later.

"Yes, I think we should." Morgan set soft eyes on Sloane. "I miss seeing you both. Breakfast and dinner once a month sound perfect."

"Then it's settled." Sloane was pleased with the extra twinkle she had put in Morgan's eyes, and hoped they would follow through. She had never experienced the power of female friendship, and now she understood why so many women craved it. It was healing, comforting, and encouraging—the type of bond she didn't realize until now that she had missed all her life.

The crowd had thinned, making their exit less zigzaggy than their entrance. When they were halfway to the main door, Rita waved an arm at the group. "Thanks, ladies. See ya next time."

"Next time." Sloane waved back, her response more promise than nicety. For two-and-a-half years, she'd come here off and on with Eric until their falling out, and Rita had served them more times than not. Starting a new tradition with Finn and her new gal pals felt right.

At the door, Sloane held it open for the others to go through. Morgan and Kyler went first, holding hands, both with an extra pep in their step. Before Finn slid past the threshold, she gave Sloane a kiss on the cheek. "You look happy."

"I am. I have you, wonderful friends…" Sloane glanced at Morgan as she whispered something into Kyler's ear, eliciting a giggle, "…an amazing daughter, and a great new career. What more could I ask for?"

When they reached the sidewalk, Finn slid an arm around Sloane's waist and drew her in close. "Forgiving Eric comes to mind."

"I'm working on it." Sloane's emotional buzz from breakfast lost much of its intensity. She'd spent six months thinking the worst of Eric, thinking that he'd been a coward and fled the scene of her parents' accident. But she had learned yesterday that he hadn't. She believed him when he said he didn't know what he'd caused at the time and had dedicated his life to making up for it once he knew. Of all people, she understood the weight of guilt; she was beginning to think he deserved her forgiveness.

A car parked on the opposite side of the street caught Sloane's attention. She recognized the seven-year-old imported sedan as Eric's. Her grin returned in full force at the thought he'd changed his mind. Maybe forgiveness was on the horizon. She nudged Finn's shoulder. "Eric made it after all."

As Finn adjusted her stare to focus in the direction where Sloane had cast her chin, the car lurched forward into traffic, traveling away from Sally's. Sloane narrowed her eyes. What was Eric doing? Maybe he figured after seeing her and the others on the sidewalk that he'd arrived too late. But then his car made an abrupt U-turn against oncoming traffic, forcing the other cars to come to a screeching halt.

What the hell?

Eric's car wobbled as it settled into its new lane on the same side of the street as Sally's. She heard the engine rev, but then the vehicle yawed to a slow pace. Standing at the group's furthest end from the oncoming car, Sloane felt her antenna go up. Something was amiss. She'd never been in a high-speed pursuit with Eric at the wheel, but every other time he drove, he was sure and steady. This wasn't like him. Not one bit.

Every detail about the oncoming car came into sharp focus as Eric closed in. It seemed to slow even more, like a cat lurking behind an unsuspecting prey. The tall buildings lining the street had blocked the sun's rays from illuminating the shadows inside the car's cabin, but Sloane could make out enough of the figure behind the wheel to recognize its shape didn't resemble Eric's. Every hair on her arms stood on end. The world around her slowed to a fraction of its average speed, as it did each time she sensed mortal danger.

Pedestrians and other cars faded into the cityscape. Urban sounds dwindled into white noise. With every fraction of a second that passed, the shape in the driver's seat became clearer. Older, balder, and more haggard, the man behind the wheel had a vaguely familiar look. Not like someone she'd passed regularly and never learned the name of. More like someone she'd run into once or twice, who'd left her with a bad taste in her mouth. Whoever this was, she sensed he was trouble.

Both windows on the passenger side had been lowered. Gang members on Peralta Street had done the same thing before they ambushed her months earlier. That instant of recognition had saved her life.

As the car inched even with Sloane's group on the sidewalk, the driver's right arm extended toward the open windows. He was clutching something dark in his hand. Sloane turned her head in what felt like super slow-motion.

"Gun!"

On instinct, she reached for her waistband, the place where she'd kept her service Sig Sauer for years. Her fingers touched nothing but fabric. She'd fallen out of the habit of carrying what used to be her trusty backup too, because it reminded her too much of her years with Eric. She had needed to distance herself from those raw memories. Now, she needed her beautiful black metal micro-compact Barretta Nano more than ever.

With no other way to protect the woman she loved, Sloane maneuvered to position herself between Finn and the danger. Without thinking, she turned her body into armor. Her arms enveloped Finn like a mother swan wrapping its wings around her young. Inches taller, her physique and head shielded every inch of Finn.

At the first crack of a shot piercing the air, she forced Finn to bend at the waist, curling her into an oddly shaped fishhook. A second shot. A third. A fourth. She lost count as she pushed Finn to the sidewalk, covering her like a Kevlar shroud.

When Finn squirmed beneath her, time resumed its normal speed. Screams coming from all directions made it impossible to hear anything else. The chill she felt earlier had left, replaced by the heated rush of blood pumping at an accelerated rate.

Finn shifted again, but Sloane couldn't be sure if the danger had passed. So much damn screaming. "Be still," she ordered.

Then another shot rang out. More screams followed. She cupped both hands over Finn's ears as if shielding her from the noise would protect her from the bullet. Wheels screeched unbearably like nails against a chalkboard. The sound culminated in a thunderous, distinct crash of metal meeting immovable object.

Sloane lifted her head and turned toward the racket. Between her and the billowing wreck several car-lengths down the street stood Morgan, her service weapon still pointing in its direction. Her upper body heaved as if she were keeping pace with the quick rhythm of Latin salsa.

"Is everyone okay?" Morgan yelled over her shoulder, still facing the commotion in the street, her gun trained on it. The screaming escalated, and others continued to stampede away from the danger.

"Finn and I are good." Sloane glanced down the street in both directions in search of threats, but detected none, only Eric's crumpled car. She locked gazes with Finn. Her pale face and determined eyes hinted she was shaken but ready for Sloane to take off her superhero cape and let her help.

"Kyler?" Morgan asked over her shoulder. When no answer came, she turned toward the section of sidewalk where Kyler last had stood before the deranged driver unleashed chaos.

Sloane rolled off Finn and pivoted her head in Kyler's direction. "Oh, God."

Kyler lay motionless on the sidewalk, an arm and leg haphazardly bent as if she had had no control as to where they landed. A dark stain had appeared on the front flap of her tailored gray blazer, and it was expanding. That could only mean one thing—she was bleeding fast. Sloane glanced back at Morgan.

"Kyler! Nooooo!" Life rushed out of Morgan's face, turning it as pale as the clouds dotting the sky. Sloane had assumed the worst seconds earlier, and if the panicked look on Morgan's face was an accurate barometer, she was doing so too.

Sloane was closer by several yards, but pushing herself from a prone position on the sidewalk slowed her. Morgan holstered her weapon on the fly and rushed toward her lover. Her fiancé. And if Sloane read her face correctly, her entire purpose for living.

Morgan reached Kyler first. She knelt and clutched Kyler's face with both hands, one on each cheek. "No, no, no, no, no."

Kyler's eyes didn't open. Morgan lifted her limp head off the sullied cement, away from stains of various colors, shapes, and sizes. Kyler's dark, bobbed hair appeared damp and mussed. Was it more blood or something else?

"I'll call it in and check for more wounded." Finn's voice served as an island of calm in a sea of pandemonium. Another reason Sloane loved her so much.

Sloane double-checked Finn, making sure she wasn't hurt. She appeared unharmed and unshaken despite Sloane having dived on top of her. That would've calmed her under any other circumstance, but the situation was still uncertain.

"Baby, open your eyes," Morgan cried out, massaging both sides of Kyler's face with her thumbs. The pain in her voice grew sharper. "Baby, wake up."

Sloane moved closer to help. Blood had trickled but not pooled around Kyler's arm—an excellent sign. Maneuvering to Kyler's other side, she pressed her index and middle fingers across a wrist. She found a sturdy beat. "She's alive."

"Baby, don't leave me. Wake up." The panic in Morgan's voice had peaked. Sloane had never seen her like this. More precisely, she'd never seen her even the least bit flustered. Morgan had always been stoic no matter the situation, especially so when Avery was killed. This must have shaken her to the core.

Sloane knew firsthand that during times like this words of optimism never helped. They only made the one saying them feel better. Instead, she remained silent, placed a steady hand on Morgan's back, and rubbed in gentle circles, letting her know she wasn't alone.

While the surrounding commotion settled, Morgan repeated her plea again and again, tears streaking her cheek. Then, in less than a minute but what must have felt like an eternity to Morgan, Kyler released a deep groan.

"That's it, baby. Come back to me." When Morgan slumped, Sloane gripped the fabric of her jacket to steady her.

Kyler's legs shifted, and then her arms, signs she was coming to. She rocked her head side to side on the hard cement before lifting the hand of her uninjured arm to her forehead. "Mo?"

"I'm right here, baby." Tears tracked down Morgan's face, one after another. She squeezed the hand Kyler had sent searching. "Don't move. An ambulance is on the way."

Sloane felt the relief pouring out of Morgan and withdrew her hand from her back. She glanced at Finn, who gave her a confirming nod. "Yes, it's coming."

Kyler shifted more but winced and stopped. "It hurts."

"You've been shot." Morgan used her textbook calm, reassuring voice. She wasn't entirely composed, but the rattled sharpness of her voice had disappeared. "I don't know how bad, baby."

Kyler shook her head from side to side. "Not baby. Sexy. You promised."

A grin slowly emerged on Morgan's frazzled face. "I almost forgot. Sexy."

She leaned down and pressed her lips against Kyler's. She lingered for several beats but didn't deepen it. There was no need to. Her love and passion for the woman lying beside her glowed as brightly as Times Square. When she pulled back, a mischievous grin built on Kyler's lips. It disappeared a moment later, replaced by an intense grimace and a rocky moan. She gripped Morgan's hand tighter.

At the first sound of whirring sirens, Morgan glanced at Sloane. "Eric." She reached behind her back and handed Sloane first her service weapon and then a pair of handcuffs.

"On it." Nothing more needed saying for Sloane to understand Morgan wouldn't leave Kyler's side until she was stable.

Stuffing one cuff into the back of her waistband, letting the other dangle until it bounced against the small of her back so they wouldn't fall, Sloane gripped the Sig Sauer tight in her right hand. Standard department issue, it was the mirror image of the one she carried for years. She knew every detail about the P229, including its compact dimensions, weight when loaded and empty, and recoil velocity when fired. The only thing she couldn't be sure of was the sighting. Did it pull left or right? But in close quarters, pull wouldn't matter. A quarter-inch one way or the other would still find her target.

She wrapped her fingers around the stippled rubber grip, stretching her index finger along the trigger guard. It felt as familiar as Finn's body. Sloane cupped her left hand beneath her right, raised the level of the barrel toward Eric's mangled mess of a car, and began a rapid advance in a slight crouch. She glided on the balls of her feet to keep herself agile. A tuck and roll might become necessary. She ignored the sweat beading her temples and pushed down and across the street. Thankfully, pedestrians and traffic had come to a halt along the two-lane road, providing a clear path.

The front end of Eric's car rested askew on the sidewalk, centered on a teetering light pole that had absorbed the hit. Its engine idled. A white SUV was parked two feet from the driver's side, leaving barely enough room to open the door.

Sloane approached that side, slowing her pace and shortening her stride as she came even with the rear fender.

She peered into the back window. The backseat was unoccupied. Another step forward. The front passenger seat also appeared empty. The lone occupant in the driver's seat had slumped and was unmoving against the steering wheel. She trained the Sig Sauer on him.

"Hands! Show me your hands!"

Her pulse picked up like she was on a double-time march. During her days on patrol, responding to dispatched calls, where she knew what she was walking into, were a snap compared to traffic stops. Walking up to a driver behind the wheel, particularly at night, was a crapshoot, and each time she prepared for the worst-case scenario. This qualified as the worst case—a mad man with a gun.

The driver didn't move. She repeated, "Hands! I said, hands!"

Sloane sidestepped toward the driver's door inches at a time, exposing as little of her torso as possible. Without body armor, she was a sitting duck for a gun hidden under the driver's armpit. She sucked in a deep breath to steady herself.

Through the side window, she spotted the driver's head resting against fluffy white fabric. Airbags had deployed. With her left hand, she tried the door handle, but it was locked. Of course.

She pounded her fist on the window. "Unlock the damn door!"

His head turned toward the window, causing the airbag to billow like a deflating beach ball. Blood had smeared his nose and cheek. His left eye fluttered open several times.

Sloane repeated her command through the window. "Unlock the door!"

A click.

She lifted the handle again and pulled the door open. When the man elevated his head and raised his right hand to it, she pressed the muzzle of her gun against his temple. "Careful, or I'll shoot."

She scanned the front compartment. A gun lay on the passenger floor.

A muffled voice and pounding sound to her right split her attention from the driver. Something wasn't right. The man remained dazed, but she wasn't taking any chances. She cuffed his right hand to the steering wheel, making sure the gun on the floor was out of the reach of his left.

Banging continued to come from inside the trunk. After she located and popped the trunk release, it stopped. Sloane maneuvered to the rear of the car, her gun at the ready. The trunk lid was ajar but not raised. Her heart reverberated fiercely in her ears as she faced the unknown again. She peered around the fender and inside the trunk.

A man lay on his side with his back toward Sloane, handcuffed at the wrists, duct-taped at the ankles. He craned his neck, revealing his face. "Eric?"

"Thank God. You're alive." He slammed his eyes shut.

"I should say that to you. Are you okay?" Both relief and confusion consumed Sloane. Whatever was happening, Eric was alive. She wedged the pistol inside her waistband at the small of her back before helping him to a sitting position.

"Other than a splitting headache, I'm fine. Now get me out of these." He inched up his hands behind his back.

Sloane couldn't put into words how she felt, but she was sure she'd be devastated if he was seriously hurt again. She choked back the emotion constricting her throat. "I don't have a cuff key."

"You've turned civilian." He grinned and cast his chin toward his feet. "Inside my right shoe. Tied to the lace."

Why hadn't she remembered his hiding place? She used to have one too. Retrieving the key, she unlocked the cuffs. While Eric rubbed his wrists, she used the end of the key to work on the tape around his ankles. Seconds later, the wail of the sirens silenced at the arrival of two police cruisers.

She glanced toward Sally's. Finn had dashed across the street and was making her way toward her. Morgan had taken charge, pointing and directing the arriving officers while remaining at Kyler's side.

"You okay?" Finn wheezed in between breaths. "My God, Eric. What the hell happened?"

Eric's face turned to a shade of red Sloane had seen only a few times. He was spitting mad. "Peter Rook happened."

"I thought I recognized him." A chill went down Sloane's spine. Their paths had crossed twice but briefly. Both times she got a bad vibe, as did Avery the one time she was the target of his caveman thinking. "I'm glad I cuffed him to the wheel." She turned to Finn. "How's Kyler?"

"She's alert. Morgan stopped the bleeding."

"We need to talk to L-T." A panicked look had filled Eric's eyes, one Sloane had never seen before. "Hurry, Sloane."

Sloane ripped the remaining section of duct tape from his ankles, releasing Eric, who then shimmied out of the trunk. Before they took a single step, a uniformed officer ran up beside them. He scanned the wreckage.

Eric spoke to the officer. "You're Franks, right?"

"Yes, sir," he replied wide-eyed but also with bright recognition. When Sloane left the department, Franks had been on the job for less than a year and still had a lot to learn. Apparently, a drive-by culminating in vehicle versus light pole was still new to him.

"You'll do fine, Franks. You've seen me around, right?" Franks nodded. "These two are with me." Eric pointed at Sloane and Finn.

"What do we have?" Franks asked.

Eric glanced over his shoulder toward the arrival of additional patrol cars, which meant the surrounding chaos would soon come to order. His eyes narrowed. "A suspected drive-by shooter got away. The driver of this car was collateral damage. He'll need medical attention."

Collateral damage, my ass. Sloane cocked her head. Eric was onto something, and her instinct was to back his play. "He looked pretty bad."

More sirens blared. A fire truck and rescue rig approached from down the street but were slowed by blocked traffic.

"We'll deal with the driver." Eric rushed his words to Franks. "You handle traffic for the rescue crews."

"On it." Franks placed a hand over the firearm strapped to his Sam Browne belt and took off running. Sloane used to do the same. The damn thing would bounce against her hip whenever she ran hard.

"We need to get Peter out of here." Eric maneuvered around to the driver's door and uncuffed Peter. "You wrecked my car, asshole."

"I'll get the gun." Sloane peeled around to the passenger side and retrieved it from the floor. When she came back around, firefighters and paramedics had parked. They were rushing toward both the wreck and the wounded across the street. She glanced toward Eric on the driver's side, who was swinging the handcuffs by his right index finger like it was some kinky foreplay. Sloane didn't want to know whether it was a practiced activity.

"We got him, sir." One of the two medics parked a gurney several feet from Eric's wrecked car.

While the paramedic tended to Peter, Eric and Sloane regrouped with Finn in the middle of the street. "I need to talk to the L-T before she gets on that rig." Eric broke out in a fast march toward the medical crew that was working on Kyler Harris. Sloane and Finn sprinted to keep up with him.

"What the hell is going on, Eric?" Sloane slowed him down by grabbing his arm.

He came to an abrupt halt and locked eyes with her. "Trust me. We can't take Peter back to Bryant."

Sloane searched his brown eyes. They contained the same determination they had when he agreed to help her go after Caco and avenge Avery's death. He had her back then. Now, despite the once unscalable chasm between them, it was her turn to have his. She gave him a heartfelt nod.

They continued their march together with Finn a step behind. Paramedics had hoisted Kyler onto a gurney and were wheeling her toward the back of the rescue rig. Morgan clung to her hand, matching the medics step for step. Color had returned to Morgan's face, which meant the uncertainty of Kyler's survival had thankfully passed.

While the crew prepared the gurney to go inside the first ambulance, Eric grabbed Morgan by the arm. "I'll go with the driver on the other rig. Don't call it in. Not yet."

Morgan's eyes danced with anger when her spine stiffened. "He shot Kyler. There's no way in hell—"

Sloane closed in and whispered in Morgan's ear. "Trust him."

Those words should've felt foreign to Sloane or at least should've had a bitter taste. Instead, they had a sweetness and rolled off her tongue as if time had rewound and Eric's confession of six months ago never happened.

Morgan's brows squished together in apparent skepticism. She paused, staring Eric in the eyes. "This had better be good."

As paramedics stowed Kyler aboard, Sloane returned her Sig Sauer. "Felt like old times."

After holstering her service weapon, Morgan briefly cupped Sloane's hands. "I wouldn't have trusted anyone else."

The other firefighters arrived at the second nearby rescue rig with Peter strapped to the gurney, groggy and partially covered by a blanket. Franks followed alongside and proudly reported he'd blocked off traffic.

"Good job, Franks." Eric waved him off. "We'll take it from here."

"But—"

Morgan's eyes widened with recognition when she glanced at Peter's face. She paused before swiping her blazer flap back with a hand to reveal a seven-point gold shield with Lieutenant arced across the top in blue capital letters. Her scowl matched her sharp tone. "We got it, Franks."

The firefighters loaded Peter and locked the gurney in place. Eric followed. As Morgan stepped inside Kyler's rig, one of the two paramedics inside called out, "It'll be a tight fit."

Morgan flashed her badge again and launched her words like arrows. "Make it work."

The doors slammed shut, sirens chirped, and both rigs took off. Sloane checked her watch. Less than fifteen minutes had passed since she had held the door open for Morgan and Kyler following a mutual promise to cultivate their friendship. She'd never seen Morgan so happy and then, minutes later, never so terrified.

"We'll need your statement, ma'am." Franks sounded overly official, an obvious sign that he didn't recognize Sloane. That was a good thing.

Uniformed police had cordoned off the city block. Yellow "Do Not Cross" tape was going up in both directions. Now that victims were en route and the wreckage appeared to be declared safe, the firefighting crews would soon be released. If Sloane and Finn didn't leave now, they'd be stuck there for hours providing statements along with Sloane explaining her part in apprehending the so-called bystander. She needed to touch base with Eric and Morgan before she said anything. In other words, she needed a diversion.

"Officer." Sloane put on her baffled and unnerved face, hoping the woman-in-distress thing would be enough. "With all the confusion, we…" She glanced at Finn and the handbag slung over her shoulder. She quickly shifted pronouns. "I need to get my purse. It should be inside Sally's."

"Umm." Franks glanced at the quickly forming command post. "I really need—"

"I'll only be a minute." Sloane begged with her eyes.

His shoulders drooped. "Make it quick."

She grabbed Finn's hand and tugged with a sudden jerk. "We'll be right back."

Stepping toward the café, Sloane took in the havoc Peter had wreaked with his wild west show. Blotches of blood stained the sidewalk where Kyler had lain. Two ragged bullet holes in the restaurant's tempered glass storefront served as centerpieces of two intricate spiderwebs of cracks. Only luck and quick reflexes had saved her and Finn from the bullets' paths.

They slipped inside the café. The place had emptied, all but the servers and the cook. From behind the diner's counter, Rita called out. "Sloane. I'm so glad you're okay. What happened?"

"I'm glad you're okay too." Sloane didn't break her stride, pulling Finn along. "I don't have time to explain, but we need to duck out the back door."

"Of course. I expect a full report next week."

Rita's voice faded when they turned the corner to the restroom hallway and the rear delivery exit. Once out the door and in the narrow, littered alley, the smell of stale urine took over. When they reached the end of the alley and turned onto the next street, Sloane silently thanked Sally's for its notorious parking problem. The three blocks to her car were well outside the police cordon.

Ten yards away, Sloane pressed the key fob and the taillights on her SUV flashed twice, signaling their getaway was within reach. She and Finn simultaneously pulled the door handles, slid into the seats, and slammed the doors shut.

"What the hell is going on?" Finn's words came out breathy.

"I'm not a hundred percent sure, but Eric said to trust him. This is me trusting."

CHAPTER EIGHTEEN

Eric's text was clear. He'd babysit Peter, whom he'd tucked away in an emergency room cubicle until they'd figured out what to do with him. Despite Sloane's mounting curiosity, solving a murder mystery would have to wait, because the text from Morgan left much to a runaway imagination. *Surgery. Waiting until she's in recovery*, Morgan had written. Did it mean Kyler was touch-and-go? Would she be all right?

The moment Sloane stepped through the emergency room doors of Bayside Hospital, shivers coursed up her spine. The hospital kept the temperature low, but it was the memories that made her shudder. From Shellie Rodriguez's overdose death to her own recovery from surgery when she realized she was a widow, this was the hospital where so much of her life had unraveled.

"I hate this place."

She took Finn's hand in mid-stride, seeking comfort. Finn gave her hand an extra squeeze but said nothing—an unstated affirmation that provided everything she needed. Sloane already considered Finn her partner in both work and in life, but right then, she realized she wouldn't feel complete until she called Finn her wife.

Signs tacked to the walls guided Sloane and Finn to the surgical waiting area. Morgan was sitting in a far corner, away from the noise of the television and the toddler pandemonium in the room's center. Normally polished and focused, she appeared disheveled and anxious with her perpetual knee bobbing and hand wringing.

Morgan raised her head and rose to her feet when Sloane and Finn closed in. The deep lines on her face told of endless worry. "I'm so glad you're here."

Sloane opened her arms and offered Morgan an embrace. She'd loved two women in her life and had seen one shot, the other killed. She knew the pain, fear, and guilt consuming Morgan. Wishful thinking without knowing the facts wouldn't help, but something had to be said. "You couldn't have prevented any of this," Sloane whispered into her ear.

Morgan trembled, clutching Sloane's jacket with both hands. "I should've been faster."

"You did everything right. You stopped him."

This was a first, Sloane thought. After Avery died, Morgan had twice offered her comfort, but she had rebuffed each overture to friendship, a reflexive instinct she now regretted. An understanding shoulder was precisely what she had needed back then, and today that was what her friend required to get her through the endless waiting.

When Morgan loosened her grip, Sloane extended her arms to look at her. "Any news yet?"

A confident yet relief-filled nod followed. "It was a through-and-through. The bullet missed bone and arteries. They're repairing a muscle, but she should be fine in a few weeks."

"That's great news. Will they keep her overnight?"

"I hope not. The doctor said the surgery was minor, but they're concerned about the concussion she got from hitting her head on the sidewalk." Morgan pouted. "Besides, I'm not sure who would have a more uncomfortable night."

"How's that?"

"It's been months since I've slept alone."

"I know how you feel. The bed feels empty when Finn isn't in it."

The lines between Morgan's brows grew more pronounced. "Is that a problem?"

A year ago, the probing question would've sent Sloane's defenses into high gear, but this "friends" thing had grown on her, and the question didn't bother her in the least. She glanced at Finn a few feet away. A surge of confidence built in her chest. "Not anymore."

Morgan's cell phone chimed. She dug it out of her front blazer pocket and raised an index finger, telegraphing she had to take the call. "Captain...Yes, she was shot...a flesh wound... I need to take some personal time...Thank you..." Morgan motioned for Sloane and Finn to sit and then continued her call. "It was chaotic. I'm not sure who else was on scene...I'll email my statement tomorrow..."

Morgan completed the call and sat on the corner vinyl chair, perpendicular to Sloane and Finn. Before she could explain what Nash had said, Finn brushed her on the knee. "I'm relieved to hear Kyler's okay."

Morgan grinned in lopsided fashion and shook her head with the vigor of a child's wonder. "She was more worried about missing court today than getting her arm fixed."

Finn smiled. "Sounds like her."

Morgan took in an uncharacteristically sharp breath. Sloane got the impression Kyler's injury wasn't the only thing that had her rattled. "Captain Nash knows about Kyler, but not about Peter, Eric, or you two." Morgan rubbed her lips with a hand— her tell that she was unsettled. "I can stall with my statement for a day at the most."

"Why do we need to stall?" Sloane asked.

"What has Eric told you?"

"Nothing yet." Sloane's spidey senses were up. At some point, Eric must somehow have told her something that convinced her to blow off her chain of command. "We wanted to hear about Kyler first."

Morgan's expression turned serious. "I'm glad you said to trust him. After what he told me when we first arrived here, there's no way we can book Peter Rook into Bryant."

"That's all he told us. What's going on?" Sloane asked.

Morgan scanned the waiting room and the various occupants. If she couldn't trust the people here or at headquarters, this must be big. "Better he tells you. He's guarding Peter in the ER."

"So you've reinstated him?"

"Verbally, yes, but I can't officially without raising questions. I'm convinced Eric and his dad had nothing to do with the cold case murders."

"That's good to hear." Sloane averted her eyes. She shouldn't have doubted Eric. After two-and-a-half years of having each other's backs and placing her life in his hands countless times, how could she think him capable of cold-blooded murder? His carelessness had taken her parents' lives, but he was by no means a murderer.

"Go." Morgan furtively shooed her with a hand. "We need to do something with Peter quickly."

Minutes later, Sloane pulled back the curtain leading into the furthest, most private bay in the emergency department. Glassed in on three sides and buffered by a utility room between it and the next bay, that was the location nurses assigned disruptive patients to until they slept it off, whatever *it* was. Bottom line: they had about as much privacy there as the floor allowed.

Eric popped his head up from his seated position. Next to him, Peter sat reclined and handcuffed to the hospital bed, a small bandage covering his nose.

"Good." Eric stood. "You made it quick."

"We ducked out before questioning." Sloane gave him a wink.

"Even better."

"Care to fill us in?"

Eric turned his stare to Peter. "You talking yet?"

"No deal. No talk." Peter rolled over on his side, clanking the handcuff against the bedrail with a huffy tug. The bad vibe Sloane got the other times she had been in Peter's orbit hadn't changed. He was an ass, through and through.

"You shot my friend, asshole. That was some pretty crappy shooting if you were trying to hit me." Sloane slung her one arrow at Peter. Insults usually proved ineffective, but she had nothing else to throw at him. Saying it still felt good, though.

"He's not going anywhere." Eric led Sloane and Finn down the hallway a few feet and into an interior entrapment area. The door guarding it featured a small rectangular pane of tempered glass, providing him with an excellent view of Peter's bay.

"Before we start…" Sloane put up her hand in a stopping motion. "Kyler's doing fine. It was only a flesh wound, and she should make a full recovery."

Eric rubbed his left arm as if he had sympathy pains. "Good. I wouldn't wish this on anyone, except for the asshole I have cuffed to that hospital bed."

"I'm sorry about that." Sloane swallowed hard at the thought he took that bullet to protect her family.

"Thank you."

The way he replied with a hint of emotion made her realize that this marked the first time she'd said anything about his injury. She choked back the swelling in her throat. "You're right, you know."

"About what?" he asked.

"About me going all civilian. I gotta get back in the habit of carrying the essentials."

"Like a damn cuff key." A lopsided grin formed on Eric's face.

"Yes. Like a damn cuff key." Sloane gave him a playful shove in the shoulder. He winced. "Oh, God. I'm so sorry. That's your bad arm."

"Gotcha." He silently chuckled through pressed lips and then rolled his shoulder. "It's fine."

"Damn it, Eric. Don't scare me like that."

"Sorry, Sloane." His grin grew wider. "Couldn't help myself."

Their playfulness marked a final turn. It took almost losing Eric again for Sloane to realize his friendship meant more to her than holding a grudge. They weren't partners anymore, but at least they were friends again.

Sloane stuffed her hands in her back pockets. "Morgan led me to believe you have enough to clear you and your dad. I'm glad." Finn placed a hand on the small of her back. She'd apparently recognized the full thaw between her and Eric.

"Thanks." The bob of Eric's Adam's apple signaled he felt the thaw too. "Peter confessed to killing Hewey because Hewey killed his brother."

"Agent Walker is Rooks' brother?" Finn asked, incredulous.

"Half-brother." Eric glanced at Finn. "He said he only wanted to hurt him, but he snapped."

"And then he burned the body to cover up the murder?" Sloane asked.

"He said an old partner did that."

"His partner? Great. Two cops are murderers. Who was it?"

"He won't say. He had a string of partners back then. It could've been any one of a half dozen. The one thing he told me after they patched up his nose was that he could prove who it was."

"Did he ask for a lawyer?" Finn asked.

Eric shook his head. "Not yet. He knows the odds of a deal go down if he does."

"What about the bullet? Why did it match your dad's gun and not his?" Sloane glanced at Peter through the small window. Solving this mystery and finding justice for three dead people rested on the fate of a cop killer, nonetheless. Making a deal was too much to fathom.

"Peter and my dad used to be partners. He knew that Dad collected every bullet he shot at the firing range and made art pieces out of them. Peter took one. His partner, whoever the fuck it was, swapped it out in transit to the lab."

"If he's not talking, what do we do now?" Sloane asked.

"We need an ADA to take the death penalty off the table, but the only one I trust is recovering from a gunshot wound," Eric said. "A wound he inflicted."

"I have to agree with you on that one." Sloane blew out a long, frustrated breath. The District Attorney's office was deeply interwoven in police department operations, working side by side with everyone from street cops to the chief of "D's" every day of the week. One verbal slip and Peter's accomplice would know they were on his trail. They needed to wait. "Kyler should be up and around tomorrow. Until then, we sure as hell can't book him into any department holding cell."

"I could call in another favor with Nate Prichard." Finn lowered her voice to almost a whisper. "They can hold him at the Federal Building until we sort things out."

"I love a woman with connections." Squeezing Finn's hand, Sloane glanced at Eric. The three of them working together felt right, like old times. "Let's do this."

* * *

Sloane closed the driver's door to her SUV after Finn closed hers. The aroma of oregano wafting from the cardboard box in her hand, though mouth-watering, meant she'd broken a promise. Dead tired or not, she'd let herself down too. When she quit the force, she'd made a pact with Reagan and Finn that fast-food dinners were a thing of the past. A home-cooked meal or the occasional trot down to The Tap with family and friends would be an acceptable substitute. Reagan would love the pepperoni, but Sloane didn't like the implication she still wasn't in control of her time.

When Finn shimmied between both cars toward the house door, Sloane grinned in sympathy. "I'll be glad when the basement office is finished, so you won't have to sidestep your way out of the garage every night."

"It's only a few more weeks, but yes, I feel like I need you to cue the music every time."

Sloane caught up with Finn at the door and wrapped her free arm around her waist. She whispered in a low, seductive tone, "I'd love to watch you dance for me."

Finn leaned back into the embrace. "That can be arranged."

The image of Finn in a skintight, thigh-high black cocktail dress, doing a slow, sexy striptease until every stitch of lace lay on the floor had Sloane breathing ragged. That was one fantasy they'd have to make a reality. "I'm holding you to it."

Finn turned around and captured Sloane's lips, forcing her to grip the pizza box extra tight to prevent it from becoming the next ant attractor. Finn dipped her tongue inside Sloane's mouth, swirling it around hers. The kiss melted away the day's tension, and a relaxing warmth spread through her like a spring day. She'd stay there all night if she could, connected to the softness of Finn's lips, but family awaited them inside. She pulled back.

"I've wanted to do that all day." Finn held her focus fixed on Sloane's tingling mouth.

"After your father leaves?" Sloane arched an eyebrow.

"I'm holding you to it."

Light flowed into the entry hall from the living room, along with the sound of Kruk and Kuip. Their bantering momentarily paused for the roar of the crowd at the baseball field.

Sloane turned the corner first.

"It's outta here!" Chandler and Reagan sang in chorus. He sloshed his bottle of beer, and she tipped over the bowl of popcorn in her lap.

Sloane glanced at the television graphics. A first-inning leadoff home run had rocked the house. The Giants' early lead meant conversation might stay on the game, making tonight's impromptu gathering a welcome distraction from today's harrowing events.

She lifted the box in the air. "Pizza's here."

"Hey, pumpkin." Chandler wiped drops of beer from his pant leg, still grinning from the Giants' home run.

"Hi, Daddy," Finn said.

Reagan looked over her shoulder and glared at Finn. The freeze between Sloane and Eric may have thawed, but Reagan had a death grip on hers. It had reached the point that the temperature in the room dropped every time she locked eyes with Finn, and everything Sloane did to address it failed miserably.

"I'll get the salad out." Reagan's tone had turned as flat as the pizza box.

Sloane sighed and followed her into the kitchen. If she called Reagan out on her behavior again, she'd likely be met with another door slam. Not a thing she wanted to start with Chandler there, so she dug deep for more patience.

"Thanks for making it, honey." Sloane placed the box on the counter and pulled plates from the cupboard. "I'm sorry we were late for dinner, but things were crazy today."

"Things are always crazy around *here*," Reagan mumbled loud enough for Sloane to hear.

Sloane dipped her head. How was she supposed to respond to a moody teenager? With more patience, of course. "Don't forget the Thousand Island."

"I know. It's Chandler's favorite."

"And Finn's."

"Whatever." Reagan punctuated her damning appraisal with a dramatic eye roll. The quirk she inherited from her mother, while usually cute, was disrespectful in this case—something Sloane wasn't willing to tolerate.

"When is this going to stop, Reagan? Finn did nothing wrong."

"So she says."

Sloane set her focus on the stack of plates. It was time to put the grounds for Reagan's hostility into perspective. "If anyone did anything wrong, it was me."

"What are you talking about? She's the one who kissed Kadin."

"Kadin kissed her, but Finn didn't encourage it. That's a completely different thing. I did exactly what you're accusing Finn of doing, and she forgave me."

"You kissed Kadin?" Reagan's eyes went round as if Sloane had confessed to a triple murder.

"What? Of course not. If I'd done what I did when your mother was alive, she'd have me sleeping in the guest room for months. Finn has nothing to feel guilty about, but I sure as hell do."

"What did you do?"

"The specifics don't matter." Sloane averted her eyes, the memory of stale cigarettes making her stomach turn. "What's important is that we've been completely honest with each other, and we've forgiven and trust one another. Sometimes I wish you didn't have your mother's stubbornness."

Moisture had pooled along the lower rims of Reagan's eyes. The way her lips quivered, Sloane suspected she was upset at more than her own behavior. She placed both hands on Reagan's forearms and squeezed. "What's wrong, honey?"

"I miss Mom." The residual sadness in Reagan's voice, while not as strong as it once was, meant she was still grieving—a reminder that the two of them were in this together.

"I miss her too." *More slack*, Sloane thought.

"You guys never fought."

Sloane chuckled herself into a full belly laugh, remembering the fiery tongue Avery often unleashed as her primary defense. Thinking back, though, she had feared the woman's silence more than her verbal onslaughts. "We were newlyweds, of course we fought. We just never let you see it."

"You must've done something pretty bad if Mom would've exiled you to the couch."

"It wasn't a matter of what but with whom."

Reagan arched an eyebrow. "Not Michelle?"

Sloane's eyes widened. She and Avery had been careful not to bring up her old fuck buddy in front of Reagan, leaving her quietly in the past. "What do you know about her?"

"Only that Mom hated her. She said Michelle would make a play for anyone with a pulse."

Sloane snickered before tucking away the grin. "Your mother was a very discerning woman."

"So it *was* her."

"That, young lady, is between Finn and me. Now how about you give Finn a break?"

Reagan rolled her eyes without the snark this time. "I'll try."

"Good. Now, let's set out dinner before Chandler complains about the service around here."

After Sloane and Reagan set up the food family style, everyone served themselves at the dining table. Chandler positioned himself to have the best view of the television and the on-screen action with the ballgame muted. At the next inning break, after devouring a good portion of pizza, he said, "I heard on the news that ADA Kyler Harris was shot in a drive-by today. Aren't you two friends of hers?"

"We were with her when she was shot." Finn's declaratory statement tumbled from her lips as if their front-row seat to the morning melee was nothing. Reagan's mouth fell agape, prompting Sloane to kick Finn in the shin under the table, who grimaced behind reddening cheeks. They hadn't discussed how much of today's happenings they should reveal, and Finn effectively had dropped a bombshell.

"You were what?" Chandler stopped in mid-chew.

Finn's sheepish grin earned her the prize of explaining the rest of the story, at least the parts that didn't include Peter or Eric, Sloane hoped. Sloane propped an elbow on the table and rested her chin in an upturned palm. Her furtive head shake signaled Finn to keep it short.

"We were having breakfast with Kyler and Morgan." Finn waved her hand in a futile attempt to assuage Chandler's concern.

"So you were almost shot too?" Reagan drilled her eyes at Sloane. Her nearly shrill tone cut Sloane to the quick. Turning in her badge had come with the expectation that perilous situations were a thing of the past. Today, however, demonstrated that danger still lurked around every corner.

"Is that true, pumpkin?" Chandler's posture stiffened.

Finn locked gazes with her father. "Short answer, yes."

"And the long answer?" If skeptical had a look, Chandler's narrowed eyes and pursed lips were it.

Finn reached for Sloane's hand. "This wonderful creature saved us."

"I just fell to the ground. Finn beat me to it." Sloane kissed the back of Finn's hand. When she had recognized the threat, her training kicked in. She didn't think, just reacted. The fact she reached for her nonexistent service weapon told her a lot of cop still lived in her.

"Yeah, right." Finn smiled impishly. "She had us on the ground before the first shot."

Chandler dropped a slice of pizza, which landed atop the Thousand Island in his salad bowl. "First? Was there more than one? Who was the gunman aiming at?"

The conversation needed reeling in, so Sloane tapped Finn's shin under the table with her foot, signaling she'd take over. "We didn't stay on scene long enough to find out. We were more worried about Kyler, so we went right to the hospital."

"How is she?" Chandler picked up the slice and took a bite from the end that was still dripping Thousand Island. He inspected the unlikely combination and shrugged. "Not bad."

"It was only a flesh wound, so Morgan took her home tonight."

"I'm glad she's okay."

Reagan's lack of questions unsettled Sloane. Much like her mother, Reagan's silence meant the news was more upsetting than she let on. It was time to change the subject. "Me too. She's helping us with a contract problem."

"Is it a legal issue?" Chandler's inquisitive expression bordered on disappointment. "You could've consulted me."

"It's nothing like that, Daddy." Finn patted the top of his hand. "We're concerned the mayor has an underlying agenda and might use our work to do something we're not comfortable with. Kyler was doing some digging."

"A little oppo research, huh?" Chandler cocked one eyebrow up. "Do you think it had anything to do with the shooting today? Politics can be a dirty game. Even if Kyler was discreet, I wouldn't be surprised if she ruffled a few feathers."

"I doubt it. She only ran some reports." Sloane knew exactly whose feathers had been ruffled, but this wasn't the time to tell all. They still had a murder to solve. "You sound like you're speaking from experience."

"Out of law school, I thought I wanted to go into politics. I even went to work for Senator Benson on her legislative staff. I quickly learned I didn't have the stomach for it."

"I could totally see you as a politician." Sloane inspected Chandler's features. Not only did he carry himself like a politician, but he also looked the part. His height, fit body, chiseled features, and perfect posture could easily command a room.

"Oh, not me," Chandler chuckled as if Sloane had suggested he looked good in a pink tutu. "I made some great connections, but I left politics to the ambitious ones a long time ago."

"Come on, Daddy. You love being on the periphery." Finn focused her gaze on Sloane. "He's on the lieutenant governor's invitation list. He's always attending exclusive dinners and parties."

"You didn't seem to mind when I'd take you as my plus-one," Chandler scoffed.

"Come to think of it. You haven't brought me to one in a while, not since before the wildfire." Finn's mouth fell open to an exaggerated gasp. "You've been taking Sharon, haven't you?"

"Guilty as charged."

"I thought I was your plus-one." Finn pressed her lips tight. *Holy hell. Her pouty lips are so cute*, Sloane thought.

"I thought you didn't like those stuffy events."

"I don't. It's the idea of being replaced."

Chandler patted the top of Finn's hand. "No one could replace you, pumpkin."

"Then I know how you can make it up to me."

"I have a feeling I'm about to be used." Chandler drew his hand back to the safety of his lap.

"If things with the mayor go south, we may need you to make a phone call."

"You want me to pull strings."

"Only if we can't."

Sloane whispered in Finn's ear before kissing her on the cheek. "Brilliant. You can be my plus-one anytime."

CHAPTER NINETEEN

A powerful sense of disappointment hit Finn when she stepped off the elevator leading to the DEA's San Francisco Division. While she had loved the action that came with serving as a field agent, dealing with the agency's bureaucracy was like navigating a minefield. When she had stepped up to serve as the division's assistant special agent in charge, she had hoped to make some genuine changes for the better, and she did. Word had it, though, that most of her positive changes now lay in the trash heap.

As she approached her old office, she thought she and Sloane had arrived early enough for a brief side tour down memory lane. Seeing her one real ally in the office seated behind a desk brought back the few pleasant memories she had of this place. She cleared her throat.

Carol removed the reading glasses from the bridge of her nose, exposing a jovial smile that extended to her eyes. "Twice in three days. This *is* a treat." Following a quick but tender hug, she returned to the chair behind her now neatly arranged desk.

Its tidiness was a good sign that she had a better handle on working with Finn's replacement.

"I know we're early for our eight o'clock with Agent Prichard, but I was hoping you could do me a little favor." Finn peeked over Carol's shoulder to determine if they were alone. "Does Shipley still arrive at eight?"

Carol punctuated her nod with a devious grin. "He does."

"Can we wait for Nate in my old office?" Finn met Sloane's curious expression with a wink.

"For you, Finn, anything." Carol stepped to the door and swiped her ID badge over the card reader. A green light flashed, and she pushed the door open. "I'll buzz you on the intercom when either of them arrives."

"You're the best." Finn rubbed Carol's arm through her white cardigan before stepping into the office and closing the door.

Like a flashing neon sign, Agent Shipley's "I love me" wall behind his desk confirmed Finn's opinion of him. She chuckled at the number of framed citations, news clippings, photographs, and degrees, marking the highlights of his career. If not a keen management sense, Shipley had a well-developed ego.

"Oh, my." Sloane's stare had focused on the same wall. "He's a climber or compensating for his son-of-a-bitch partner."

"I'm guessing both." The fact Finn had supervised Shipley's partner for almost a year and had not a single inkling that he was on a cartel drug lord's payroll gnawed at her still. Former Agent Barnes was indeed a son of a bitch. "I still can't believe I didn't pick up on what Barnes was hiding."

Sloane closed the distance between them and gently stroked both her arms. "I didn't pick up on Eric's big secret, either."

Finn saw other similarities between the former partners. Eric had helped make Sloane an orphan, Barnes had made her a widow. One by accident, the other by design. One took Sloane away from her, the other brought her back. Eric's part was conceivably forgivable but not Barnes's. It sickened Finn to think if not for his despicable act, she wouldn't have Sloane.

"Neither is important." Sloane clasped Finn's hand and led her to the large window overlooking the city. She wrapped her other hand around Finn's and brought them both to her lips, kissing each one. Shivers rolled through Finn when Sloane whispered, "This is the exact place where I told you I loved you for the first time."

"It was." Finn leaned into Sloane's caress when she rested a palm on her cheek, savoring the tingles that trailed her warm fingertips. "I'd wanted to hear those words for weeks."

Sloane searched her eyes as if looking for a secret treasure. "I felt those words grow inside me each time we touched and take shape with every kiss. That night, I was never so sure that we were meant to be together since the first time you held my hand after choir practice."

Those words melted Finn into a blissful state, relaxing every muscle. "I feel the same way."

Sloane's hands slid around her waist, her eyes steeping with emotion. "I remember rushing over here the day I feared El Padrino had gotten to you after his men ambushed me. I couldn't think straight until I knew you were safe."

Finn wrapped her arms around Sloane's neck and nestled her head into its crook, pressing the remainder of their bodies together. "Though you hadn't said it yet, that was the day I knew you loved me."

"I could've lost you yesterday." Sloane squeezed tighter. "Hell, I thought I had twice with the whole Kadin and Michelle nightmare. My stupidity almost broke us."

"That's behind us—"

"Finn," Carol's voice cracked through the desktop phone intercom, prompting Finn and Sloane to end their embrace. "Agents Prichard and Shipley just stepped off the elevator."

"We better make our escape before Shipley walks in." Sloane scanned the ego wall one more time. "He may think you're trying to steal your job back." She ended with a playful wink before they entered the outer office.

Shipley stopped in mid-stride, locking eyes with Finn as they exited his office. *Shit!* Finn squared her shoulders and decided to head off the cold war. She walked up to him and offered to shake hands. He accepted. "Love what you did with the office, Tom."

"Thanks, Ms. Harper." His tone was surprisingly void of tension. Perhaps his show of respect meant he appreciated the challenges that came with management.

"Please, call me Finn."

"You must be here for the John Doe in holding." Finn gave him a nod. "When Decker brought him in, I figured you weren't too far behind."

"It's all still hush-hush."

"I figured as much." Tom Shipley glanced toward his office door. "I should start the day."

"It was nice seeing you, Tom."

After taking a few steps toward his door, he stopped and turned back toward Finn. "I never knew how hard your job was. You made it look easy."

"You'll pick it up, Tom. Just give it time, and remember that Carol is your greatest ally. She was running this place years before Agent Prichard or I came along."

"Thanks, Finn. I'll remember that."

After he disappeared into his office, Finn glanced at Carol. She sat sentinel over the command section from behind her desk, controlling access like a bar bouncer. In the few moments Finn had chatted with Tom Shipley, she'd repelled two agents vying for a minute of Prichard's time. "Now, shoo." Carol's hands swept them out of her path with the force of a bulldozer. She marked her return to fighting form with a pronounced harrumph and sweater tug full of impatience.

"They all think they're king of the hill." Carol's gaze shifted to the bank of elevators down the hallway. "Oh, my."

Sloane did too. "She made it."

Eric brought the wheelchair to a halt near Carol's desk, followed by Morgan, who placed a hand on Kyler's knee and asked, "Do you need your water?"

Kyler caressed Morgan's hand. "I'm fine, Mo."

Without a strand of her dark bobbed hair out of place, Kyler was flawlessly dressed in sensible flats, a white silk blouse, and gray pinstripe slacks. She'd also done up her makeup. She was spotless. If not for the black Velcro arm sling over which a matching blazer was draped, Finn would never have guessed she'd been shot yesterday.

"You look amazing." Finn's gaze drifted and pointed at Kyler's feet. "But what happened?"

Kyler inched up her pant leg, exposing a tightly wrapped first-aid bandage. "I rolled my ankle when I fell to the sidewalk yesterday. Normally I'd use crutches for a few days, but I found it impossible with this arm."

"I'm so sorry you were hurt, Kyler." Sloane's drawn expression conveyed her regret. "This is all my fault, poking around Bernie's cold case."

"Nonsense." Morgan grazed a hand across Kyler's shoulder as she took a position behind the wheelchair, gripping the handles for another trip down the hallway. "This is Peter Rook's fault, and we're both here to make sure he doesn't get away with it."

"Any of it," Kyler barked with emphasis. "He deserves to be behind bars. Isn't that right, Nate?"

"I can confirm he had a very uncomfortable night." Nate Prichard stepped from his office doorway toward Kyler. He shook her left hand. "It's an honor, Ms. Harris. When Finn Harper told me you were injured, I was more than happy to help."

"When can we interview him?" Morgan moved a protective hand to the shoulder of Kyler's injured arm.

"I had him moved to interrogation before I arrived." He extended his arm toward the DEA offices deeper to his right. "Shall we?"

Morgan pushed Kyler, following Nate toward a secure area. Eric walked evenly with Sloane but remained silent in his jeans and suede jacket. He was carrying himself with more assuredness than Finn had seen in months. Perhaps his and Sloane's reemerging friendship had brought this on, but whatever the reason, she liked having the old Eric back.

Nate buzzed them through a metal security door flanked by an impossible-to-miss camera on one side and signage warning of federal imprisonment for violating some obscure law on the other. In her twelve years with the DEA, Finn never bothered reading those signs beyond the bold print. Why bother? Blatantly breaking the rules was never in her wheelhouse; she never left a trail on those rare occasions when she did bend them a little.

After spending weeks inside Bryant headquarters' moldy dungeon, walking into the high-tech observation area between interrogation rooms was like entering a time warp. Finn missed the bloated federal budget and all the toys she had had at her disposal at the headquarters level. Scanning the wall of new recording equipment, she thought the Sloane-Harper Group should drop a few dollars on some new tech toys of their own.

Sloane launched her observation with an appreciative whistle. "I thought your technical ops center was nice, but this is mind-blowing." She whispered into Finn's ear. "We need some of this stuff."

"I was thinking the same thing," Finn whispered back.

Nate maneuvered behind Chuck, the twenty-something, smartly dressed, dark-skinned technician operating the intricate electronics console. He'd split his attention between the two-way mirror leading into the interrogation room and the video feed displayed on the center monitor. In both, next to a lawyer in a five-hundred-dollar suit, Peter Rook sat dressed in his new uniform, federal orange from head to toe. One hand cuffed to a metal bar running the length of the table, he had a mix of boredom and impatience plastered on his face.

"We've got it from here, Chuck." Nate patted him on his back, prompting him to exit the room without question. Nate focused on Morgan. "I thought you might want to keep a lid on this."

"I do, thank you." Morgan gave him an approving nod.

"Finn…" Nate motioned to her. "Would you mind doing the honors?"

"Sure." Finn forced a smile. *Good to see nothing has changed.* Nate couldn't operate any of the high-tech equipment if his life depended on it.

Giving Kyler's wheelchair a wide berth in the cramped quarters, Finn claimed Chuck's chair. She wasn't as familiar with this console as she was with the ops center, but once she reviewed the levers and switches, she was confident she wouldn't screw up the recording. She patted herself on the back for training on every piece of equipment in the headquarters.

Nate turned to Morgan. "He's all yours."

After Eric wheeled Kyler toward the interrogation room door, Morgan pulled a small leather case from her front coat pocket. She handed it to him. "I can't make it official yet, but as far as I'm concerned, you're cleared."

Eric opened the familiar case, revealing his gold seven-point badge. Never had that hunk of metal meant so much to him, but not for the reason he expected. Holding it said that he hadn't let his father down and had preserved both of their reputations. That and having Sloane back in his life meant more to him than the job itself. For the first time, he didn't fear being forced out.

"Thank you, L-T. This means a lot to me." He removed the badge with its leather backing and clipped it to his belt before sliding the case into his back pocket.

Morgan pushed the interrogation room door open before stepping in. She held the door while Eric wheeled in Kyler. Peter instantly locked eyes with Eric. If Eric had his way, he'd wrap his fingers around Peter's neck and squeeze until he choked the life out of him, but they needed him to reel in the other dirty cop.

Eric maneuvered Kyler to the center of the table, opposite Peter. He and Morgan flanked her on either side. He hoped sitting in front of his handiwork would entice Peter to cooperate. Though his posture and the presence of a defense lawyer told him otherwise.

"Walls closing in on you, Peter?" Gauging the roll of his shoulders, Eric surmised the answer was yes. "What's it gonna take?"

"I—"

Peter's lawyer raised his hand, sharp like a sword, stopping him in mid-sentence. "My client has advanced lung cancer with less than six months to live. He wants to spend his remaining time in a minimum-security prison where no one knows he was a cop."

"That's never going to happen." Kyler's tone remained dry. Eric hoped whatever pain medication she'd taken had given her what she needed to call his foreseeable bluff. "Thanks to the little present you gave me"—she jutted out her right arm in the sling—"I still haven't finished outlining all the charges from yesterday's rampage. Attempted murder of a police officer. Attempted murder of a government official. Assault with a deadly weapon. Kidnapping. Grand theft auto. Reckless—"

"We get the picture." The lawyer appeared unfazed, unamused.

"There's no way I'll let your client live out the rest of his life in a Club Fed atmosphere for killing a police officer twenty-two years ago. He'll end up in a state penitentiary where everyone knows he's a cop."

"That's a death sentence." For the first time, Peter's face appeared pale. He was on the ropes.

"Not my problem." Strangely, Kyler's voice didn't modulate, convincing Eric pain meds were definitely in play. He'd acted the same way after he was shot and was pumped up with opioids, an uncomfortable period he'd rather forget.

"You need the name of his accomplice. Unless—" The lawyer began to say.

"We already have a name." Morgan failed to keep her tone monotone like Kyler's. It dripped with disdain. "Personnel records might be sketchy regarding partner pairings, but police reports aren't, even ones from twenty-two years ago. It's Carter Nash."

The sweat forming on Peter's brow meant Eric and Morgan's digging through old reports overnight had paid off. Peter leaned in, whispering back and forth to his high-priced lawyer, confirming their findings.

"You'll need proof. We have it." The lawyer spoke to Kyler as if they were the only two in the room.

"Specify." Both Kyler and the lawyer used a tone more suited for negotiating a business deal than for vying for a man's life.

"My client has blood and DNA evidence that will link Carter Nash to the murder of Jesse Houston."

"How do I know this supposed evidence will tie Nash to the murder?" Kyler asked. "What is it?"

"A ring."

"With whose blood on it?"

"Houston's."

"Insufficient," Kyler said. "I want Nash tied to both Houston and Officer Sellers."

"Then we have a problem."

"Your client has a problem. Either you want to save his life, or you don't."

After Kyler brilliantly pitted client against lawyer, more whispering between Peter and the lawyer ensued. Peter's stiff body language built into gesticulation, culminating in a defiant head shake.

Eric craned his neck to whisper in Kyler's ear. "Remind me to never be on the opposite side of the table as you." Under the table, Kyler tapped Eric's shin with her uninjured foot but added a slight, unsmiling nod for the rest of the room.

The lawyer's perfectly erect posture faltered. His shoulders slumped, signaling a crack on his icy facade. "What are your terms?"

"A confession from both."

"You want him to wear a wire?"

"Yes." For the first time, Kyler's face grimaced in pain. All too familiar with the sudden stabbing sensations that could course through a fresh gunshot wound, Eric rested an arm across the back of the wheelchair, ready to comfort her. She waved him off. "He gets a confession from Nash on tape, and I'll place him in medium-security state prison."

"Insufficient. A cop's life expectancy behind bars in any state prison is less than three months. That's essentially a death sentence."

"Not my problem." Kyler's voice contained not a hint of hesitation. She wasn't budging.

"And if he agrees to testify?"

Slam dunk. Christmas bow. Served on a platter. Whatever the metaphor, twenty-two-year-old cold cases were nearly impossible to solve without a confession, and snagging all the players involved was the icing on the cake.

"Low-security federal prison." A decent compromise. The walls would keep Peter in, but at least he wouldn't be surrounded by anyone with the mind to shank a dirty cop.

"We have a deal, but we hold on to the ring until he's checked that box and we have a signed deal."

"No confession from Nash, no deal." Kyler wagged an index finger. "Until then, Mr. Rook will confess now for the record."

The lawyer threw Peter a consenting nod. Eric sat straighter in his chair. This is what he'd worked for since all of this began—getting him and his father publicly cleared.

Peter cleared his throat. "When my brother's partner told me who killed him and that he was in San Francisco, I had to do something. Nash and I tracked him down. I only wanted to beat him to within an inch of his life, but I lost it. I shot him with my service weapon while Carter held him down."

"And disposing of the body." Kyler leaned in as if preparing for the kill. "Whose idea was that?"

"Carter's." Peter shifted in his chair and tugged on his handcuffs, producing a loud clank. "He knew of a crack house that would be the perfect spot, so we threw him in the trunk. He said detectives would assume it was a gang hit, which they did, and that a fire would burn up any other trace evidence. We checked the place first, and it appeared empty. We must've missed the junkie under all that filth. We carried the body to a back room, and that's when Carter lost his ring. I picked it up for safekeeping. Carter set the fire, and we left."

"Explain about the bullet."

"Carter had been banging a CSI tech who was dispatched to the scene. He said he could swap out the evidence before it made it to the lab but that I only had a few hours to find a bullet of the same caliber that wouldn't link back to either of us. I knew Eric Senior fired the same caliber as me and where he kept his spent bullets for his damn art projects, so I paid him a visit."

Eric cocked his head, searching his memory. "Son of a bitch. I remember that visit."

"It was my last." Peter shifted his gaze from Eric to Kyler. "I stole a bullet and gave it to Carter. What he did with it after that, you'll have to ask him."

Kyler cast her chin toward the lawyer's cell phone sitting neatly atop a luxury leather portfolio that screamed money. Peter must be telling the truth about having months to live. A lawyer like that probably cost every cent he had squirreled away for retirement.

"Set it up for tonight," Kyler said with a certainty that left no room for debate.

The lawyer picked up his phone, swiped his thumb against the screen, and held it out to Peter. "Call him."

Peter reacted as if he'd been offered a piece of trash, refusing to take it. "Carter won't answer if he doesn't know the number."

"Leave a damn message, Peter." Eric pounded his right fist on the table, the reverberation punctuating his message. "I want this over tonight."

"He won't listen to it. I need my flip phone."

"Which is where?" Eric gritted his teeth to contain his seeping impatience over Peter's stalling.

"You should know." Peter shrugged. "It was with my clothes in the hospital."

Eric snapped his head toward the two-way mirror, hoping someone in that room was reading his message to scramble and find that damn phone.

Less than a minute later, the door opened. Finn stepped inside, carrying an evidence bag containing a single flip phone. She laid it on the table in front of Morgan and left. It seemed Nate Prichard remembered enough from his field days to be prepared during interviews.

Morgan inspected the bag before holding it up. "Is this it?"

Peter rolled his head left to right, looking at the bag.

"Stop the damn thumb-sucking, Peter." Eric's irritation had peaked. Morgan removed the phone and slid it across the table. "Put it on speaker and make the damn call."

"All right, give me a second to think." Peter's eyes darted back and forth as beads of sweat trickled down the sides of his face. He picked up the phone, flipped it open, and thumbed several buttons. He let it ring three times, then ended the call.

He dialed again, but this time spoke when voice mail connected. "This has gotten out of hand. Unless you want me to activate my insurance policy, meet me, nine o'clock tonight at the place where this all began." Peter flipped the phone closed and slid it across the table. "He'll show."

"Where this all began?" Morgan asked. "You're not referring to the crack house?"

Peter shrugged again. His "don't give a fuck" attitude had become grating. "It's now an unmanned parking lot with controlled entry. It's perfect."

CHAPTER TWENTY

Like a toddler loose in a toy store, Sloane couldn't stop tinkering with the DEA surveillance van's tempting collection of knobs, switches, and touchscreens. She envisioned her and Finn starring in a futuristic movie as the latest badass detectives, using this van to catch the bad guys. Of course, they fell in love in the end.

"You're like a little kid on Christmas morning." Finn swatted her hand away when it wandered dangerously close to the recording controls and Chuck, the technician operating them from his position at the console.

"I can't help myself. We never had gear like this." Sloane was sandwiched between Finn and a handcuffed Peter Rook on the upholstered bench that ran the length of the windowless back compartment. She leaned closer to Finn and whispered so only she could hear, "It's quite the turn-on."

Finn pulled back enough to look her in the eyes with a matching naughty grin. "Remind me to stop by the tech center and pick up a copy of their equipment catalog." Her tone verged on the seductive, but doing anything about that flirtatious timbre would have to wait.

From each side of the Mercedes Sprinter, four monitors displayed external video feeds in vivid high-definition. They showed diffused red twilight hues that back lit buildings and other vehicles as the van maneuvered in traffic. When the van crept to a stop, its interior pocket door slid open, revealing the driver's compartment and captain's chairs with Agent Shipley at the wheel and Morgan West in the passenger seat.

Shipley craned his neck to peer into the back of the van. "I had the area scouted this afternoon. We're a block over to the north. That's about as close as we should get. Otherwise, we risk being made. There are three directions of egress. Team Two is covering the east, and Team Three is covering the west. The south is blocked by a hillside, so I put a spotter from Team Four on the tallest roof to the north. We should have three-sixty-degree coverage."

"Well-planned op, Tom." Finn's compliment was more than ego-stroking, Sloane decided. She'd effectively handed over the reins to a reluctant leader.

"Thanks, Finn." His perceptible grin suggested that he readily accepted her gesture. "We're all linked on tac two."

Peter Rook shifted on the bench, pinching the fabric of Sloane's jean jacket. Given that there were four people crammed onto a seat designed for three, she'd put up with his squirming for the last twenty minutes. It was annoying. But with the possibility of getting Carter Nash's confession on tape, her best option was to keep her mouth shut. She wouldn't be surprised, though, if he got a few elbow jabs from Eric, who was sitting at the end of the bench, smashed between the Sprinter's tail end and the man who had framed his father for murder, hit him over the head, and totaled his car yesterday.

Fifteen minutes before the meeting with Nash, the van remained quiet and overstuffed. The air was stale and heavy with anticipation and the faint smell of cigarettes radiating from Chuck.

The longer Sloane sat next to Peter Rook, the more her skin crawled. She brusquely pushed Peter's leg back into his personal space with her thigh.

"You're a little testy, Sloane," Peter said.

"Cop killers have that effect on me."

"Him, I regret."

"He had a name."

"I know. Bernie Sellers." Peter sighed.

"Bernie left behind a daughter." Sloane slowly turned her head to lock gazes with Peter. She drilled him like a jackhammer with her eyes. "Whatever happens to you in prison, you've earned it." A side of her hoped someone in that low-security prison he was heading off to would put him in the ground before cancer did.

"On that cue, I think it's time for me to get in place." Peter extended his handcuffed wrists for Eric to unlock them.

"We have multiple teams watching your every move, so don't get any ideas." One at a time, Eric slid the skeleton-like key into each tiny lock, releasing the metal restraints. "If you do, Sloane and I will make it our life's mission to hunt you down."

"And we're damn good at our jobs," Sloane said with an added self-assuredness. Calling themselves a team again was like applying a salve to a fresh wound. It soothed away the sting with the knowledge she would soon heal.

Peter rubbed his wrists once they were free and followed Eric out the back door. "I'm starting to think you don't like me, Junior."

"Whatever gave you that idea?" Eric pointed to the button that secured the breast pocket flap on Peter's corduroy jacket and had a hidden camera and microphone embedded inside it. "Remember, we have eyes and ears on you. As soon as you get the confession, we'll close in."

Peter patted down his pockets. "Anyone got a smoke?"

"Sure." Chuck pulled a pack of gold Marlboros from his breast pocket and tapped it on the console until one cigarette peeked out of the open end on the top. He extended the pack out the open door. After Peter took one, Chuck sparked his blue plastic Zippo to life and held it out. Peter leaned forward with the cigarette dangling from his lips until the flickering flame lit the tip into an orange glow. Chuck withdrew and resumed his position at the console.

Peter took a long drag. The glow brightened as more of the tobacco burned, sending tendrils of smoke rising like ribbons flapping in a soft breeze. He removed the cigarette from his mouth and coughed something awful as he blew out the smoke. A man with lung cancer shouldn't be smoking, but what more harm could it do in Peter's case?

"Thanks." Peter gave Chuck a grateful nod and then focused on Eric. "See you on the flip side, Junior."

"Can't wait." Once Peter disappeared around the corner, Eric climbed back into the Sprinter and secured the rear doors. He mumbled, "Asshole."

"Exactly what I was thinking." Sloane patted a section of the bench next to her, inviting Eric to sit. "This will be over soon."

The extra elbow room helped Sloane shed the claustrophobic feeling she had since Agent Shipley had crammed them in like sardines back at DEA headquarters. At least he'd arranged for their top-tier surveillance van, as Finn had called it.

Removing noise-canceling headphones that looked like a 1970s throwback, Chuck slung them around his neck. "You guys want to hear the audio feed?"

"Please, Chuck," Finn replied. Finn's practice of using first names and making people feel important didn't escape Sloane. That unique skill likely had helped put her on the DEA fast-track, propelling her to management faster than her contemporaries.

Chuck flipped a switch, activating the system speakers. Crystal clear, the sound of heavy breathing, shuffling clothes, and sneakers thudding against concrete filled the cabin. "Geeze, I knew he wasn't in the best of shape before he retired," Eric said, "but he sounds like Darth Vader."

"Luke, I am your father," Chuck said right on cue while fiddling with some toggles. Laughter filled the van with Morgan howling the loudest. Sloane couldn't recall ever seeing her laugh that hard, ever. She liked it.

Sloane's gaze focused on the console's large center monitor. The sun had gone to bed, leaving behind a dark sky, but the city streetlights had come on, casting an amber glow that followed Peter as he walked. The high-definition quality of the images, when compared to those of the SFPD's surveillance video, was like comparing ultra-4K to grainy talkies. *I gotta get one of those.*

The video feed showed Peter continuing down this once run-down side neighborhood. Section Eight housing and drug dens had been renovated into a mix of tightly spaced middle-class townhouses, small businesses, and public parking lots. It didn't surprise Sloane that Peter hadn't passed a single pedestrian traveling from the direction of his destination at this time of night. In this neighborhood, shops and local residents battened down the hatches after dark.

When the concrete sidewalk in front of Peter turned into asphalt, motion on the center screen slowed. He had entered the parking lot where once stood the crack house where Carli Thompson and Bernie Sellers lost their lives. Where Jesse Houston became charred beyond recognition.

Sloane's mind drifted to the morning when she sat on the curb in front of her grandmother's townhouse waiting for Bernie to take her to see Finn and the anger she felt when he didn't show. She was ashamed to think when she saw the smoke rising beyond her neighborhood in the distance that she cursed him while he was trapped, trying to save a stranger's life.

Sloane slid closer to Finn until their thighs touched. She needed her comfort to get past the shame. When her leg bounced uncontrollably, Finn pushed a hand on top to still it. Sloane clutched that hand, squeezing it for dear life. The energy from Finn flowed in strong and steady. Without it, she would've melted into a puddle of nerves.

"I wanted none of this to happen, Junior." Peter's voice was glaringly clear through the feed. "I was blinded by rage and then panicked by what I'd done. Even though the fire wasn't my idea and I didn't set it, I went along. Finding out a cop died in that fire changed me. I was a cop killer and never felt proud wearing the badge since. I'm sorry about your dad. He was a good cop and an even better man. Let's chalk that part up to being a coward. Not a day has gone by that I didn't wish the shoe to fall, so this would finally be over. It's poetic justice that it was you, the man whose father I set up, who ended up taking me down. Whatever happens to me, I hope Carter Nash meets the same fate."

Though it barely qualified as one, Peter's apology left the six people in the Sprinter speechless. It sounded prophetic. Like he expected his future to include something worse than a prison cell and hospital bed.

Sloane stared at Eric. She expected a stoic expression, but he met her with tears pooling in his eyes. Something Peter said had penetrated the unconditional wall he'd erected for cop killers.

Eric stood. Too tall for the Sprinter's interior, he crouched two steps toward Chuck's console. "Mind if I use the mic?"

"Sure." Chuck removed the tactical radio microphone from the U-hook mounted above the console and stretched the curly cord to Eric.

Eric gripped the hard plastic of the block mic and held it to his chest for a moment. He then raised it to his mouth, depressed its button, and spoke. "Do you remember what you told me the first day we partnered up?"

"I told you that you were a good cop and street smart. That you knew the difference between the law and justice and that the two don't always mean the same thing." Peter's voice contained a hint of nostalgia, prideful of better times.

The back of Sloane's throat thickened. The first day she wore her gold badge, as she sat in the front seat of an unmarked sedan with Eric behind the wheel before entering her first crime scene as a detective, Eric had given her exactly the same speech.

Eric pressed the button again. "You weren't wrong about law and justice. You just took it too far. Some lines aren't meant to be broken. But you already knew that, which is why you're standing in that parking lot. Nothing you do or say can ever—"

"This is Team Four. I got movement on a rooftop south of Pawn's location."

Shipley picked up the microphone to the van's main tactical radio in the front compartment. "Team Two, this is Team One. One of you break off and find out what it is."

"Team Two, copy."

The images in Peter's video feed to the monitor wildly spun left, right, and in a circle as if he were trying to make out what was on the rooftop.

"Team Two, this is Team Four. It's the three-story apartment complex with wood siding."

"Copy. Two Alpha en route."

Sloane squeezed Finn's hand harder. Movement on a rooftop could be anything from a teenager sneaking up there to smoke pot to... She didn't want to complete that thought. Everything they needed to bring down Carter Nash rested on that man in the parking lot and what was in his head.

A sharp noise through the speaker.

Peter's video feed shook and then settled, displaying only pavement.

"Shots fired. Shots fired," someone yelled over the air.

"Converge. All units converge," Shipley yelled through the mic.

"Shit." Eric flung open the back door so hard the Sprinter wobbled on its tires. Sloane dashed out behind him. Eric increased his lead, taking longer strides, despite Sloane kicking it into high gear. Her heart beat wildly. The seconds running down that dark unpopulated street felt like an eternity. She didn't have time to think, but she had the comforting sense Finn was just steps behind.

When she reached the corner of the adjacent building, the sparsely filled parking lot lit by the amber glow of streetlights came into view. Eric was kneeling near a late-model imported SUV.

Three dark-suited agents converged on the lot, their semiautomatic service firearms drawn and searching for targets—one was trained on her and then behind her. Sloane came to a screeching halt, arms up to demonstrate she was unarmed. She hoped Finn had stopped on a dime, too. The agent pointed his weapon at Sloane again. She stared down the barrel, hoping he hadn't had an extra cup of caffeine while on stakeout. A jittery hand could cost Sloane her life.

From behind her, Finn's voice roared. "Friendly. We're with Pawn."

When the agent lowered his weapon, Sloane finally exhaled. *That was fucking stupid. Me, not him.* A quick glance over her shoulder confirmed Finn had stopped a few feet short. *Thank goodness someone had a clear head.*

Agents had their guns at the ready, searching for threats as they formed a makeshift perimeter around where Sloane suspected Peter Rook was lying. She and Finn rushed to Eric's side. His upper body heaved, desperately sucking in deep swaths of the cool night air. He had turned Peter over onto his back and was clutching the lapels of his coat. He leaned over him while a pool of what Sloane assumed was blood crept from beneath his body and spread like the stink of death on a battlefield.

"Damn it, Peter. It didn't have to come to this. You should've turned yourself in when I first gave you the chance." Peter's legs twitched as Eric clutched harder. He was alive. "We could've found another way."

A winded male voice sounded from behind. "Two Alpha report." Sloane glanced over her shoulder. Shipley spun on his heels, apparently stopping in each direction long enough to get his bearings. He held his left wrist close to his mouth, barking more orders into his mic. "Who's on that damn roof? Team Three, come in."

A gagging, spitting sound came from Peter's direction. Sloane snapped her head around in time to see his body convulse and then stop. Eric shook him by the lapels, but his eyes remained closed.

The faint sound of a siren grew louder as the first responders approached, but they were too late. There was no sign of life. Peter lay limp. Still. The life had drained out of him and, along with it, the location of that damn bloody ring. Without it, Carter Nash would walk. Despite her relief that Eric had secured vindication for him and his father, anger built in Sloane. Justice for Bernie and Carli had slipped through their fingers.

CHAPTER TWENTY-ONE

Sloane nudged open the door leading into Reagan's dark bedroom, cringing at the long, steady creak of the hinge that resulted. She'd thought once or twice about spraying some WD-40 on it, but it served as an effective, low-tech, middle-of-the-night alarm for sneaky teenagers.

It was past two o'clock in the morning. Sloane expected to see a Reagan-sized lump under the bedcovers. Other than the empty dinner plate on the nightstand, she wasn't disappointed. Her daughter was sound asleep, nestled between a myriad of pillows. Sloane inched the door back, once again flinching at the horror movie sound effect.

"She's fine," Sloane whispered to Finn in the softly lit hallway. Another missed family dinner added to her list of regrets of the day. Or was it yesterday? She promised herself to make up for it in five or six hours with a home-cooked breakfast before Reagan went off for another day of her internship at Chandler's law firm.

Before they returned to the stairs leading up to the main level, Finn opened the new white six-panel door guarding the half-finished home office. "I wanna check it out. The drywall went up today." Her hand went to the wall switch, turning on the ceiling can lights. Inside, contractors had leveled the floor, installed electrical, framed, and hung drywall, still unfinished and untaped. Every sound echoed off the flat walls and cement floor.

Though tired, hungry, and disappointed, Sloane welcomed the diversion of scouting the home office she'd soon share with Finn. With the woman she planned to propose to soon, she thought with an easy smile. She'd already decided on where she wanted to do it, but getting Finn there without raising her curiosity was her primary stumbling block. For it to be the best surprise of Finn's life, she'd have to wait until the time was right.

"This is turning out so much better than I envisioned when you first suggested it." Finn ran a hand across the long wall of the ten-by-fifteen-foot space, her fingertips bumping over the unfinished seams of the drywall sheets. "I'll miss having a window, but as I'm learning in The Pit, I work better without the distraction."

When Finn reached the far end of the room, Sloane came up behind her, wrapping arms around her waist. Pressing their bodies together, from thigh to chest, she nuzzled Finn's neck. "I have a feeling you'll like my type of distraction."

"I think you're right." Finn arched her back and slung an arm up, hooking it around Sloane's neck. Her chest rose, inviting her to touch her.

"Mom?" Reagan's groggy voice broke the spell, prompting a retreat of the hand Sloane had slid dangerously close to a tempting breast. "It's late. What are you guys doing down here?"

Sloane kissed Finn on the cheek and murmured, "Raincheck." She released her embrace and turned toward Reagan. "Sorry we woke you. We got in a few minutes ago and wanted to see the progress after checking on you."

"It's fine." Reagan yawned. "The contractors were gone by the time I came home from work."

The word "work" coming from Reagan's mouth never failed to astonish Sloane. Avery would've never imagined her as an intern in a prestigious law firm and toying with the idea of attending law school. Neither had Sloane until that first morning when Finn helped her pick out an outfit. Reagan had no longer looked like a spirited teenage girl. She'd looked all grown up like a professional young woman, and that melted her heart.

Sloane's stomach gurgled loudly, announcing her hunger to the room. When was the last time she ate? She scratched her head. *A sub sandwich and chips for lunch*, she thought. *No wonder!* "Anyone else hungry?"

"For hours." Finn placed a hand over her belly, making Sloane's hunger pangs more pronounced.

"I could go for some ice cream." Reagan waggled her eyebrows, an invitation Sloane couldn't resist.

"At two a.m.?" Finn's mouth fell open.

"There's never an inappropriate time for ice cream." Sloane playfully swatted Finn on the butt as they ascended the stairs. In the kitchen, Reagan took out the bowls, Finn the utensils, and Sloane the quart of Oreo cookie dessert.

"Let me, ladies." Finn held up the scooper. After Finn filled the bowls, everyone settled into a soft, cozy spot on the couch. Not a single word of chitchat. Only the occasional moan of satisfaction with their early, early morning indulgence.

Once the clank of spoons against porcelain slowed, Reagan asked, "Why so late tonight?"

"Work." Vague and impersonal. Sloane fell back to her typical response when danger was involved.

"Must've been something bad that you don't want me to know about." Reagan snatched up her bowl and huffed toward the kitchen. "You don't have to protect me, you know."

"Tell her, babe." Finn gave Sloane an encouraging nod.

"You're right," Sloane said after a moment. Minutes ago, she had been musing about how grown up Reagan looked. She should start treating her like she was. She followed Reagan into the kitchen. Finn, close behind her, put a reassuring hand on her back and started stroking it in circles. She cleared her throat and started in.

"Finn and I have been working with Eric on a cold case as part of our contract."

Reagan's eyes lit up with anticipation. "With Eric?"

After explaining about Officer Bernie Sellers, Eric's involvement, and the nameless former partner, Sloane recounted the drive-by shooting at Sally's café and Peter's involvement. She ended with, "So our friend Kyler was collateral damage because of our snooping around. Eric's old partner agreed to help us get a confession from the other man who helped him kill those people, but tonight he was killed by a sniper before he could."

Reagan gasped. "That's horrible. So the dangerous part is over?"

"We think so." This was more wishful thinking than certainty, but Sloane couldn't be sure of anything when it came to Nash. "We're just disappointed the other man, the one who killed Bernie and the woman he was trying to save, might get away with murder." Sloane dipped her head. Her failure still stung, but having Finn at her side was making it bearable. "I wanted to make it right."

"I'm glad you had Finn." Reagan's sheepish eyes were as soft as her words. The cold war in the house had finally ended. "You kept each other safe and sane."

Sloane exchanged glances with Finn. "Yes, we did."

Tonight they had turned a corner. The distrust that had enveloped the house like a dark cloud finally had cleared. Like the air following a cleansing rain, the mood in the room now had a freshness about it. And with it, a renewed sense of family. That was it. Sloane had to get a ring.

* * *

"Best view in the whole damn city."

Eric lay on his side, naked beneath the sheets covering him from the waist down. He'd propped up his head by the palm of his right arm bent into a triangle against the pillow. The view? Kadin strutting back into his bedroom dressed only in one of his white long-sleeve button-down dress shirts, unbuttoned, of course. In her hands? An opened bottle of wine, red. And two stacked cups. Plastic. Also red.

"These were all I could find." She held up the Solo cups.

"That's because that's all there is." Eric sat up straight and patted the section of the mattress she'd occupied for the last hour. She'd left to retrieve the wine she'd brought in response to his late, late booty call. After watching his old partner die, he desperately needed the release. "I mostly eat out."

"Yes, you do." She followed up her reply with a seductive wink before handing him a cup. She poured until it was half full, filled hers the same, and placed the bottle on the cheap Ikea nightstand. "It should be a crime to drink Chateau Leoville Barton Saint Julien from plastic."

"I have some Bud Light if you'd like that instead." He maintained his best straight face until she playfully swatted his chest.

"Not when my best Bordeaux is in danger of going bad. I've opened it, for God's sake." Her wine splashed over the edge of her Solo, blotting the front of his poplin shirt. Three spots started out pea-sized but quickly grew into silver dollars. A panicked look filled her eyes.

"Oh, I'm so sorry. Let me clean it." She narrowed one eye. "I won't bother asking if you have any baking soda or hydrogen peroxide. Do you have any club soda?"

"Nope. Bachelor."

"Laundry detergent?"

"That I have. It's under the bathroom sink."

"I'll be right back."

Eric thought the view of Kadin strolling into his room had been spectacular, but this one almost put him in a coma. She slid the shirt off her shoulders as she walked away, letting the cotton cascade down her arms and back. With every step past the bedroom door into the hallway, she exposed alluring thewy flares, more and more skin and a figure that would bring traffic to a grinding halt.

Dear Lord. How did Finn let you go?

When the shirtsleeves gathered at her wrists, she glanced over her shoulder, narrowing her eyes into a seductive tease. After two nights with her, Eric realized Kadin was a master at flirtation. Every word carefully chosen. Every movement strategically planned. She designed every action to titillate the senses and evoke the desired reaction, and he was her willing victim.

When she stepped through the bathroom door, she flexed a hand, sending one end of the garment toward the floor, revealing the entirety of her teardrop bottom. After collecting the shirt in one hand, she stepped further into the bathroom, keeping the door open. At the vanity, she bent at the waist instead of at the knees, providing Eric an exquisite view. Seduction, indeed.

"Got it." Kadin straightened, effectively ending the best part of the show.

He considered telling her the shirt was old and the stain didn't matter, but what was the fun in that? He waited out the hum of running water and the several rounds of body jiggling and arm shaking at the sink, thoroughly enjoying the view.

When the water stopped, she bent again at the waist and closed the cabinet. She faced him, presenting every inch of her body. With a fingertip, she slowly pushed the bathroom door closed. Her naughty look gave him the impression she enjoyed the fun and games as much as he did.

Eric flopped flat on the bed, his arms bouncing off the mattress. "She's gonna kill me."

He couldn't remember the last time a woman had him both physically and mentally intrigued. Scratch that. He couldn't remember it ever happening because he never allowed himself to enjoy a woman's company beyond his physical needs.

The only woman who had occupied his head was Sloane. He'd secretly kept up with her life to make up for what he'd done as a teenager. But all of that was behind him. Sloane was on the road to forgiving him or at least accepting him back into the fold.

Kadin was an enigma. Smart, sexy, ambitious, and well off. Why weren't men and women lining up at her door? Had she beaten them all back with her sharp wit? Was she hiding some wicked secret? Would he soon discover he was no match for her outside the bedroom? From what he'd seen, that would likely be the case. Until then, he'd enjoy the ride.

A flush.

The hum of running water again.

The bathroom door flew open with a rush of air. Then Kadin marched through, naked and flat-footed, not on the balls of her feet like before to make her body sway. Her eyes narrowed again, not in a sexy tease, more like a raging bull. If not for the searing stare directed at him, he'd have zeroed in on her curves.

"Are you a dirty cop? Were you suspended because you hid evidence?" Kadin's march continued until she reached the bed. "I'm an officer of the court, Eric. I can't be associated with a dirty cop."

"What are you talking about?" He pushed himself to a sitting position. "And I sure as hell don't like the implication that I'm dirty."

She threw a sealed plastic bag atop the sheets covering his lap. "I dated law enforcement long enough to know you don't take home evidence." The cocked hip, he assumed, was her fighting posture.

His gaze drifted from her glowering face to the item she'd tossed on the bed. The telltale printing on the exposed side of the pint-sized clear plastic bag told Eric it was a police evidence bag, but not of a type he'd used before. It appeared dated. Whose ever it was, it wasn't his.

He lifted it at the corner with his thumb and index finger, careful not to smudge any more fingerprints than Kadin already had. Inspecting the front, Eric noted the description and chain of custody lines were empty. This wasn't official evidence.

He flipped it over to the unobstructed side, taking a moment to focus on the contents. He let a broad grin emerge on his face as an adrenaline-tinged lightness filled his chest. It was a ring. A beautiful, bloody man's ring. "Holy shit. Where did you find this?"

"In the tissue box. Are you saying it's not yours?"

He laughed—a half-sinister one that wrinkled Kadin's brow into a suspicious recoil. "You may have been a son of a bitch, but at least you did one thing right."

"Who are you calling a son of a bitch?" She placed both hands on her hips, balling them into fists. Her face reddened almost to the shade of the wine she'd spilled. When her nostrils flared, one thought came to mind. She was damn sexy when she was mad.

His laughter turned into a lighthearted chuckle. He reached for Kadin's hand, but she withdrew. "Not you. Peter."

"Peter? Your friend from the other night?"

"He's no friend. And he's dead."

"Dead? When?"

"Earlier tonight."

"You better start explaining."

He carefully placed the evidence bag on the nightstand next to their cups of Bordeaux and then pulled her onto the bed. She didn't resist when he rolled on top of her. "After."

* * *

"This had better be damn good," Sloane mumbled as she slammed the driver's door of her SUV. It was four o'clock in the morning. No matter what had gotten Eric all worked up, this had better wrap itself up within two hours. Otherwise, breakfast with Reagan would be a bust. Missing dinner was one thing, but breakfast? That was an unspeakable crime in their house.

"He said it was important, right?" Finn closed the passenger door and met Sloane near the rear bumper.

"He made it sound like he'd won the lottery."

"Then Reagan will understand."

"She shouldn't have to. I quit the force so this very thing wouldn't happen." Stuffing her key fob back into her front jeans pocket, Sloane questioned the logic of listening to Eric's two words—"trust me." A week ago, she wouldn't have considered meeting him, let alone crawling out of bed after an hour's sleep.

"Come on, you." Finn extended her hand to Sloane and then led her through the parking lot toward Eric's apartment.

Two hours before sunrise, Sloane's senses were heightened. Movement several cars over raised her defenses. Her pulse increased two-fold. She inched up the side of her jacket and rested her right hand on her Beretta Nano. Peter's drive-by had convinced her to never be without it again. Kyler being shot and the sniper taking out Peter had Sloane justifiably spooked.

She stopped and protectively positioned herself between Finn and the danger. A second later, something small darted from beneath a nearby car. "Fucking cat."

"Want me to protect you?" If Finn's playful tone was meant to lighten the mood, it did.

"You weren't supposed to hear that."

"You're still my big, badass superhero."

"I'd rather be an asleep superhero curled up next to my damsel in distress." Sloane wrapped an arm around Finn's waist and pulled her close.

"I can make that happen after we meet with Eric." Finn gave her a peck on the lips and pulled Sloane along.

At the apartment door, Sloane rang the bell. If she annoyed anyone at this time of the morning, it would be just Eric, not his neighbors with the door banging she had in mind. She pressed it again and again, ensuring she'd achieved her goal.

The door opened with a force. "Geeze, Sloane. I heard you the first time." Eric's tight expression, mussed hair, and randomly thrown together wardrobe were priceless.

"It's four o'clock. That's what you get."

"You *have* gone civilian." Eric snorted. After he motioned for Sloane and Finn to come in, he closed the door and followed them into the living room. "According to L-T, I might join you."

"Why? What did she tell you?" Sloane grew concerned at Eric's sulky expression.

"At the hospital, she told me why she and Kyler were meeting you and Finn at Sally's."

"We hope Kyler has found enough to leverage the mayor into rethinking her plan." Finn used a more optimistic tone than Sloane would have. Nicci Cole struck her as a woman who wouldn't easily back down.

"Well, I can't pass the physical. The mayor will probably force me and others like me into early medical retirement." Eric's voice had thickened. Being forced out apparently troubled him, but not as much as she expected. He cleared his throat. "Enough of that bullshit." Using a partially folded handkerchief, Eric picked up a plastic bag lying on the coffee table. His expression brightened into a devilish grin. "This was hidden in my bathroom."

When he flipped it around to the see-through side, a single item came into view. Sloane rocked her head, determining its shape. "What is it?"

"I think it's Peter's ring."

"Not *the* ring? How did you find it?"

"I didn't exactly find it." Eric's expression turned sheepish when the rushing sound of the toilet flushing came from the hallway.

"Really?" This just became interesting, and Sloane didn't intend to cut him any slack. Eric was a gentleman, but it was about time she paid him back for walking in on her and Finn during several pivotal moments. She slinked toward the hallway, grinning as she traveled backward. "I think I gotta pee."

The bathroom door opened. A woman stepped out. Sloane hung her mouth open wide enough to park her SUV in it. "What the fuck?" Kadin's was the last face she had expected to see. The casual clothes meant she wasn't about to do the walk of shame after a wild night of clubbing, which hinted Eric was comfortable enough to call her in the middle of the night. "I thought you were gay."

"You thought wrong." Kadin turned sideways to shimmy past Sloane in the narrow hallway, making sure to not brush up against her.

Everything about that woman bothered Sloane. She was smart, sexy, and knew Finn in a way that drew out her jealous streak. Out of all the straight or bi women in the city, how in the world did Eric pick her? Sloane might have to rethink this forgiving thing with him.

Kadin stepped out of the hallway shadows and into the well-lit living room.

Finn's mouth dropped open as Sloane's had. "What the—"

Kadin snapped her palm up near Finn's face in a stopping motion. "Don't you start either. Yes, we're sleeping together."

"Not much sleeping," Eric mumbled with a hint of subdued pride.

"What happened to Four B?" Finn jerked her head back. She looked as confused as Sloane felt.

"I should've followed my instincts. Too vain."

"How long?" Finn rapidly shifted an index finger between Kadin and Eric.

"Not long." That translated to not new. Meaning this wasn't the first time.

"Eric's a great guy. I'm happy for you." Finn's concern for Kadin didn't escape Sloane, but it didn't bother her either. They'd turned the corner on Kadin Hall.

"I should get going." Kadin pointed toward the evidence bag Eric still held between his fingertips. "If you need a statement, I can attest to discovering it."

Kadin kissed Eric on the cheek, lingering an extra beat. Whatever this was between them, it was clear the newness had yet to wear off. Walking out the door, she glanced over her shoulder. "Good luck with the case."

After closing the door, he turned to face the gallery of gawkers. "Ring or Kadin first?"

Without looking at each other, Sloane and Finn said at the same time, "Kadin."

Eric slumped his shoulders. "It started the night I got suspended. We're just having fun. Now, can we talk about the ring?" He raised his hand with the evidence bag.

"In a minute." Sloane placed both hands on her hips. "Of all the women, why her?"

"With all due respect, Sloane, it's none of your business."

"Just last week, she was all over Finn, so it *is* my business."

"Whatever happened in the past doesn't matter." Eric emitted a breathy, complex sigh. "Look, Sloane, I don't want this to be awkward between us. I appreciate your concern, but my seeing Kadin is off-limits."

"Babe," Finn rested a hand on Sloane's back, "let's table this."

Finn was right, but Kadin weaving her way into Eric's bed and potentially Finn's life again couldn't be coincidental. She hoped for Eric's sake that Kadin wasn't using him to stay connected to Finn.

Sloane cast her chin toward the evidence bag. "So you think that's the insurance policy Peter talked about?"

"Absolutely." Eric's voice had a sense of confidence she missed. His great instincts never let them down.

"Let me look at that." Finn reached for the bag via the handkerchief. She examined the ring inside. "There's definitely blood on it. There's a Greek symbol. Could it be a fraternity ring?"

Sloane leaned forward to focus on the ring details. She remembered thinking about a fraternity recently, but she couldn't recall where. It would come to her. "Does Morgan know about this?"

"Yes," Eric replied. "She didn't want to leave Kyler in the middle of the night, so we're meeting at Bryant at eight."

"Are you thinking what I'm thinking?" Sloane asked. A lopsided grin sprouted on Eric's face. Simultaneously, they said, "Todd."

CHAPTER TWENTY-TWO

The migas that were in their final stages of digestion in Sloane's stomach meant two things: She hadn't broken another promise to Reagan, and she, Finn, and Eric were several hours closer to taking down the high-ranking chief of detectives. With Peter Rook dead, connecting Captain Carter Nash to the twenty-two-year-old murder required rock-solid proof. Ironically, a drug dealer's vanity could do just that. Matching Jessie Houston's DNA from that gaudy gold tooth to the bloody ring would get them halfway there. To seal the deal, they needed Nash's DNA on that ring too.

New rapid DNA technology had revolutionized law enforcement and compressed the wait for testing results from two days to two hours. But that meant that waiting had become a bigger part of the process. Why do anything else when you could have another lead before lunch?

Paper plates, plastic utensils, five large paper coffee cups, and one half-empty pie tin littered the usually empty conference table in Morgan West's office. Sloane and Finn had picked up the perfect comfort food from Sally's for today's waiting crew. The decision was primarily selfish. Sloane had gotten into the habit of indulging in sweets to ease her anxiety, and she'd obviously corrupted Finn. She was already halfway done with her slice.

Morgan continued to dote over Kyler in her wheelchair, stirring sugar and cream into her second cup of coffee. Eric sat brooding at the end of the table, having resisted engaging in idle conversation for the last two hours.

Kyler sipped on her lovingly prepared coffee before turning to Sloane. "Since I'm working mostly from home this week, I had my assistant drop off the files on Nicci Cole's declined cases with that law firm I told you about. I've sifted through a few, but so far, the list of reprobates she let go is quite colorful."

"This is exactly what we'll need to throw at the mayor when we make our report to her at the midpoint of our contract."

The hard fact was that Nicci Cole's contractors had played a pivotal role in solving a twenty-two-year-old murder of a police officer. That proved the mayor's point: the SFPD needed a thorough housecleaning. Sloane had wracked her brain over coffee and pie, but other than making use of Chandler's connections, she couldn't think of anything more she and Finn could do to shift the mayor from her warpath. She hoped what they had would be enough.

The room settled into an uncomfortable silence that reminded Sloane of the night El Padrino had kidnapped Reagan and Chandler. Except for a handful of intense moments, long periods of anxious waiting had marked the entire ordeal. Like that night, Finn remained close, caressing her hand or kissing her on the lips whenever she needed the comfort and added encouragement.

Finally there was a knock on the door.

Todd, dressed in his white lab coat, held up a piece of paper in his hand. His expression was unreadable, which didn't bode well. "Got it."

Morgan waved him in. "Close the door."

The seconds he needed to shut the door and face the small crowd in the room took way too long for Sloane's patience.

More precious seconds ticked away at sloth-like speed as he stood there, mouth closed, staring at Morgan.

"Well?" Morgan asked.

"The blood on the ring is a match to the gold tooth."

They'd dotted an "I." Now, they had to cross the "T" and link the ring to Nash.

"Anything else?" Their case rested on the answer to Morgan's open-ended question.

"Sorry, Lieutenant." Todd shook his head. "I couldn't find any other identifiable DNA. Though I found the word 'Callahan' engraved on the inside."

"Thank you, Todd."

He handed Morgan the report and scurried out of the room. Sloane would've scampered out too, but she was too disappointed to move.

"I'm sorry, Morgan." Kyler's sad smile and soothing tone signaled they'd come to an impasse. "With Peter dead, his signed statement isn't enough. Unless I directly link Nash to the ring, he has to walk."

Bernie Sellers, Carli Thompson, and Jesse Houston were all dead in part because of Carter Nash. And Peter likely had been killed by his sniper's bullet. Sloane suspected Nash's SWAT training had seen to it the only person who could put a virtual noose around his neck was lying in the morgue. While each of those victims deserved justice, Sloane took her failure to secure it for Bernie and his family hard. Until she put Nash behind bars, this would never be over for her. She patted her Barretta Nano, hoping Nash wouldn't get any wild ideas about eliminating threats and force her to use it.

* * *

Two weeks had passed, and the last thing Sloane wanted was to stand in front of Carter Nash and serve up a status report on her and Finn's work. She'd leave out the part where they'd unearthed him as a killer, but providing a summary of everything else was a necessary evil.

Yesterday, she cursed Detective Jim Shaw all afternoon for reminding her of the contractual requirement. He noted if she failed to show up, Nash could declare her in breach of contract with the city. Rock and a hard place. Over a barrel. In a jam. Every idiom came to mind, but they all said the same thing: she didn't have a choice.

Sloane stepped off the elevator with Finn, wishing she could grab her hand and take her anywhere else but Bryant's fifth-floor command section. The printed report she carried contained numbers, charts, and high-level summaries as their contract required. It lacked the most crucial piece of news, though: Carter Nash is a fucking murderer!

"Is this making your skin crawl too?" Finn's matter-of-fact tone left no question. This part of the job bothered her equally.

"At least we have to do this only a few more times."

Sloane squirmed in her flats as if shaking off a disgusting layer of slime before knocking her knuckles extra hard against the frosted glass office door. She waited for the disembodied voice from the other side to invite her in. She shook the virtual goo off her once more and pushed the door open.

Inside, Captain Carter Nash sat behind the oversized desk that matched his inflated ego. Angled so his right side faced the sunlight cascading through the equally large window to their right, Sloane had a perfect view of his profile. Though he'd focused his attention on reading the papers in his hands, she imagined him holding up a felt board with his name spelled out in individual plastic letters. A throwback to the past—she'd conjured up an impeccable booking photo.

When she drew even with him, keeping a generous buffer between her, the desk, and the stink seated in the executive chair behind it, the muscles in her jaw tensed. If she had any hope of someday putting him in prison, the most challenging part of this meeting would be not letting on she knew his dirty past. Her back teeth ground against one another as she forced herself to greet him.

"Good morning, Captain. We're here to provide you our required status report."

He snapped his reading glasses from the bridge of his nose, angled his chair toward the front of his desk, and focused his attention on Sloane and Finn. "I'm eager to hear about your progress."

Was he toying with her? The smug look on his face made him appear overly confident. After Peter's killing made the top of the news and front page, he must've felt hunted, like the noose would soon close around his neck. When homicide detectives didn't beat down his door the following day and week, he must've decided he was in the clear.

How she wished she could wipe that superior look off his face. She averted her stare to his wall of fame. The framed awards for his alleged heroism and the pictures of him accepting those medals from mayors and governors grated on her nerves worse than snarled city traffic.

Her focus shifted to the next set of pictures. They were older, showcasing the youthful college-aged Carter Nash about to embark on a distinguished career in law enforcement. The trim, angular body from his past looked nothing like the soft, rounded physique he presented to the world today. Still, he appeared to be in good enough shape to put a bullet in Peter's chest from a cowardly hundred yards away. He even looked capable of making it down three flights of stairs before Shipley's team could catch up with him, but not much beyond.

The preppy white cardigan with bold blue Greek letters in that college photo made her want to puke. He looked like all the other frat boys resting on their white privilege.

Frat boy? She fixed her gaze on the picture, zeroing on the semicircle of clean-cut man-boys. Each had extended a fist at waist level, displaying their matching silver rings. She'd seen that ring or something like it before.

"Sloane?" Finn gently elbowed Sloane in the ribs, forcing her back to the present. "He asked if we found anything interesting."

"I think I have." She ignored whatever Nash had repeated. His question became white noise. She stepped toward the side of the desk and then slid herself between the wall and Nash's plush leather chair with him still in it.

"Excuse me?" he huffed.

Sloane ignored his condescending objection and reached for the framed photo. She pulled it down, making sure not to damage it, not for his sake, but for Bernie's. She examined the distinctive rings in the photo. The photo was at least thirty years old, and the resolution wasn't as crisp as they were today. Still, Sloane could make out the outline of the Greek symbol on it. The same one that was imprinted on Peter's insurance policy. When she looked closer, she noted below each man in the photo, someone had handwritten a name in quotation marks, fraternity pledge nicknames perhaps. Below Carter Nash was the name "Callahan."

"Callahan, it's nice to meet you."

She tore her focus from the picture to lock gazes with Nash, noting his confused expression. She'd found the link Kyler needed to secure an indictment. Justice was long overdue, and he had no O.J. glove defense. A corner of her mouth slid upward into a devilish grin.

"Got you, you son of a bitch."

* * *

Inside the plush outer office, Chief of Staff Mark Gandy gave Sloane the same warning about the mayor's tight schedule as he had during their first meeting three months ago. She ignored him; she would leave when she, not Nicci Cole, was finished.

Doris, the perfectly coiffed, smartly dressed secretary, still sat quiet sentinel like a Queen's Guardsman protecting Windsor Castle. Expressionless, she pressed a button on the headset wrapped around one ear. "The mayor will see you now."

"Thanks, Doris, you're doing a noble job." Clutching a manila folder in her hand, Sloane gave her a wink before passing by.

The mayor's face beamed when she locked eyes with Sloane. "Ms. Sloane. Ms. Harper. I'm so glad to see you." She motioned them toward the leather guest chairs lined up in a row in front of her antique wood desk. "You two made a splash in the news, putting a cop killer behind bars for life."

"It helped to have a personal stake in the outcome." Sloane confidently crossed her legs at the knee when she sat.

"I understand Officer Sellers became the reason you entered law enforcement."

"He was."

"Well, solving his decades-old murder through modern technology was the very thing I was trying to prove. There is no reason our city should have the highest cold case rate in the state. Big changes are coming because of the excellent work you two did."

"We're glad you're pleased with our work, but I think you may want to hear what we have to say next privately." Sloane didn't blink, savoring what would come next.

The smile dropped from the mayor's face. "Why would I want to do that?"

"Colby and Jones."

Mayor Cole's expression turned stony. She turned to Gandy. "Please excuse us, Mark."

"But—"

"I'll call if I need you." Before he closed the door to exit the room, Mayor Cole called out, "Tell Doris to cancel my next appointment." Sloane didn't envy the firestorm awaiting him in the outer office. Doris would be on a war footing. "What is it you want to talk about, Ms. Sloane?"

"Your plan to gut the police department."

"I see." Mayor Cole reclined in her high-back chair, slowly tapping her desktop with a fingernail. "Your loyalties still run deep."

"Not loyalties. My sense of right and wrong. You were elected on a platform of holding the police accountable, and they should be."

"I'm glad you agree."

"I may agree with your goal but not your approach. A wholesale gutting will do more harm than good. Besides causing chaos, you'll ruin the lives of hundreds of good detectives and street cops."

"A necessary step to keep my campaign promise."

"And which promise is that?" Sloane leaned forward and rested both elbows on her knees, preparing for her attack. "The one you made to the voters? Or the one you made to Colby and Jones to not prosecute their dirtbag clients in exchange for hefty campaign donations?" Sloane slapped the manila folder on the mayor's desk and sat back in her chair. "Your constituents won't be too happy to discover that as the District Attorney, you let the worst of the worst go free in order to fund your aspirations for this office."

"I don't know what you think you've unearthed, but San Francisco voters care about the things we tell them to care about." Nicci Cole opened the folder and scanned the list of thugs, ruffians, and all-around lowlifes she had refused to prosecute—all represented by Colby and Jones. "I have no intention of backing off from my campaign promise."

"I thought you might take that position." Sloane focused her attention on Finn. "Make the call."

Finn had her phone at the ready, swiped the screen, and placed it to her ear. "We will need Travis to make that call." She waited silently for several moments. "Thank you, Daddy." Hanging up, she turned to Sloane. "Done."

"We understand you're on the shortlist for State Attorney General." Sloane paused when Mayor Cole's eyes formed into daggers. Sloane had her attention. "I don't think you want to jeopardize that."

The mayor's intercom system came to life with Doris's discreet, professional voice. "Sorry to interrupt, Mayor Cole, but I have Lieutenant Governor Travis Buchanan on the line. He says it's critical."

The mayor's eyes twitched, a sign Sloane had hit her soft spot. Sloane pointed toward the desk phone. "You better take that."

Minutes later, chin high and chest puffed out proudly, Sloane strutted out of the mayor's suite. Everything about this week was going right. For his own safety Carter Nash had been transferred to Pelican Bay to serve out his life sentence. She'd gone toe to toe with a political powerhouse and won. And now,

Eric's and Morgan's jobs were safe, along with those of dozens of other good cops she knew. Only one other thing could make this day better.

As they exited the long historic hallway that memorialized the city's past leaders, the Grand Staircase came into view. Sloane stopped and took Finn by the hand. She slowly filled her lungs and let the warmth radiating from their laced fingers take over.

"I still can't believe how beautiful it is." Finn had fixed her gaze on the majestic stairs, the centerpiece of the stunning central rotunda. As sweeping as the Golden Gate, its nine marbled steps rose from the main floor in concentric ovals to a landing at the base of the straight ascending staircase. The spectacular sight made a perfect backdrop for what Sloane was about to do.

For the second time in her life, Sloane wrapped sweaty fingertips around a small velvet box hidden in her front pants pocket. She silently promised herself this would be the last. Finn had been her soulmate since the day they held hands in choir over twenty-two years ago, and no matter what the future might bring, no one would have her heart like Finn.

For weeks, she tried to come up with the right words, but nothing captured the essence of what Finn meant to her. As she'd done when they first reconnected, she'd let the words come naturally.

"Come with me, Finn." Sloane gave her hand a tug and guided her toward the freshly polished tiles at the top of the staircase. Murmurs from passersby and the sound of clicking heels echoed in the rotunda. She faced Finn and drew their clasped hands close to her chest. "Do you love me?"

Finn's eyes searched hers as if asking what this was all about. "Of course, I love you."

"Count with me like we used to do when we were kids."

"This is silly."

"Trust me."

Sloane tugged again, and they began their descent like they had every day after choir when they were teenagers. With each step downward, she and Finn counted. "One, two, three...

eleven, twelve, thirteen." She pulled Finn to a stop and faced her. "Thirteen was the age when I discovered who I was. I didn't have a word for it, but I knew I liked girls." Sloane paused when Finn's wide smile caught her by surprise. "Well, one girl in particular. We planted a seed that last day after choir. It grew inside me all those years, and the day we reconnected, it finally blossomed."

Her heart thumping as fast as a speeding train, Sloane retrieved the red box from her pocket and opened the lid to expose a simple, yet meaningful silver infinity ring. Finn covered her mouth with a hand. "Finn Harper, you've been a part of me since we were thirteen. Now that we've found each other again, I can't imagine a life without you. I want you to become my wife, right here, on the thirteenth step. Will you marry me?"

Finn's eyes welled with moisture. She nodded up and down. "Yes, of course, I'll marry you."

Those were the words Sloane wanted to hear. They were already a family and partners in every sense, and the only thing that had been missing was the ring. Sloane removed it, stuffed the box into her pocket, and slipped the ring onto Finn's slender finger. "I've wanted to do this for months."

"What took you so long?"

"I wanted it to be on these steps, but I didn't know how else to get you here."

"Why here?"

"This is the place where I first realized I was ready to marry you."

Finn slowly rested one arm and then another around Sloane's neck. "You sure know how to romance a woman." She pressed their lips together in a long, passionate kiss, sealing their engagement. "I love you, Manhattan Sloane."

"I love you, Finn Harper." Sloane took Finn by the hand and they continued their walk down the grand stairs. She rubbed a finger against Finn's ring, sensing their connection was complete. It may have taken two decades, but they'd finally come full circle. Sloane's heart was whole.

EPILOGUE

Four months later

Sloane dabbed at the collar of her pearl white tuxedo jacket, attacking the oblong dollar-sized silver stain there with a damp paper towel. *At least it was champagne and not Kyler's red wine.* Staring into The Tap's uncharacteristically clean restroom mirror, Sloane had a hard time judging her progress. The wet spot was simply growing bigger. She half-hoped the stain wouldn't come out and would remain a fond memory of this perfect day.

The restroom door flung open.

"I'm so clumsy." Morgan rushed in, carrying a freshly poured glass of club soda on the rocks and a clean bar towel. She placed the cup on the light brown laminate sink counter and handed the cloth to Sloane. "This should get it out."

"No worries, Captain," Sloane emphasized Morgan's new rank, a promotion years overdue. "If it doesn't, I'll swap with you."

Morgan eyed Sloane's reflection in the mirror. "You're still a size smaller. I don't think I'll fit." She smoothed her matching tuxedo jacket against her much flatter abdomen. "One good thing about it being our wedding day, I can eat whatever I want. So you better keep scrubbing."

"Oh, come on. You look great."

"I do, don't I?" Morgan turned sideways to inspect her much trimmer self in the mirror. "We both look great."

"So do our brides." Sloane turned around and leaned her bottom against the counter, continuing to dab at the champagne stain.

"I thought I'd pass out when I first saw Kyler in her chiffon strapless."

"Same here. Finn was so stunning in her dress I couldn't take my eyes off of her."

"It made for some comic relief when the pastor snapped her fingers in front of your face to get you to say your vows."

The tips of Sloane's ears burned with embarrassment. "Can you blame me?"

"Not one bit. How did we both get so lucky?"

Sloane dipped her head at the memory of her first wedding reception held here at The Tap. That day, she felt like the luckiest woman in the world. Sloane had tucked away the guilt she'd carried from killing her own parents two decades earlier and had opened her heart to Avery, the woman who taught her a life without love was not worth living. If not for her, Sloane wouldn't have been ready for Finn.

"What's wrong, Sloane?"

"Nothing's wrong." Her eyes burned with tears. Dare she say it? Yes. "How did I get so lucky twice?"

Morgan rested a hand on Sloane's shoulder. "Avery was a wonderful woman."

"But Finn is my soulmate. She has been since we were thirteen."

"It shows." Morgan pulled her hand back. "We better get back to our wives before they send out a search party."

Closed for the reception, The Tap's main dining room bustled with dozens of guests from the joint wedding. Police officers, lawyers, law clerks, family, friends, and neighbors filled the pub, which had been specially decorated with white tablecloths and floating candle centerpieces. White balloons and bright clear Christmas lights strung across the walls and around the posts completed the festive atmosphere.

All four brides had contributed to the music playlist and based on the recent string of 1970s soft rock songs on the speakers, Dylan was currently playing Morgan's set. A clanky crash punctuated by the distinctive sound of glasses breaking roared over the music and the hum of dozens of conversations. Sloane glanced in its direction.

Dylan snapped a towel against the top of the bar. "Damn it, Michelle. That's twice today. Niece or not, one more accident, and you're outta here."

"I'm sorry, Uncle Dylan." Michelle had bent down on her three-inch heels, her tight jeans stretching at the seams and her form-fitting white T-shirt revealing a tramp stamp on the small of her back.

"Keep your mind on the drinks, not the stud in the white tux," Dylan huffed as he retreated behind the bar.

Sloane's gaze searched the room. She stopped when she caught sight of beautiful white chiffon, but then focused on the dark, bobbed hair. It was Kyler. Morgan tapped Sloane on the arm before stepping toward her wife. "There's my beauty. I'll catch up with you when it's time for the cake cutting."

Sloane continued her scan until she found the matching dress. Stunning. Breathtaking. Sexy. Alluring. Captivating. Pick the adjective. It described Finn tonight. She'd grown out her hair a few inches past her shoulders for today. The stylist had curled and weaved sections into an intricate pattern, tying them up in the back. Every inch of Finn's enchanting neck drew Sloane in like a magnet.

As Sloane drew closer, the people surrounding Finn came more into focus. Chandler and Sharon to her left. Janet and Caleb Tenney, her former in-laws, across from her. And an older woman in her sixties she didn't recognize to her right. The woman, dressed in white slacks and blouse, layered with a black and white cheetah print three-quarter sleeve sweater, gestured as if she and Finn were in the midst of a meaningful conversation. Had she been at the wedding? Sloane couldn't remember seeing her at the City Hall ceremony. Then again, she hadn't noticed anyone but Finn and the pastor.

When the crowd gave way to clear a path to her, Finn glanced her way, giving birth to a smile that could light Giants' stadium. Finn tapped the arm of the woman next to her and then left her, stepping toward Sloane and meeting her halfway. "There you are."

"Miss me?" Sloane slid an arm around the soft fabric encasing Finn's waist.

"Always when you're not with me." Finn arched her torso back far enough to inspect Sloane's lapel. "The club soda worked."

"Like a champ."

Finn loosened Sloane's hold and turned toward the mystery woman. "I want to give you your wedding present."

A sinking feeling beset Sloane's stomach. "I thought we weren't doing presents today."

"I know, but this has to be tonight." Finn gave Sloane a loving yet determined look. She took her by the hand, leaving no room for argument. When they reached the spot Finn had last staked out for conversation, Caleb wrapped an arm around Sloane's shoulder while holding a champagne glass in his free hand.

"Great shindig, Sloane," he said.

"I'm so glad you and Janet came. Did Reagan get you settled into the guest room?"

"We're all set, dear." Janet's puffy, rosy cheeks told the tale she'd already indulged in the champagne. "You just concern yourself with this wonderful party."

"And my incredible wife." Sloane slid an arm around Finn's waist again.

"Ready for your present?" Finn whispered into Sloane's ear, receiving a swift nod. Finn motioned to the mystery woman she had been speaking to earlier, who waved over another woman about half her age from a few feet away.

"Babe, I'd like you to meet Barbara Cotton and Lisa Sellers."
Sloane extended her hand to the older woman without processing their names. A second later, she knitted her brow. Did Finn say Sellers? "Barbara, it's a pleasure."

"It's so very nice to meet you finally, Sloane." Barbara accepted Sloane's hand.

"Finally?" Sloane turned to Finn for an explanation.

"Barbara is Bernie Sellers' widow."

Sloane brought her left hand to her mouth to cover a gasp. A fluttery sensation filled her belly as she locked eyes with Barbara. A perceptible head bob of her short salt-and-pepper hair confirmed what Finn had said.

"When your wife called me last month and explained who you were, I couldn't wait to meet you." Barbara's grin grew wide when she glanced at Finn. "She insisted we surprise you today."

Still wrapping her head around who this woman was, Sloane's breathing stalled. She couldn't find the right words. "I— My God. How?"

"Your wife is an amazing investigator. She found us in Illinois."

"Us?" Sloane turned toward the younger woman. "Lisa, you must be—"

"Bernie was my father."

Sloane's head spun, replaying in her head the conversations she had had with Bernie. She slowly picked out the words he had said during their one lunch together. "He told me about you. He said you liked algebra when you moved."

Lisa's eyebrows arched. "He was right. I did."

Sloane stared back and forth between Barbara and Lisa in a short-lived tennis match, still absorbing their presence. "I can't believe this is happening. This means so much to me."

"It means a lot to us, too." Barbara caressed Lisa's shoulder. "Resolution of his cold case made the national news, but the reports left out details about what he meant to you. I remember him telling me about you and how scared you were the night of the accident. He wanted to make sure you were settling well into your new life."

Sloane clutched Finn's hand and held it against her thigh, fighting to hold back the tears threatening to escape her eyes. "He and I had lunch right here once. The day he died, Bernie promised to take me to see Finn." Sloane shook her head and voiced the lingering guilt that accompanied that statement. "I'm so sorry, Barbara. If not for me—"

"There's nothing to feel sorry for. Bernie was born to protect others. When others ran away from danger, he ran toward it. He died doing what he loved. Knowing the men who set that fire are dead or behind bars is a comfort. I can't thank you enough for bringing us peace of mind."

With those words a massive weight lifted and decades of guilt evaporated. Sloane squeezed Finn's hand, thanking her for the precious gift even as a tear dropped down her cheek. "Thank you, Barbara. I felt responsible for so many years, and once I learned his case was a mystery, I swore not to stop until I solved it. I wish I'd done it sooner."

"Well, it's done now." Barbara scanned the crowded room. "I don't want to keep you from the rest of your guests."

"But there's so much I want to ask you."

"Lisa and I are in town for several days, staying with Chandler in Atherton. Your wife suggested brunch on Monday before you leave for your honeymoon."

"She's thought of everything." Sloane turned her lips into a cheerful smile and shook Barbara's hand goodbye. "Monday then. I hope you like pie."

After Barbara and Lisa excused themselves, Sloane glided both hands up Finn's back, skimming her fingers across her smooth, alabaster skin. Her body tingled with excitement. "You are wonderful."

"So you like your gift?"

"It was priceless." Sloane pressed her lips against Finn's ear and murmured, "I can't wait to show you how much it meant to me." The twitch in Finn's ear meant she had grinned. When the lead-in to Journey's "Open Arms" began to play softly in the background, she whispered, "Dance with me."

"Always."

Sloane led Finn to The Tap's dance floor and wrapped her arms around her torso. Finn's around Sloane's neck. Sloane swayed to the song's slow, romantic beat, her chest swelling with emotion. "Your gift was perfect. You always know what I need."

"That's because you're a part of me."

"You've helped me shed every piece of guilt from the accident to Avery's death to Bernie's." Sloane released one hand and grazed Finn's cheek with her fingertips. Those deep hazel eyes held only love for her. "I'll always love you."

During the next song, a tap on Sloane's shoulder drew her attention, forcing her to pause her dancing. "Hey, Mom." Reagan's sheepish eyes forecasted either a request for money or a speedy departure. "Emeryn and I are meeting up with some friends."

Sloane placed both hands on Reagan's upper arms. Every day she looked more and more like her mother and had grown into a smart, responsible, independent young woman. To think in a short four months, she'd be eighteen and soon after that off to college. *You'd be so proud, Avery.*

"Of course, honey. If you think you'll be past midnight, send me a text."

"Will do." Reagan kissed her mother on the cheek. "You two look beautiful tonight. I'm so happy for you."

Sloane narrowed a single eyebrow. "Thank you, but flattery won't buy you an extra few hours."

After saying goodbye, Sloane took Finn into her arms again. "Now, where were we?"

Before Sloane swayed her through a single verse, Eric appeared behind Finn and tapped her shoulder. "Mind if I cut in?"

"Of course not." Finn gave Sloane a slow, suggestive wink and lowered her arms. Before stepping off the dance floor, she pecked Eric on the cheek. "I'll be watching you."

"Kadin said the same thing." Eric pulled out his signature lopsided grin. "I promise to keep a respectable distance." He held out his right arm. "You'll have to lead."

Sloane accepted, placing her palm against his and letting him put a hand on her flank while she rested an arm on his shoulder. They began a basic box step. "You and Kadin have gotten serious."

"I wouldn't label it as serious yet, but yes, we've been seeing each other."

"Is that what the kids call it these days?" Sloane snickered.

"I like her, Sloane."

"I can see why. Just be careful."

"I will."

"Wasn't your department physical last week?"

He shrugged. "Yeah."

"And the verdict?"

"Forced retirement."

"Oh." Sloane's playful tone disappeared. Eric took that bullet in his shoulder out of some sense of an unpaid debt to her. He'd paid enough. "You know, between Chandler's firm contracting us for their investigative work and the national attention we've gotten from Nash's arrest, Finn and I have more clients than we know what to do with. We need to bring on more detectives."

"Really?" Eric slowed his dance pace.

"But I'm sure that sort of work wouldn't interest you."

Eric stopped. "Are you going to make me beg?"

"The thought had crossed my mind." Her smile and playful tone returned. "But no. Finn and I are dying to have you join the firm."

Eric cleared his throat following an apparent hard swallow. "I'd love to but under one condition."

"What's that?"

"Don't stick me under the men's room."

"Deal." She threw her arms around Eric's neck in a tight hug. He was her friend, mentor, and now partner again. Having all of that back filled Sloane's heart, erasing every bad feeling she once had about him. They'd come full circle, just like she and Finn had.

* * *

Motion from Finn nudged Sloane and rustled the cotton sheets encasing them. In her sleep, Finn rolled to her other side, sliding her naked leg from atop Sloane's midsection. The skin-to-skin contact served as an echo of the passion they shared not an hour earlier, sparking another pang of desire, but Finn needed her sleep. Sloane did too. The day had filled her mind with too many memories, though, keeping her awake.

After carefully lifting the covers, Sloane slipped out of bed. Streetlights provided enough illumination through the window for her to locate her sleep shorts and tank top. Finn had tossed them on the wood floor hours ago during the seductive dance she'd promised her months ago.

Taking care not to disturb the Tenneys, who were sleeping in the neighboring guest room, Sloane tiptoed in the dark to the kitchen. She hoped the champagne they had, prompting them to retire early, kept them comatose for a while longer. Typically, she'd soothe her middle-of-the-night wanderings with a cup of hot tea, but the several glasses of champagne she had earlier at their reception dictated water as the wiser choice.

It was a rare cloudless winter night, and stars and lights from the Oakland hills were shimmering through the sliding glass door in the dining room. Sloane pushed it open and crept onto the deck, leaving the door open to let the crisp air into her stuffy living room.

She leaned her elbows atop the wood railing as she'd done thousands of times before during the twenty-three years she'd lived there. She stared into the night, across the dark bay waters toward the dotted Oakland hills. The addition of buildings and streetlights over the years magnified the hills' resemblance to a manmade Milky Way and made them infinitely more mesmerizing.

A light breeze raised goose bumps on her arms, but rubbing them for warmth proved inadequate. Sloane placed her water glass on the deck railing before padding over to the storage chest tucked into a corner. She opened it, intending to pull out a blanket, but a gray wool sweater was lying on top. Dozens of memories flooded back when she raked her fingers across it.

Avery wore this sweater on the deck most evenings to end their day. She'd said the ridged weave provided enough warmth to prevent her from going inside and missing out on watching the sun wane at dusk. Reagan was wearing it the day of her kidnapping. Sloane was convinced that connection to Avery had protected Reagan during that ordeal and saved her from burning in the fire Padrino had set. It was also the sweater she had worn when she said goodbye to Avery on this same deck months after her death. Without question, she needed to keep it.

She slipped it on and resumed her position at the railing, taking in the view that had comforted her for years. She recalled her first few weeks here following her parents' deaths, getting accustomed to living with a grandmother she barely knew. Bernie had given her fleeting hope of holding on to her past, but his death ended it for decades.

"Nana," she whispered, fondly recalling their twenty years together in this house. "You would've loved Finn. She's everything I ever wanted. Everything I'll ever need."

From behind, two hands wrapped tightly around her waist. "I wish I could've met your grandmother."

Sloane covered Finn's arms with one of her own, pushing them firmly against her midsection. "She was an amazing woman. You would've loved her."

"Come back to bed." Finn nuzzled her chin on Sloane's shoulder, the touch sending tingles radiating through her chest. "Family day starts in a few hours with a home-cooked breakfast."

Sloane rotated on her heels until their lips were inches apart. "And what do you propose we do until then?"

"I have a few ideas."

Bella Books, Inc.

Women. Books. Even Better Together.

P.O. Box 10543
Tallahassee, FL 32302

Phone: 800-729-4992
www.bellabooks.com